The Paper Bracelet

RACHAEL ENGLISH

REVIEW

For Eamon

Chapter 1

Then, Patricia

They skulked in the dark like animals, the only illumination coming from the fanlight over the front door. It was safer that way, her father said. You'd never know who might be rambling about. He eased open the door and peered left and right. Stars were splashed across the sky, and a swing-boat moon hung over the street. It was cold for April.

'I hope there hasn't been an accident,' he said.

'He'll be here soon,' replied her mother. 'Ten o'clock was the time he gave us. It's only five past.' She twisted around, her long face creased with irritation. 'Stand back, Patricia. You don't want anyone catching sight of you.'

Already they were using her new name, the name she would be known by in Carrigbrack. It was for her own good, they insisted. She'd have more privacy that way. And privacy was vital. One stray word, and a young woman's life could be damaged beyond repair. She might never find a respectable husband or enjoy a proper family life. Judgement would follow her, and no good man would want to be tarnished by association.

She suspected that using a different name made the situation a little easier for them. It wasn't their daughter who'd disgraced herself, it was Patricia. Their daughter was dutiful. She sang in the choir and passed every exam. She obeyed the rules. Patricia was a messy imposter.

The secrecy didn't end there. They'd found a wig and instructed her to wear it. The hair was long and black and smelled of plastic and cigarette smoke.

'It's for fear anyone sees you in the car with Father Cusack,' her mother had explained. 'We don't want people asking questions.'

'Sooner or later someone will enquire after me. What then?'

'They'll be told you're in England.'

'What about work?'

'We'll tell them the same.'

For a time, she had denied the truth. She hadn't said anything because she hadn't been able to admit it to herself. Then she'd bargained with God or the universe or whatever was out there. *Make it go away, and I'll change. I promise.* When, finally, she'd confessed, time had speeded up. The questions, the looks zipping between her parents, her mother's weeping, her father's controlled fury; they'd all blurred together. She regretted not running away. She'd considered getting the bus and boat to London, but she knew no one there, and the few pounds she'd saved wouldn't have lasted long

'Where did we go wrong?' her mother kept asking.

'We didn't,' her father said. 'Some girls are raised to be no better than tramps, but that was never the case in this house. Her failings are her own.'

Although neither parent was given to displays of affection, Patricia had always assumed they loved her. Their love had shown itself in polished shoes and a new school coat, dinners on the table and drives to the sea. Compared to many parents, their use of the wooden spoon had been sparing. Sometimes they spoke about the sacrifices they'd made. Other girls were forced to leave school at fifteen and earn their keep. She'd been allowed to complete the Leaving Cert. They spoke too about how girls were a constant worry. She remembered fragments of conversation; her mother saying to a neighbour, 'You're always nervous with girls. You're better off with boys. Boys are straightforward.'

After a couple of hours, her father's rage had eased. He'd left, only to return thirty minutes later with the parish priest. Father Cusack's white hair was combed into an elaborate arrangement, but it wasn't thick enough to mask his pink scalp. The lines on his face were deep, like cracks in dried mud. Her parents brought him into the good room, where he sat on the brown sofa and lit a cigarette. He took a pull and exhaled a long curl of smoke. Save for a brief admonishment for the shame she was bringing on a well-respected family, there was no anger. He had the air of a man performing a familiar ritual.

Patricia focused on the strip of green and orange wallpaper that was peeling from the wall behind him. Out on the street, some girls were skipping. In giddy voices they chanted, 'Cinderella dressed in yella went upstairs to kiss her fella.'

'Remind me again,' said Father Cusack, 'how old are you? Nineteen, is it?'

'Twenty, Father.'

'And how many months, do you think?'

'Four,' she replied, her voice stronger than she felt. 'Perhaps five.'

'The baby's due in August, then. There's no chance the father would be willing to marry you, is there?'

'Oh God, no. That definitely won't be happening.'

'Hush,' said her mam. 'You're in no position to be speaking like that.'

'All I'm doing is telling the truth.'

'Very well,' said the priest. 'I think it would be best if you went out to the kitchen and made us some tea.'

She eavesdropped from the hall. Her parents' words were easy to make out. They were telling him about Mike. The priest was softly spoken, however, and she caught only snatches of what he had to say. 'A reliable institution', she heard, then 'right from wrong', followed by 'surprisingly common' and 'tomorrow'.

Outside, the girls had changed their rhyme. 'Vote, vote, vote for de Valera,' they sang. 'Here comes Annie at the door-io.'

Later, Patricia's mother accompanied Father Cusack to the parochial house. They had a telephone there. He called the home in Carrigbrack and spoke to a woman called Sister Agnes. Her mam came back with instructions.

'One small suitcase,' she said. 'Two nightdresses, a face cloth, a toothbrush. Underwear. Practical shoes. No fripperies, books or make-up.' The girls wore uniforms, so there was no need for a change of clothes. 'Not that your own clothes will fit you for much longer,' she added.

Twenty-four hours later, and they were standing in the grainy light, pretending that everything made sense. The atmosphere was septic, all their rancour and disappointment lingering in the air.

Patricia pressed her fingers against her forehead. 'What if I decide I want to keep the baby?'

The question prompted another snap of anger from her father. 'Please,' he said, 'we don't need any foolish talk.'

'But I've heard of girls holding on to their children. It happens in Dublin, apparently. No one here need know.'

'Don't mind what they're doing in Dublin. What's wrong is wrong. Do you want to kill your mother? Is that it?'

There were a thousand replies she could have given, but there seemed no point. She was flat-on-the-floor exhausted. There was a dull pain around her eyes, a heavy feeling in her chest. She worried too that if they argued, she'd start crying again. Crying would be a mistake.

Presently, they heard the putter of an old Hillman Minx.

Her father opened the door just wide enough to confirm the priest's arrival.

He nodded in her direction. 'You'd better not keep the man waiting.'

She paused, wondering if they'd give her a kiss or even a hug. She hoped for a sign, no matter how slight, that they would forgive her. Neither parent moved, and eventually she picked up her suitcase.

'This is it, so,' she said.

Her mother turned away. 'Please God, we'll see you later in the year.'

Chapter 2

Now, Katie

Katie Carroll sat on the edge of the bed. Every day she sat in the same place and recited the same lines, and every day she walked away again. Was there a specific word, she wondered, for the one task you couldn't do? A special way of describing how your brain turned to sludge and your limbs refused to function? If not, she ought to invent one.

The bedroom was filled with milky sunlight. Dublin had enjoyed a rare hot summer, and while the temperatures had dipped, the days remained bright. In the near distance, a lawnmower buzzed. On Griffin Road, untidy gardens were taboo.

If there was one job Katie couldn't tackle, there were a hundred questions she couldn't answer. Two months on, and they continued to ripple through her head. What will you do now? Is the house too big for you? Would you consider selling? What about moving home?

Margo had been the first to ask about her plans. Others had followed. It was funny how she could ignore the enquiries of friends and acquaintances, yet Margo whittled away at her. There was something about her sister's tone, its blend of sympathy and condescension, that made Katie want to give an inappropriate answer. To say she was thinking of moving to Thailand or finding a young lover. Of course, she hadn't said any such thing. She'd mumbled about not being sure and needing more time.

There were moments when she forgot. She'd get irritated by the creaking board at the top of the stairs and think, I'll get Johnny to fix that. She'd roll over in bed, expecting to inhale his warm, soapy smell. Or she'd wake up, and for one happy minute her mind would be blank.

That was when the truth would find its way in.

People, well-meaning people, maintained her behaviour was normal. 'Don't be too hard on yourself,' they'd say. 'Honestly, you're bearing up well. Considering.' The last word was an acknowledgement of the suddenness of Johnny's death. From the day of his diagnosis, he'd had four months. Her time as a nurse had taught Katie that no disease was as unfair as cancer. Receive one diagnosis, and a year down the road you could be sitting in Lanzarote swapping hospital stories. Receive another, and you barely had time to say goodbye. She told herself that there was nothing exceptional about her husband's passing. He'd been seventy-four, not a grand old age, but a decent one. Old enough for his death not to be considered a tragedy.

At the funeral, she'd been restrained. She'd been brought up to be suspicious of showy demonstrations of grief. That had been the way back then. Wasn't it crazy that a sixty-nine-year-old woman could be influenced by what she'd been told as a child? But she was. Truth to tell, she'd just wanted to be alone. Oh, she knew she shouldn't be ungrateful. It was wonderful that so many people had made the effort to be there, to say 'Sorry for your troubles' and swap soft reminiscences. It had been years since she'd seen some of those who'd travelled from her home village of Danganstown. Others had come from abroad. One of Johnny's nephews had made the journey from Madrid, and Margo's daughter, Beth, had arrived from London.

For the following month, Katie had been busy. Friends had swooped in, offering meals and chats and cups of tea. She'd written thank-you notes and attempted to tackle the endless stream of paperwork. But lives moved on. Even close friends had other priorities, other concerns and demands.

Besides, Katie had never been one for relying on others. Early on, she'd learnt it tended to lead to disappointment. For most of her life, Johnny had been enough. He'd said the same about her. Through a mix of accident and design, they'd had a tight circle of friends. She'd always preferred small gatherings to the dazzle and noise of the crowd.

Now, here she was, back in the bedroom, bags at the ready. All she had to do was parcel up Johnny's best clothes and take them to the Vincent de Paul. She rose from the bed, opened the mahogany wardrobe and removed a pale blue shirt. Instead of stuffing it in a bag, she rubbed its fabric across her face. For some minutes she stood there, rocking on her heels, a familiar burn at the back of her eyes. This was stupid. The clothes were in good condition. There were men who could put them to use. But, as life had taught her, there was a wide gulf between recognising the foolishness of your behaviour and doing something about it.

She returned the shirt to the wardrobe. 'Another day,' she whispered. 'Another day, but not yet.'

Katie's grief was a slippery thing. Much of the time she was crippled by tiredness. She wanted to curl up with her loss and mourn in peace. There were other times when she felt a throbbing anger. She was angry with neighbours for coming out with platitudes about time being a great healer. She was angry with Johnny for leaving her. She'd been happy with their life together; there'd been no need for anything to change. Mostly, though, she was angry with herself. Why hadn't she spotted that something was wrong? What sort of nurse was she? Why, over the years, had she wasted energy worrying about nonsense? Why hadn't she made the most of what she'd been given? She would march around the house like a madwoman, wanting to kick and scream. Then it would hit her: maybe what she felt wasn't anger. Maybe it was guilt.

She'd fret about this until she remembered one of Beth's favourite phrases: get over yourself. Katie was doing too much thinking. She had to get over herself.

Rather than shutting the wardrobe, she reached into the

back and took out a box. Once upon a time, it had contained a pair of cork-heeled sandals. As she recalled, Johnny hadn't been keen on them. He'd also had mixed feelings about the current contents of the box. 'Seriously, Kateser,' he'd said, 'you shouldn't go upsetting yourself. Anyway, most of those women are probably dead by now.'

She didn't believe this was true. Yes, the women would be old, but then again, what was old? Age, she'd discovered, was a complex business. If the news referred to a woman as being sixty-nine, Katie would picture a small lady with white hair, ill-fitting dentures and a wardrobe of Crimplene and tweed. It was an image from her childhood, when anybody over pension age was left to wither in a corner with a blanket on their knees. But that wasn't how she looked or felt. The knowledge that women of her age were expected to shrivel and fade made her doubly determined not to. Even on her worst days, she put on lipstick and mascara. Two weeks after Johnny's death, she'd had her blonde highlights refreshed. She liked to think he would have approved.

She sat down again, lifted the lid from the box and sifted through its contents. The notebook and the fragile curls of paper took her back almost fifty years. She'd been twenty-two when she'd started work in Carrigbrack. In those days, most people had said little about what happened there. If they did, they spoke in euphemisms. It was a home for girls who 'got themselves into trouble', a place where they could 'reflect on their failings' and 'get back their self-respect'.

The notebook had a mottled brown cover and its

pages were crisp with age. She opened it at random. The writing, in fountain pen, was small and precise. *19 October 1971*, the entry read. *Boy, 6 lb 10 oz. Mother aged 19, from Co. Limerick. Named Goretti. Says she will call her baby Declan. Her boyfriend is in Birmingham, and she wants them both to join him there.*

No doubt some of Katie's memories had been warped by time, but she could still picture the young women and their babies. The 'fallen women', as some had insisted on labelling them, as if they were characters from the Bible or a Regency novel. She'd be going about her business when·a sound or a smell would return her to another era. To a time of flared trousers and platform boots, black-and-white televisions and Vietnam. A time of calculated cruelty and unexpected kindness. She could still hear lonely sobs echoing through the building. She could smell the disinfectant and boiled dinners; see the spots of damp on the walls; sense the isolation and hopelessness.

She would also recall her own failures.

An outsider might assume that Johnny had forbidden her from doing anything with the bracelets. That wouldn't be fair. He'd been a protective man but not a controlling one. She'd been held back by her own fears. And yet, no matter how hard she tried to push her memories aside, they continued to seep in. Like her childhood in Danganstown and her marriage to Johnny, Carrigbrack was part of her story. And if that story finished now, it wouldn't have the ending she wanted.

*

'Carrigbrack?' said Beth with a wrinkle of her nose. 'Yeah, of course I've heard of it. It's in north Clare, up near the Burren. Wasn't it a big mother-and-baby home?'

'Mmm. Not as massive as some of the others, but pretty sizeable all the same.'

'So what were you doing there?'

'I was a nurse,' said Katie, trailing a hand along the edge of the shoebox. The two of them were in the kitchen, drinking the milky coffee that Beth had bought from a café near the college in Drumcondra.

A month after Johnny's funeral, Katie's niece had returned to Ireland for good. 'I'd forgotten how much I like Dublin,' she'd explained. She'd found a job with one of the large internet companies near the docks. Securing an affordable flat was altogether more difficult, and she was staying with old college friends in Stoneybatter. Despite the age gap, Beth and Katie had struck up a rapport. This was helped by the fact that, unlike her mother, Beth had shown no interest in rearranging Katie's life.

For years, their contact had been infrequent. Katie had rarely returned to her home village. Nevertheless, she'd always been fond of her niece. She'd been a chatty, lively child, full of questions about Katie's life in Dublin. Margo had seemed exhausted by her. But what mother of six wasn't perpetually exhausted?

'Didn't you have to be a nun to work in a place like Carrigbrack?' asked Beth.

'Most of the staff were nuns,' said Katie, 'but two or three of us weren't. We were just … well, I suppose you'd say we were helping out. I was newly qualified at the time.'

'Was nothing else available?'

'Not much. Getting a job wasn't easy. And, in the grand scheme of things, Carrigbrack was close to home. Danganstown's only thirty or forty miles away.'

'I hear what you're saying, but didn't working there make you uncomfortable?'

Katie was beginning to question the wisdom of confiding in Beth. That was the problem with her niece's generation: everything was black or white, spectacular or unforgivable. They had a certainty about the world – and their place in it – that Katie had never acquired. They were direct, too. There was none of the let's-pretend-everything's-fine behaviour of the past. This was, she reckoned, a change for the better. Still, she wasn't always equipped for Beth's candour.

'I didn't have much choice,' she said. 'Mam and Dad heard about the job, and that was that. What I wanted was irrelevant.'

'How bad was it?'

'If you mean was there physical punishment, the answer is no. Not officially, at any rate. The regime was harsh, though. The girls were expected to work right up until they went into labour. And conditions were bleak. You couldn't have called it a happy place.'

Beth shook her head. 'What gets me is why everybody put up with this carry-on for so long. Did people really think that packing your daughter off to an institution was a good idea?'

Katie attempted to put some order on her thoughts. She didn't want to be evasive, but neither was she able to give a full answer. Before replying, she took a deep breath. 'I've thought a lot about it, and looking back, it can be hard to tell where misguided ended and cruel began. People were scared. Scared of the Church. Scared of their neighbours. Scared of being seen as less than decent.'

'But—'

'I suppose what you've got to understand is that for most ordinary people, life was far more limited than it is now. When we were growing up, there was no contraception. You were warned not to have sex before marriage. If you did, and you became pregnant, you were marched up the aisle. If that wasn't possible, you were sent away and the baby was adopted. That was how it was, and mad as it sounds, most people accepted it.'

'It sounds mad because it *was* mad. It was absolutely mental.'

Katie recoiled at the sting in Beth's voice. Five years in London had stripped most of the Danganstown from her accent, but it was still there around the edges, especially when she became emotional. 'Mad' sounded more like 'mid', and 'mental' came out as 'mintal'. Katie remembered how, in their early years, Johnny had poked fun at her own country accent. She, in turn, had laughed at his Dublinisms. At 'banjoed' and 'spanner' and 'get up the yard'. They'd both marvelled at how such a small country could have so many ways of speaking.

For a while, the two of them sat in silence. On the street, a group of children were enjoying the summer's last hurrah. Their squeals and hollers crashed through the quiet.

'I'm sorry, Katie,' said Beth. 'I was wrong to snap at you. I do appreciate you telling me this. I just find it all so grim, y'know?'

Katie leant over and tapped her niece's wrist. 'You're fine, pet. I won't put a gloss on it. Grim's the right word.'

'So what's the story with the box?'

'Ah. Well, when I was working in Carrigbrack, I decided I ought to record the births in some way.' She stopped to remove the lid and take out the notebook. 'New babies were a non-event. Celebration was forbidden, and no one was allowed to make a fuss. The mothers were told to reflect on the sin that had brought them there. "The more pain you suffer, the better," one of the nuns, Sister Sabina, used to say. Anyway, I knew what would happen. In most cases, the mother would be given a few weeks, perhaps a few months, with her baby, and then – *whoosh* – the child would be whipped away.'

'And the mother wouldn't be entitled to any information about where they'd gone?'

'That's right. In a way, the longer a baby stayed, the worse it was. Even though the girls were told not to form an attachment, many of them did.'

Katie paused, and an image drifted in. An image of a frightened young woman who'd been able to keep her boy for five months. She'd wanted to hold on to him. She'd been adamant she could cope. One dank Friday afternoon, he'd been taken away. Later, when she'd accepted that she would never get him back, she'd stretched out on the floor and howled with misery.

It was just one image. One story in an ocean of stories. But it never went away.

Katie was surprised to realise that her eyes were wet. 'Sorry, love,' she said. 'There's no call for me to get maudlin. That's not what this is about.'

'I don't blame you,' said Beth. 'I can't imagine what it must have been like. So ...'

'You're wondering about the notebook? Well, I decided to keep a record of the births – a few details about the mothers and their babies. And I also kept these.' She reached into the box and plucked out two paper bracelets. 'The babies were given identity bands. As you can see, they're not like the high-tech things they have in hospitals nowadays; just bits of paper with the name of the mother and her baby and so on.' She handed over one of the bracelets.

'Boy. Eugene,' read Beth. 'Fifth of January 1972. Seven pounds two ounces. Mother: Loretta.'

'Loretta wouldn't have been her real name,' said Katie. 'They were all given different names in the home. And I can tell you, they used to get a right talking-to if they didn't use them.'

'Presumably Eugene's name was changed after he was adopted,' said Beth, running a finger over the tiny lettering.

'I'd say so. The Lord only knows where the little chap ended up.'

'But wherever he is, he'd probably love to have this. It might even help him find his birth mother.'

'If that's what he wants. Or maybe he already has. Remember, he's forty-six now. And I guess Loretta's nearly seventy.'

Beth's round blue eyes were suspiciously misty. Along with her small mouth and narrow nose, she'd inherited those eyes from her mother's side of the family. But while Katie and Margo had been cursed with flat faces, Beth had been blessed with her father's delicate cheekbones. At twenty-eight, she was a remoulded version of her mother. 'How many bracelets have you got?' she asked.

'Forty-seven. I was in Carrigbrack for a year and a bit, long enough to see the births of more than fifty children. There were three stillbirths, and three others died when they were very young. Oh, and I missed a couple of bracelets. Obviously, we weren't supposed to hold on to them. If my stash had been found, I'd have been in serious trouble.'

As she spoke about the babies who'd died, Katie noticed Beth's mouth tighten. Although the number was higher than it should have been, she'd tried to console herself with the knowledge that other homes had been worse. That being said, practices in Carrigbrack had made a mockery of her training. There had been unnecessary suffering, and she had contributed to it.

'And you've kept the bracelets all this time?' asked Beth.

'To be fair, it wasn't as though I was looking at them every day of the week. I just couldn't bring myself to get rid of them.'

Going back to her school days, Katie had always been embarrassingly organised. She'd been the child who did her homework so that others could copy it. Throughout her career, she'd valued detail, record-keeping, lists. Odd as it might have seemed to others, she could never have thrown away her box of names.

Beth handed back one bracelet and took another. 'Girl. Jacqueline. Tenth of November 1971. Six pounds four ounces. Mother: Hanora Culligan,' she read.

'I remember her. Bless her, she was only fourteen, and a young fourteen at that. Christine was her real name. She called herself Chrissie. She'd been raped by a neighbour.'

'Jesus.' Beth swiped at a tear. 'The poor girl. I hope life turned out well for her, though she must have been totally screwed up by the time she left Carrigbrack.'

'But you never know, do you? I'm amazed by what people can survive. Maybe she marched out and never looked back.'

'Do you really believe that?'

'I'm not sure. It's what I'd like to think, though.'

'It'd be great to find out.'

'It would,' said Katie, in a low voice. The more they spoke, they more convinced she became. Yes, there were risks. Some of the stories were likely to be upsetting. She might be drawn into contact with people she'd rather forget. Plus, she had only a hazy idea of how to go about this. What she did know was that if she could help someone to unlock a door, that was what she should do. She smiled at Beth. 'Like you say, the men and women born in the home might appreciate some information about where their story began.'

'Except ...' Beth hesitated.

'Go on.'

'Don't get me wrong. I think it's a brilliant idea, but I was wondering if this is the right time. Look at the two of us. We're all teary just looking at pieces of paper. I can hear Mam giving out. "Are you mad?" she'll say. "Bringing all that hassle on yourself, and Katie's husband not long in his grave."'

'We'd better not tell her, then.'

'That's cool with me, but what about my question?'

'There doesn't have to be hassle. And as far as the timing's concerned ... as much as I always hated those clichés about death, it turns out they're true. When someone close to you dies, you begin to measure your own time. If I don't do this now, there's a danger I'll regret it. Some of those involved mightn't have many years left. Besides, it's not as though I can go hunting down women and harassing them. I'll put an ad in the paper, and if anyone gets in touch, I'll talk to them.'

'The new job doesn't start for a couple of weeks,' said Beth. 'I can give you a dig-out if you like.'

'Thanks, love. I'd really like that.'

'And if people do contact you, what then?'

'I'll pass on what I have, and that'll be it. Believe me,' said Katie, 'I've no intention of getting involved in anybody's life.'

Chapter 3

Katie

According to Beth, an online adoption forum was what they needed. They could put up a post to let people know about the bracelets. At the bottom, they'd include a dedicated email address. If anyone wanted more information, they could send a message.

Katie wasn't convinced. 'Don't look at me like I'm some sort of behind-the-times old woman,' she said. 'I've a feeling the folks we want to reach are more likely to see an ad in the paper.'

'In the short term, maybe so. Only it would disappear after a day. A post on an adoption message board would be there indefinitely. I promise you more people would get to hear about it. They'd be the right people too. If you put an ad in the paper, there's a danger the rest of the family will come across it. And from what you were saying yesterday, you'd rather do this on the down-low. Am I right?'

'It's not as though I'd put my name in the paper. I'd call myself "Carrigbrack Nurse" or some such.'

'All the same, if Mam saw the dates, she'd guess it was you. There's far less chance of her spotting a message board post.'

'Hmm. Show me this forum you're talking about, so I can see whether it's suitable.'

Beth laughed. 'You're a hard woman to please.'

They were back in Katie's kitchen in Drumcondra. Apart from the occasional student house, Griffin Road was a street of tidy red-brick homes where the railings shone, the roses were pruned, and the bins were left out – and taken in – on the correct day. Katie and Johnny had bought number 89 in the mid 1970s. Now, youngsters would laugh at how small their mortgage had been. Back then, however, Katie had stalked the bare rooms saying, 'Thirty thousand pounds' in a way that someone might say 'A million euro' today. She'd been torn between the safety of owning something so solid and her fear that the loan was too big.

Johnny, being Johnny, had taken everything in his stride. Gradually, his carpentry and building skills had transformed the terraced house. Furniture and decorating had been Katie's responsibility. She'd haunted Roches Stores, Clerys and Guineys. She'd visited every wallpaper shop, auction and warehouse sale, and spent her every spare hour painting and sewing until Number 89 was just right. She remembered her husband's hand on her back and the way he'd liked kissing the top of her head. They'd had big plans back then.

Looking around now, she could see the kitchen was outdated. There was a stain in the bath, an annoying creak on the landing, and two light switches needed repairing. And, yes, a three-bedroomed house was too large for a woman on her own. Yet there was one thing Katie could say for sure: she wouldn't be moving.

She pulled her chair closer to Beth and looked at the computer screen. *Born May '67 in Cork – Hoping to Find Birth Mother*, said one heading. Another asked: *Should I Take a DNA Test?* A third was titled: *A Message for My Daughter, Born in Mayo, January 1982.*

Beth clicked on the next post. A man called Richie was seeking advice. A woman had turned up at his mother's funeral and sat at the back crying. Later, she approached the family. Their mother had also been her own birth mother, she said. The two of them had been reunited, but the elderly woman had been scared to tell her family. By way of proof, the stranger showed them her birth certificate. It contained their mother's name. *The thing is*, Richie wrote, *Mam had a very common name. How can we be certain this woman is our sister?*

'You know what, Richie?' said Beth. 'You're an almighty tool. Do you think the unfortunate woman gets a buzz from travelling the country and having a weep at the funerals of strangers?'

'Maybe you should tell him that,' said Katie. 'In slightly more diplomatic language.'

'Don't worry. Half a dozen other people already have.'

'You've spent a bit of time on here, then?'

'This and several other sites. And, honest to God, I'm raging. I'd no idea that tracking down your birth parents was so difficult. Not just difficult; in plenty of cases it's impossible. Half of the files appear to have been destroyed in mysterious fires and floods. And the official channels take forever. You can be on a waiting list for months, and even then, there's every chance you'll get nowhere. No wonder people take matters into their own hands.'

Katie watched her niece's shoulders stiffen. For the first time, Beth was seeing how the sins of the past reverberated around them. She'd realised that the story wasn't confined to black-and-white film and bleached-out Polaroids. The women weren't exhibits in a museum.

'The lack of records is amazing,' said Katie, 'because, as I remember it, everything was catalogued and recorded. Be it a baby's nappy or a bar of soap, it was on a list somewhere.'

'So,' said Beth, 'will you give the message board a try? Please?'

'All right, you've won me over. But if we find it's not working, we'll do things my way.'

Beth grinned. 'Katie, I promise you, it'll work.'

For an hour or more, as rain tip-tapped against the windows, the two played with words and phrases until both were happy.

Were you born in the Carrigbrack Mother and Baby Home in County Clare between July 1971 and December 1972, and were you adopted from there? Would you like to know more about the circumstances of your birth? If so, I may be able to help.

I worked as a nurse in Carrigbrack at that time and collected the discarded identity bracelets of many of the babies born there. I still have those bracelets. I also have a small amount of information about the young women who gave birth.

Even if you don't want to trace your birth family, you might like a memento of your earliest days.

If you think this may be of assistance to you, please contact me. My email address is CarrigbrackNurse@gmail.com.

I promise your query will be handled with strict confidence.

I regret that I can't answer any questions about births before July '71 and after December '72. Neither am I able to help with any wider queries about the operation of the home. I was an employee, not a member of the order that ran Carrigbrack.Good luck with your search. My thoughts are with you.

'There we are,' said Beth a few minutes later as she refreshed the screen and their post jumped to the top. 'The replies and emails will soon start rolling in. Then we can go sleuthing – like Miss Marple and her assistant. Except without the dead bodies, obviously.'

'Like I told you yesterday,' said Katie, swallowing a smile, 'there'll be no detective work. If someone contacts me, and I can help, I will. If I'm certain they're the right person, I'll put the bracelet in the post. Oh, and I'll have you know I'm years younger than Miss Marple.'

'Consider me told.' Beth tucked her long fair hair behind her ears. 'Can I ask you something?'

'Okay.'

'What did Mam make of your job in Carrigbrack?'

'I'm not sure. Remember, Margo's nine years younger than me, so she was only thirteen. And our parents were strict. I don't think she was allowed an opinion.'

'You can bet that wouldn't hold her back now.'

Katie said nothing. Margo had an opinion for every occasion, and a few spares in the cupboard. When her sister had been very young, Katie had been delighted with her. She'd toted her around like a doll. After the novelty had faded, however, there'd been nothing there to replace it. Unfortunately, their connection had never been strong. Katie should probably have made a greater effort to understand her sister, but she feared it was too late for that now.

At twenty-two, Margo had married Con Linnane, the eldest son of the largest landowner in Danganstown. It was decent land too, not like the marshy fields of their neighbours, where only ragwort prospered and only snipe could be assured of a decent meal. The Linnanes had renovated and decorated a mini mansion and filled it with children. Given that Beth was the lone girl, Katie had expected Margo to be thrilled by her return to Ireland. Yet, for some hard-to-pin-down reason, their relationship was uneasy. She'd been tempted to ask if there was a problem, but decided against it. Besides, what she'd said to Beth about Margo and Carrigbrack wasn't the full story. In Katie's experience, too much honesty could be as dangerous as too little.

For three days, nothing happened. Again and again Katie returned to her new email account, hoping that someone would get in touch. On the forum itself, some of the responses were hostile. One poster demanded to know why it had taken her so long to offer help. Another questioned why she'd worked in Carrigbrack to begin with. In capital letters, he accused her of being a collaborator and an accessory to cruelty. Poison dripped down the screen.

She wanted to explain, but Beth urged her to hold back. 'Don't feed the trolls,' she said.

Not for the first time, Katie had to ask for a translation.

With her inbox remaining empty, she pored over the forum, reading the stories of others, each one sadder than the next. After that, she turned to other message boards. If your mood was already low, she discovered, internet forums were not your friend. Although the adoption board contained plenty of empathy, there was scant sign of it elsewhere. Politicians were pathetic; television presenters were talentless; most neighbourhoods were dangerous; the country was broken and corrupt; and if you doubted any of this, you were stupid.

That night she dreamt about Carrigbrack, one of those vivid dreams where every tiny detail was magnified and every scene, no matter how implausible, seemed real. She woke up coated in sweat, her nightdress stuck to her skin.

When morning came, she was sluggish, her head filled with concrete. Every step felt as if she was walking up a down escalator. It occurred to her that in trying to dodge the 'What will you do now?' questions, she'd made a mistake. Yes, she needed a task to fill her days, but this wasn't it. Would Beth be able to take down the post? she wondered.

And then it arrived.

The email was titled *All Help Appreciated*:

Hi,

I've just come across your online message and I was hoping you might be able to help.

I'm forty-seven years old, and for reasons too complicated to go into here, I've only recently discovered I was adopted.

It turns out that my birth certificate is a fake. It gives my name as Gary Winters, but that wasn't my original name. My adoptive parents are registered as my birth parents.

According to my adoptive mother, I was born in

Carrigbrack. She says she doesn't know any more than that.

My date of birth is 12 August 1971. Do you have a bracelet for a boy born on that date? And do you remember anything about my birth mother?

Yours in hope,

Gary Winters

Co. Wicklow

Katie tingled like a child with a surprise present. Even if she did ask Beth to take down the post, she would reply to Gary. No sooner had she sent her email than he came back again. He said he'd learnt to expect complications but was confident her information was important. *If I hop in the car,* he wrote, *I can be with you in less than an hour.* Katie rang Beth for advice. No answer. She texted, then rang again. Still no answer.

Twenty minutes later, Beth called back. 'I take it there's been a development,' she said. While Katie read out the email, her niece made small humming sounds. When she reached the end, Beth jumped in. 'Gary Winters? As in *the* Gary Winters?'

'Should I know him?'

'Not necessarily, but if he is who I think he is, lots of people do.'

Katie was sitting in front of her laptop. She ran the name through Google. A Wikipedia page popped up, as did several images of a dark-haired man with a sprinkling of tattoos. In most of the pictures he wasn't wearing a shirt.

'Oh,' she said.

'Is he the right guy?' asked Beth.

'He's definitely the right age for our Gary. In fact ...' she opened the Wikipedia page, 'the date of birth listed here is the same as the one he gave me.'

'Wow.'

'Are you doing anything tomorrow morning, by any chance? I arranged to meet him.'

'You're not serious?'

'I'm afraid I am,' said Katie, already regretting the combination of curiosity and politeness that had made her agree to Gary's request. She'd known that in some cases a meeting might be necessary, but in this instance, she feared it was pointless. 'The snag is,' she said, 'I've been through my notes and examined all the bracelets and I'm certain there were no births in Carrigbrack on the twelfth of August 1971.'

'Right,' said Beth. 'That means ...?'

'That someone's not telling the truth.'

Chapter 4

Gary

Gary couldn't remember when he'd last been this nervous. Was it the first time Black Iris had played the Hollywood Bowl, and it had felt as if every star in the universe was backstage? Or was it when they'd headlined the third night of Rock in Rio, and two hundred thousand people had spread out in front of them like ants on a highway? Or was it all the way back when he'd told his parents he was dropping out of college to go on tour with a rock band?

He picked up a teaspoon, passing it from one hand to the other. 'You see,' he said to Katie, 'I keep thinking about the times I came across those pictures on TV – the girls in convents and boys in reform schools and that place in Galway where the babies were buried in a tank – and I never had any idea I was part of the story. But now that I do, I've got to find out who my people are.'

'Your people,' said Katie, her voice soft. It wasn't a

question, he decided, so much as a comment on his choice of words. Gary was aware that he sounded slightly American. People in Ireland smirked at the way he said 'garaage' and used phrases like 'touch base', 'reach out' and 'cell phone'. But he'd spent so much of his life in the States that the words of his adopted country were first on his tongue. He had to focus on being Irish.

Katie didn't tally with his expectations. She was old, sure. But not old old. He'd pictured a large woman with thick legs and steel hair. Someone forbidding. Instead, he'd been met by a small blonde lady wearing beige trousers and a navy jacket. He was taken by the way she'd described herself as a widow, like she was trying out the word. He guessed the bereavement was recent. Neither had he expected an assistant, but from the way Beth and Katie finished each other's sentences, he sensed they were close.

'We know who you are,' Katie had said as she rose from the black leather armchair to greet him. 'Well, to be honest, Beth here had to fill me in. Grunge passed me by, I'm afraid, but I gather you're very successful.'

He was touched by her use of the present tense. Black Iris had had their heyday – three *Billboard* number one albums, nine Grammys, four *Rolling Stone* covers – in the nineties. They hadn't been on stage or in a studio for three years. One or two heads had turned as he'd entered the Gresham Hotel and walked towards the bar, but even at the height of the band's fame, he'd rarely caused an out-and-out stir. After all, Anton had been the charismatic front man, Ray the famed guitarist, Liamo the crazy-as-hell drummer. Gary was the bass player. And unless you were Paul McCartney or Phil Lynott, who remembered the bass player?

Although Katie had warned him that she didn't have a bracelet for the relevant day, he hadn't been too disheartened. If his natural parents could be erased from history, it was hardly surprising that his given date of birth was wrong. He figured the details on the certificate couldn't be that far out. If he could get all her records for July, August and September 1971, he'd be able to find his birth mother.

Katie took a delicate sip of tea. 'You said in your email that you've only recently found out you were adopted. That must have been tough.'

'Yeah, at the start I refused to believe it. The thing is, I look like the rest of the family. I have two sisters, my parents' biological children, and we all have dark hair and brown eyes. And if you've been told a lie often enough, it becomes hard to accept anything else. For a while, I railed against my folks. In the end, though, I ran out of anger. You do, don't you? Anyhow, it's not like I have any complaints about my childhood. The three of us were treated the same – and we were treated well.'

The recognition that he'd been raised by kind, generous people had helped Gary to accept his situation. He'd never approve of what they did, but he'd heard enough stories about miserable childhoods to make him appreciate the Winters family. His bandmate, Ray, had suffered a horrific upbringing, with regular beatings and a mother who defended her husband no matter how cruel his behaviour. Complaining to Ray was like moaning about a paper cut when the guy beside you had a bullet wound to the chest.

'If you don't mind me asking,' said Katie, 'why did your parents wait so long to tell you?'

Gary's first impulse was to flim-flam around the question, but he had a hunch she'd see through him. 'It's kind of complicated. In my thirties, I had a relationship with a woman called Posy Fuente. You may have—'

'She's an actress,' said Beth to Katie.

'Oh, yes,' said Katie, with a deep nod, 'she won a prize at the Sundance Festival.'

Gary doubted that Katie was genuinely familiar with Posy's work. She'd done her research.

'So,' he said, 'Posy and I have a daughter. Allegra's her name. She's ten. I don't get to see her as often as I'd like, but … we're in regular touch. And we're good now, her mother and me. A year or so back, Allegra began having seizures. They were fairly bad, and her doctors couldn't track down the precise cause. They wondered if there might be a clue in her background. Like, could she have inherited some sort of genetic disorder? When they couldn't find anything on Posy's side, they asked about me. I wasn't aware of any issues, but I thought my folks might be able to help. To begin with, they were vague. There was a lot of shilly-shallying and staring at the floor. A week or two later, Allegra was no better, and the doctors were still asking questions. By that stage, I was in LA. I called home and said, "Listen, if there's anything,

anything at all, you've got to speak up." That was when they came clean. I can hear my old man's voice crackling down the line. "We can't tell you," he said, "because we don't know."'

'How's Allegra doing now?' asked Beth.

'She's a lot better, thanks. She's on medication and everything, and Posy has to keep an eye on her, but she's a great kid.'

'That's good to hear,' said Katie. 'I assume you haven't been able to find out if there's a family connection to her illness?'

Gary rearranged his legs. He felt too long for the chair. 'No. Only that's no longer such a big issue. I want to find my birth mother because I want to hear her story. I need to know why she didn't keep me. Oh, and I'd like to know if she's okay. Did she ever get married? Do I have brothers and sisters? And, if she needs anything, I'm not short. I could help.'

'I understand,' Katie said, reaching for the tea strainer and placing it over her cup. It was a while since Gary had seen proper tea with leaves. 'I know it might feel like your birth mother didn't want you, but, believe me, there's every chance she did. I'm sure she loved you very much. The way it was back then … girls weren't given a choice. And, awful as it sounds, quite a few of the mothers thought their babies would be better off elsewhere. Bless them, they were brainwashed into believing they weren't fit to raise a child.'

She faltered in a way that suggested she found this

difficult to discuss. Gary figured he'd be the same if he'd worked in such a terrible place. Still, her reassurance was welcome.

'That's not all,' said Beth. 'I've been reading up on this. Apparently, there was no support for single mothers. Not a penny. Unless your birth mother's family had agreed to help, she probably wouldn't have had the money to feed you.'

'What a system, huh?' said Gary.

'Did your parents say why they'd kept your adoption a secret?' asked Katie.

'I mean,' added Beth, 'isn't it unusual for someone's birth certificate to be forged?'

Gary signalled to the black-uniformed waitress for another coffee. This was going to take a while. 'Not as unusual as you might think.' He turned to Katie. 'When you were in the home, did you ever hear about birth certs being written up without the natural mother's name?'

She paused to consider the question. 'I didn't, but I wouldn't read too much into that. Carrigbrack was a secretive place. The mothers were forced to sign a document promising they'd never attempt to find their child. A certificate of surrender, it was called. They had no rights, and there was nobody to speak up for them, so the logical next step was to remove their name from the baby's papers.'

'It was as though an adoption had never taken place,' said Beth.

Gary's Americano arrived. He took a welcome mouthful.

'And that's my problem. There are no records. The arrangements were made through a cousin of Dad's who happened to be a nun. They were told next to nothing, just that I was born in Carrigbrack, I was in excellent health, and my birth mother was from a "decent" family. Whatever that meant.'

'And ...' started Katie.

'Sorry. You wanted to know why they didn't tell me the truth when I was a kid?'

'Yes.'

'First off, they'd recently moved to a new house so they didn't have to say anything to anybody. They weren't going to face any awkward questions about the sudden arrival of a baby. Plus, they genuinely thought they were doing the right thing. They worried that if the other boys at school knew I was adopted, there'd always be some lowlife giving me grief about it.'

'I see,' said Katie. 'If this nun was related to your father, it's easy to imagine her cutting a special deal for your family.' She stopped and raised a hand to her face. 'Gary, you'll have to forgive me. I've made it sound like your parents were buying a second-hand car or a barn of hay.'

He found himself smiling. 'It's cool. I understand.'

'Could the nun give you any information?' asked Beth.

'She died more than twenty years ago.'

'Ah.' Katie played with her teacup. 'Now, don't get me wrong, I'll help if I can. But I was wondering: you're a well-known man; might it not be easier for you to go public? To talk to a newspaper or a chat show? They'd be delighted to do an interview, I'm sure.'

She was shrewd, was Katie. Gary paused to gather his thoughts. Light Muzak tinkled in the background. He didn't mind; musicians had to make a living. To explain why he didn't want to make his private world public, he would have to tell Katie and Beth the story of his life. He would have to make them see that he'd moved in circles with the potential for limitless good times. From the age of nineteen, when Black Iris had first travelled to America, every rock-and-roll cliché had been available to him, and he'd tried most of them. As the warning at the start of his favourite true-crime podcast put it, his story contained coarse language and adult themes. For two decades, he'd bounced from one city to another. He'd been to all the best parties – and many of the worst. He'd been involved in every kind of excess on every continent.

He liked to tell himself that he'd fared better than most. He'd avoided alcoholism and addiction to hard drugs. His brain hadn't been liquefied. He had no infectious diseases. What he did have was a personal life that was monumentally screwed up.

His first marriage, to a singer called Lorena Sands, had produced two sons. They were adults now, and he saw them from time to time. Thankfully, his second marriage, to the model Carly McCall, hadn't lasted long enough for them to have children. He did, though, have another son, from a flirtation with a journalist. Then there was Allegra. Even though she was six thousand miles away, he liked to think he had a good relationship with his daughter. More than twenty years after the birth of his first child, he reckoned he was getting to grips with the fatherhood thing.

While he'd never had sex with a woman who wasn't willing, he hadn't always treated women well. He'd walked out on too many and considered the feelings of too few. His story had been part of the tapestry of the times in which he'd grown up, but times had changed. Talking about his life would give others the excuse to go rooting around. In the era of #MeToo and #TimesUp, he saw how his behaviour would be framed, and the picture wouldn't be pretty. He'd be vilified as a toxic love rat, a tawdry abuser, a guy who'd taken what he wanted and damn the consequences. He'd be part of the gallery of obnoxious entitled men.

A close examination of his life might also raise questions about why Black Iris hadn't played together in three years and why the bass player and the vocalist, friends since the age of nine, spoke only through their management and lawyers.

He figured that Katie already knew some of his history. Many of the bare facts were available online. He needed her to understand that speaking to the press would be a mistake, so he blundered through an explanation, emphasising his concerns for his parents. They wouldn't enjoy the spotlight, he said. If Katie didn't appear fully convinced, she didn't argue either.

She picked up her red handbag and took out a tattered brown notebook. 'Remind me,' she said to Beth, 'to get a new cover for this. Otherwise there's a danger it'll fall apart.'

'Will do.'

Next, she took out a pair of gold-rimmed reading glasses. 'Now, Gary,' she said, 'like I told you in my email, there were no babies born in Carrigbrack on the twelfth of August 1971. Neither do I have any mention of a Gary, so your adoptive parents must have chosen your name. There were, however, three boys born during the month of July and another two in August. Either side of those dates, there's quite a gap. In fact, it was October before another boy was born. Taking that into account, the chances are that you're one of the five. Have you a piece of paper so you can take all of this down?'

'I can put the details in my phone.' Gary took it from the pocket of his leather jacket. He also put on his glasses. 'It happens to all of us eventually,' he said to Beth, hoping he didn't sound too pathetic.

'Right,' continued Katie, 'there's a chance, then, that you are one of these five boys.'

She spoke slowly and clearly, giving the women's real names rather than the ones they were forced to use in the home. Even so, Gary had trouble recording everything she said. His hands trembled. This was the closest he'd come to finding out the truth.

The names fluttered around him. His mother might have been Gráinne. She might have been Tina or Edel, Noreen or Olivia. He might have been called Paul. Or he might have been Séamus or Kevin, Martin or John.

'Thank you,' he said to Katie. 'Thank you. Thank you. Thank you.'

She smiled. 'You haven't got anywhere yet.'

'But it's a start,' said Beth.

'Can you …' he asked, 'can you remember any of the women?' He then thought better of his query. 'Sorry, that was a dumbass question. It was almost fifty years ago. I can barely remember people I met last week.'

'As it happens,' said Katie, 'I do recall two of them. I remember Olivia because she attempted to escape. The guards brought her back, though what business it was of theirs, I don't know. She was a real beauty, a gorgeous young woman.'

Gary gave a nod of encouragement.

'And Edel has stuck in my memory because she was older than most of the others. She was in her mid thirties.'

'Which means she'd now be in her eighties,' said Beth.

'That's if she's still alive,' added Gary. 'I figure I ought to begin with Edel. Edel Sheehan.' There was pleasure in just saying the name. And if Edel wasn't the right woman, it had to be Olivia Farnham. Or Tina McNulty. Or Noreen Nestor. Or Gráinne Holland. All he had to do was whittle down the list and he would find his birth mother.

'Good luck,' said Katie. 'It's not an easy task. And … well, I'm not certain how to put this, but please tread lightly. If you do find your birth mother, it may take her a while to adjust.'

Gary's head was full of possibilities. 'Thanks,' he said. 'I … um, I was hoping there was one other thing you could help me with.'

Chapter 5

Then, Patricia

'What you'll learn here in Carrigbrack,' said Sister Agnes, 'is that actions have consequences. I'm aware that nowadays some girls dismiss this as an old-fashioned concept. "Sister," they say to me, "the world has changed. We can do what we want." You may even have thought something similar yourself. But,' the nun paused and focused her gaze on Patricia, 'no doubt you're beginning to understand how misguided such notions are. We can't abandon personal morality, and we can't fill the country with illegitimate children.'

Patricia had been sitting in the wood-panelled office for ten minutes, and most of Agnes's speech had been unexpectedly low-key. From behind a heavy desk, she'd rattled through a series of petty rules with the mechanical demeanour of a woman who'd done this a thousand times before, which she probably had. Save for a Sacred Heart lamp, the walls were bare. A tall bookcase was devoted largely to stories about female saints. A dark corner of Patricia's mind imagined the nun hiding contraband copies of *The Country Girls* or *Valley of the Dolls*.

This was her first encounter with the woman who oversaw the day-to-day running of the home. She'd arrived in Carrigbrack late the previous night. While Father Cusack had been brought to the parlour for tea and cake, a pencil-thin nun in a thick black dress and veil had shown Patricia to a dormitory. There, she'd been instructed to change for bed as quietly as possible. 'The other girls won't thank you for disturbing their sleep,' the nun had said. Patricia's request for a glass of water had been met with a raised eyebrow and a slow shake of the head. In the far corner, a girl had been crying, her muffled sobs amplified by the silence.

Agnes had a comfortable look that belied her position. With her pudgy face, small glasses and rosy cheeks, she looked kindly. Soft, even. Patricia had already seen enough of Carrigbrack to know that there was nothing soft about the place.

She'd heard about the homes. Who hadn't? From the age of ten or eleven, every show of disobedience had been met with a warning: if you don't watch yourself, you'll end up in Carrigbrack. Reality appeared to be even harsher than rumour. A substantial entrance hall, its floor gleaming, gave way to a series of sombre corridors. The mothers-to-be slept in dormitories, the children in a spartan nursery. There were no photographs or personal items, and few toys. Every room was decorated with religious statues and holy pictures. The penitents, as Agnes called them, wore indigo uniforms made from stiff cloth that seemed designed to rub and scratch. They ate in a draughty refectory. The nuns, and the nurses who helped deliver and care for the babies, had a separate dining room. Mass was every morning at seven, the rosary was at six, lights-out at nine.

New mothers could hold their babies only while feeding them. For much of the day, talking was forbidden. Any attempt to escape was likely to fail. The nearest village was more than a mile away, and most of the locals were supportive of the home. Runaways were easily spotted and returned. Anyone breaking the rules could expect to be disciplined. The punishments ranged from extra work to extra prayers to having your hair cut off. Happiness was viewed with suspicion.

Patricia had learnt some of this from a whispered conversation with the girl in the next bed and some from Sister Agnes. From what she had seen of the other women, many were cowed and docile. She had the impression that even if the doors were unlocked and the gates thrown open, few would leave. After all, where would they go?

Agnes was still speaking. There was more force to her words now.

'What you'll have to do,' she said, 'is reflect on the sins that brought you here and on how you can atone for them. You've caused grave distress to your family. When I spoke to your mother earlier in the week, it was clear she was heartbroken. Remember, despite what some would claim, there's nothing wrong with deference and humility. Men can't help themselves, so the burden falls on women to keep society safe and close to God. Do you understand?'

As much as she would have liked to argue, Patricia's compliant streak came to the fore. 'I do, Sister.'

'We may not get much thanks today, but future generations will be grateful that we stood firm and protected children from lives of corruption and sin.'

When, finally, Patricia was allowed to ask a question, her words were stilted. 'I was wondering, Sister, if I could work in the nursery. I think—'

'That's out of the question. Such valued positions are given only to our most trusted girls, and from what I've heard about the circumstances of your downfall, I don't think I can include you in that category. Some time working in the fields will be of more benefit to you. We grow our own fruit and vegetables here, and there's plenty to be done.'

'But—'

'I said no.'

To her annoyance, Patricia felt tears pooling at the back of her eyes. Don't cry, she thought. You can't cry.

'There are those,' said Sister Agnes, 'including some of my own sisters, who believe your shame will be eternal. As it happens, I don't share that view. You have fallen and you can rise again. The day will come when you walk out of here and begin afresh. But I warn you, Patricia, if you behave as though you belong in the gutter, the gutter is where you'll end up.' She shuffled some papers and gave a watery smile. 'Now, before we lose any more of the day, I'm going to bring you out to the garden. Sister Sabina is in charge. She can tell you what to do.'

That night, Patricia couldn't sleep. She hadn't been able to accept that she was pregnant. Now, she couldn't grasp that she was here, in a place of strangers, forced to use a name that wasn't hers, bound by rules that made no sense. A place without colour or comfort, where she had no control and no voice. Even her body was no longer her own.

She thought of Mike and of how sweet everything had been at the beginning. She thought of how they'd kissed the hours away. Of how she'd believed what he'd said. She wondered if he would hear about what had happened to her. If so, what would he think? Would he, too, think it was for the best?

In the dark, alone with her thoughts, she allowed herself to cry.

To begin with, Patricia cried every night, mopping her tears on the starched sheets. Her brain was clogged with 'what ifs' and 'if onlys'. She was regretful and angry and a hundred other emotions besides. The chaos in her head matched the awkwardness of her body. She was the wrong shape for sleep. During the day, she was too hot; at night, her limbs became rigid from the cold. If she learnt nothing else, she learnt that complaints were futile. Worse, they might lead to punishment.

Gradually, she came to terms with her situation. It wasn't what she would have chosen, but there was a person inside her. A boy or girl who kicked and squirmed. They might go on to achieve great things. They might play football or sing in a pop group or cure cancer. Or maybe they'd have a regular life with an ordinary job and a standard family. For the first time, she saw the appeal of a straightforward existence with someone who loved you. No hiding or game-playing; just honesty and commitment. Either way, the baby was real, and it was hers. It didn't belong to Mike or her parents. It didn't belong to Sister Agnes or Mother Majella or Sister Sabina. The dreaded Sabina had an extensive line in insults and a voice that could strip paint. Under her watch, even those in the final stages of pregnancy were forced to keep on working. Patricia had looked on in horror as the nun shouted at a girl who'd got sick while picking cabbages.

'I don't care if you're here until midnight,' she'd said, 'you'll finish your work.'

When Patricia had asked her parents about keeping the baby, she hadn't been serious. She'd been trying to shock them. As time passed, however, she wondered if it might be possible.

The more she got to know the other women, the more interesting she found them. It was easy to dismiss them as all the same when, in truth, no two were alike. Some were silent and downtrodden, while others appeared to have only a hazy idea of how they'd got pregnant. More were clever and funny. In snatched moments, they'd forget about their circumstances. They'd tell stories of home or impersonate the nuns or, imaginations soaring, dream up plans for the rest of their lives.

A few of the girls were in bad shape. One was bruised and emaciated, another had ringworm on her face, while a third had a permanent barking cough. Little was done to help them. Surely, thought Patricia, the nurses could do more? She'd taken a dislike to the nurses, who strutted around as if they belonged to a superior species.

From the nuns, and from Agnes and Sabina in particular, the mothers were subjected to regular diatribes about their own failings and those of others. Mini skirts, maxi skirts, long hair, short hair, English television, American music, depraved novels, the spread of the vernacular Mass: all were blamed for the rise of godlessness and the sorry state of the nation. More than once, Patricia caught the eye of one of the other girls, and they were forced to suppress a giggle.

After a few weeks, life fell into a rhythm. Every day was the same: prayer and work and more prayer and more work. As the evenings grew brighter, Patricia and the others spent endless hours in the fields, picking cabbages and cauliflowers, lettuces and scallions. They sowed and thinned and pruned until their swollen bodies screamed for rest.

'At the start, I thought you were stuck up,' said Winnie, 'but you're all right.'

'Thanks, I think,' replied Patricia, who was planting

cucumber seeds in small mounds of earth, the way Sister Sabina had shown her. Sabina had been called away, so they were free to chat.

'No offence, but you do have a stand-offish look about you. It's like you're more educated or something. Still, I reckon that behind that, you're the same as the rest of us.'

'We're all in the same position, anyway.'

'Knocked up and abandoned, you mean?' said Winnie, and they both laughed. The humour in Carrigbrack was dark.

Winnie was from County Sligo. She had bouncy black hair, a smattering of freckles and a wide, full-lipped smile. By comparison, Patricia felt washed out and drab.

'Jesus, this is uncomfortable,' said Winnie. 'Crouching's definitely not good for pregnant women. Sit down there for a minute.'

Patricia hesitated.

'Don't worry. We'll see Sabina coming.'

'Or if not, we'll definitely hear her. I'm more afraid that if I do sit down, I won't be able to get up again.'

Winnie tilted her face towards the sun. 'What's your story, then?'

'Not too different to yours, I'd say. I met the wrong man and … well, you know yourself.'

'Did he run off?'

'Yes and no.' *Oh, why not tell the truth?* 'He's married.'

'Ah. And did he used to tell you he'd leave her?'

'I never asked.'

'Weren't you the brazen hussy?'

Winnie's tone sounded amused rather than judgemental, and Patricia smiled. 'What about you?'

'Pure eejitry, to be honest. When we first met, I was cracked about him. He pestered me for sex, and I gave in. I hope he enjoyed himself, because it didn't do much for me: lots of pushing and panting and not many thrills. I remember Sabina saying, "All this for ten minutes' pleasure." And I thought, ten minutes? That'd be a miracle. Anyway, before I knew where I was, I'd missed three periods. I threw up at school, they sent me home, my parents put two and two together ... and here I am.'

'What did your boyfriend say?'

'Not much. After I told him, he moved to Manchester.'

Patricia attempted to clean one fingernail with another. 'That's desperate.'

'I know. The miserable fecker. When I get free of this place, I've a mind to head that way just to haunt him. I have this fantasy where he's sticking his tongue down some young girl's throat, and I pop up behind him shouting, "Surprise! Remember me?"'

As Winnie spoke, her curls bobbed in time with her voice. Patricia felt laughter rising in her throat like a cat's purr, and before she knew it, they were both laughing hard.

'I can see you, all right. The poor lad, I almost feel sorry for him.'

'I wouldn't go that far. To be fair, he might have been

worried about my father calling the guards on him. I'm sixteen now, but I was only fifteen then.'

'Oh. I thought you were older. As Sister Agnes would say, you've got your whole life ahead of you.'

Winnie ran a hand through the dirt. 'Is that what she said to you? She told me I only had myself to blame and that, chances were, I'd never amount to anything. "You messed up your own life," she said, "so we're not giving you a chance to mess up the life of an innocent child."'

Patricia decided to change the subject. 'When are you due?'

'Next month. You?'

'August.'

'That's one big baby you're carrying. Could you be having twins, do you reckon?'

'Jeekers, that's an awful thought,' said Patricia, a drop of sweat trickling down her back.

'Don't panic, I'm only messing.'

'Do you know what you want to do? Like, if it was possible, would you keep your baby?'

'Every day I change my mind. I'm not certain I'd be any good with a child. But, at the same time, I'd like to have a choice. Does that make sense?'

'It does, yeah. Will you go back and finish school?'

'You're codding me,' said Winnie. 'They wouldn't let the likes of me infect the place with my filthy ways. Believe me, I've a better chance of becoming Miss Ireland than doing the Leaving Cert.'

'By the time we leave here, you'll be an expert gardener anyway.'

'That's if I stay.'

'What do you mean?'

Winnie leant in close. 'I've spotted a gap in the hedge that runs around the back of the building. Even in this state,' she patted her stomach, 'it should be possible to squeeze out.'

Patricia was about to ask where Winnie would go when she saw a couple of the other girls scrambling to their feet. 'Damn, Sabina's on her way back.'

From then on, she kept an eye out for Winnie.

Every two weeks, Patricia received a letter from home. Mostly they were dreary, and she suspected her mother filtered out anything worth knowing. More often than not they were accompanied by an article torn from *The Sacred Heart Messenger* or the *Saint Martin Magazine*. Not being allowed to write back was a relief.

The letter that arrived in mid June was different. Her mam mentioned Mike – or Mr Langan, as she insisted on calling him. Her father had arranged to meet him, and they'd had a conversation. The thought brought bile to Patricia's mouth.

She couldn't remember when she'd first seen Mike. He was one of those people who'd always been there, a fixture of village life. When she'd been in her early teens, she'd fancied him. He had the sort of straightforward good looks that appealed to fourteen-year-olds: floppy black hair, toffee-brown eyes and skin that tanned easily. Locals maintained he had 'a touch of the Armada' about him. (This claim, of descent from one of the Spanish men whose boats had foundered off the west coast, was made about anyone who wasn't as white as a handkerchief.) Mike was seven years older than Patricia, a grown-up with a job selling insurance door-to-door. By the time he looked her way, she was nineteen. And he was married.

She recalled how it began. They'd met on the street, and she'd been surprised by his friendliness. No, it had been more than friendliness. It had been flirtation: sparkle and flash, push and pull. She'd walked away in a glow of compliments. A couple of weeks later, they'd met again. This time in Sheehy's bar. Patricia's father hadn't approved of her spending time in pubs; they weren't for respectable girls. If he'd had his way, she'd have kept her confirmation pledge until she was fifty. Mike had suggested they go outside – 'To talk in peace,' he said.

She remembered standing in the long west-of-Ireland twilight, her back to the wall. The night was mild, with barely a breath of wind. He cupped her chin, and they kissed. One moment he kissed hard, the next he paused to nuzzle her face and neck. He smelled of cigarettes, beer and spicy aftershave. She remembered the lurches and whooshes of pleasure. She remembered thinking, so this is what proper kissing is like.

Yes, she'd known that what she was doing was wrong. Mike was another woman's husband. Just thinking about him was a mortal sin. But, in truth, hadn't that also been part of his appeal? Her life had been heavy with duty, light on thrills. Her tightly regulated world hadn't allowed for excitement. All the same, in her idle moments, guilt crept up on her and told her she deserved to be punished.

After the evening in Sheehy's, Mike and Patricia met whenever they could. The first time they had sex was in a disused barn. Afterwards, they shared a cigarette and joked about rolling in the hay. To begin with, she didn't like doing it out in the open like a farm animal. She fantasised about a more sophisticated setting. She wanted to make love in a proper double bed with music and gentle light. As time passed, she accepted that this wasn't going to happen. By then, she was in love. Or, at least, she thought she was. It was more like a sickness, really. She craved Mike's company, his touch. She wanted to be with him all the time. And when they weren't together, she fantasised about him. Despite what some might want to think, she never felt pressured or bullied. She desired him as much as he desired her. She tried not to think too far ahead. She tried not to think at all. For a brief, glorious time, she considered herself special. He told her she was special.

He didn't complain about his wife or make any claims about Vera not understanding him. If he spoke about her, it was in passing, like he was talking about a friend or a sibling.

Patricia was aware that this sounded naïve. Others would be more severe in their judgement. As her mother put it,

'What kind of imbecile messes around with a married man? Nobody will have you now.'

Before she told her parents about the baby, she'd spoken to Mike. He asked what she wanted to do, as though there was a range of options. Then he said, 'It's probably best if we avoid each other for a while. People will talk.' She shivered as the truth worked its way in: she couldn't expect support from Mike or anyone else. The baby was her burden.

Now, she stood near the entrance to the nursery and read on. According to her mother, the meeting had been useful. *Mr Langan admitted he'd made a mistake, and he apologised. He said his head had been turned and he would never be tempted again.*

Patricia's forehead was damp. In the nursery, a baby cried, its thin wail cutting through the silence.

The letter continued: *He told your father that his wife is expecting. Their baby is due shortly before your own, but you probably know that.*

Again, Patricia paused. One of the nurses passed by, sent a concerned look in her direction, but walked on.

Mr Langan pleaded with your father not to take matters any further, and he agreed. As your father pointed out, it takes two to tango, and you share the blame. We talked it all through and decided that Mrs Langan is better off not knowing about her husband's infidelity. In every other respect, they have a good marriage. Please God, he's learnt his lesson. For your sake, and for hers, it's best if this matter isn't discussed again.

Patricia stopped reading. Her parents' initial reaction

had been easier to accept. Tears and spiky fury she could understand. In the circumstances, she might have behaved the same way. She could also forgive how distant they'd been on the night of her departure. They'd been in shock. But this was colder, more calculated. This was a swift punch to the stomach followed by a kick to the back of the knees. She wanted to fall to the floor, crumple up and hide.

She could see why, on leaving places like Carrigbrack, many young women went to England or America. It wasn't because they were ashamed. It was because they'd been abandoned.

In the nursery, another baby began to cry. Sister Eunice scurried by, then stopped and returned.

'Did you get bad news from home, Patricia?' she asked.

'No, I'm grand, Sister.'

Eunice, who wasn't much older than most of the girls, patted her arm. 'Well, if you need to talk, let me know. You're very pale.'

'Thanks, Sister.'

Patricia folded the letter and walked to the dormitory. Thankfully, it was empty. There, she tore the paper into narrow shreds and threw them in the bin.

Chapter 6

Katie

'Weren't you the woman who wasn't going to get involved?' said Beth as they rounded the corner from North Frederick Street onto Dorset Street. The day had turned out fine with just a scattering of thin white cloud, and they'd decided to walk back to Drumcondra.

'Strictly speaking, I don't think I've broken my word,' said Katie. 'It's not like I'm hammering on anyone's door making a nuisance of myself. And it'd be a terrible trip for him to make on his own.'

Gary's suggestion that she accompany him to Carrigbrack had caught her by surprise. Without stopping to think, she'd agreed.

'I reckon you just want a spin in a Ferrari – or whatever it is he drives,' said Beth.

She chuckled. 'I hope he brings something more sensible, because, let me tell you, a sports car wouldn't last long. When

I worked there, the nearest road was no better than a dirt track, and I've no reason to believe things have improved. The place was abandoned years ago.'

What Katie didn't say was that she'd found the morning fascinating. Now that she'd started the process, she wanted to see where Gary's search would lead. Of course, this was partly because of the sprinkle of stardust surrounding him. (At one point, she'd spotted two women staring and she'd wanted to say, 'Yes, ladies. It is!') But that wasn't all. Trying to piece together Gary's background was like doing a particularly complex Sudoku.

Also, the more she engaged, the less time she had to think about herself. She'd enjoyed the previous night's research, tracing Gary's glamorous life and complicated times. She'd sat in her fluffy dressing gown and slippers, a glass of white wine at her side, and tapped and scrolled until she'd found everything worth finding. While she would never be as internet savvy as her niece, she liked to think she was improving.

Despite this, she'd struggled with some of Gary's questions and observations. She needed to be better prepared.

'When did Carrigbrack close?' asked Beth.

'Sometime in the early eighties, but the numbers began to dwindle in the mid seventies. After the nuns left, it became a centre for people with disabilities. That shut a few years later. If you see the place, you'll understand why. It's very isolated. The back of beyond – and then on another bit, as Johnny used to say.'

'Have you ever been back?'

'Gosh, no. I was so happy to get out of there, I never had any desire to return.'

Katie had made her escape from Carrigbrack – and escape was how she thought of it – in the winter of 1972. The previous summer, on a day trip to Lahinch, she'd been sitting on the low wall at the top of the beach when a wiry, wavy-haired man had sat down beside her.

'That's some day,' he'd said, before introducing himself as Johnny Carroll. Along with a group of friends, he was spending a week in Clare. Katie was with another nurse from Carrigbrack, a marble-hard Galway woman called Rita Farragher. Although they weren't especially strong friends, Rita had a car, and Katie never said no to a few hours of freedom.

Forty-six years later, she remembered the briny air and the power of the waves as they surged and fizzed towards the shore. She remembered eating salty periwinkles from a paper bag, the tinkle of pennies sliding down the coin cascade and the thump and scrape of the bumper cars. Mostly, however, she remembered Johnny's good humour and his insistence that she accompany him to the dance in the seafront ballroom.

'I've got to get back to work,' she said. 'I'm on duty first thing in the morning.'

'I'll stay off the gargle and drive you back,' he promised. He did, too.

At the time, she'd found it hard to describe Johnny's

appeal. He was an average-looking man of average height holding down a steady but unspectacular job with Dublin Corporation. Yet there was something about him, something that allowed Katie to shake off her reserve. Now, she realised that she'd fallen for his enthusiasm. Johnny saw the positive in everything. No day was dismissed as too wet, no dinner too tasteless. No neighbour was too cantankerous, no colleague too dull. Every item had its merits, every person their saving grace. In some, this near-constant sunniness would have been grating, but Johnny got away with it. It was as if he gave everyone, Katie included, permission to have a good time. He taught her that it was okay to hug people, to compliment them, to tell them you valued their friendship. Simple acts, but important ones. It seemed to her that Beth's generation possessed an easy intimacy, and she envied them that.

A year working in Carrigbrack had hardened her. So immersed was she in the home's rules and practices that she began to ignore all but the worst instances of cruelty. On more than one occasion, she snapped at a young woman over some minor issue when she should have offered comfort. True, she continued to collect the babies' bracelets; true, she jotted down the details; but she did so by rote rather than through any sense of solidarity or affection. With hindsight, she saw how she'd had to grow a shell for self-protection. Back then, she'd worried she was being brainwashed. To this day, some of her decisions gnawed at her.

The second time she met Johnny, she told him about her

unhappiness. All she wanted was someone to listen. Instead he said, 'We'll have to get you out of there, Kateser.' At their third meeting, in the Imperial Hotel in Lisdoonvarna, he proposed.

Neither Oliver nor Mary Ann O'Dea was impressed by the idea of their elder daughter marrying an unknown Dubliner. In Oliver's view, the capital city was a nest of thieves and chancers where sin was rampant and women were losing the run of themselves. 'Soon enough, we'll be no better than the English,' he'd say to anyone willing to listen. He also argued that Katie was too malleable, and that Johnny was after her money. Whatever about his first claim, the second one was complete nonsense. The O'Dea family was long on respectability, short on cash. Their house was cold and rickety, with an outside toilet and mildew-infested bedrooms.

For once, Katie was determined to make her own decisions. Her parents boycotted the wedding and confined their communication to the occasional letter. No matter; she floated through those months, as light as a dandelion clock. She felt as if her life was beginning, which in a way it was. For her, Dublin was liberation. It helped that Johnny was from one of those happy families where the most serious fight was over who got to eat the skin of the rice pudding.

While her mother softened with the years, her father never fully accepted Johnny. Katie was struck by how old-fashioned this sounded. She'd effectively waited for a man to rescue her. Then, she'd been cold-shouldered by her father.

Beth would be appalled. In 1972, however, it had all seemed logical.

'So, what did you make of Mr Rock 'n' Roll?' Beth was asking. They were striding along Dorset Street, past a jumble of shops: a pizza place, a bookmaker's, a Polish supermarket and a black-windowed 'adult store'.

'Do you know,' said Katie, 'I quite liked him. He's interesting. He strikes me as someone who got lucky but never quite knew how to handle his luck.'

'You're very charitable.'

'Why so?'

'When he was talking about his children, I wanted to say, "Listen, bud, if you're that careless with the family you already have, I'm not sure you deserve to find any others." There he was, talking about a son here and a daughter there. At one point, he sounded like he'd lost track of the precise numbers.'

'Did you not get the feeling that he's making more of an effort now?'

'Yeah, but only because he's knocking on a bit and the pretty ladies aren't falling at his feet.'

Katie smiled. From her vantage point, Gary was as young as the morning. She'd warmed to his low rumble of a voice and his slightly lopsided walk. Also, with his tattoos hidden beneath a shirt and jacket, he'd looked quite presentable. Still, she couldn't argue with Beth's observations. Judging by what she'd seen online, he'd lived much of his life like a bee in a field of clover. Why had his behaviour changed? she wondered.

They were approaching the Royal Canal. On one side,

Croke Park rose up, more like an alien spaceship than a sports stadium. On the other, the water stretched out to Kildare and the country beyond. All these years later, Katie still got a lift from walking in her adopted city.

'I'm sorry,' she said. 'I never asked if you wanted to come to Carrigbrack. I just assumed you would.'

'Oh, you can count me in,' replied Beth. 'Now that I've heard more about the place, I'd love a look around.'

'That's great. One thing, though. Even though we won't be far from Danganstown, it's probably best if you don't mention our trip to your parents. Like I said before, I doubt your mother would understand.'

'You can relax. There's no danger I'd say anything to them.'

'I see,' said Katie, sensing this might be the time for some gentle prying. 'Is there an issue with your mam and dad?'

'Nope. Not with Dad, anyway.'

'What's my sister been up to?'

'Is it okay if we talk about it another day?'

'No bother, love. I don't want you to think I'm sticking my nose in.' This was precisely what she was doing, but an idea was beginning to take shape in Katie's head and she didn't want to fall out with Beth.

As they approached the bridge, Beth took her phone from the pocket of her denim jacket. 'I've felt several notifications,' she said as she peered at the screen, prodded it, then grinned. 'Well, what do you know? Two new enquiries, and both appear genuine.'

'Really? May I have a look?'

They turned down by the canal and found a quiet spot for Katie to examine the emails. The dark water flowed silently past.

'The first one's important,' she said. 'We'll have to tell Gary not to waste his time trying to find Edel Sheehan. She wasn't his birth mother – and she's dead. The email's from her son.'

Edel's son revealed that she'd managed to track him down. They'd become close in her final years, and he would like the wristband as a keepsake. *She was a wonderful woman,* he wrote, *who deserved much more than life gave her. I was fortunate we had some time together.*

'What about the other email?' said Beth. 'The one from the woman called Ailish?'

Katie leant back against the rough gable wall. With her free hand, she massaged her forehead. 'Do you remember the other day, when I told you about a young girl who'd been raped?'

'Uh huh.'

'I think Ailish Dwan's her daughter.'

'Oh,' said Beth. 'Oh.' She paused. 'God, that's desperate. But it's also good, if you know what I mean. What are we going to do?'

'By the looks of things, she didn't travel far. She's still in Clare. In Kilmitten. I reckon we ought to go and have a chat.'

Chapter 7

Ailish

If you asked Ailish, they did it deliberately. There was, she believed, a certain type of person who got their kicks from causing as much damage to a hotel room as a one-night stay would allow. Five-star hotel. One-star behaviour.

'Animals,' she said as she walked into Room 15. 'Out-and-out animals.'

The first thing she saw was the red-wine stain on the pale blue carpet. Then she noticed that one of the pictures had been knocked from the wall. And the smell was putrid. You'd swear someone was decomposing under the bed. She opened the windows as wide as they would go and inhaled several lungfuls of morning freshness.

A quick look at the bathroom confirmed her fears. There was a ring of scum around the bath, a layer of tan make-up on the white bath towel, and the toilet ... Well, the less said about the toilet the better.

The couple who'd spent the previous night in Room 15 deserved a particularly hot corner in housekeeping hell. A special kind of hell, Ailish had invented it years earlier to house the very worst guests. The people who tore the bed linen and spilled nail polish on the dressing table. The people who insisted on wearing muddy boots and using the wastepaper bin as an ashtray. Oh, and the people who clicked their fingers and shouted 'Maid!' in her direction.

Sometimes she wanted to say to them, 'Would you do that at home?' She knew full well, though, that the answer would be yes. Many of Rathtuskert Manor's guests could do whatever they liked at home because they had cleaners there too. Ailish divided the world in two: those who cleaned and those who let them.

And yet she enjoyed her job.

She'd had been working at the Manor for twenty years. Save for a brief period of maternity leave when her younger boy, Stevie, had been born, she'd barely taken a break. She felt as if she'd cleaned each of the forty-five rooms a million times. She was familiar with every suspect floorboard, every troublesome tap, every temperamental socket. There was nothing she didn't know about polishing smeared mirrors, unblocking sinks and removing the smell of vomit. Once, she'd been offered a promotion. The head housekeeper had left, and the general manager had suggested to Ailish that she might like to take over. She'd decided against it. Her reasoning was hard to explain. What sane person would understand why she'd prefer to push an iron cart around the

Manor's uneven-floored halls and clean up the filth of others? Why would she choose to have an aching back and hands that reeked of cleaning products? Why wouldn't she want to spend her day planning and inspecting?

The truth was that she got satisfaction from her work. She took pride in her ability to transform a room. She cherished the calm of working on her own. And, daft as it sounded, she prized what the wealthier guests left behind: pricey shower gels, high-end moisturisers, American magazines, and a library's worth of books. She wouldn't be able to buy any of these luxuries for herself, and she'd be a long time waiting for anyone else to buy them for her.

Deep down, she knew that this wasn't the complete story. She just couldn't picture herself as anyone's boss. She didn't have it in her.

She was an unusual housekeeper. An outlier. She'd seen scores of others come and go. Almost all her colleagues were either under thirty or from eastern Europe, but that suited her fine. She liked the banter in the staffroom, the young ones with their stories of raucous nights out and the Polish and Lithuanian women with their tales from home.

Jodie, her daughter, maintained that cleaning had become cool.

'Honestly, Mam,' she'd said, 'there are women on Instagram and YouTube making fortunes from cleaning tips. It's all about the best way to polish your windows, or how to stop your bin from smelling.'

Ailish hadn't believed her until she'd had a look for herself. It was a mad world, and no mistake.

She hadn't told Keith about the spurned promotion. He wouldn't have understood. He was forever complaining about how little she earned. Just the other day, she'd mentioned something about saving for Christmas, and he'd got all snarky, saying there was no point in buying presents for ungrateful children or for grandchildren who'd already been given too much. Then he'd delivered a speech about her low wages. It wasn't as if he earned much himself. Ailish resisted the temptation to say so. That would be asking for trouble.

Neither would she tell her husband about the message she'd spotted that morning on the adoption noticeboard. Before caution could take over, she'd fired off a reply.

Twenty years earlier, before the nuns had handed their files over to the authorities, Ailish had attempted to track down her birth mother. She'd told them everything she knew, including her belief that she'd been born in the mother-and-baby home in Carrigbrack. No, they said, we have no record of you, and even if we had, you probably wouldn't like what you found. It was best to leave well enough alone, they claimed.

She tried again a couple of years later. Once more, she was given the run-around. Keith, voice stained with disapproval, maintained she was deluding herself. 'Listen,' he said, 'children were given away for a reason. If you turned up on your birth mother's doorstep, she'd probably die a thousand deaths.'

Ailish abandoned her search.

She knew that not everyone wanted to find their biological mother. That was grand. That was their choice. But she did. The older she got, the more she wondered about the woman who'd given her away.

Who are you? she'd think.

What happened to you?

How has life been for you?

Do you ever think about me?

She suspected that if her experience of adoption had been happier, she might not feel so haunted. While her parents had been upstanding, they'd had no warmth about them. 'You're lucky we rescued you,' her mother used to say. 'Imagine the squalor you'd have grown up in if we hadn't taken you in.' As a child, she'd twisted herself into shapes to try and earn their approval. When her behaviour had fallen short of their standards, her mother had said, 'You didn't get that from us.' Later, Ailish had rebelled. She'd left school at the first opportunity and got married at nineteen.

Bed made and carpet scrubbed, she set about cleaning the sink. The woman in the mirror wasn't the woman she wanted to see. She'd read that, after forty, you got the face you deserved. If so, she must have been a right cow. There were grooves between her nose and her mouth and smudges as black as bruises beneath her grey eyes. Her hair was too thin, her eyebrows too wayward.

Occasionally, while buffing a table or pulling hair from a plughole, she tried on other lives. She imagined she owned the hotel and cleaned rooms for the fun of it. She ran a café beside the sea. She lived on a farm in the Australian outback and rode horses every day. She was Melanie Griffith in *Working Girl* or Madonna in *Desperately Seeking Susan*. They'd been her favourite films as a teenager and remained so today. Her taste in music was the same: if she'd liked it when she was a youngster, she liked it now. Not that long ago, 'Into the Groove' had come on the radio, and Ailish had strutted around the room like a sixteen-year-old. It was only when the song had ended that she realised the bedroom door had swung open and a guest had been watching. She'd been mortified.

Truth to tell, one of the reasons she'd shied away from trying to find her birth mother was her fear of not being good enough. She was a forty-six-year-old mother of four and grandmother of two who lived in a tiny house with a husband who would cross the road to be offended. She had a mediocre Inter Cert education, a low-paying job and a fifteen-year-old Nissan Micra. It wasn't that she was complaining. She had lots of joy in her life. She just figured her biological mother would have hoped for more.

She was bracing herself for the scummy bath, when she heard her phone make a silly *bing-bong* sound. The notification alert had been chosen by Stevie – he was an awful messer – and Ailish didn't know how to change it.

Already behind time, she told herself to ignore the message. She would finish the bathroom before taking a look. But what if the *bing-bong* meant there'd been a reply from the woman who'd posted the message on the adoption website?

Ailish had to find out.

Please, she thought. Please be good news.

As she read, a flapping sensation rose in her chest, as if birds were nesting there.

The woman's name was Katie, and she had information about Ailish's birth mother. As chance would have it, she would be in Clare the following day. Would it be possible for them to meet?

Ailish considered the question for at least ten seconds. Keith wouldn't approve, but Keith would be at work. He didn't have to know.

Yes, she replied. *That would be great. What would suit?*

Chapter 8

Katie

They left early for Carrigbrack, far earlier, Katie suspected, than Gary would have liked. For a long time, he spoke only to complain about the failings of other drivers.

Beth, on the other hand, was a morning person. She chatted away in the back of the car – a disappointingly boring Volvo – about her friends in Stoneybatter and what she was expecting from her new job. She threw the occasional question in Gary's direction, but got little in return.

'You live near Enniskerry? That must be beautiful?'

'It is.'

'And are your family nearby?'

'Stepaside,' he said, his voice gruff.

Katie felt compelled to fill the vacuum. As they passed the exit for Naas, she updated them on the responses to the forum. The night before, Carrigbrack Nurse had received another email, this time from a woman who'd already traced her birth mother. While the reunion hadn't gone well, she wanted her identity band. *Don't mind the online whingers*, she wrote. *You are doing a GOOD THING*. Katie promised that the bracelet would be with her soon. As for her critics, she found herself drawn towards their posts. Not that she'd say this to Beth. Her niece had little patience for the forum's more caustic members.

'Some folks shouldn't be allowed to have paper and crayons let alone access to the internet,' she'd said.

Katie would admit that there was something disturbing about her compulsion to read the judgements of people she'd never met.

You took part in this barbarity and now you're hoping for absolution? wrote one.

Where's your remorse? asked another.

You supported a vile regime. What did you do to stop it? added a third.

Even as her heartbeat accelerated, she continued reading.

Gary was unruffled by the news that Edel Sheehan couldn't have been his birth mother. 'It's cool that I've found out now rather than a few months down the line,' he said. 'I'll just move on to the next name on the list.'

'And will you be doing the work yourself?' asked Katie.

'I don't see why not.'

'I hope I'm not being presumptuous here, but I expect you have a few euro in the bank. Would it not be easier to hire a genealogist … or even a private detective?'

'Maybe. For the time being, though, I'll do my own thing. I've got plenty of time.'

'Won't you have to go back to the band? I mean, I know you've been having a bit of a break and …' Katie realised that she had wandered into sensitive territory, and she allowed her voice to trail off.

'No,' replied Gary. 'That won't be happening.'

He offered no further information, the conversation stalled, and for a while they travelled in silence. Katie watched the signs flash by. Monasterevin. Portlaoise. Mountrath. She remembered making the journey west with Johnny. Back then, they'd had to travel through a succession of towns and villages. These days, every last one was bypassed. It was almost as if they no longer existed. Although the morning was bright, it was the sort of bright that said, 'Don't be fooled, I could change at any minute.' Autumn was moving in.

At Katie's suggestion, they left the motorway at Birdhill and drove to Killaloe for coffee. Afterwards, they went for a walk beside the Shannon, the water clear as glass, the trees a deep green.

'County Clare,' said Gary, like a man visiting a foreign country.

'Has it been a while since you were over this way?' asked Katie.

'It's my first time.'

'Really?'

'Yeah. I joined the band when I was fourteen, and most of the gigs we played were in Dublin and Cork. I was nineteen when we went to America. There was never any reason to visit this part of the world. Well, that's not entirely true. I've been to Connemara. I was in Kerry once too ... with my first wife. But, apart from an emergency stop at Shannon Airport, this is my first time in Clare.'

'Except it's not,' pointed out Beth. 'You were born here.'

Gary came to an abrupt halt. He ran a hand through his hair and smiled his slow smile. 'I guess you're right. I guess I'm a Clare man.'

Beth laughed. 'On behalf of the natives, may I say we're happy to claim you. By the way, Katie and I are from up that way.' She gestured past the marina and upriver.

Katie felt a ridiculous pride at the simple beauty of the landscape. No matter that she'd left nearly fifty years before, she wanted outsiders to admire her home. She also had a fresh appreciation of how much Gary's world was shifting. 'There's not much in Danganstown.' she said. 'We'll spare you the tour.'

'The girls ... women, I mean ... in Carrigbrack, were they mostly local?'

'When I was there, some were from as far away as Cork and Dublin. There was a handful of mothers from Limerick and Galway, a couple from Sligo and Tipperary. But, yes, they were mostly local. If I recall correctly, two of the women on your own list were from Clare.'

Gary looked out over the river. 'So it's possible my birth mother came from around here?'

'I suppose it is.'

'She might be in this area now?'

'Yes.'

Afterwards, Gary opened up, and as they motored towards Carrigbrack, he offered small pieces of information. Before retirement, his father had been a teacher, his mother a school secretary. He hadn't told them about today's trip because he wasn't sure how they'd react. Neither had he spoken to his sisters.

Beth told him about growing up as the only girl in a large family, and about her tricky relationship with her home village. 'I'm fond of the place,' she said, 'but I don't think I could live there. If that makes sense.'

'It does,' he said, his tone that of a man who'd run away from home at nineteen and kept on running. His escape Katie could understand. What she found harder to fathom was his return. If Gary wanted a strong relationship with Allegra, why wasn't he in Los Angeles?

'The problem with being from a small place,' said Beth, 'is that you're expected to have an opinion about everybody. And I could never be bothered.'

'What about your own kids?' Gary asked Katie. 'Do they live in Dublin?'

'Johnny and I didn't have children.'

'Oh, I'm sorry. I just assumed … Nah, scratch that, it's none of my business.'

Katie wasn't surprised by Gary's assumption or by his ham-fisted attempt at recovery. In her experience, strangers often asked the questions that friends couldn't. More than ever, she wished they'd had a son or daughter, if only because it would mean some part of her husband had been left behind.

'We're not far away,' she said. 'You'd want to keep an eye out for the sign.'

Gradually, the landscape was changing, the fields turning to stone. The former mother-and-baby home was a mile or so from the village of Carrigbrack, on the edge of the Burren. Beth began a commentary on the area. She spoke about the limestone, the rare plants, the dolmens, the high crosses and ring forts.

'Sorry for sounding like the sixth-class geography book,' she said to Gary. 'I can't help myself. Dad used to bring us here as kids, and every time he'd give the same lecture about the wonders of the place. We'd all be wriggling in the back, asking when we were stopping for ice cream. He never mentioned that this was also a convenient spot for hiding a pregnant daughter.'

By now, they were on one of those narrow west-of-Ireland roads with a stripe of grass along the centre and unruly hedges on either side. Even to call it a road was to exaggerate its status. The hedges were laden with blackberries and rosehips. When the lane snaked to the left, they abandoned the car and walked the last short stretch. Gary strode on ahead with Beth a step or two behind and Katie at the rear. She couldn't quite believe that she was back.

What struck her most was the absence of noise. The breeze was too light to make a sound, the birds unusually subdued. The only sign of life came from a large hare that bounded onto the lane, took one look at them and scampered off again.

The tall iron gate, once so forbidding, hung open. The padlock and chain were smashed and scabbed with rust.

'This is it, then,' said Gary. 'The infamous Carrigbrack.'

Katie nodded.

The former home consisted of a series of grey buildings, some long and narrow, others small and squat. All were crumbling. The main house sagged. Branches and weeds poked through the roof. The windows were boarded up, and white paint peeled from the warped front door. An abandoned car was slowly disintegrating outside what had once been the nursery. Black rubbish sacks were heaped beside the main dormitory. Clumps of nettles had sprung up everywhere. The smell of decay, while faint, was unmistakable.

Beth touched Katie's shoulder. 'What's it like to be here again?'

'Odd,' was all she could say in reply. 'Odd.'

If she tried to say anything more, it would be incoherent. She'd been pitched back to a different time. A different century. And, in that moment, she was frozen. Girls milled around; some cleaning, others in the kitchen, more in the walled garden. A fortunate few were in the nursery, the unluckiest ones in the laundry. All wore the same drab blue uniform, its cloth chafing against their skin. There were determined faces, stoic faces, mischievous faces, but many of the women appeared beaten down and wary. The light had been turned off in their eyes. Sister Agnes patrolled the halls, her face round and pink-cheeked, her voice as thin and sharp as a razor. There too was Sister Sabina, permanently on the lookout for breaches of the rules. Sabina, who had the doleful eyes and emaciated face of a character from an El Greco painting, divided the girls into two groups: those she regarded as capable of reform and those dismissed as beyond redemption. In every case, she told them their shame would follow them forever. Beside her was Sister Faustina, who always looked like she'd rather be somewhere – anywhere – else. Faustina was obsessive about the rules. A couple of the other nuns were kinder, more flexible. Katie wondered, as she had all those years ago, if kindness could cut you open more effectively than cruelty. The girls, of course, said nothing. Talking was forbidden.

Her mind lurched forward again. There were few nuns left now. Those that remained tended to do good work. Others, the ones who'd had power, hid behind public relations companies.

Gary's voice broke through her thoughts. 'I was just asking,' he said, 'if there was a doctor here.'

'No. There was a midwife, an older woman who'd been in the home for years. And then there was me and another nurse.'

'What happened if a child was ill?'

'You did your best, and they either recovered …' she faltered, 'or they didn't.'

Gary looked away.

'Is it what you were expecting?' she asked.

'Yes and no. Knowing that once upon a time this place was full of life feels strange.'

The wind was getting up now, the sky filling in.

'Come on,' said Beth, 'let's go and look around the back before it starts to rain.'

At first glance, the back of the site looked like derelict ground. Katie knew otherwise. This was the part of their trip she'd been dreading.

A dilapidated wall was dotted at irregular intervals with rusty nails. Some were clearly visible. Others were obscured by brambles. A single headstone stood nearby. *In Memory of the Little Angels*, it said.

'I was reading about this,' said Beth. 'This is where the babies were buried. The nails give a rough indication of where the graves are.'

'But how can you tell which grave is which?' asked Gary.

'You can't,' said Katie. 'That was the point.' A heaviness came over her; a sense that, like the buildings, she could crumble into the ground. 'The nuns didn't want anyone making a fuss.'

'What I'll never get,' said Beth, her face shining with the zeal of the recently converted, 'is how women could be so hard on other women.'

Katie felt a snap of pain across her forehead, as if she'd been struck. 'I know I should have complained. If nothing else, I should have done something to make sure the children were given a proper burial. When I think—'

'I wasn't having a go at you, Katie. That's not what I meant.'

They stood in silence, Katie blinking back tears. Beth placed an arm around her. Gary stared at the ground.

'I think this is the saddest place I've ever been,' said Beth. 'I can't imagine how difficult it must be for you. Please forgive me for putting my foot in it. You did your job, and I'm sure you did it well.'

'You're fine, lovey,' said Katie. 'There's nothing to forgive. Unless you were here in those days, it's hard to understand what it was like – and why everyone behaved the way they did. To try and answer the question you asked: in some cases, the nuns were blinded by religious belief. In others, well ... we all like to have someone to look down on, don't we?' She turned towards Gary. 'Has coming here helped you at all? I mean, it doesn't really bring you any closer to finding your birth mother, does it?'

'No, but I'm glad we made the journey. It makes her, whoever she was, feel more real.' He paused. 'And thanks for coming with me. It's obviously not easy for you.'

When they got back to the car, the first drops of rain were landing on the windows. Gary reached into the glove box, took out a bag and passed it to Katie. 'I meant to give you this earlier. It's about the right size, I think.'

The bag contained a cover for her old notebook. Made of emerald-green leather, it was perfect.

'I wouldn't want the notebook to fall apart,' he said, 'not while you still have work to do.'

'Thank you,' replied Katie. 'That's … that's very kind.'

'Aw, it's nothing,' replied Gary, apparently embarrassed by his own thoughtfulness.

As they left Carrigbrack, Katie turned towards the passenger window, rested her forehead against the glass and closed her eyes.

The door was answered by a small, spare-framed woman in a maroon top and trousers; so small and spare-framed that Katie, who was handy-sized at best, felt like a giant.

'Katie?' said the woman.

'That's me. You must be Ailish.'

'The very woman. Come in before you get soaked. You'll have to forgive the gear. I'm just home from work and I haven't had the chance to get changed.'

The rain, which had fallen intermittently on their journey to Kilmitten, had suddenly intensified. Before stepping into the hall, Katie turned and waved to Gary and Beth, who'd spotted a café a short way down the street. The downpour hit her face like a fistful of gravel. Gary, who'd stopped to pull on a black woolly hat, waved back.

'Is that …?' started Ailish. 'No, obviously not.'

Katie shrugged off her anorak. Even in a leather jacket and jeans, with wild hair and several days of stubble, Gary stood out. He looked like someone who ought to be famous.

'What were you going to ask?' she said, finding it hard to keep the insider knowledge from her voice.

'Ah, nothing. I just thought I recognised the man you were with. Come in and I'll put the kettle on.'

'You probably did.'

Ailish's delicate face was split by a huge grin. There was a gap between her front teeth. 'You mean that genuinely was Gary Winters?'

'I do.'

'Nooo.' She clapped her hands with joy. 'I can't believe you know him. When I was young, I was a massive fan of Black Iris. Massive. I remember leaving the children with Keith – that's my husband – so myself and my friend could go and see them in Slane. The bus didn't get back until seven the next morning. I thought Keith would go insane.' She clapped again. 'But it was worth it. Totally worth it.'

'If I'd any idea you were a fan, I'd have asked him to come over and say hello.' Katie wasn't sure that this was true. Neither was she sure that Gary would have agreed. In her limited experience, he could be warm and chatty one minute, withdrawn bordering on sullen the next. Ailish might be disappointed by her hero.

By this point, they were in the next room. The house was in the middle of a pale pebble-dashed terrace, and its kitchen was small and functional. The cupboards were a yellowish cream, the table chipped brown Formica, and the fridge hummed in a manner that suggested its best days were behind it. The room was saved by little touches of life: a photo of a group of women all glossed up for a night out, a child's multicoloured painting, and, pinned to the fridge, a local newspaper clipping about a victorious football team.

Katie sat down while Ailish filled the kettle. She was still smiling. 'Forgive my nosiness, but what's Gary Winters doing in Kilmitten? Are you related? And who's the young woman? Is she his wife or girlfriend or something?'

'No, that's Beth. She's my niece. Gary's ...' Katie hesitated. While she shouldn't break a confidence, she reckoned Ailish deserved an exemption from the rule. 'We've been visiting Carrigbrack. Gary's trying to learn more about his background too.' She gave a carefully edited version of the story.

Ailish put down the mugs she'd taken from the cupboard and turned around. 'You're saying I was born in the same place as Gary Winters?'

'Yes.'

'And I may have been there at the same time?'

'There's only three months between you, so it's almost certain that you were. The difference is, I remember you. Unfortunately, I don't remember him.'

'So what you're saying is, Gary and me – we're part of the same gang?'

'I suppose I am.'

'That's amazing. I swear to God, if I learn nothing else, I'm happy knowing that.' She took a white box from a bag and placed its contents – four dainty cakes – onto a plate. The cakes were elaborately iced, like the ones served with afternoon tea in pricey hotels. 'I knew I wouldn't have the chance to get to the shop,' she explained, 'so I took these from work. Anyway, they owe me. I had to clean three extra rooms today, and two of them looked like a pack of hounds had been let loose.'

Katie knew that Ailish was a chambermaid and that she was married with four children. Her knowledge ended there. Unlike Gary, Ailish Dwan had left no imprint on the World Wide Web.

For a few minutes, the two women drank tea and traded titbits of information. Ailish revealed that, in the past, she'd made fruitless attempts to track down her birth mother and that Keith hadn't approved. This time, she hadn't told him. Thankfully, he wasn't due back from work for a couple of hours. Three of their children were in their twenties and had left home. Their youngest, Stevie, was at a friend's house. Not, Ailish added, that he'd have any difficulty with what she was doing.

'But just say he let something slip to his father,' she said, 'where would we be then?'

'Will it not be hard for you to make progress without telling your husband?' asked Katie.

Ailish's large grey eyes were troubled. 'For years, I tried not to think about it. I told myself there was nothing more I could do, and that maybe my birth mother wouldn't want to meet me anyway. The problem is, I can't stop wondering. I hear other people's stories and, even when they don't work out, I find myself thinking, at least they did their best. Every day, I follow the stuff in the papers and online. I read the forums and whatnot. And I've never been more certain about anything. I've got to do this.'

'What if Keith finds out?'

'We've been married for twenty-seven years, and I don't want to fall out with him, so I've decided I'll do as much as possible without telling him. But, in the end, he'll have to accept my decision.'

There was a slight wobble in Ailish's voice, enough for Katie to gather that this was hard for her. 'Are your adoptive parents still alive?' she asked.

'No.'

She waited while Ailish picked the icing from one of the cakes.

'Mam and Dad were "good" people.' Ailish didn't make the air quotes; she didn't need to. 'I was their only child, and I think the nuns chose them for their devotion to the Church rather than any fondness for children. No matter what I did, they were unimpressed. I was never smart enough or polite enough. I never looked right. They'd hoped for an obedient girl, someone they'd be able to shape. Instead, they got scrappy old me.'

'I'm sorry it didn't work out.'

Ailish nibbled the cake before responding. 'They did their best. I did too. We kept in contact after I left home, but we were never close.'

Although she said no more, there were worlds of information in her silence.

'So, then,' said Katie, 'you'll be wanting this.' She handed over a padded brown envelope. 'It contains some information, and I'll do my best to answer your questions.'

Ailish opened the envelope and took out the paper bracelet. She passed it from one hand to the other and back again. 'So tiny,' she said. Then she read the details, the same details that a few days earlier had moved Beth to tears. 'I was Jacqueline. Jacqueline Culligan.' She took a deep breath. Then another. When she spoke, her voice was flecked with pain. 'My mother picked a lovely name for me. Was Hanora her real name?'

'No. Her name was Chrissie.'

'Do you have any idea where she was from?'

'She was from somewhere in County Clare, but I'm afraid I can't remember the exact spot.'

Although her voice remained low, Ailish's smile returned. 'She's local, though. Isn't that brilliant? She might be down the road. Do you know anything else about her?'

Katie wasn't sure how much was hers to tell. She'd run it all past Beth, and they'd agreed that one fact would emerge anyway. The rest was up to Chrissie.

'There's something you should be aware of,' she said. 'Your mother was young.'

'I see. Like seventeen or eighteen? I was only twenty when my eldest was born, and, believe it or not, she got pregnant at the same age. I was ripping with her. Jodie's not like me. She's clever. I remember shouting at her, "You could have done anything with your life, and now you'll be stuck here like the rest of us."'

'Where is she now?'

'She's three hundred yards away, in the new houses beside

the church. And you know what? I was wrong. Her partner's a great fellow, and everything's worked out okay for them. They have two kids, and Jodie's in college, studying business, no less. I wish I knew where she got her brains from.'

'That's great to hear.' Katie swallowed. While she prepared herself for the next part of the story, Ailish placed the bracelet back in the envelope and put it in her bag.

'I don't want anything to happen to it,' she said, 'not after you've minded it so well.'

'The thing is …' Katie paused, 'when I said Chrissie was young, I meant very young. She was fourteen.'

The words floated between them.

Ailish raised a hand to her mouth. It was older than her face, the hand of someone who'd done decades of cleaning. 'Oh, bless her. Imagine being sent to that place when she was only a baby herself. She must have been petrified. Was she all right? Were people nice to her?'

'From what I can recall, she was fine. Or as fine as she could be. When I left Carrigbrack, she was still there. You know the way it worked: she had to spend another while in the kitchen or the laundry to meet the cost of her stay.'

'Pfft. I've read about that carry-on. The fucking pettiness of it, if you'll excuse my language.'

'No apologies needed. It was a terrible practice.'

'Do you know what happened? Like, did she have a boyfriend?'

'I don't know,' said Katie, hoping her lie wasn't obvious.

Ailish's eyes filled with tears. 'Don't mind me. I swore I

wouldn't get emotional, but it's hard, isn't it? Do you recall what she looked like?'

'Petite. Red hair. Big eyes. A lot like you.'

Ailish's mouth twisted and she began to sob, spasms passing through her thin body. Her shoulders rose and fell, rose and fell. 'The poor thing. All these years, I thought she'd given me away because I wasn't good enough. You'll probably say that's stupid, but it's how I felt. And there she was, only a little girl. I doubt anybody asked what she wanted.'

Katie reached over and rubbed Ailish's hand. 'She wouldn't have been able to care for you. You see that, don't you?'

'But her family would. They could have looked after us.'

'You can't say that. You don't know their circumstances.'

'I suppose.'

'They may have been given no choice.' Katie took a packet of tissues from her bag and handed them across the table. 'No doubt you've heard what it was like: the whispers and the nasty looks and all the local busybodies gathering around until the priest knocked on the door. Many ordinary families were given no say in their daughter's fate.'

Ailish blew her nose and dabbed at her face. 'Trust me, it wasn't much better when I was a teenager. There were people around here who got their entertainment from looking down on the rest of us. Anyway, that settles it. I need to find her.'

Earlier, in Carrigbrack, Katie's doubts had returned. She'd questioned whether she was robust enough for the task. Dedicated enough. Those misgivings had evaporated. She was helping Gary and she would help Ailish.

Something else occurred to her. 'I'd better get going,' she said, 'but before I do, I'll give Gary and Beth a ring. I'd say he'd like to meet you. You've got a lot in common.'

Panic flashed across Ailish's face. 'Oh no, I couldn't. Not here. The state of the place. And the state of me! In my manky uniform with my face all blotchy and my eyes red.'

'Don't worry about any of that. You look grand. And Gary will understand that this is an emotional day for you.'

'I'm pleading with you, Katie. I know you mean well, but Gary Winters wouldn't want to meet the likes of me. Please.'

'If you're sure …'

'I'm sure.'

They heard the front door open, then close again with a sharp click.

'Oh hell,' whispered Ailish. 'I hadn't expected him for hours yet. How are we going to explain—?'

'Ailish!' came a roar. 'Who owns the coat in the hall?'

A man entered the kitchen. A solid slab of a fellow with shaggy eyebrows and skin like corned beef, Keith was as tall as his wife was tiny. 'What's the story?' he asked.

'Well …' said Ailish.

Katie stood and put out her hand. 'Mr Dwan, how nice to meet you. Katie Carroll's my name. My niece and I have been staying in Rathtuskert Manor. Ailish looked after us so well that when we were leaving we went to say goodbye. Well, we were devastated to learn that she'd already finished for the day. Thankfully, the manager was kind enough to pass on her number, and I invited myself in for a cup of tea.' She smiled what she hoped was her sweetest smile. 'My niece is having a look around the village. I was just about to leave.'

Reluctantly, he shook her hand. 'You do know there are laws against that class of thing. A worker is entitled to privacy.'

'Mrs Carroll's been very good,' said Ailish, her tone suggesting that cash had changed hands.

It was enough to placate Keith. 'That's decent of you. Plenty of rich folks have stayed in that hotel, some of them rotten with money, and they haven't left as much as two euro for Ailish.'

'That's shocking,' said Katie. 'I find manners aren't what they used to be.'

'How right you are,' he said. 'Mind you, Ailish can be her own worst enemy. I'm worn out from telling her she's too timid.'

Katie guessed that this wasn't all he told her. Keith struck her as a man who valued his own opinion. No wonder his wife was so nervous. She picked up her bag. 'I'd better make a move. It was a pleasure to meet you, Mr Dwan. Your wife's a fantastic woman. And Ailish, promise me you'll stay in touch.'

'Don't worry,' she said, 'you haven't heard the last of me.'

Chapter 9

Then, Patricia

It started with the rat.

They were in the walled garden, picking strawberries, when it ran across Jacinta's foot. Jacinta was a tall, snippy girl from the Ennis Road in Limerick. Patricia knew where she was from because she mentioned it – a lot. Although the Ennis Road meant nothing to most of them, they guessed it was a well-to-do area and that Jacinta wanted everyone to understand that she wasn't a lower-class scrubber. She also moaned – a lot – about getting fat.

'I wonder,' said Winnie, 'if she's noticed that she's single, nine months pregnant and living in a prison full of women. She might have more serious problems than putting on a few pounds.'

The rat – a greasy, long-tailed creature – scurried over Jacinta's foot before veering left into the blackcurrant bushes. Many girls would have shuddered. A hardy few would have taken it in their stride. Jacinta began squealing. In a blink, she was bawling like a banshee.

Sister Sabina, who was a short distance away, shouted at her to stop. When her instruction was ignored, she tried again.

'Quieten down, will you,' she said, her voice twanging with irritation. 'It was only a mouse.'

'It was a rat,' said Jacinta. 'A dirty, disgusting rat. He could have bitten me. My baby could have died.'

'Whatever it was, it's gone, so put an end to your snivelling and get back to work.'

Jacinta resumed her keening.

The June day was warm, the sun prickling their skin. If you asked Patricia, Jacinta shouldn't have been at work. She should have been inside with her feet up, waiting for her big day. Her baby was due within the next couple of weeks. Patricia herself was hot and uncomfortable, and her baby wasn't due for two months.

Jacinta was a messy crier, her face scrunched up with misery, her body shaking. Eventually, Sabina walked over and slapped her – *thwack* – across the cheek. For half a moment, Jacinta stopped, only to start up again even louder than before. Sabina administered another slap and received the same response. Jacinta had worked herself into a frenzy.

Patricia was disturbed by the scene. Although they were treated like errant schoolgirls, most of them – Jacinta included – were grown women. No matter that the regime was strict; the nuns weren't supposed to engage in physical punishment.

Winnie stood up. 'Ah, Sister,' she said, 'will you look at the cut of her … and her about to give birth at any minute. She's in a bad way.'

'Winnie, this is none of your concern. You've a job to do. Those strawberries won't pick themselves.'

'She has a point, though,' said Patricia, getting to her feet too. 'Imagine if Jacinta was so upset that something happened to her or the baby. I gather her parents are well connected.'

Jacinta gave a loud sniffle of acknowledgement.

Patricia raised an eyebrow at Sabina, her way of saying *I have the measure of you*. The letter from her parents, in which they'd essentially said that Mike's happiness and well-being were more important than hers, had knocked something loose in her. She was less deferential than before. Less respectful. She also dwelled on what they'd said about Mike's wife. Patricia hadn't known that Vera was pregnant. The information made her feel dirty.

Winnie looked at her and nodded. 'As I understand it, Sister, Jacinta's people have a fair bit of money.'

As often as the Carrigbrack women were told that they were all the same, they knew this was untrue. Some sinners were more equal than others.

For at least a minute they stood there, staring at each other. Six girls who'd been working nearby also got to their feet. One of them, a tiny little thing who said she was fourteen but might be younger, looked terrified.

Finally Sabina sighed and said, 'This pathetic behaviour is distracting us from our task. Come on, Jacinta, you'd better go indoors for a while so you can regain control of yourself. The rest of you can return to the strawberries. I'll be back shortly, and have no doubt, if I hear any chatter, there will be consequences.' She glanced at Jacinta. 'Like I always say, empty vessels make the most sound.'

In Sabina's absence, they worked slowly. As Winnie put it, 'One strawberry for the bucket, one for the mouth.' Patricia and the others followed her example. It wasn't as though they were stealing from their own table. Most of the soft fruit was either sold or turned into jam. The girls rarely got jam, and, on such a hot day, the strawberries were delicious.

The food in Carrigbrack was meagre and poorly cooked. Their diet consisted of porridge, soup, bread and fatty bacon. Everything was either too watery or too lumpy, too cold or guaranteed to scald your mouth. They suspected the nun who ran the kitchen went out of her way to ensure the meals were borderline inedible. Otherwise, they might get pleasure from their food, and pleasure was forbidden. They ate because they were hungry and because their babies deserved the nutrition.

'All we need is a jug of cream,' said Patricia, wiping the juice from her chin.

Winnie grinned. 'Aren't you the fancy one with your cream?'

'My father used to say, "I don't know where you get your notions from."'

'Are you sure he's not related to my old man? He says exactly the same thing.'

When she wasn't chewing, or teasing Patricia, Winnie was singing to herself. After Sabina returned, she continued. While her friend wasn't especially tuneful, Patricia thought she recognised 'The Mountains of Mourne'.

'How many times do you have to be told to work in silence?' asked the nun.

'We're not allowed to talk. Nobody told us not to sing.'

'I'm telling you.'

'Grand, so,' said Winnie, who hummed instead.

Sabina walked towards her. 'You're determined to cause trouble, aren't you?'

'Not really.'

'We've had some cheap straps in here, but you're among the worst of them. I've always thought that some girls are led astray and others, God help them, are abused. But the likes of you? You're pure bad. If I had my way, you'd be kept in here indefinitely.'

Patricia wondered if Sabina genuinely believed this. If so, what had happened to sour her view of human nature and strip her of empathy? Yes, Winnie could be cheeky. But she was also as kind as the day was long. She'd been the first to support Jacinta, a girl she didn't particularly like.

Winnie stood up. 'Hold on a—'

Sabina was warming to her theme. 'You're a disgrace to your family. No wonder they threw you out. Mind you, they've questions to answer themselves. If they'd made any attempt to teach you right from wrong, you'd still be above in Sligo studying your books. Now do as you're told.'

Again, Winnie looked like she wanted to say something. Instead, she paused, stuck out her chin and began to sing.

'*I believe that when writing, a wish you expressed …*'

She faltered, and for what felt like an agonisingly long time, there was silence. Patricia looked at her friend. There were tears in her eyes, a reminder that, for all her bravado, she was only sixteen. Patricia stood and finished the line: '*As to how the fine ladies in London are dressed.*'

From the other side of the garden, a third girl joined them: '*Well, if you'll believe me, when asked to a ball …*'

And then a fourth: '*They don't wear no tops to their dresses at all.*'

By the time they'd reached the final line, all eight workers were singing.

'That's enough,' said Sabina, with a brisk clap of her hands. 'In fact, that's more than enough. I want you to get back to work. Except you, Winnie – you're coming inside with me.'

Patricia didn't know many songs, and most of those she did know were religious. But the warmth of the day and the nastiness of Sabina's words had combined to create a restive atmosphere. This was no time to give up. She cleared her throat and began:

'When boyhood's fire was in my blood,
I read of ancient freemen,
For Greece and Rome who bravely stood,
Three hundred men and three men.'

Once more, Winnie and the others joined in. That only a couple of them had strong voices didn't matter. When they all came together, they sounded formidable.

Sabina hadn't bargained for mass insubordination. 'You'll stop that racket,' she said, 'and you'll stop it immediately. Do you hear?'

Emboldened, they sang on. Their repertoire was short but varied. After 'A Nation Once Again', they tried 'Daydream Believer'. This segued into 'Hey Jude' which somehow led to 'An Poc Ar Buile'. Here they were, cut off from the rest of the world, with no audience but themselves, their voices lifting and soaring. They sang with spirit and exuberance, and occasionally they even sang in tune. When they forgot the words, they *la la la*-ed. When a girl paused for breath, another took over. At one point, Patricia's baby delivered an almighty kick, but still she sang.

They were a ragtag bunch, their stomachs swelling against their ugly uniforms, their hair tied up in topknots, their faces pink from heat and exertion. They'd been assaulted, abandoned, discarded, left in the lurch. They'd been branded, insulted and punished. They were sluts, tramps, whores, fallen women. Their babies would be taken from them without consideration or permission.

And still they sang.

At first, Sabina shouted at them. When this didn't deliver, she poured scorn upon them, their families and their pregnancies. She spoke in an assortment of monosyllables and grunts. At one stage, she mentioned the devil. She was no fool, however, and after a while she went in search of reinforcements. Presumably, she also hoped her absence would bring their singing to a halt.

Briefly, they did stop. The sun was scorching through the cloth of their uniforms and beating down on their bare heads. They needed a rest. The arrival of Sister Agnes rekindled their enthusiasm. Oh, and there was something else. Something remarkable. The respite was long enough for them to hear the faint but unmistakable sound of 'Black Velvet Band' drifting from the main house. Their protest had spread.

Agnes was white with anger. Two deep pleats formed at the top of her nose. She made no attempt to silence the women, however. She told them to leave the buckets of strawberries behind and return to the house. Two by two, they linked arms and, like refugees from a musical Noah's Ark, did as she asked. On their way, they sang 'The West's Awake'.

Inside, they were met by more singing. From the kitchen, they could hear 'All You Need Is Love'. The girls in the laundry sang 'The Raggle Taggle Gypsy', while in the nursery a lone voice performed 'Oklahoma'. Several babies did their best to follow the soloist's lead. Sister Agnes and some of the other nuns ushered all the women into the refectory and closed the doors. They would be corralled there until thirst, exhaustion or the need to go to the lavatory forced them to stop.

Patricia saw Sister Eunice standing beside a dresser. The nun smiled before quickly turning away.

For an hour or more the women continued, pausing only to listen to Bernadette, a shy slip of a girl from Tipperary. It was unusual to hear her speak, let alone sing. She stood at the top of the room, closed her eyes and sang 'We Shall Overcome'. Her voice was powerful and pure. None of them would have guessed at her talent.

Even as Bernadette's voice floated over the room, and even as Patricia hummed along, she knew it was a lie. She doubted that all of them would overcome. She also knew that this harmless revolt would be punished. In that moment, though, they were united against a common opposition: not just the nuns, but every damn thing that had caused them to be trapped in Carrigbrack.

What Patricia felt then was as close to joy as she had experienced in a long time.

Chapter 10

Gary

It was odd that such a bleak experience could be so energising, but after his visit to Carrigbrack, Gary was doubly determined to find his birth mother. At the start, he'd been irritated by Katie's plans for a detour. He hadn't wanted to drive to some throwback of a village so she could hand over a bracelet to a woman lucky enough to know her own mother's identity. Now, he regretted not calling in to Ailish's house to say hello. It wasn't so much the news that she was a Black Iris fan that had changed his mind, as something Beth had said while they waited in the café.

'This could have been your life,' she'd said, as rain pecked the window. 'You could have been brought up in Kilmitten. Maybe you'd still be here, working nine to five and looking forward to a quiet pint in some kip of a bar.'

She had a no-nonsense way of speaking that made her pronouncements difficult to challenge. That didn't stop him from trying.

'I suppose. But who's to say I wouldn't have ended up in a band anyway? I might have had the same experience only with a different bunch of guys.'

Beth blew across the top of her cappuccino. 'That's true. I'm not saying you wouldn't have had the talent. I'm just suggesting there would have been more obstacles in your way.'

'So I should thank the stars I was born two months before Ailish and got my parents rather than hers?'

'That's about the size of it, yeah. It's unbelievable to think the two of you were in that awful place at the same time. You're part of the same tribe, if you get my drift.'

He did, and it was.

She was an attractive woman, Beth. Gary liked how animated she was. Physically, she was right too. He'd always preferred his women on the chiselled side. He'd considered making a move, but had a feeling he might not be her type.

The following morning, he sat at his desk, making lists, jotting down possibilities, adding and subtracting. According to Katie, his birth mother was likely to be one of four women. Two had been from Clare, one from Galway and one from Kerry. Of these, he reckoned Olivia Farnham was the leading candidate. Admittedly, he had no hard evidence to support his theory. He just liked the fact that she'd tried to run away. The idea of his birth mother being a bit of a badass appealed to him. He pictured her, dark and gangly, setting out from Carrigbrack, giving hell to the nuns and whoever else got in her way.

He already knew that officialdom was unlikely to be of much assistance. Officially, the boy born in Carrigbrack in the summer of '71, the bass player, father and sometime husband, didn't exist. Olivia Farnham hadn't given birth to a son; Lillian Winters had. All the authorities could do was confirm this.

There must, though, be a record of Olivia. According to Katie's notebook, she'd been twenty in August 1971, which meant she'd been born in 1951 or in the last five months of 1950. The notes also said she was from Clare. It was a substantial county but an underpopulated one, and Farnham wasn't a common name.

'I'm going to find you,' he said aloud.

That was the trouble with being on your own in a large house in the countryside. You ended up talking to people who weren't there: to ghosts and former friends and women who might be your mother.

After he'd abandoned LA, Gary had spent a few months in the apartment he owned in Dalkey. For twenty-five years, most of his visits home had been brief. He'd returned for concerts or big family events. Actually living in Dublin was strange. He'd left in 1990, when the city had felt suffocatingly small. Everyone you met had been to school with someone you knew or had slept with your cousin or played a gig with your neighbour. The place had teemed with bands, all of them sharing the same teenage dream, all of them wanting to be the next U2 while insisting that wasn't the case. A&R men had trawled the city for youngsters who sounded and looked like they might be famous. They'd all competed to be the wildest and the hottest, and Black Iris had won.

In 1990, kids had still got unreasonably excited about a trip to McDonald's, and the opening of a British high street store had been regarded as a national event. Girls in bikinis had made a living from photo shoots at the top of Grafton Street, the dole had been less than fifty pounds a week, and everything had been faded and broken. Dublin had been parochial, homogeneous, more of a town than a city. By the time Gary returned, many of his reference points were gone. Unknown people lived in unknown suburbs. Teenage girls spoke like they were from Calabasas and dressed like junior Kardashians. There were fewer bands, but everyone had a YouTube channel, a blog or a podcast. The city wasn't uniformly white. Women wore Repealed sweatshirts, and guys held hands in the street.

There were troubles, too, troubles from which Gary was insulated. News bulletins warned of the growing scourge of homelessness. The papers reported that qualified people with responsible jobs were living four to a room while families with children were spending months in tiny hotel rooms.

Still, in almost every other way, this Dublin was better than the one he'd left behind. It had thrived without him. The problem was, it no longer felt like home. Then again, he wasn't sure that anywhere else did either.

That wasn't all. Gary had spent twenty-five years behind a velvet rope. Life in Ireland was less sheltered. To show that success had changed you was to invite mockery. To begin with, his family was delighted to see more of him. After a while, his novelty value dimmed, and his parents became suspicious. Why had he returned on his own? Was he sick or in trouble? What would he do with his house in America? Where were the rest of the band?

He dodged and deflected until they gave up.

It didn't take long for him to grow tired of the apartment. When you were accustomed to thousands of square feet, a two-bedroom flat was never going to be more than a bolthole. Eventually, he found a modern five-bedroom house down a winding road in north Wicklow. Rowanbrook – not Gary's choice of name, but he couldn't be bothered changing it – had been the dream home of a businessman who'd lost everything in the crash and was starting over in Dubai. It was all light and space with heated floors and an indoor pool. The kitchen contained more marble than the average cemetery, and the view was stunning. Even on the murkiest of days, it looked like the entire county was on display before him.

Gary wasn't a hermit. He met up with old friends, he saw his family, he'd had a couple of short-lived relationships (these aside, he'd have to admit his sex life had been unusually fallow). In so far as he was isolated, he'd imposed the isolation on himself. He wouldn't claim he was happy, but he'd needed to escape the noise, the mayhem and, frankly, the rank seediness of his final years in America. He'd also had to get away from Anton Toland, his collaborator and best friend.

*

In his innocence, Gary had expected to find Olivia online. A general search yielded plenty of Olivia Farnhams, but they were either too young or too far away. He'd assumed the birth records for 1950 and '51 would be digitised and easy to find. Again, he was wrong. He emailed Katie, who advised him to go to the General Register Office, where he could inspect the index books for the relevant years.

He did so with trepidation. His origins must have been obscured for a reason. Perhaps his birth mother had wanted to make sure she would never be found. After a few minutes, he dismissed this thought. The women in Carrigbrack had been given no say in either their own fate or that of their children. They'd had no voice. Literally. He couldn't forget what Katie had said about the enforced silence in the home. For someone who'd spent most of his life revelling in being heard, that felt like the most poisonous of punishments.

The Register Office was not what he'd expected. He had imagined that the records – decade after decade of births, deaths and marriages – would be housed in grand style. Instead they were kept in an ugly grey building surrounded by high walls and prison-style gates. The registers themselves looked to have passed through hundreds of anxious hands. It was impossible not to think of all the people who had pored over the pages. For two, three hours, Gary scoured every line. The writing was looped and sometimes indistinct. His back grew sore, his eyes tired. And then ... there she was: Olivia Mary Farnham, born Coolerra, County Clare, on 27 February 1951. Her father was Timothy Farnham, a tradesman. Her mother was Geraldine Farnham, formerly Clancy.

Gary was surprised to find that his hands were shaking. He was giddy with a mixture of pleasure and relief. Okay, he had another distance to travel, but having found a record of Olivia's birth, he was confident he'd be able to find more. Track down a marriage certificate, and he'd be almost there. He felt a surge of what his bandmate Ray called 'famous person confidence': the belief that if you wanted something badly enough, it would be yours.

He decided to order the full version of Olivia's birth certificate. First, though, he needed a walk and a coffee. Outside, he switched on his phone to find a message from Katie. 'Gary,' she said, her voice even more precise in recorded form, 'I'd appreciate it if you'd give me a ring. I have news.'

Convinced that whatever she had to say would be positive, he called back. After a minute of bland chatter, Katie revealed that through a friend of a friend, Olivia Farnham – *the* Olivia Farnham – had heard about the message board.

'And?' he said.

'Well, I know you had a notion that she was your birth mother …'

Keep going, thought Gary, his free hand clenched into a fist. Keep going.

'… but she was reunited with her son quite a while ago. Back in the late nineties, I think. And then – oh, you won't believe this – wasn't he killed in a car crash?'

'I see.'

'She'd put her number on the email, so I rang, and we had a nice long talk. I feel desperately sorry for her. Imagine finding your child, only to lose him again.'

'I see.'

'She asked if I'd send on the baby bracelet. She'd like it as a keepsake. She sounds like a lovely woman.'

'That's good.'

'Now, Gary, I get the impression you're disappointed, but you shouldn't be.'

'But I'd thought she was the right woman.'

'I understand, only you've got to see this for what it is: a positive development. This time yesterday, you were looking for four women. Today, the list is down to three. You're getting closer to finding your birth mother. You do see that, don't you?'

Gary thanked her and returned to his car. The first setback had hardly registered. This was different. He told himself to consider Olivia and the tragedies she'd suffered. She'd lost her son. Twice. In contrast, the chances were that his birth mother was still out there. He was lucky. He needed to believe that.

Allegra was in high good humour, brimming with chat about school and friends and the competition she'd won with her track team. Ten was a perfect age: old enough to have lots to say, young enough to say it. Even at six thousand miles' remove, Gary got a buzz from watching his daughter. He loved the way she paused before answering a question, how she could be thoughtful one moment and bubbling with life the next. She had Posy's wide green eyes and sleek brown hair, but she was tall and narrow like him. He wondered if their Skype conversations were all the sweeter because her childhood was nearly over. Soon, she'd be more guarded, less given to sudden enthusiasms and wild inventions. Rather than being the smart, funny guy, he'd be that old fool who used to have a thing with her mother.

It was late afternoon in Los Angeles, after midnight in Wicklow. In all the time he'd been doing this, Gary had never got used to watching his daughter in glowing sunlight while his skies were dark.

'Are you coming to see us soon?' she asked.

'I hope so, but remember how I told you about trying to find my original mom?'

'Uh huh.'

'Well, I'm fairly busy with that at the moment. I'll definitely see you before Christmas, though.'

'Okay.' Allegra frowned, and Gary assumed he'd given the wrong answer. 'Mom wants to talk to you,' she said.

Gary's conversations with his former partner tended to be short. They spoke about their daughter and occasionally about mutual friends. While no one would describe her career as stellar, Posy earned a decent living. She'd managed to make the role transition from quirky girlfriend in cut-off jeans to anxious wife in flannel shirt with less difficulty than many. Still, in as much as Gary prayed for anything, he prayed that Allegra would steer clear of show business. He knew how pretty girls could get mangled and crushed.

For a talented actress, Posy had a transparent face. Gary could tell that something was up. His immediate fear was that, despite appearances, Allegra was ill. Then he guessed she wanted to talk about herself. She'd been seeing a guy. Maybe she was pregnant, or they were getting married.

It was his day for being wrong.

'So,' she said. 'I met Anton last night. At a party.'

'Oh?'

'He was asking after you. I told him about how you'd discovered you were adopted and were looking for your birth mother. He said to wish you all the best.'

'Did you have to tell him?'

'Aw, Gary. He was being friendly. He seemed genuine. The two of you can't go on punishing each other. At some stage, you'll have to talk it through. Either that or announce that you've left the band.'

'Now's not the right time.'

'There's never going to be a right time, though, is there?'

'I can't say.'

'Do you not miss making music? You should be doing something with your life rather than talking to the frigging trees or whatever it is that fills your days.'

'I do stuff.'

'You mess around. It's not the same.'

Gary was about to defend his production and soundtrack

work, but Posy gave an impatient flap of the hand before continuing.

'Okay, so here's the other thing.' He should have known there'd be another thing. 'Anton mentioned that next year it'll be twenty-five years since *Overboard* was released.'

'I'm well aware of that.' *Overboard* was the band's biggest album, the record that had bounced them to a different level. From arenas to stadiums. From tour buses to private jets. From being four Dublin lads having a laugh to the cover of *Time*.

'Anyhow,' Posy continued, 'the record company wants to do an anniversary reissue.'

'Good luck to them. Nobody buys CDs any more.'

'Your audience does.'

'Old people, you mean?'

She laughed. 'You said it. Seriously, though, from what I can gather, they're talking about packaging it in different ways, including vinyl and downloads. They also plan on releasing out-takes and old footage. They hope the band will record a few new tracks too. And, well … they want you to go on tour to support it all. Not a huge tour, just a few dates in the US and Europe. Oh, and you'd get the full Rock and Roll Hall of Fame treatment.'

'Nobody told me about this.'

'I'm telling you, and Frank's likely to get in touch later in the week.'

Frank O'Toole was the band's manager. He'd spotted them early on when they'd been churning out lousy cover versions in McGonagles. He'd assured them that their own material couldn't be any worse. Frank was a seminary dropout with the professional and personal morals of a jailhouse snitch. He was also the best in the business.

'I don't want to be a heritage act,' said Gary.

At the best of times, Skype tended to make people sound hollow and shouty. Posy's voice might only have risen by half a notch, but it filled the room. 'Yeah, that's right,' she said. 'You stay over there and wallow in your misery. You don't think Anton regrets what happened?'

'No doubt he does. Only a monster wouldn't.'

'Short of crucifying himself, what more can the guy do? It's not as though you're entirely blameless. Besides, from what I hear, he's been leading a clean life.'

'He can't have changed that much, because he obviously worked his charm on you.'

No sooner had the words left Gary's mouth than he wanted to reel them back in. This was how it always was with Posy. They became enmeshed in an argument, and all subtlety disappeared. They were two kids in a schoolyard. Two drunks at closing time.

'Screw you,' she said.

'Aw, please,' he said, 'you don't want Allegra to hear.'

She'd already cut the connection.

Gary considered calling back, but there was no point. She wasn't going to change her mind, and they'd fall out all over again. He poured a large measure of Canadian Club and stepped outside to the deck. The high black sky was filled with stars, the fields bathed with silvery light. He sat and savoured the slow burn as the whiskey washed down his throat.

'This is a mess, isn't it?' he said to the sky, half expecting it to offer an opinion.

He had screwed up his life, and somehow he'd convinced himself that finding his birth mother would give him a chance to begin again. Roll up, roll up for the new improved Gary Winters. The problem was, no matter how far he ran, his regrets came with him. He'd wanted to press delete and start over, but everything was on a loop in his head, as real as the day it had happened.

Chapter 11

Ailish

Ailish hid the bracelet at the back of her underwear drawer. This was also where she put the few euro she had managed to save. Stevie, her youngest and smartest child, was in his final year of school, and she wanted him to do the course of his choice, even if that was in Dublin. Everybody knew that Dublin was ruinously expensive, so each fortnight she tried to put a little aside. Ailish regretted her own lack of education, not because she would like more money – who wouldn't? – but because she was frustrated by her ignorance. People would mention places or books or historical events, and she'd have to nod as though she knew what they were talking about. How she wished she had something to contribute.

As well as the money and the bracelet, she stored a handful of other mementos in the drawer. It was where she kept a lock of each of her children's hair and a thin silver chain given to her by Keith when they'd started going out. Oh, she knew it was sentimental, but she liked a reminder of the days when everything had felt simple.

These days, all her thoughts led back to Chrissie. She wondered if, having had a baby at fourteen, her birth mother had been able to return to school. Probably not. She guessed the Culligans had been poor. Those had been poor times. Had Chrissie been able to recover from the stigma of being an unmarried mother? Or had she become one of those sad, withdrawn women who spent a lifetime drifting from one institution to another, hair matted, eyes empty?

If Chrissie had stayed in County Clare, there was a chance they'd seen each other. They could have stood side by side in the supermarket or the pub. They could have walked the same lanes, travelled on the same bus, breathed the same air.

Ailish had to stop herself from becoming obsessed with the bracelet; from taking it out and staring at the tiny writing. The narrow strip of adhesive that had fastened the slip of paper no longer worked. Otherwise the bracelet was as perfect as it had been five decades before. She was amazed that Katie had kept it safe for so long.

Optimism crept over her. She was meant to find Chrissie.

An internet search gave her a shock. The first entry on the page was a recent death notice. She cried out in disappointment before realising that she was reading about the wrong woman. Christine Culligan had been the deceased's married name. Next, she looked at several Facebook pages. Katie had said there was a strong resemblance between the two women, and Ailish kept hoping she was one click away from seeing a mirror image of herself. Unfortunately, none of the Christines or Chrissies sounded right. Most didn't appear old enough, while one looked about twenty years too old. Aware that a considerable number of the women had gone to the United States, she decided to try some American sites. A search unearthed fourteen Christine Culligans in New York, New Jersey, California, Florida, Texas and Wisconsin. While it was possible that one was her birth mother, contacting them would be sensitive work. Plus, there was every chance that Chrissie had married and changed her name. She could be Chrissie Aaron or Chrissie Zysman or anything in between. This was, Ailish concluded, a needle-and-haystack task.

She could try a DNA test and see if there were any matches out there, but it was a long shot, and taking the test would cost more than she could afford to lose. That left her with one obvious option. Although the rest of the family had always made fun of her for following the rules, Ailish decided to try the official route. If the authorities couldn't provide her with more information, she'd think again. Not that she looked forward to any of this. Officialdom made her nervous. Even when asking for what was rightfully hers, her hands became clammy and her throat tightened. Confrontation made her unwell.

She soon discovered that pass-the-parcel had been played with her files. The information once held by the nuns and St Saviour's Adoption Agency had been transferred to the old health board, which had become the new health executive, which, in turn, had given its files to the newer Child and Family Agency. She pictured sheaves of paper being stuffed into filing cabinets, and cabinets being wheeled between offices. Thousands of lives being hawked from place to place. No wonder so much paperwork was missing.

Giving the hotel as her return address, Ailish wrote to the relevant office and to the Adoption Authority and filled out all the necessary forms. Then she prepared for a long wait. She contemplated talking to one of her daughters. She was sure they'd encourage her. On the flip side, they might reveal something to Keith. That wasn't a risk she was willing to take. And, honestly, just thinking about Chrissie, just having the information and running it around her head, was enough.

It could never mean as much to anyone else.

The weeks passed, one fading into another with no word from the authorities. Despite telling herself not to visualise an ideal outcome, that was exactly what Ailish did. She pictured herself receiving a letter saying that Chrissie had been searching for her and would like to make contact. Her old daydreams were replaced by a new set in which the two became firm friends. The desire to find her birth mother pulsed through her. That she might not be everything Chrissie had wished for no longer mattered.

This fantasy life shielded her from the worst of Keith's crabby humour. The factory where he worked as a forklift operator had been sold, and the new management weren't to his liking. They insisted on changing the rosters and shaking up work practices. He dismissed them as 'kids who know feck-all about feck-all'. She pretended to listen. Meanwhile, Stevie continued to hum and haw about his university choices. Sometimes, Ailish suspected his vagueness was a ploy to annoy Keith. If so, it was effective.

One morning, after she'd cleaned her first three rooms, she sat down on the bed in Number 24 and made a phone call.

'Hello, stranger,' said Katie. 'I've been thinking about you. How are you getting on?'

Ailish explained her predicament. 'I didn't call you before because I didn't want to make a nuisance of myself. I'm trying to do the right thing, but I don't know if I have the patience.'

'It's funny you should say that. Beth and I are learning such a lot about how to work around the system. Of course, she doesn't have as much time now that she's started work. Did I tell you that she's a data analyst with Google?'

'That sounds impressive.'

'Doesn't it? To tell you the truth, I haven't a notion what it means.'

Ailish laughed. 'That reminds me of Stevie and his college plans. "What do you think?" he says to me, and I have to say, "Stevie, I don't understand the title of the course, not to mind what you'd actually be studying."'

'So,' said Katie, 'let's talk about your search. What you've got to do is find your birth certificate – which should be fairly straightforward. Then you need Chrissie's birth cert. Oh, and if you could find a marriage cert for her, you'd be well on your way.'

'That sounds great, only ...'

'... only the records are in Dublin, and you're in Kilmitten?'

'That's the snag. I'll have to find a way of escaping for the day without Keith getting wind of what I'm at.'

'Why don't I have a look for you?'

'Seriously?' Although this was precisely what Ailish had hoped for, she'd been too nervous to ask. 'I'd be very grateful. I mean, I'll pay you for your time or—'

'You will not,' said Katie. 'I'd be delighted to give you a dig-out. I'd love to find out what happened to Chrissie.'

Ailish was amazed by Katie's efforts on behalf of people she barely knew.

Two days later, when she was scrubbing the bath in Room 11, her phone rang. In her haste to answer it, she tripped over a mound of linen and went flying into the dressing table.

'Hello?'

'There you are,' said Katie, 'Jacqueline Ann Culligan, daughter of Christine Marie Culligan of Hackett's Cross.'

'You found us!'

'Didn't I tell you I would?'

Ailish stopped to consider the information. The words danced in front of her.

Katie was still talking. 'There's no mention of your birth father. That was often the case, though, so I wouldn't read too much into it. While I was there, I had a look through the marriage records. I didn't come across anything. Then again, we knew that'd be a tougher task. I'll have to get Beth to give me a hand. She's very sharp-eyed. Mind you, so was I when I was twenty-eight.'

Ailish felt dizzy, as though the room had tilted and nothing was quite where it belonged. She perched on the edge of the bed. 'I think I know Hackett's Cross. Isn't it over in the west of the county?'

'That's right, not far from Kilkee. Chrissie must have grown up beside the sea.'

'If memory serves, it's only a little place.'

'So little it's hardly a place at all.'

Ailish could hear the smile in Katie's voice. She tried to steady her thoughts, which were swerving in every direction. 'That means the Culligans should be easier to find.'

'It does. You need to think carefully about what you want to do next. I know you're impatient, but there's a reason why social workers get involved in reunions. They can be delicate matters.'

'I … I can't thank you enough. Sorry if I'm a bit stuck for words. This is all brilliant. Just brilliant. How do I go about getting copies of the certificates?'

'They're already in the post.'

Ailish inhaled with surprise – and panic. Before she could say anything, Katie intervened.

'Don't worry. I sent them to the hotel. With any luck, they'll be with you in the morning. But ...' She hesitated.

'Go on.'

'I wish you didn't have to do everything in secret. If you're going to continue, you'll have to talk to Keith at some stage.'

The truth of this was dawning on Ailish. She knew, however, that not only would her husband's reaction be hostile, he would probably stymie her attempts to trace Chrissie. 'I will tell him,' she said. 'I promise I will. Just not yet.'

'I understand,' said Katie. 'Believe you me, I know what it's like when a job feels too big.'

The certificates arrived on schedule the following morning. Thankfully, Ailish's first room was a nice handy one: a couple on the second of five nights, no need to change the sheets, no excessive wear and tear. She settled onto the bed and opened the large brown envelope. The first certificate confirmed what she already knew. The second belonged to her natural mother. Christine Marie Culligan had been born on 12 June 1957. Ailish couldn't stop herself from doing the maths. Chrissie had been only thirteen when she'd got pregnant. Far, far too young to consent to anything. Her parents were named as Patrick and Bridget Culligan. Patrick was described as a labourer.

For a short while, Ailish sat and thought through everything she'd learnt. Afterwards, she went about her work without comment or hesitation. All the while, her brain crackled and whirred.

Stevie had texted to say he was going to a friend's house, so when Ailish got home, she decided to go for a walk. She needed to think everything through. She put on her red anorak and set off towards Toomey's Hill. Kilmitten, like many of the neighbouring villages, was small and ramshackle. Despite the best efforts of the Tidy Towns committee, it had a bruised, dishevelled look. The supermarket was forever running out of stock, and the most popular bar was like an outpost of the 1980s. Outsiders might question how anyone could be fond of such a place, but Ailish was. Briefly, she wondered what Gary Winters had made of it. The thought made her smile.

Whatever the village's shortcomings, the surrounding countryside was gorgeous. After a hard October rain, the sky was clear, and as she climbed, Ailish could see for miles. The lanes surrounding the hill were carpeted in brown leaves, with the occasional shot of yellow or red. While Chrissie was at the forefront of her thoughts, memories of her adoptive parents, Deirdre and Jarlath, were there too. How often had she walked these fields with her mam? At this time of year, they'd collected blackberries. In December, they'd searched for holly. In the spring, they'd picked cowslips and primroses while in the nearby woods they'd gathered bluebells. Those had been some of the best days of Ailish's childhood.

Often, on their way home, Deirdre had stopped at the church to say a prayer. She'd been old-style devout, given to First Fridays and novenas. The family had eaten fish on Fridays and recited the rosary every evening. When they'd left Kilmitten, it had been for trips to Knock or Croagh Patrick. Late in life, Deirdre had travelled on the diocesan pilgrimage to Lourdes. She'd regarded it like a round-the-world cruise, a once-in-a-lifetime treat rather than five days saying prayers and tending to those frailer than herself. Ailish had never heard either of her parents complain about their drab lives. Indeed, she suspected that even a lottery win wouldn't have changed them. Martyrdom came in many forms.

For her, religion was a conundrum with too many sorrowful mysteries and not enough joyful ones. She reflected on what had been done to Chrissie: wrenched from home, sent to a place that was no better than a prison and forcibly separated from her child. No doubt she'd also been branded a sinner and made to endure endless mumbo-jumbo about hell and shame. Religion had treated her like a criminal when in reality she'd been a victim. Ailish's parents had adopted her through a sense of Catholic duty rather than any affection for children. So no, she wouldn't call herself religious. And yet, neither could she sever all ties with the Church. Once a month or so, she went to Mass. She usually sat at the back on her own and allowed the prayers to wash over her. She found it restful.

By the time she began her walk back to the village, the

last light was seeping from the sky. Someone was burning turf, its distinctive smell lingering in the chill air. On Main Street, she called into the shop for a few groceries. June Mangan, a woman with crow's feet so deep it looked like she was she wearing winged eyeliner, was at the till.

'Aren't we blessed to have such a grand evening?' she said.

'Indeed we are,' agreed Ailish.

As soon as she entered the house, she sensed that something was wrong. Keith was there ahead of her, his face slightly off kilter.

'I went for a walk and lost track of time,' she said, as she removed her anorak and threw it over the banister. 'I'll put the dinner on in a minute. I bought sausages below in Mangan's.'

'Where's Stevie?' asked Keith.

'Round in Declan's house. He'll have his dinner there.'

'It's well for him. I thought he was supposed to be studying.'

'He is. They're doing their homework together.'

'A likely story. The pair of them are probably smoking at the back of the church. Or hanging out with young ones. You're far too soft on him. I'm tired of telling you that.'

Ailish noticed a twitch in Keith's left cheek. There must have been more hassle at work. She bent to scoop up her handbag. The birth certificates were tucked inside, and she needed to put them in her hiding place.

'I'm popping upstairs,' she said. 'I'll be back in a tick.'

She opened the drawer and, without thinking, sought out the envelope containing her baby bracelet. It had been moved. She looked inside. The bracelet was gone.

Before she had the chance to absorb what had happened, she heard Keith's footsteps, slow and heavy, on the stairs. Quickly, she shut the drawer and slid the certificates under a pillow. She turned and stood in front of the dressing table.

Keith took several steps into the room. He opened his mouth, then paused. 'It's about time we changed this,' he said, scuffing the toe of his boot against the pink and green carpet. 'I'm sure you'd prefer something more modern. What have they got in the hotel at the minute?'

'Powder blue. It's nice.' She stared straight at him, at the moss-coloured eyes she'd once found irresistible.

'Any chance of an offcut?' He was toying with her.

'I can ask.'

He stepped forward again. The air felt taut. 'Why do I get the feeling you're looking for something?'

If he wanted to be cagey, she could be cagey too. 'I don't know. Like I say, I'm about to go down and cook the dinner.' She attempted a 'nothing to see here' smile, but her mouth was too stiff.

'You were keeping money from me.'

She edged away until she couldn't go any further. 'I wasn't keeping anything from you. I've been trying to save for Stevie's college fund, that's all.' There was an irritating crack in her voice. Stay composed, she thought. He's taken what belongs to you, and you've got to get it back.

'Isn't Stevie the lucky fellow? I hope he appreciates you. Anyway, there I was, getting ready to go out … I'd arranged to meet the lads for a quick pint in Pilkington's … when I realised I needed a few euro. "Not to worry," says I. "Can't I borrow from Ailish? Haven't I seen her slipping money into the drawer?"'

Silently, she cursed her stupidity. She should have been more careful. 'You could have asked me,' she said. 'I'd have given it to you.'

'You weren't here.' His tone became harder. 'I don't hide anything from you. Every cent I earn goes towards keeping this family.'

This wasn't true, but Ailish was scared to argue. 'I'm here now.'

She was frightened that he would hurt her. That he would twist her arm behind her back or pull her hair or punch her in the stomach. He was always careful to avoid her face, and she was skilled at hiding her bruises.

Instead, he reached into his jeans and pulled out the bracelet. Already it was folded over. Damaged. 'What's this?' he asked, waving it in front of her.

Her stomach lurched. 'You know what it is.'

'Why are you keeping secrets from me?'

'I'm not. It's just a scrap of paper. I figured it wouldn't mean anything to you, so I didn't mention it. It means a lot to me, though. Can I have it back, please?'

'Where did you get it?'

'Does it matter?'

'If my wife has been lying to me, of course it matters.'

'You can take all the money you want, but give me back the bracelet. Please.'

Blotches of colour had risen in Keith's face. 'It was that old woman, wasn't it? The one I found here a few weeks ago sitting in the kitchen like Lady Muck. Where did she get it?' He passed the bracelet to his other hand. 'Here, she's not your real mother, is she?'

'No. She's ... she's someone who worked in the home where I was born.'

He laughed, a brittle sort of laugh. 'She's a good liar, I'll give her that. A crafty one. I wasn't convinced she was giving me the full picture, but I didn't see this coming.' He held the bracelet up again. 'When you think about it, though, what class of sad old biddy holds on to the likes of this?'

'If you'll just hand it back to me, I'll put the dinner on. You'll want a bite to eat before you go out.'

The blotches deepened. 'Forget the fucking dinner, would you? What I want is the truth. Why did you lie to me? I was reasonable about this adoption bullshit before, but you got nowhere. And do you know why that was? Your mother doesn't want to be found. She didn't want you then, and she doesn't want you now.' He leant in and, with his free hand, tapped Ailish's head. 'Why can't you get that into your little skull, huh?'

Ailish flinched, and her eyes began to water. 'You don't know that. You don't know anything about her.'

'And neither do you. You can be certain that whatever

airy-fairy crap you've got in your head is wrong. I'll bet any money there's nothing special about her. Chances are she was like all the rest: some dizzy young one who got herself knocked up because she was too stupid to know any better.'

'Don't say that.'

'Listen to me, Ailish. You've lost all perspective here. You probably think I'm being unkind, when I'm doing you a favour. If you get all worked up about this nonsense, you'll end up hurt. Again. The last time, there was no talking to you. You went around with a face as long as Lent until you made everybody in the house as miserable as yourself. You've got to realise how selfish you're being. And there's no call for the whimpering. You know how thin the walls are. If you don't shut up, we'll be the talk of the village.'

Keith looked at her with the bottomless distaste in which he specialised, a look that made her feel like the detritus in the sink after the washing-up water had drained away. It hadn't always been like this. It wasn't always like this now. Back in June, they'd had a week in Spain, their first genuine break in years. Along with Stevie, they'd spent the days laughing and messing, playing in the pool and coating themselves in factor 30. They'd got burnt all the same. But it had been great. A proper family holiday.

Still, this was no time for getting wistful. Ailish had to focus on the bracelet. She considered making a lunge for it, then decided against. Keith was far stronger, and there was a danger the fragile paper would rip in two. Or he might hit her. She wiped her eyes with the cuff of her cardigan.

'Okay,' she said, 'I hear you, and I'm sorry I didn't tell you about the identity band. That was wrong of me. I would like to keep it, though … as a reminder of my roots. I won't go looking for my birth mother, if that's what you're concerned about. I swear I won't.'

'So you say.' He stepped back, turned away and walked over to his side of the bed. 'Except I don't believe you. You know what your problem is, Ailish? You're a fucking liar.'

'I'm telling you the God's honest truth, Keith. The bracelet … well, it's a sentimental thing, no more than that.'

He placed the bracelet beside the glass of water on top of his bedside locker and took a purple lighter from his pocket. One click, and a long orange flame appeared. With his other hand, he picked up the bracelet and held it to the flame. Before Ailish could move, the edge was alight. It curled towards him, glowing slightly at first. Then the paper truly caught fire.

For a moment, she froze. Then she hurled herself in her husband's direction, shrieking, 'Stop it! Stop it!' She was too late. He dropped the ashy remains into the glass and returned the lighter to his pocket. The smell of smoke hung between them. Katie had kept the bracelet for almost forty-seven years. Ailish had managed less than two months. She went to speak, but no words came. Instead, she collapsed onto the bed, buried her face in the pillow and balled her hands into fists.

A thick silence fell over the room.

After a minute or two, Keith left. A short while later, she heard the front door closing and the sound of his feet on the street below.

Chapter 12

Katie

Katie and Beth had established a ritual. On Saturday mornings, they sat at Katie's kitchen table and reviewed progress. In the two months since they'd placed the notice on the adoption forum, sixteen bracelets had been returned to their original owners. Katie had bought a special notebook to keep track of developments. She'd also printed the emails and placed them in a new blue folder. Beth made fun of her, but there was something pleasing about having all the details on file. She kept the shoebox in her wardrobe, bringing it out only when she was certain a bracelet should be passed on.

She'd spoken to several of the recipients. It was fascinating to hear how life had turned out for them. Although they used different words and displayed different emotions, they shared a yearning to reconnect with the woman who had brought them into the world. They didn't want to interfere, they insisted; they just wanted to know that she was all right. Most said this desire had intensified as they'd got older. One man, a lovely fellow from Tipperary called Larry, told Katie that every time he heard something on the news about mother-and-baby homes, it ripped him apart. 'I had no idea how badly the women were treated,' he said. 'To my shame, it never occurred to me.'

Even before her feet hit the ground in the morning, Katie was thinking about the bracelets and their original owners. There were days when she found the task almost unbearably difficult; days when fear and darkness tugged at her, and she felt as if she'd returned to a place and time she wanted to forget. On those days, she muddled on, hoping that no one, especially Beth, noticed her struggle.

This had been one of those weeks when she'd felt Johnny's absence as keenly as if he'd just left her. Every song on the radio, every picture on the wall, every story on the news had rekindled her sorrow. The previous evening, she'd been flicking through the television channels, looking for something other than a cookery programme or a soap, when she'd chanced upon the channel with all the quiz shows. Johnny had been addicted to *The Chase*. She could hear him shouting out answers: 'fear of butterflies', 'the Bee Gees', 'Saturn'. A wave of tenderness had come over her, and she'd realised she could no longer watch. Even though it was only seven o'clock, she'd swallowed two sleeping tablets and climbed into bed.

These Saturday-morning sessions with Beth made the

weekends feel a little less lonely. For many years, Katie and Johnny had gone walking on Saturdays. Sometimes they'd travelled to Wicklow; occasionally they'd spent a couple of days in Mayo or Galway, but the Cooley peninsula in County Louth had been her favourite destination. She'd loved the gentle slopes, the coconut scent of the furze bushes and the view over Carlingford Lough. She could, of course, make the journey on her own. But she knew she wouldn't.

Now, as Beth tapped at her laptop, Katie reviewed her to-do list. Some of their correspondents, like Larry, were content to take the official route. He trusted he'd eventually trace his natural mother. Others were less sanguine, and Katie found herself offering advice – and cautioning against moving too quickly. She remembered suggesting that Gary hire a private detective, and it occurred to her that she'd become a detective of sorts. Gary was in her thoughts that morning, as was Ailish. Above everyone else, Katie wanted to help Ailish. This was partly explained by the sad circumstances of her birth, but there was more to it than that. She had known too many Ailishes: people who spent their lives facilitating others and getting little in return. In particular, she'd worked with nurses who'd given everything to everybody only to find themselves burnt out and alone.

Having found Chrissie's birth certificate, she'd made several unsuccessful attempts to unearth her marriage records. Ailish's birth mother appeared to have vanished, and in her gloomier moments, Katie suspected she might be dead.

'Ailish has gone quiet on me,' she said to Beth, who was reading an email from a Carlow man. While he thought he'd been born in Carrigbrack, he was vague about the details, and they weren't sure how to handle his case.

'Have you rung her?'

'I don't want to make a nuisance of myself. I might give her a shout next week. I have to be careful in case her husband's around.'

'From the way you described him, it sounds as though Keith Dwan's a man who needs to get over himself.'

'Ah, no. That's far too generous. As they'd say in Danganstown, he's a ferocious gobshite altogether.'

Beth looked up from the computer and winked. 'I'd say you were great crack in your youth.'

'I thought I was great crack now,' Katie said, and they both laughed.

To be honest, Katie didn't think she had been much fun as a teenager. It wasn't that she'd been especially earnest or dour. More that she'd been too needy. Thirsty, she believed was the modern-day term. She'd maundered around the village, grateful for any scrap of attention that came her way. If that attention was male, so much the better. It would be easy to blame her insecurity on Margo, but her sister had been a small child at the time. Plus, while the lack of affection at home hadn't helped, it was hardly unusual. Katie had grown up in austere times, when showy displays of endearment were frowned upon, and 'spare the rod, spoil the child' was viewed as sound parenting advice. She'd been fifteen the last time her father had slapped her. She'd skipped Mass in favour of sharing a cigarette with a buck-toothed charmer named Billy Tuite. Unfortunately, they'd been spotted by a local gossip-merchant. She wondered where Billy was now. Buck teeth seemed to have gone the way of hand-me-down clothes, corned beef sandwiches and the measles: not extinct, but no longer commonplace either.

Had Katie ever been as outspoken as Beth? Probably not. She liked to think she'd had a certain spirit about her, but spirited girls had been viewed with suspicion back then. Time and experience had dulled her edges. It seemed to her that nowadays, young women were allowed to make a splash. Older ones were still expected to colour inside the lines.

Beth took a deep breath. 'I hope you don't mind me asking, but was there a reason you didn't dust down that old shoebox and start looking for people while Johnny was alive?'

'You mean would he have disapproved?'

'Seeing as you've put it like that, yes.'

'It's not that simple. It's not like he agreed with what went on in Carrigbrack, far from it. If I'd been keen to return the bracelets to their original owners, he'd have supported me. But, at the same time, he'd have been wary. He used to say that if you went around turning over logs, you mightn't like what crawled out.'

'Fair enough,' said Beth, but her tone suggested the answer was less than satisfactory.

'Besides, if I'd done it any sooner, I wouldn't have had you to help me.'

'I'd say you'd have been just fine. Oh, you know what I meant to tell you. I saw a piece online this morning about Black Iris. They're re-releasing one of their old albums. Rumour has it they're going back on the road too – but without Gary.'

'That's odd,' said Katie. 'Why wouldn't he go with them?'

'I haven't a clue. Have you heard from him lately?'

'We spoke the other day. I get the feeling he's struggling. He thinks he's found another one of the contenders, if we can call them that. A woman named Gráinne Holland. He wrote to her but hasn't heard anything back. So far, he's got nowhere with the others.'

'He's a funny fish.'

Katie lifted her reading glasses. 'He speaks highly of you.'

'Yeah, right.'

'No, seriously, he's got great time for you. He says you're very clever.'

'In Gary's lexicon, I'm not sure that's positive. I reckon I'd need to be called a "foxy chick" or a "hot piece of ass" for it to be considered a compliment.'

'Now, Beth Linnane, even I know those phrases are old hat. I doubt Gary speaks that way any more.'

'Okay, then I'd need to be a "total honey" or a "lush babe", or whatever this week's term is.'

'I get the idea that something else is on his mind. I tried asking, subtly of course, but he didn't give a proper answer.

He's an enigmatic sort of character.' Katie pushed her glasses down again. 'Mind you, he does have quite a complicated life.'

'Understatement of the century, right there,' said Beth, before returning to her laptop.

Katie closed her notebook and rose to fill the kettle. The tree in the back garden was beginning to take on its spindly winter form. The sky was quilted with pale grey. She watched next door's cat streak past. He was always in a hurry, was Grover.

'Time for a break,' she said, spooning coffee into two striped mugs.

Beth leant back in her chair. 'Great stuff. Is there cake?'

'There's a cupboard full of cake. I got a bit fidgety during the week, so I did some baking.'

While Katie cut thick slices of apple cake, Beth spoke about work and about her unsuccessful attempts to find a flat of her own.

'Would you consider …' said Katie, 'and I promise I won't be offended if you don't want to, and take as much time as you need to think it through … would you consider moving in here with me?'

For a moment, the kitchen was quiet, so quiet they could have heard a piece of dust drop. (Not that this was likely. Along with the baking binge, Katie had indulged in a manic clean. It really had been a challenging week.)

Then a smile spread across Beth's face. 'I thought you'd never ask.'

'Honestly?'

'I'd be delighted to be your tenant.'

'Gosh, pet, you wouldn't be a tenant. You're family. I couldn't take money from you.'

'Katie, I'm paying rent, and that's that.'

'Something small, then. Anything more, and your mother would never forgive me.'

'Don't mind Mam, I'm paying my way.'

'We'll see. I would have asked sooner, only I didn't want you thinking I was meddling, or, worse, that I wanted someone to look after me. You've always been the independent type.'

Beth looked over the rim of her mug. 'Sit down there and stop your old guff. You're the last person who needs looking after.'

Katie joined her at the table. 'Well, this is great. Have you any questions? You know the house as well as I do. You can have either of the spare rooms.'

'I have three requests,' said Beth, selecting a slice of cake.

'Oh?'

'First off, we need to get Netflix ... and a coffee machine. Don't worry, I'll sort both of those.'

'Fair enough, though what's wrong with instant coffee, I don't know. You young people and your fancy ideas. What's the third request?'

'That you keep making apple cake.'

'We have a deal. Apple cake was Johnny's favourite, too.' Katie slapped herself on the cheek. 'Listen to me, getting all nostalgic. You needn't fret that I'll rattle on about Johnny all the time, because I won't.'

'You're fine,' said Beth. 'You can talk about him as much as you like.'

'That's something else I meant to say. Don't hesitate to bring friends – or boyfriends – home. I promise not to interfere or ask about their intentions.'

Another silence, this one longer. Katie realised she must have said something out of turn, but for the life of her, she couldn't see what.

Finally, Beth spoke. 'This is kind of awkward, but I don't want you getting the wrong end of the toothbrush. The truth is, I'm unlikely to bring men home, because I'm not interested in them. Admittedly, I had a couple of teenage boyfriends; nobody wants to be different when they're sixteen, or at least I didn't. Since then, all of my relationships have been with women. I'm not seeing anyone at the minute. But if I ever do bring someone back, it'll be a woman.' She looked down. 'Please tell me you're cool with that.'

Katie had a sensation of missing jigsaw pieces slotting into place. She needed to choose her words carefully. 'Oh, Beth, love, of course I am. I just ... well, it never occurred to me. I feel like a bit of an eejit.'

'Katie, there's no reason for you to feel foolish. It's not as though I go around with a sign over my head – warning: lesbian in the room. Although to listen to my mother, you'd think I should.'

'Ah, I see. Has she known for long?'

'Only since last year, which was ridiculously late, I know.

For ages, I figured the less Mam and Dad knew about my life, the better. But, honestly, pretending to be someone you're not becomes exhausting.'

'Do I take it they didn't react well?'

'Dad was brilliant.'

'That doesn't surprise me. He's a decent man. Don't get me wrong, I'm not suggesting my sister isn't. It's just – how do I put this? – she's very fixed in her views.'

'You can say that again.'

That Margo had snared Con Linnane had always been a source of fascination to Katie. She thought of Con as the definition of fair-minded. His wife, on the other hand, had a gift for highlighting the shortcomings of others. However buoyant you felt at the start of a conversation with Margo, by the end you'd be flat as roadkill. In Katie's charitable moments, she didn't believe her sister intended to offend. She was so single-minded, so determined that everything match her idea of perfection, that she didn't notice the harm she was doing.

Beth cradled her mug. 'Dad's one of those people who spent a long time believing what had been drummed into him at school. All the usual rot about sin and suchlike. Then, at some point, he realised that you can't live other people's lives for them; that, basically, there's nothing wrong with being nice to folks and accepting them as they are. He wants me to be happy, simple as that. With Mam, nothing's straightforward. It's not like she's an out-and-out bigot. She's friendly with Paddy McElligott who runs the newsagent's in Danganstown, and he's as camp as Christmas. She even voted yes in the marriage referendum. Yet she behaves like I've let her down. Like I'm not quite what she ordered.'

'I'm sorry to hear that.'

'The problem with Mam is, she wants everyone to conform to her version of the ideal life. According to her, we should all live in a bee-you-tiful detached house with a Lexus in the driveway, a hairdresser on speed-dial and a clatter of photogenic kids in the back garden. Anyone who doesn't want that is somehow lacking.'

'I fail on all counts, I'm afraid.'

'You're not alone. Most of all, though, she's annoyed that I won't supply her with grandchildren. Or, should I say, the right kind of grandchildren.'

'But don't four of your brothers have children?'

'She has nine grandkids … and another on the way.'

'Is that not enough for any woman?'

'Apparently not.'

'Correct me if I'm wrong,' said Katie, 'but could you not have a child all the same? If that's what you wanted, I mean.'

'I could, and I may well do. Who can say what's in the future? Except in Mam's view, that wouldn't be quite right.' Beth rolled her eyes. 'Ideally, I should have forgotten about college, stayed within a ten-kilometre radius of home, married some local yokel and started reproducing in my early twenties. Actually, better still, what's that thing they teach you about in biology? The thing that keeps splitting in two?'

'An amoeba?'

'That's the one. If I could be an amoeba, she'd be beside herself with happiness.'

Katie tried, and failed, to hold back a smile. 'That's quite an image.'

'You've no idea how crazy she is. The last time I was talking to her, she started yammering on about this young one down the road – Sophie Fitzgerald – who's expecting. I had to listen to a monologue about how fabulous Sophie looked and how heartening it was to see young people settling down close to home. The thing is, not only is Sophie unmarried, she's been going out with the baby's father for about five minutes. And, let me tell you, he's not the brightest bulb in the chandelier either.'

'It's amazing how the world changes, isn't it?' Katie tipped her head towards her notebooks, old and new. 'All of the women in there were banished for something similar.'

The heresy of one generation becomes the orthodoxy of the next: Katie had read that somewhere. How true it was. She considered the situation. Not for a moment did she think that Margo didn't love Beth. Nor did she believe her love was conditional on Beth being a certain type of person. And yet she could see how Margo, one of life's planners, would react badly when those plans went awry. Tact had never been her strong suit. Reluctant as she was to draw her sister upon herself, Katie reckoned she should say something to try and heal the rift. After all, she would have to mention that Beth was living with her.

'Should I have a quiet word with your mother, do you think?'

'Lord, no,' said Beth. 'She'd take offence. Big-time offence.'

'I'd be very subtle.'

'I appreciate the offer, but I'd prefer it if you let matters rest. When it comes to what she sees as family business, Mam can be very sensitive. You might only make matters worse.'

'Okay, then. But I hope you sort out your differences. Take it from me, when these situations fester, they can get out of control.'

Later, Katie decided to go for a short lie-down. No sooner had she made herself comfortable than Beth bounded into the room, cheeks so flushed they matched her coral jumper.

'I'd wondered if this would happen,' she said, waving her phone like a semaphore flag.

'Sorry, love,' said Katie, scrambling to sit up. 'You'll have to explain.'

Beth folded herself into the brocade armchair beside the bed. 'It's an email from a woman called Robyn Bennett. She's writing on behalf of her husband, Brandon. He was born in Carrigbrack in August 1972.'

'What date in August, does it say?'

'Um, the fourteenth. Does it matter?'

'It does, as it happens,' said Katie. 'Go on.'

'The fascinating part is this: Brandon's in Boston. That's

where he was raised. He's an American.' Beth said 'American' as though describing a particularly rare and beautiful beast. 'I knew lots of babies were adopted, or let's be honest, *sold* in the States. What I didn't know was that Carrigbrack was involved. You never mentioned it.'

Katie scratched her neck. She was genuinely taken aback. 'I didn't know myself. No one told us where the children went. Does Robyn say whether Brandon is up to speed with what she's doing?'

'She doesn't. Why don't you read the email and see what you think?'

'Pass me the phone, there. Oh, and my glasses too, if you wouldn't mind. They're on the dressing table.'

'No bother,' replied Beth, practically pirouetting across the room.

The window was slightly ajar. Outside, magpies and crows were cawing and rattling and clicking.

Katie scanned the email. Then she read it more slowly. She didn't remember every birth in Carrigbrack. Some memories were muddled, others clear as spring water. She hadn't been there on the day Brandon was born, but she knew what had happened and she knew that a crucial detail was missing from Robyn's account. No matter how they handled this, it would be tricky.

'Well?' said Beth, who was back in the armchair, arms wrapped around her knees.

'I don't think Robyn has the full story,' said Katie. 'Then again, perhaps Brandon doesn't either.'

Chapter 13

Brandon

They were walking on Summit Avenue, the November air biting at their cheekbones, when Robyn told Brandon about the email. By now, he was accustomed to her passions and foibles, but this was different.

'Can you run through that again?' he said, steps accelerating as they passed the red-brick colonial that reminded him of his parents' house. (Important as it was to reach their daily target, Brandon would prefer to do so without freezing to death.)

'I emailed a woman in Ireland who worked as a nurse in Carrigbrack in the early seventies. Apparently she held on to the babies' identity bracelets. She replied this morning saying she wants to help. She asked for our address so she can send us what she knows.'

'She didn't ask for our bank details too? A credit card number maybe?'

Robyn squeezed his arm. 'Don't be silly.'

'I'll bet it's a scam.'

'And I'll bet it's not. She's called Katie Carroll, and she sounds lovely.'

'So lovely she worked in a baby factory, churning out nice white Catholic kids for the export market.'

'Aw, Brandon, don't get all political on me,' said Robyn, her breath forming plumes in the air, her cheeks glowing from a combination of exercise, enthusiasm and youthful good health.

'I'm only kidding. What I don't get is why this Katie lady kept the ID bracelets. Isn't that kind of odd?'

Robyn chose not to answer. 'I've a feeling this could be the breakthrough we've been looking for.'

A sudden gust picked up some dry leaves, sending them hurtling in a circle. Brandon shivered. He didn't point out that he wasn't looking for anything.

Not that long ago, a guy at work had called him a 'status-quo warrior'. The guy had been baffled when Brandon had taken it as a compliment. But why would he agitate for change? He lived in Brookline, one of the most beautiful neighbourhoods in one of the most beautiful cities in America. He had a high-paying job with a prestigious investment firm and a dazzling – if slightly eccentric – wife. From time to time, he measured his life against those of friends and acquaintances. He usually came out on top. Yes, this sounded superficial. That was why he would never say it out loud. But he'd thought about it many times, tested himself from every angle, and he was satisfied there was nothing missing. Well, nothing that wouldn't in due course, and with the grace of God, be provided. No nagging questions. No gaping void. Even if a void did appear, it wouldn't be filled by learning the name of the woman who'd given him up for adoption.

Brandon had made sacrifices to achieve his position in life. When others had been partying, he'd been working. When others had been settling down and having kids, he'd still been working. But that was okay. He was content with the choices he'd made. He bore his biological parents no ill will and hoped his birth mother had gone on to have other children in better circumstances. In the unlikely event she ever came looking for him, he'd be happy to meet her, but he couldn't imagine they'd have much in common.

Also, to be blunt about it, wasn't there a danger that complications would trail in her wake? What if she wanted to involve herself in his life? What if she had other children, his half-brothers and sisters, who decided to seek him out? He had a vision of convoys of raucous Irish people invading his house.

Here was the problem: Robyn saw things differently. She was *fascinated* by Brandon's backstory. How can you not want to know? she'd say. How can you not be curious!? (When Robyn got worked up, she tended to speak in exclamation points and italics.) Too many episodes of *Who Do You Think You Are?* combined with countless internet articles about family trees had fuelled her interest in amateur genealogy. Unfortunately, her own background was as bland as oatmeal. For generations, the Archers had enjoyed lives of uneventful middle-class rectitude. By contrast, Brandon's origins were as intriguing as they were obscure.

She was constantly urging him to sign up to one of the main genealogy websites. So far, he'd resisted.

In recent months, Robyn had become an expert on Irish adoptions and mother-and-baby homes, seizing upon every article for nuggets of information. Given the secrecy surrounding foreign adoptions, most of her findings had been general in nature. She'd been angered by statistics or saddened by individual stories. Brandon had been touched by her interest.

He had also underestimated her tenacity.

Although careful in their choice of words, Brandon's friends had been sceptical about his marriage. He'd been forty-four on their wedding day, and he'd got to that age without so much as a starter marriage. Robyn had been twenty-nine. The mistake outsiders made was to judge the book by its cover, or to be more precise, the woman by her Lululemon leggings. With her honey-coloured ponytail, large brown eyes and pert body, Robyn was the ideal advertisement for her job as a personal trainer. What most people didn't know was that she also had a communications degree from Northeastern. She took pleasure in soaking up patronising comments before flooring her tormentor with an astute observation or well-honed put-down. (Brandon applauded her career change. While the traditional media were dying, wellness was a booming industry.)

Following the email from Ireland, Robyn obsessed about Carrigbrack and the bracelet. If she wasn't talking about them, she was poring over online message boards or Dublin news sites. He did his best to divert the conversation with anecdotes about the office or mutual friends, but she invariably worked her way back to Katie Carroll.

Every morning, she waited for the mail like a child waiting for Santa Claus.

'A letter from Ireland's bound to take at least a week,' he said. 'Why doesn't she email you the details?'

'Well, *duh*. Because she's going to send us your ID bracelet, that's why. I wonder if she remembers you and your birth mother, or if she's relying on the date I gave her.'

Brandon had always known he was adopted. When he'd been six or seven, his mother and father, Art and Ellen Bennett, had given him the basics. He'd been born in an institution called Carrigbrack, they'd said, and almost a year later he'd arrived in Boston. 'We were specially chosen,' his mother had added, 'so you could have a wonderful life in America.' Fanciful as that sounded, they hadn't let him down. While both of his parents were from Irish families, they'd never shown any strong attachment to the place.

Once, his mom had asked if he'd like to learn more about the country of his birth. He'd replied, truthfully, that he'd heard enough. In sixth grade, his friend Davy McGann had spent two weeks with cousins in County Mayo. His report had been alarming. 'Straight up,' he'd said, 'it's the Third World over there. You know how many television channels they have? Two. And the food? Yee-uch. It's like having every meal at your grandma's house.'

Being adopted hadn't always been easy. At school, a kid called Scott Miller had revelled in giving him a hard time. While Miller's taunts had varied, his theme had been constant: Brandon was in America because nobody in Ireland had wanted him. He'd been too ugly or too slow or his mother had already had too many children. Sometimes, the bullying had taken on an extra dimension. Not only was Brandon personally inadequate, the country of his birth was a backwards dump where people took pleasure in killing each other. That no one else had behaved like Miller hadn't mattered; every jibe had left a mark. Brandon hadn't complained – who wanted a reputation as a snitch? – and after a while, Miller had moved on to fresh targets. But neither had he forgotten. His experience had taught him that standing out from the crowd was for other, braver souls. He wanted to belong.

Back then, he'd been called Brendan. At eighteen, with the approval of his parents, he'd filed a petition and changed his name. He'd prefer to sound more American, he explained. In truth, he'd been ambitious and hadn't believed there was much to be gained by sounding like a bartender from Southie with ginger hair, cornflake-sized freckles and an accent thick as chowder. In those years, he too had viewed the Irish as less than appealing. Several of his friends, including those of Irish ancestry, had agreed. Their people were either rough as a cat's tongue or overly sentimental about the land that had rejected them. Oh, and they were ugly. In the contest for the world's least attractive race, the Irish – with their small mouths, big noses and blue-white skin – would be finalists. Obviously, Brandon would never cast such a slur on any other race, but he was entitled to think what he liked about his countrymen. He thought of his own face as a composite sketch: all the features were solid, but nothing quite matched.

Religion didn't play much part in his life. He'd made his confirmation at St Mary of the Assumption, but, save for the occasional wedding or christening, he wasn't a guy for going to church.

In more recent times, his attitude towards Ireland and the Irish had mellowed. He knew the country had changed. Most places had. But if he didn't have any animosity towards it, he didn't have any great enthusiasm either.

The parcel arrived two days before Thanksgiving.

Brandon was late home from the office. He was working for a particularly lucrative client and couldn't afford to skimp on his hours. Robyn was in the kitchen chopping vegetables. He could tell from her preoccupied face, and the fact that she'd already chopped enough peppers to feed the five thousand, that she was on autopilot.

'It came,' she said.

'And?'

'I decided to wait until you were here.' She put down her knife and shrugged. 'I'm kind of nervous.'

'No kidding,' he said, nodding towards the vegetable mountain.

Outside, a storm was gathering, the wind picking up then dying down again.

Inside Katie's parcel, there were two smaller envelopes. One, he presumed, held the bracelet. The other contained a letter.

They read the letter first.

Dear Robyn and Brandon,

My apologies that this has taken a few days longer than expected. It's an unusual situation, and I wasn't sure what to do for the best. Rest assured, I have given it a lot of thought. I have also discussed everything with my niece, Beth, who's of great assistance to me.

When you open the accompanying envelope – if you haven't already done so! – you will find two identity bracelets. One for Edward Markham, the other for Brendan Markham, both born on 14 August 1972.

Brandon, from what Robyn told me in her emails, I have the feeling you grew up without knowing that you have a twin. I believe that you were originally named Brendan and your brother was Edward, or Eddie as he was known in the home.

Even though I worked as a nurse in Carrigbrack, I wasn't informed about what happened to the babies after they had left. I can't say for certain, but given the secrecy of those times, it's unlikely your parents in the United States were aware you had a brother.

Your birth mother is named Linda and is from County Galway. I remember her well. She was a beautiful young woman with long light-brown hair and blue eyes. She was twenty years old when you were born. Please know that she loved you very much, but in those times very few unmarried women were allowed to keep their children. The consequences of those decisions are still being felt today.

I understand that your parents in Boston are good people who gave you a fantastic upbringing. Robyn spoke highly of them in her emails. May I say, you also have a lovely caring wife!

Brandon, I could be wrong, but I sense that this search has been instigated by Robyn. No doubt the information in my letter is hard to take on board. I have sent both bracelets in the hope that one day, if you so choose, you will be able to meet your twin and pass it on.

Whatever you decide, I would urge you to call me so we can talk this through. I'm sure you'll have questions and I'll do my best to answer them. My number is at the bottom of the page

With all best wishes from Dublin,
Katie Carroll

Robyn and Brandon exchanged a look, her eyes suggesting she was as bewildered as him.

'Oh my God,' she said finally. 'Oh. My. God.'

Brandon's hands were shaking so hard he had difficulty opening the second envelope. As Katie had promised, it contained two narrow curls of paper, for Brendan and Edward Markham. Brendan had been the heavier of the pair, weighing a shade under five pounds.

How can this be happening? he thought. How can it be real?

'Are you all right?' said Robyn. 'We should sit down.'

Still without speaking, he followed her to the living room. They sat side by side on the sofa. Robyn clasped his hand.

'I had no idea,' she said. 'No clue. How could I?'

'Why is she so confident that I'm Brendan?' was the first thing he said.

'Guesswork, I'd say. I told her that Brendan was your name as a kid. Most adoptive parents change their child's first name, but some don't. Or so I've read.'

'It's wild,' he said. 'I assumed I had half-brothers or sisters. It stood to reason. But this? This never occurred to me. Never in a million years would I have thought it possible.'

'From what I've read, when it came to those homes, anything was possible.'

'I suppose. Did you notice that she didn't say whether we're identical?'

'No, I hadn't thought of that. Perhaps it means you're not, but—' Robyn came to a sudden halt. 'What about your mom and dad?'

'They can't have known. They wouldn't have lied to me.'

Or would they? Brandon needed to think, but his mind

had seized up, and his surroundings appeared to have taken life. The white walls and denim-blue chairs, the 1950s coffee table and vintage rugs, all chosen to create an atmosphere of serenity, had become a messy blur.

'I'll fix us a drink,' said Robyn. 'What would you like?'

'I'm not sure there's a liquor strong enough for how I'm feeling. I'll settle for a whiskey, though. Just ice.'

When she returned, Robyn asked the obvious question, the one he'd been avoiding.

'Do you want to find him?'

'If you'd asked an hour ago, I'd have said no. But the guy's my twin. We're two halves. So … I don't know.'

A quick internet search failed to supply any suitable Eddie or Edward Markhams. Brandon hadn't expected otherwise. Chances were his brother had a different name. Chances were the guy was living an uncomplicated life in Ireland, ignorant of the fact that he had a twin. Then again, he might also have been sent to America. He might be in LA or New York or Boise, Idaho. He might be elsewhere in Boston.

'Will you call Katie?' asked Robyn. 'She's obviously keen to hear from you.'

'Sorry to be repetitive, but I don't know. I probably will, if only to get the complete story.'

Brandon put down his glass and pulled Robyn close. He buried his face in her hair. Until an hour earlier, his life been perfectly ordered. As with the decor, he'd put considerable effort into ensuring that everything was harmonious. Now, he'd been tipped into the universe of the unexpected, a place of sharp edges and dangerous bends, and it wasn't where he wanted to be.

He woke at 3.13, his brain busy busy busy. Beside him, Robyn slept, her breathing shallow and steady. Outside, the wind had strengthened. Something – nothing important, he hoped – creaked.

Almost immediately, he was gripped by irritation. Why couldn't she have left well enough alone? Why did she have to meddle? There'd been no need to go poking and prodding and looking under stones. He thought of his childhood enemy, Scott Miller. How Miller would have enjoyed this. 'There you go, Bennett,' he'd have said, 'your mom must've held on to the better twin and rejected you.'

Stop, he thought, you're being stupid.

If he was angry – and he was – Robyn was the wrong target. He'd been born in a country where children had been sold, at a time when not telling someone they were a twin had been considered acceptable. The knowledge caught in his throat until he felt he would choke.

He wondered if some part of him had always known, and if this explained why he'd been reluctant to explore his origins. Had his instincts told him it could all get complicated? Or were these the deluded three-in-the-morning thoughts of someone who'd received a shock?

One minute, he would decide to call Katie. Hell, he'd

think, I'll do it straight away; it's already past eight in Ireland. The next, he'd consider throwing the letter in the trash and trying to forget. He switched the pillow over to the cool side and closed his eyes. He turned one way and then the other. But sleep wouldn't come.

Chapter 14

Then, Patricia

'Do you think I'm bad?' asked Winnie, examining her shorn hair in the bathroom mirror. 'I mean, is there a chance that Sabina's right, and I'm going to spend the rest of my days causing trouble?'

'Ah, here,' said Patricia, who was standing behind her, 'you've more sense than to listen to that old witch. Of course you're not bad. If there's anyone who ought to have a look at themselves, it's her. You're to forget her nonsense.'

'That's easy for you to say,' said Winnie, her tone surprisingly humorous. 'You've got all your hair.' She ran a hand over what remained of her own curls. 'The state of me. There's no danger of a fella looking in my direction any time soon. Mind you, given that I'm likely to be working here until I'm twenty-five, I'll probably never meet a fella again.'

'You don't think your family will pay to have you released?'

'Do you know how much it costs? A hundred pounds! Short of winning the Sweepstakes, they'd never be able to afford that. What about you?'

'I don't expect my family'd have the money either.'

Winnie sighed. 'Maybe I'll end up running away after all.'

When she'd first arrived in Carrigbrack, Patricia had overheard a conversation between Agnes and one of the other nuns. From it, she'd gathered that the government also contributed to the cost of running the home. She suspected that making women stay after their babies had been adopted was as unnecessary as it was unkind.

Three days after the singing protest, its repercussions rippled on. Sister Agnes, a cunning operator, had waited until they were worn out and parched for want of food and drink. Gradually, their shoulders had slumped, their voices had weakened and their solidarity had leaked away. Some had felt sick. Others had needed to feed their babies. By nine o'clock that night, they'd had to surrender.

It wasn't as though the protest had been in pursuit of any particular aim or agenda; more that, for a short time, it had made them feel like they had some control over their lives. They'd sung because it had felt good.

The retribution had started the following morning with a rare appearance by Mother Majella, who'd delivered a lengthy sermon about the evils of self-indulgence. So severe was the talking-to that Patricia had been transported back to her school days. She'd half expected a few slaps from a size 15 knitting needle or the metal edge of a ruler, both favoured punishments in St Joseph's National School. Instead, along with Winnie, she'd been transferred to the laundry. The work there was hard, the temperature unbearable. Patricia's baby had taken to dancing jigs, and she regularly had to pause and wait for him, or her, to stop. On the plus side, she no longer had to put up with Sister Sabina.

Winnie was brought to Sister Agnes's office, where her hair was cut back to her scalp. Agnes went out of her way to do a bad job. There was no hint of Twiggy or Mia Farrow about Winnie's crop. Nothing gamine or sophisticated. She looked like a boy who'd fallen foul of a short-sighted barber. Or like a convict. Patricia steeled herself for something similar, but the summons never came. She felt guilty. Did she not deserve the same fate as her co-conspirator? Winnie told her not to be silly. 'Don't draw attention to yourself for the next few days,' she advised. 'One of us looking like we belong in a horror picture is bad enough.'

To begin with, Winnie reacted with stoicism. She said nothing as she swept up her beautiful hair and threw it into the bin. Afterwards, she went about her work without complaint. Spool forward a couple of days, however, and the punishment was wearing her down.

The bathroom beside their dormitory had cracked black lino, walls the colour of cooking fat and a stench of disinfectant. The mirror was marked with brown dots. It was also one of a handful of places where it was possible to talk without facing the wrath of Agnes or Sabina.

After Winnie had inspected her hair, the two girls sat on the floor. They needed to take the weight off their swollen feet.

'Why did she have to do this to me? I mean, I was already the size of a house. Now I'm pig-ugly too,' said Winnie, before adding, 'Jesus, I sound like Jacinta.' She steepled her hands and looked skywards. 'Please, God, don't let me turn into Jacinta.'

Patricia grinned. 'I don't think there's much fear of that.'

Winnie patted her bump. 'Sorry, in there, by the way. I didn't mean to be nasty about you. I hope everything's going okay.'

'Speaking of Jacinta, I hear she had a tough time.'

Jacinta's baby had arrived the previous day. A giant of a boy, his delivery had been long and agonising. Word had it that she'd suffered a bad tear. The nurse had argued that she needed stitches, but Sister Agnes wouldn't hear of it. 'Let her mend in her own good time,' she'd said.

Winnie grimaced. 'Her story put the frighteners on me, all right.'

'Anyway,' said Patricia, running a hand through the pale brown hair that had become increasingly streelish during her time in Carrigbrack, 'don't worry about your curls. When they grow back, they'll be lovely again. Some of us are stuck with wishy-washy hair.'

'Would you ever go blonde?'

'My father would have a conniption. He says that dyed hair is cheap.'

'I hate to break it to you, but if he survived the news that his daughter was in the family way and the baby's father already had a wife, he'll probably survive anything.'

'Blonde it is, so,' said Patricia.

'Feck. Did you hear footsteps?'

'Can we pretend we're saying a prayer?'

Winnie giggled.

'Shush,' said Patricia, but she was laughing too.

'Hello,' said a young voice. 'What's going on in there?' It was Sister Eunice. 'What are you doing on the floor?'

'We were dying for a rest, Sister,' said Winnie. 'We were melting below in the laundry. You won't tell anyone, will you?'

'No, I think you've had more than enough bother for one week.' With that, Sister Eunice hitched up her skirt and eased herself to the ground. 'Move over there, if you wouldn't mind. I could do with a rest myself.'

Although Eunice was the friendliest of the nuns, Patricia was taken aback to see her joining them on the floor, especially given their reputation as troublemakers.

If Winnie was similarly surprised, she didn't let it show. 'You must be roasting in that gear,' she said, glancing at the nun's heavy black dress and tights as thick as bandages.

'I'm used to it, but yes, at the minute, something lighter would be nice.' Eunice removed her clumpy grey shoes. 'I was sorry to hear about your hair, Winnie, but it'll be back to normal in no time.'

'Thanks.'

'Don't tell any of the others I said that. Obviously.'

'You're grand. Do you mind if I ask: how old are you?'

'I'm twenty-three.'

Patricia was wary. She assumed Eunice would give them a lecture, however gently worded, about their wayward behaviour. Still, there was nothing to be gained by being rude. 'That's only three years older than me,' she said.

'Did you always want to be a nun?' asked Winnie.

Eunice smiled. 'Now, there's a question. Not always, no. But I was happy to take on the challenge. I'm fortunate that my faith is strong.'

Patricia was tempted to ask how she felt about imprisoning women who'd committed no crime, but she didn't want to make Eunice uncomfortable. 'Do you ever miss the outside world?' she asked.

'She means, would you like to go out with men,' said Winnie. 'She's got a terrible dirty mind, that one.'

'I do not.'

Eunice gave a nervous tinkle of laughter and sidestepped the question. 'This is the life I've chosen, and I've got to make the most of it.'

'If I had a few hours' freedom, do you know what I'd like?' said Winnie. 'I've a fierce longing for chips from the chip shop, steaming hot, with a good shake of salt and plenty of vinegar. What about you, Patricia? What would you do?'

'I wouldn't mind a proper sleep in my own bed.'

'Ah, stop, you can do better than that.'

'Okay, then. I'd go to the pictures.'

'What would you see?'

'I'm not sure. Something with Paul Newman … or Omar Sharif.'

'Aren't you the wild one? You see, Eunice, there you are thinking we're right bold hussies, when all we want to do is eat chips and watch soppy films. Oof.' Winnie placed a hand on her stomach. 'Whoever's in there is doing a fair amount of dancing today. I reckon they're learning the hucklebuck.'

'You haven't long to go,' said Eunice.

'Three weeks or so, I think.'

The nun arched her feet. 'If I had to pick a small pleasure, I'd choose nicer shoes. And I wouldn't mind wearing lipstick occasionally. A nice pale pink, perhaps.' She blushed. 'I probably shouldn't have said that.'

'Your secret's safe with us,' said Patricia.

'If all else failed,' said Winnie, 'I'd settle for a day without any sin-and-misery talk.'

'Amen to that.'

Eunice closed her eyes. 'Don't worry,' she said. 'I promise you, it won't always be like this.'

The hot weather continued into July, and the laundry became ever more hellish. Every day, they washed sheets, towels, baby clothes, nappies, uniforms and habits. The sheets had to be passed through an enormous metal machine called a calender. Its roller was red hot, and many of the girls suffered nasty burns. Without exception, their hands were raw and blistered. Some had developed a rash as far as their elbows, but if you scratched and drew blood you were in serious trouble. As well as the steaming heat and dust-filled air, they had to endure constant noise: the roar of the boiler and the whine of the machines.

What made the laundry bearable was the camaraderie of the workers. Despite being forced to carry out their tasks in silence, they supported each other through smiles and shrugs. Patricia marvelled at their ability to communicate without making a sound.

One day, when the nun in charge, Sister Faustina, had left the room, they had a chance to talk.

Winnie asked a familiar question. 'Suppose,' she said, 'you could have anything you wanted, what would it be?'

Without hesitation, one of them replied, 'Cream for my rash.' She displayed her hands, which were a mess of weals and sores.

The others voiced their agreement.

The following day, Winnie told them that if they went to the toilet beside the refectory, they'd find a treat. 'Don't all go at once,' she said. 'I can't risk Faustina or any of the others finding out. I've no more hair to give.'

Somehow, she'd managed to steal a tub of Sudocrem from the nursery and hide it in the cistern. One by one, the women went to the bathroom and applied the cream to their sore hands. They had to rub it in well for fear Faustina noticed. Thankfully, she wasn't overly observant. When the theft was discovered, there was an inquiry, but no one told tales, and the fuss died down again.

As her time drew closer, Winnie became more skittish. When they were able to talk, she mused about how awful giving birth might be. 'I'm sure it's rough no matter where you are,' she'd say. 'The difference is that here they actually want you to suffer.' Patricia would try to change the conversation, but her successes were rare. In a way, she envied Winnie's ability to speak about what frightened her. All her friend's emotions were on the surface. In contrast, Patricia could barely acknowledge her fears, not to mind articulate them.

They were in the laundry when Winnie started to complain that she was in pain. Without looking up from her prayer book, Sister Faustina told her to wait a while. It became increasingly apparent, however, that Winnie's baby was in a hurry. At least, that was how it looked to Patricia. One of the others, who'd already given birth, agreed.

'Patricia, this is no concern of yours,' said Faustina. 'It's a well-known fact that first labours are slow. Just because the contractions have begun, it doesn't mean the birth is imminent. Some of the penitents have taken a couple of days to deliver their baby.'

Winnie, who was as white as one of the sheets she was supposed to be ironing, squealed. 'I can't put up with this for another two days.'

'Nobody's suggesting you'll have to stay here for that long. Whisht a moment, will you? You're distracting the rest of us from our work.'

'Please, Sister,' said Patricia, 'I think she needs to go to the delivery room.'

The others murmured their agreement.

'Aaaargh,' called Winnie, gripping the side of the sorting table.

'You do know,' said Faustina, 'that Sister Agnes frowns upon too much noise during labour. You're expected to offer up your pain for the poor souls in purgatory.'

'Fuck the souls in purgatory. They can take care of themselves.'

Faustina shook her head and blessed herself. 'That's a desperate thing to say, Winnie. Desperate entirely. One of these days that mouth is going to get you into serious trouble.'

'She's in trouble right now, Sister,' said Patricia, wiping the sweat from the back of her neck.

'I've already told you to stay out of this. Winnie, describe the pain for me.'

For a while, Winnie said nothing. Or, rather, she said nothing intelligible. Eventually, the terror lifted from her face, and she spoke. 'Everybody told me it was like very bad period pain. But it's not like that at all. It's really intense … as though … as though everything in my back is twisting. And I feel like all my insides are going to pop out – not just the baby. Please, Sister, I can't take any more.'

'Sit down over there. We'll wait until the next contraction comes and monitor the situation then.'

Ordinarily, Sister Faustina wasn't the worst of the nuns. Tall, and thin as string, she had a face that appeared to have been carved from the limestone that surrounded them. Patricia thought of her as someone who'd had the religious life foisted upon her. She'd encountered a few similar figures. Often the youngest girl in a large family, they'd taken their vows either because it was expected of them or because it was the only way to get an education. Faustina wasn't as prone to mentioning God or the devil as Sabina. Nor did she have Agnes's predilection for delivering speeches about the failings of modern society. Instead, she chivvied the women along with mild exhortations to do their duty. Mostly she spoke in a low monotone. If anything, Patricia felt sorry for her. On this occasion, however, she believed the nun was making a mistake.

It didn't take long for Winnie's next contraction to arrive. A sheen of sweat covered her face as she moaned and roared. Patricia walked over and held her hand. Winnie attempted a smile, but couldn't quite manage it.

At last, Faustina told her to go to the delivery room.

'May I go with her, Sister?' asked Patricia.

Faustina tilted her head. 'Why would you do that?'

'She needs a friend.'

'Indeed and she does not. If ever a girl could look after herself, it's Winnie.'

'But she's only sixteen, and she's scared.'

Winnie, who was trembling, looked at the nun with pleading eyes.

'No,' said Faustina, with a lethargic wave of her hand, 'and that's my final word on the subject. The rest of you, including Patricia, are to get back to work. We've had enough disruption for one day, and if we don't finish the laundry by our designated time, you'll have to put the hours in this evening.'

'Good luck, Winnie,' shouted several of the women, but she seemed too dazed to acknowledge their support.

The time trickled by. Patricia's head felt as if it was filled with molasses. Unable to concentrate, she burnt her hand on the roller.

Sister Faustina instructed her to hold it under the cold tap. 'If it gets infected, you won't be of any use to anyone,' she said.

Patricia took the opportunity to enquire after Winnie. 'Perhaps I could drop over and see how she's getting on. The baby might have arrived.'

'How many times do you have to be told?' replied Faustina, eyebrows drawing together. 'Winnie's child is none of your business.'

'Yerra, go on, Sister,' said one of the girls. 'We're desperate to know.'

The rest joined in until the chorus became too much for the nun. 'Very well, I'll go and find out. In the meantime, you're to continue *in silence.*' She slapped the table to emphasise her words. 'Any more of your shenanigans, and I'll inform Sister Agnes.'

Patricia found that she could barely move. Winnie's baby had become as important to her as her own. That the child was destined to be raised by someone else was irrelevant. She was filled with anticipation. They'd already decided that Winnie was having a lively girl and Patricia a great lump of a boy.

Not for the first time, she wondered why the babies and their mothers couldn't be treated with more dignity. Maybe even some kindness. Surely someone like Sister Eunice would understand that? She remembered hearing a discussion on the wireless. A woman had proposed that unmarried mothers be allowed to stay with families rather than in a home. Their parents would be saved from embarrassment, she'd said, but the atmosphere would be less judgemental. They could do housework, or help on the farm, to pay for their keep. Afterwards, the babies would be adopted. In a limited number of cases, the mother would be allowed to bring up her own child. This appealed to Patricia.

She touched her bump. 'Today's a big day,' she whispered.

When Sister Faustina returned, her announcement was terse. 'Winnie had a girl,' she said before giving a short, tight smile.

'How big was she, Sister?'

'How is she?'

'How's Winnie?'

'Did Winnie's roaring drive Sister Agnes demented?'

The questions overlapped until Faustina raised one hand. 'That's none of your concern. Settle down, and we'll all return to our jobs.'

Patricia's skin turned cold. 'Is Winnie all right?' she said.

'I've told you to get back to work.'

'Please say she's all right.'

Faustina folded her arms across her chest. 'I won't tell you again, Patricia. The rules apply to everyone here, and there's a job to be done.'

A babble rose up around them. Patricia wasn't alone in thinking there was something disturbing about the nun's behaviour. 'Sister, I asked you a question.'

'And I told you to follow the rules and finish your work.' The others stopped talking.

'I don't give two hoots about the rules,' said Patricia. 'I want to know about Winnie and her little girl.'

'If I have to tell Sister Agnes about your behaviour, I will. You were moved here because you couldn't be trusted in the garden, and I'm starting to see why.'

Had she been asked, Patricia would have said that, at eight months pregnant, she wasn't capable of running. She would have said there was no way she would break the rules and court further punishment. Before she fully appreciated what she was doing, however, she'd barged out of the laundry and was darting helter-skelter down the corridor towards the delivery room. She careened around two girls carrying pails of water before flying past a nun. The nun yelled at her to come back. She ran on.

Lungs burning, legs aching, she arrived at the delivery room. Sister Eunice was standing outside, telltale stains on her cheeks.

Patricia, who'd been clinging to the slim hope that everything was okay, pushed open the door. Winnie was sitting up in bed, her eyes red-rimmed and wild.

'They've taken my baby from me,' she said. 'Why won't they let me see her?'

Chapter 15

Ailish

In more than twenty years, Ailish had never taken a dubious sick day. This was a first. She left home at the usual time, but rather than setting off for Rathtuskert Manor, she turned left and headed towards the coast.

After Keith had burnt the bracelet, she'd felt as low as it was possible to feel. A cold sore had popped up on her top lip, while her eyes had been raspberry red. He'd behaved as if nothing had happened, roaming the house while complaining about work, the weather and anything else that crossed his mind. Yes, she should have tackled him, but she didn't want to make the situation worse. Stevie, who'd always been adept at spotting trouble, spent most evenings with friends or at Jodie's house. Several times, he asked if something was wrong, but she fobbed him off. She didn't think she could talk without getting emotional. Her son needed to focus on his exams, not some pointless parental stand-off about an old strip of paper.

A malaise came over her, a form of paralysis. She ate dinners she couldn't remember cooking. She did her job by rote. The problem with Keith was that he resented anything he considered to be hers and hers alone. She wished she could convince him that finding her birth mother would be positive for them both.

She'd considered leaving. No doubt that was what the experts would advise. But where would she go? Where would Stevie go? She couldn't disrupt her son's life. Not now.

If she couldn't talk to her husband, she also feared contacting Katie. She'd let her down. For decades, Katie had kept the bracelet safe. Ailish had allowed herself to get caught up in a fantasy world where all she could think of was meeting Chrissie. She'd been careless and she'd paid the price.

Not being in contact with Katie meant she hadn't been able to find out more about Gary Winters's search. She'd told Stevie about his visit to Kilmitten, and while Black Iris weren't his sort of music (he'd referred to them as 'old white dudes with guitars'), he'd been impressed.

For more than a month, Ailish had tried to find the strength to push on. During that time, she'd received a letter from the Adoption Authority, confirming that her request was on file. In due course, the letter said, her case would be considered. It also warned of a lengthy wait. She decided she'd waited long enough. If she was going to find Chrissie, she would have to do it herself.

*

Hackett's Cross was set back slightly from the ocean. In early December, the Atlantic was greenish-grey; white-tipped waves crashed to the rocky shore. Wind and salt water had combined to give the few buildings a battered appearance. The trees were buckled and bent. Although Ailish didn't expect to find Chrissie in her home village, she hoped someone would remember her.

In the shop, a woman in an electric-blue tabard sat behind the counter watching *Judge Judy* on a small grey television. She looked Ailish up and down, then up again. At this time of year, it was unlikely she encountered many strangers. Ailish explained that she was trying to track down the Culligan family.

'Years ago, they were friendly with my parents,' she said. 'They lost touch, and as I was in the area, I thought I'd see if I could find them again.'

'Christine Culligan?' said the woman, whose eyelash extensions crossed the line between glamorous and Daisy the cow. 'The name means nothing to me. I've only been here since 2005, mind. You'd want to ask in the Cross Tavern. One of the regulars might be able to help.'

Ailish glanced at her watch. 'Will it be open at this time of the morning?'

A smile passed across the shopkeeper's doughy face. 'What else would people be doing on a day like this? Take it from me, you'll find one or two in there.'

Ailish didn't argue. Hackett's Cross was so quiet, it made Kilmitten look like Beijing.

The Cross Tavern was two doors down from the shop. No matter that smoking in pubs had been illegal for the past fifteen years, the place managed to smell of cigarettes and stale beer. The purple carpet had a spongy quality, and the housekeeper in Ailish recoiled. In the one concession to Christmas, a lacklustre strip of silver tinsel hung over the bottles of spirits.

As predicted, there was a handful of customers. In a far corner, a man and woman were drinking tea and having a low-level argument. One man sat at the bar with a pint of stout, while three more occupied the seats closest to the television. A cookery show played silently on an old-style set. Ailish was glad to note that all the patrons appeared to be over seventy. The older they were, the greater the chance they'd recall something about Chrissie.

The barman, a fellow with a beak of a nose and a thatch of red hair, was guarded bordering on hostile.

'Why would you want to know that, now?' he asked.

Ailish repeated her line about the Culligans being old family friends.

'Patsy and Biddy Culligan?' said the man at the bar. 'Low-sized people? Quiet?'

A chill ran down her back. On Chrissie's birth certificate, her parents had been named as Patrick and Bridget. 'That's right.'

'I'm afraid they're a long time dead, pet. The Lord have mercy on Patsy, he must be gone thirty years or more. And Biddy didn't last long after him.'

'Did they—?'

'They'd a son, Collie; he's dead too.'

'Oh. Wasn't there also a daughter? That's who my parents knew. She'd be in her sixties now. Christine ... or Chrissie, maybe?'

'A daughter? No, I don't think so. I only remember Collie. A harmless lad, if ever there was one.' The man tipped his head towards his pint. 'A bit of a martyr for this stuff, if you get my drift.' His face was opaque, and it was impossible to say how truthful he was being.

The barman, who was polishing pint glasses on a stained tea towel, decided to make himself useful. 'Lads,' he called to the three men near the television, 'do any of ye remember the Culligans? Patsy and Biddy? Had a son called Collie? May have had a daughter called Christine?'

'The only place you'll find them is above in the graveyard,' replied the eldest of the three, a squat man in a loud sports jacket. 'God love them, they made no age.'

His friends murmured in agreement.

The bar became silent, and Ailish was aware that her presence wasn't welcome.

'Sorry not to have been more use to you,' said the barman. 'Can I get you anything?'

'No, thanks,' she replied, her disappointment tempered a little by the knowledge that she could visit the family grave. She'd noticed the church and graveyard on her way into the village. 'And thanks for your help.' She smiled at the man with the pint and pulled out a fiver from the pocket of her jeans.

'No bother, sweetheart.' He accepted the money without demur. 'Oh, if you want to see their house, it's up the lane there,' he pointed towards the back of the bar, 'and on a little bit. There's not much of it left, mind.'

She followed his directions, such as they were. As she walked the lane, a thin wind whipped around her. She dug her hands deep into the pockets of her navy winter coat. For some reason, she was hit by a childhood memory. Her mother, Deirdre, had attached her gloves to either end of a long piece of wool and threaded it through the sleeves of her anorak. 'You've a head on you like a sieve,' she had said. 'I can't trust you to mind those gloves.' At school, they'd laughed at Ailish. But she'd never lost her gloves.

After about five hundred metres, she arrived at an abandoned cottage. While not quite a ruin – all the walls were standing – it was ravaged beyond redemption. The once white facade was pockmarked with brown and grey. The windows were boarded up, while the faded green door was warped and peeling. Slates were poised to slide from the roof. Grass grew to waist height. Ivy and brambles wrapped themselves around every available surface. In the undergrowth, something scurried and rustled. The house where her birth mother had grown up was being reclaimed by nature.

Ailish stamped her foot with frustration. Once again, she'd thought that if she wanted something badly enough, it would be hers. Once again, she'd been wrong. She felt like she was trying to crack a walnut with her teeth. While technically possible, the task was slow and painful. She stood there letting everything sink in, tears stinging her eyes.

The men in the bar had claimed not to remember Chrissie, but Ailish didn't believe them. Rumour and innuendo lived long in a small village. How plausible was it that they could recall three of the Culligan family but not the one member about whom there must have been gossip? How absurd was it, how twisted, that half a century later, those men were still governed by a code of silence? A lot might have changed, but Hackett's Cross remained a village of blind eyes and deaf ears.

She removed a tissue from her coat pocket and blotted her tears. Then she took several photos of the crumbling cottage. Finally she bent down and picked up a tiny black stone. She wanted a token from the place where Chrissie had spent her childhood. It wasn't an adequate replacement for the bracelet, but it was something.

As she reached the graveyard, drizzle began to fall from the grout-grey sky. Two huge seagulls swooped in and perched on the wall. A third hovered, squawking all the while. St Aidan's church was mottled with lichen and moss, but its door was freshly varnished. The Culligans' house had spoken of poverty, and Ailish wondered if the family had a gravestone. To her relief, they did. To her surprise, it was shiny and well kept. Although there were no flowers, the grass around it had been cut.

The stone told her that Patrick Culligan had died in November 1984. His wife, Bridget, had died in March 1985; their son, Colm, ten years later. Her grandfather, her grandmother, her uncle. All had been tragically young. Ailish said a prayer, a few hurried lines, hoping that if there was a heaven, that was where they were. For the first time, a sliver of hope rose within her. At the very least, Chrissie must have returned for her family's funerals. Who else could have paid for the headstone? Again, Ailish got out her phone, crouched down and took some photos.

As she did so, she noticed a man crunching along the path towards her. A sludge-coloured woolly hat was pulled low over his face, and it took her a few seconds to recognise him as one of the three fellows who'd been sitting near the television.

'That wind would skin you,' he said, in a quiet rasp of a voice.

''Twould.'

He shuffled from one foot to the other. 'I was hoping you'd still be here.'

'Oh?'

'A word to the wise. The girl of the Culligans? She went to England. As far as I know, she's in London.'

'You don't happen to know whereabouts?'

'I don't.' He peered at the ground. 'I do recall that she was married, so she's no longer Culligan.'

'Thanks a million,' said Ailish. 'Would any of the folks

around here be likely to have her married name, do you think?'

'I doubt you'll find anyone willing to tell you more than I can.'

'I see. I really appreciate your help.'

The man looked up. He was older than she'd thought. His cheeks were a criss-cross of deep lines, and his blue eyes were so pale they were practically colourless. His face was damp from the rain. 'I wish you good luck,' he said. 'She was a lovely young girl, and, bless her, she was treated very badly.' He hesitated. 'You're the living image of her.'

He didn't say any more. He didn't have to.

'Thank you,' she said again, but he was already on his way.

In the car, she tried to compose her thoughts. London. It wasn't a lot, but it was more than she'd had this morning. The haystack was ever so slightly smaller. She examined the images of the Culligans' cottage and their gravestone. Then she made a call.

'Hello,' answered a friendly voice.

'Katie?' said Ailish. 'I've got to tell you something.'

Chapter 16

Katie

If Katie had mixed feelings about her conversation with Ailish, it was because she was appalled by Keith's behaviour. Even as Ailish told her about the progress she'd made in Hackett's Cross, all Katie could think of was the burnt bracelet. In the grand scheme of things, it didn't matter. It was just a slip of paper. What disturbed her was Keith's malice – and how Ailish kept apologising for it. Katie didn't want contrition. She wanted anger. That wasn't all. More than once, Ailish made excuses for her husband. 'He's under pressure at work,' she said, 'and, to be fair, I could have done a better job of handling things.'

Katie tutted and clucked but managed to avoid raising her voice. Altogether more pleasing was the news about Chrissie. Okay, they still had a distance to go, but Ailish's birth mother being in London rang true. Many women had left the country. Katie had heard them on the radio, talking about their teenage experiences in one institution or another, their accents shot through with Liverpool or New York.

She'd assumed that this would be a quiet time of year for Ailish. Not so, apparently. Between dinner dances and Christmas parties, Rathtuskert Manor was constantly busy, and a lot of the partygoers stayed overnight.

'All one-night stays,' said Ailish, 'which is a complete pain. But now that I'm on Chrissie's trail again, I'm determined to make enquiries whenever I can.'

Katie convinced her that she too should make some calls. 'I've plenty of time,' she said, 'and I've got a willing assistant.'

Ailish asked about Gary's progress. Katie told the truth: there hadn't been any. Neither had she had much contact with him lately. They'd both seen pieces in the paper about Black Iris playing concerts the following year. The speculation still had it that Gary wouldn't be there. Katie wished she knew why but was scared to ask. She didn't want to appear meddlesome. She'd watched several Black Iris videos on YouTube, as well as a documentary about one of their most popular songs. 'Overboard', it was called. The music was more melodic than she'd expected, joyous and sad in equal measure. How cruel was it that Gary's biological parents didn't know what he'd achieved?

The priest in Hackett's Cross was taken aback to receive an enquiry about long-dead parishioners. Although he might have guessed at the story behind Katie's query, neither of them acknowledged it. In a hesitant voice, he explained that he was new to the parish and couldn't say what had happened back in the eighties or nineties. Katie asked if his predecessor might know.

'Ah,' came the answer. 'That'd be a bit tricky. His health isn't the best, and he's wandering a little.'

Recognising this as west-of-Ireland-speak for 'That's out of the question because he's seriously ill and has advanced dementia', she moved on.

The funeral director was brusque. His father would have known who'd arranged the Culligans' funerals, he said, but the old man had died ten years earlier. The records didn't go back that far, and he wasn't aware of anyone else who would know.

Katie decided she'd have to try a different angle. In the meantime, she had other work to do. There was momentum to the process: one person would see the online noticeboard and contact someone else, who would mention it to a third person, who would talk to a fourth. In quite a few cases, she hadn't been able to help. The person didn't have enough information, or they'd been misled, or they hadn't been born during her time in Carrigbrack. Nevertheless, she was now on friendly terms with the staff of the post office in Drumcondra, who were amused by the woman with the padded envelopes.

So far, twenty-two bracelets had found their way home, and she was at the kitchen table parcelling up number twenty-three. It belonged to a woman called Maeve, whom

Katie remembered because she'd been such a sickly baby. How brilliant was it that she'd grown up to become a marathon-running orthopaedic surgeon? Even better, her birth parents had reunited. Maeve had two sisters and a brother to add to the two brothers from her adoptive family. Hers was one of those sweet, sweet cases – and they did exist – where everything was out in the open and everybody got along. It lifted Katie's heart.

Other stories continued to gnaw at her. Every day she thought of Brandon. She'd received an email from Robyn, who said he was finding the news hard to process. Robyn promised to stay in touch, but, three weeks on, Katie was less optimistic. She feared that sending both bracelets had been a mistake.

Beth was unimpressed. 'That fellow has no manners' and 'What sort of loo-la wouldn't want to know about their *twin*?' were two of her milder observations. Katie was slower to judge. His world had been upended. He needed time to adjust.

The longer she spent at her task, the more she treasured contact with the Carrigbrack children. She was fascinated by how their unorthodox beginnings had moulded their lives. Since the first contact from Robyn, the Carrigbrack Nurse account had received another query from the United States. Sadly, that adoption had taken place five years before Katie's stint in the home, so she wasn't able to help. She replied to the man, a plumber from Philadelphia, offering advice about the best way to proceed.

'What are you like?' said Beth, who was patrolling the kitchen, waving her freshly painted nails in the air in preparation for a Christmas party. 'Could you not give it a rest for one evening?'

'It's good for the older person to have an interest. Isn't that what the magazines advise?'

Beth smiled. 'I think they mean golf or yoga or something.'

'Can you see me playing golf? Anyway, as you might say, I've got to look after my posse.'

There was another job on Katie's to-do list, one she was dreading. For the first time in her adult life, her Christmas cards would have only one signature at the bottom. Her mind skipped back to how Johnny had scrutinised their lists. 'Why are we wasting a stamp on that old killjoy, Kateser?' he used to say, or 'Are you certain she's still in the land of the living?' But he'd only been messing; he'd loved sending and receiving Christmas cards. Beth's generation weren't so enthusiastic. She'd assured Katie that no one would blame her for giving the cards a miss this year. She didn't understand the importance of ritual.

'So,' she said now, 'will you be coming home with me for Christmas?'

'I'm not sure you need me around the place.'

'Sorry, I made that sound like a question. It's an order. Mam said no sister of hers would be spending Christmas on her own.'

'You're determined to make me suffer, aren't you?'

Margo remained in the dark about the bracelets. When

they spoke, Katie reeled off a list of make-believe activities she claimed were occupying her time. 'I'm unbelievably busy,' she'd say.

Beth laughed, then sat down beside her. She was wearing a cornflower-blue leopard-print dress. On many, it would have looked garish, but Beth was pretty enough to carry it off. 'You'd be doing me an enormous favour. Relations are still a bit on the strained side, and it'd be great to have another ally about the place. Besides, I'd feel like an almighty cow if I left you here on your own.'

No matter what Katie did or where she went, this was going to be a difficult Christmas. She and Johnny had created a lifetime of traditions – Midnight Mass, chicken rather than turkey, a walk in Howth on St Stephen's Day – and they'd been stolen from her. She'd had no opportunity to prepare. Twelve months earlier, she hadn't even known he was ill. She didn't want to go to Danganstown, wear a paper hat and eat an overly fussy dinner. Deep down, Margo probably didn't want her there either. She was fulfilling what she saw as her obligation, and Katie didn't want to be anyone's obligation. She'd prefer to stay in Dublin and mark the day in private. Alas, she didn't have a choice.

'Go on, then,' she said to Beth. 'I'm not staying past the twenty-seventh, mind. I'm a busy woman.'

Three days later, the email arrived. Brandon was ready to talk.

Beth fixed up her phone so they could use FaceTime.

Call her old-fashioned, but Katie could never adjust to watching people on the telephone. It was too science fiction for her. This was what Brandon had suggested, however, and she was keen to accede to his wishes. She took a moment to reflect on the strangeness of it all. Here she was on Griffin Road in Dublin, talking to a man in Boston, Massachusetts; a man she'd known as a baby but could never have expected to see again.

She'd already seen him online. The first picture she'd found was on the website of a company called Longwalk Investments, where he was a senior fund manager. With his neat hair, navy blazer and cautious smile, he looked like he'd stepped out of a back-to-school catalogue. The images on Robyn's Instagram were more interesting. He was pictured at a barbecue, on a beach, in a bar. There was something wooden about him. Although she told herself not to judge a person's character from a handful of photos, Katie suspected that Brandon was one of those people whose eyes scoped the room at parties. Not because he wanted to hook up with a different woman (he would have to be completely mad), but because he was permanently on the lookout for someone important or successful.

Robyn, on the other hand, was born to have her picture taken. Like many young people, she knew how to pose without appearing gormless or drunk or double-chinned. When she looked at the lens, she was fully engaged. Oh, and she was beautiful, with the glossy hair and dewy skin of the wealthy and the blessed.

The Brandon who called was a little less manicured, a little more baggy-eyed than his photos had suggested. His shoulders were in a tense line, his hair in need of a trim. For a minute or two, they swapped nervous chit-chat. Katie had expected him to have a strong accent, but it was disappointingly neutral. He sounded only slightly more American than Gary. He told her that, while he'd been to London and Paris, he'd never returned to Ireland.

A flock of butterflies had set up home in her stomach. As a nurse, she'd often had to face challenging questions, and she feared that in many cases, she'd flubbed the answer. She'd told patients less – or more – than they'd needed to know. Still, her uniform had been her chain mail. It had helped her feel like a woman in control. This was different.

'So then,' she said, after they'd tiptoed through the initial pleasantries. 'I'm sure you're anxious to hear what I remember about your birth, your brother and your mother.'

'Yes. A little nervous, too.'

That makes two of us, thought Katie. 'I should say that I wasn't there for your delivery, so any knowledge I have is second-hand. But I'll do my very best to answer your questions.'

'Okay.'

'Like I mentioned in the letter, your birth mother's real name was Linda. She was a bright spark, a fine young woman. While her bump might have been bigger than average, no one, including Linda herself, suspected she was having twins.

Afterwards, lots of people said, "I should have spotted this", or "You should have noticed that." Folks wondered why she hadn't guessed herself. But it was her first pregnancy, and while she did report a lot of kicking and thrashing, that was dismissed as a good sign. "A fine healthy baby," everyone said.'

Brandon blinked. 'That sounds kind of odd. Was there genuinely no way of knowing she was carrying twins? Shouldn't you or one of your colleagues have had suspicions?'

'You've got to understand that we're talking about almost fifty years ago … and we're talking about an isolated home in the west of Ireland. We had no tests, no ultrasound, nothing. That's not to say we shouldn't have considered the possibility.'

'All right.'

'As is often the case with twins, Linda went into labour early. Even before the first baby was delivered, the midwife suspected there were two of you in there. You were wrapped around each other, so, as you can imagine, it was a challenging birth. Your mother suffered a lot, and afterwards there were fears for her well-being. Some of the nuns wouldn't have been particularly sympathetic, and they usually expected a new mother to return to work a week or so after the birth. In Linda's case, it was three weeks before she had the strength to go back to her job in the laundry.'

'Three weeks?' said Brandon. 'Is that normal? I'm no expert, but would she not have needed more recovery time?'

Katie stopped herself from telling him that, by Carrigbrack standards, a three-week break was an eternity

– and an indication that Linda had been seriously ill. 'Yes. Your mother was badly treated, Brandon, and I wouldn't try to defend it. She should, of course, have been given more time.'

'So tell me about us. My brother and I. Were we identical?'

'You were. You were small and delicate, but you were fine. There were no immediate signs that either of you had a problem. After a short while, the other young mothers were lining up to admire you.' Katie remembered everyone cooing over Linda's twins. She also remembered Sabina shooing them away as though there was something sinful about wanting to cuddle a baby.

Brandon looked to the side. There was a delay before he spoke again. 'When you say "no immediate signs", do I take it a problem emerged?'

Katie swallowed. 'Yes. No doubt you've asked yourself how I could be certain that you were the twin called Brendan. It wasn't just the name that answered that question for me. Within a couple of months, it became apparent that there was something different about Edward, or Eddie, as we called him. Sometimes he was too floppy. At other times, too rigid. There were no issues with your development. Right from the beginning, you were sharp and alert.'

A hint of understanding ran across Brandon's face, but he said nothing.

'Because she'd had a hard time of it, Linda had trouble feeding you both, and one of the nuns – Sister Sabina – accused her of not looking after you properly. She said that if there was something amiss with Eddie, it was his mother's fault.'

'That was a crock of BS anyway,' said Brandon. 'I can't believe they were allowed to speak to her like that.'

'They were, and unfortunately some of them did. Now, obviously, whatever was wrong with Eddie wasn't Linda's fault. But I do remember she was distraught. Bless her, she was so upset, the nuns threatened her with the psychiatric hospital.' Katie paused to collect herself. This was proving to be harder than anticipated. 'They sometimes made those threats, but in reality, few girls were sent there.'

'But some were?'

'I'm afraid so.'

'So, correct me if I've got this wrong: a pregnant young woman was abandoned by the father of her child, or, as it turned out, children. Then she was banished from home and sent to a brutal institution. After she'd endured a terrible birth, she realised that one of her babies wasn't well. Sick, and no doubt exhausted, she found it hard to cope. Despite this, she received no help. Worse, she was forced to do manual labour. Oh, and she was told that everything was her own lousy fault. When that upset her, she was threatened with an even harsher institution, one where she might be locked up for the rest of her days.'

'Yes. I … I can't argue with any of what you've said.'

Brandon was becoming increasingly agitated. Katie might not know much about him, but she could tell he was someone who didn't like the unexpected. Momentarily, she thought of Johnny. He'd been skilled at soothing the anger of others. It wasn't so much that he'd said the right words; more that he'd known how to sound reassuring. Stop it, she thought. This isn't the time to get wistful.

She was also conscious that Brandon could see *her* expressions. This amplified her awkwardness. Did her face look too stiff? Too unfeeling? Oh, why couldn't they have spoken on the phone in the old-fashioned way?

'Allow me to be blunt here,' he said, 'but how could you work in a place like that? How did you get up day after day and watch what was happening?'

Beth, who was sitting nearby, attempted to interrupt, but Katie waved her away. She repeated her well-rehearsed lines about not being given a choice and trying to do her best. She didn't make a good job of it. Brandon's face barely moved. Like many others, he didn't accept her explanation.

'I left Carrigbrack in December 1972,' she said, 'when you were four months old. You were both still there, as was your mam. After my departure, I tried to cut all contact with the place. From time to time, I did talk to another nurse. I always asked after Eddie. I don't want to sound patronising, but he was a very likeable baby. And, by all accounts, he grew into a lovely child. By the time he was eight or nine months old, it was clear he had a disability of some sort. He couldn't move his hands or sit up properly. Eventually, the staff realised he had cerebral palsy.'

'Is that because our delivery was screwed up?'

'The simple answer is, I don't know. I promise you, I'm

no defender of what happened in Carrigbrack, but, as far as I'm aware, it's just as likely he was starved of blood or had a stroke in the womb. If you want to read up about it, you'll find that twins are at greater risk of being born with cerebral palsy. It'd be wrong to describe it as common, but it's not unusual.'

Brandon frowned. 'Are you saying it was my fault? That I deprived the guy of blood and oxygen?'

Once again, she'd got it wrong. 'Of course I'm not. That never crossed my mind. I'm so sorry. Please don't think I was …' She instructed herself to remain calm. To try and describe everything in a logical way. As she did so, she noticed Robyn's hand rubbing Brandon's arm. 'Like I told you, it happens. Not enough was known about cerebral palsy back then, but that's all changed.'

The conversation faltered. After what felt like a very long time, but was probably five seconds, he spoke again. 'Can I ask you,' he said, 'about Linda's folks? Given the trauma she must have been through, did they not come to take her home? Did they not intervene?'

'No. That wasn't … that wasn't how things were done.'

'What a fucked-up way to behave. Those people should be ashamed of themselves. Frankly, I'm ashamed to be related to them.'

Katie should have foreseen Brandon's reaction. Wading into a situation in which she had no expertise had been a mistake. Technology might advance and mutate; emotions were more constant. What had happened to Linda, and to many, many others, had been outrageous.

Fearing she was losing control of the conversation, she started afresh. 'I've given this a fair amount of thought down the years, and the best word I have for those times is "mean". There was a meanness about, a lack of generosity. We all liked to see ourselves as generous. We had our collections and our sponsored fasts, and we were always going on about how much we gave to the Missions, but ...'

'... generosity was for faraway children, not your own family,' said Brandon.

Faraway children, she thought, and the dead. Usually, back then, the dead had been well treated. In Carrigbrack, however, even that hadn't been true.

'And after I was sent to America,' he said, 'what happened to Eddie?'

'I'm sorry. I don't know.'

'And our mother?'

'Again, I'm afraid I don't know.'

'Should you not have found out before you contacted me?'

'Oh, Brandon, I wish it was that simple. Robyn asked me to pass on the information I had, and that's what I'm doing. The fact that you're only finding out about Eddie now shows you how everything was wrapped in secrecy. If you want to find out more, there's a process you can follow. Who knows, you might discover that Linda and Eddie have been looking for you.'

'If you don't mind me saying so, Mrs Carroll—'

'Katie, please.'

'If you don't mind me saying so, I feel I'm being manipulated. That's why you sent both bracelets to me. Eddie's probably not in any position to ask for his.'

'I know this isn't easy,' she said, 'but I promise I'm not being cagey or playing games with you. I simply don't have all the information. Like I said a moment ago, facts can be hard to come by.'

Katie heard Robyn say, 'That's right.'

There was another pause. Brandon ran a hand through his hair. 'What you've got to appreciate,' he said, 'is that I didn't ask for this. I was completely taken aback by your letter, so I thought about it, and in the end, I said, "A twin, yeah. I should meet my twin. We can have a few beers, compare our lives." And then I thought a bit more, and I said, "Well, maybe it'd be good to get in touch with my birth mother too." From what you're telling me, though, she was put through ten kinds of hell. It'd be a miracle if she held onto her sanity. Oh, and the brother I was looking forward to meeting? He mightn't even know who I am.' He shook his head. 'I'm sorry, this is all too much for me right now.'

'I'm not sure you're reading Eddie's situation correctly,' said Katie, failing to keep the irritation from her voice. 'He has a mild disability, that's all.'

Immediately, she chastised herself. Her memory was of a contented baby. But what if Eddie's disability was more severe than she remembered? While no expert, she was aware that in some cases, cerebral palsy could be extreme. It would be wrong to mislead Brandon.

'The truth,' she said, 'is that I don't have much information about your brother. But, honestly, wherever he is, there's every chance he's perfectly happy.'

'You don't know that.'

'And you don't know otherwise. Either way, if we can find him, I'd say he'd be absolutely delighted to meet you. Please don't be blinded by the fact that he's disabled.'

On the screen, Brandon's eyes narrowed.

As soon as the words left Katie's mouth, she regretted them. 'Sorry,' she said. 'Sorry. I didn't mean that. As I say, I'm conscious that this is a lot to take on board. I shouldn't have sounded judgemental. Please forgive me.'

'No, I'm sorry,' said Brandon. 'We're wasting each other's time here. It's a bleak story, and I feel desperately sad for Linda, but there's nothing either of us can do to change what happened.'

'What are you saying?'

'I'm saying that my first instinct was right, and we should leave the past where it belongs.'

Katie thought she noticed Robyn attempting to say something, but before she could intervene, the line went dead.

Chapter 17

Then, Patricia

Winnie named her daughter Diane. She was buried at the back of the main building, in the same small plot as the other children. The grave had been dug by two girls who'd already had their babies. Later, they would replace the dry stony soil and flatten it out again. Save for a nail knocked into the adjacent wall, Diane's grave would go unmarked. No one would know that an infant girl was buried there. It was better that way, Sister Agnes said.

Four people attended the ceremony: Winnie, Patricia, Agnes and Eunice. Because Diane had died before she could be baptised, there was no priest or funeral Mass. Instead, they said two decades of the rosary at the side of the grave.

According to Agnes, the baby was in heaven. 'Diane left the world in the same hour she entered it,' she'd said. 'She did no harm.' Sister Sabina had loudly disagreed. She'd insisted that, while the child hadn't committed any sins of her own, she'd been tainted by original sin and was trapped in limbo. Winnie hadn't been allowed to hold her daughter. The first time she saw her, she was wrapped in white cloth and ready for burial.

The sky was an uninterrupted blue, the breeze like a warm breath. Patricia felt as if the beauty of the day was mocking them. She imagined how the scene would appear from above. There they were, a tight huddle surrounded by pale grey rocks and bright patches of grass. A hundred yards away, women went about their work: planting and harvesting, chopping and boiling, washing and ironing. Babies gurgled and cried.

Despite the heat, there were goose pimples on Patricia's arms.

Throughout, Winnie was uncharacteristically quiet. Her uniform, which had always been too large, looked absurd, as did her cropped hair. She joined her hands together and kept her gaze on the tiny body. Not once did she cry. Patricia couldn't comprehend her friend's composure. How could she be so strong? She tried to force back her own tears, but they spilled out. At one point, she made an involuntary sound. 'Glug,' she went, prompting a glare from Agnes. Warmth rushed up her neck. If the girl who'd lost her baby was able to maintain her dignity, she should be capable of it too.

In the hours leading up to Diane's burial, Winnie had barely spoken. Patricia believed that one of the few things she did say would stay with her forever:

'Just because I couldn't keep her, it doesn't mean I didn't want the best for her. I wanted her to be brilliant. She deserved to be brilliant.'

Patricia hadn't known how to respond. Every line that entered her mouth sounded like a platitude, like something you'd say on the death of an aged aunt. She simply squeezed Winnie's cold hand.

News of the tragedy had spread through the home, fast as fire. Although a baby had died the previous month, he'd been several weeks old and had already been baptised. There was sympathy for Winnie, but unease too. Those yet to give birth became more anxious. Those with babies in the nursery wanted to spend more time there, something disapproved of by Sister Agnes.

Patricia hadn't expected to attend the burial. Agnes had summoned her to the office, where she'd been scolded for running out of the laundry and for asking questions about Diane's death.

'It may be difficult for us to understand,' she'd said, 'but the Lord works in mysterious ways. You must pray for the grace to accept that.'

Patricia wasn't satisfied. 'But suppose Winnie had been able to go to the delivery room when she'd first raised her concerns? And suppose …'

Her voice had trailed off. What she'd wanted to say was 'Suppose the nurse in charge had taken more care? Suppose her mind had been on her job rather than on a dance or the pictures or whatever she does when she's not here?' Even in her unsettled state, she realised this would be an accusation too far.

As it was, Agnes's tone was icy. 'I don't ever again want to hear an uncharitable suggestion about Sister Faustina. She could have done many things with her life but she followed her vocation and devoted herself to the service of penitents such as yourself. She deserves your gratitude. Do you follow me?'

'I do, Sister, only—'

'No, Patricia. You've said enough.' Agnes removed her glasses. 'You asked if you could accompany Winnie to the burial. My initial instinct was to say no. However, Sister Eunice tells me you've been a good friend to Winnie. So, given her young age, I've decided to bend the rules. Let me warn you, though, any further disobedience will be punished. Severely.'

Patricia's burnt hand throbbed. 'Thank you, Sister. Have Winnie's parents been told?'

'I don't know why you have to ask so many questions. Meddling is not an appealing trait. Can you not accept that we're dealing with the situation?'

'I was only—'

'Her parish priest has been contacted. In due course, he will inform her father and mother. Now listen to me, Patricia. You're not a stupid young woman, yet you persist in acting like one. I only wish you could see that everything we do here, we do for the right reasons. If it wasn't for Carrigbrack, and other institutions like it, the country would be in chaos.

We do our best to help people and to keep Ireland safe. Only the very selfish would think otherwise.'

It probably wasn't the right time for her next question. She thought she'd try anyway. 'Sister, do you ever allow women to keep their babies? Like, say if you knew a mother would be able to take care of her child? That she'd love them and mind them and be able to earn a living? What then?'

'That's a dangerous notion,' said Agnes, a flare of anger in her voice, 'and one you'd do well to forget. We can't allow silly young girls to harm innocent children. As for earning a living: what respectable employer would give work to the mother of an illegitimate child? And what about the good Catholic couples who can't have children of their own? Have you thought about them? Should they be made to suffer?' She gave a brisk shake of her round head. 'Tell me, where does a girl from a decent family hear such ludicrous ideas?'

'I didn't hear the idea so much as think about it myself. I mean, with the way the world is changing and …' The rest of the sentence vanished. There was no point in having this argument now. She would have to make her move at an appropriate time.

After Diane was laid to rest, Winnie was told to spend the rest of the day in silent prayer and contemplation. Patricia returned to the laundry. The atmosphere was sombre. The others glanced at her, then quickly looked away again. She felt as if the connection between her brain and hands had been severed. She knew what to do, but the actions were impossible. Sister Faustina instructed her to sit in the corner.

'Strictly speaking,' she said, 'I should force you to carry out your duties. At the moment, though, you're more hindrance than help.'

'I'm sorry.'

'Sorry isn't of any use. Considering the circumstances, you can sit there for the afternoon, but tomorrow you'll need to be back at full strength. If one person is allowed to shirk, it's not fair to the others. Do we understand each other?'

'Yes, Sister.'

In her heart, Patricia would always blame Faustina for what had happened. She blamed herself too. She should have been more insistent. She should have taken Winnie's arm and marched her out of the laundry. It was what a proper friend would have done. She dwelled on what Sister Agnes had told her at their first meeting. 'Actions have consequences,' she'd said. How, then, could the death of a baby be glossed over and described as God's will? Maybe negligence hadn't been responsible for Diane's death. Maybe Patricia was being unfair. What was clear, though, was that consequences were for little people.

If the burial was handled in a perfunctory manner, Winnie's treatment was devoid of feeling. Three days after her baby's death, she was ordered to return to work. The one concession was that she'd be employed in the kitchen rather than the laundry. The work there wasn't quite as onerous. Patricia suspected the change had more to do with Faustina's guilt than any consideration of Winnie's grief.

Physically, she was in a poor state. She was sore, and her breasts continued to produce milk. It was her mental condition that worried Patricia most. Her speech was staccato, her eyes blank. The real Winnie didn't smother her emotions. She sparkled and fizzed. But that Winnie had disappeared, to be replaced by a hollowed-out person who seemed unaware of what was happening around her.

The following week, she received a letter from home. She showed it to Patricia, who was shocked. Written in pale blue ink on a thin sheet of paper, its contents read as though dictated by Sister Agnes.

The baby's death is sad, wrote her mother, *but it wasn't as if you could have held onto her anyway. You're young, and your chance will come again. Hopefully, next time you'll find a husband first.*

'Daddy would have been more sympathetic,' said Winnie, 'but writing isn't his strong point.'

The letter also revealed that Winnie's eldest sister, to whom she was close, had moved to London.

Patricia did everything she could to make Winnie feel better. She made fun of the nuns and the other girls. She fantasised about what they both might do with the rest of their lives. They could go to London themselves, get good jobs and a flat. They could meet men who cared about them, exotic men with grand English accents who drove sports cars and hung about with pop stars. While Winnie gave a weak smile, it was obvious her mind was elsewhere.

*

Eventually, she snapped. Two weeks after the burial, she sought out Sister Agnes to ask when she could leave. 'I've no baby to mind,' she explained. 'I've nothing to contribute. May I go home?'

Agnes told her that this wasn't how Carrigbrack operated. She had to pay for the cost of her stay. 'You'll need to work here for another six months,' she said. 'Possibly longer.'

Winnie left the office. Rather than returning to the kitchen, she turned in the opposite direction and went to the nursery. Patricia, who was in the laundry, didn't witness what happened at the start. She had to rely on rumours and second-hand stories. What she did know was this:

Since Diane's death, many of the women in Carrigbrack had been kind to Winnie. Take the young girl with whom they'd worked in the fields. At considerable risk, she'd stolen several strawberries, wrapped them in a handkerchief and given them to Winnie. 'I remember how you liked them,' she'd said, with a nervous smile.

Others, though, were less supportive, and some effectively shunned her. In their superstitious minds, she was damaged. She was bad luck, and bad luck was contagious. They might as well have rung a bell and shouted, 'Unclean, unclean.'

In the nursery, Winnie asked two of the new mothers if she could hold their babies. Both turned their backs. The one person to step forward was Jacinta, who'd been feeding her son, Lorcan, a calm boy with solemn grey eyes and a full head of deep brown hair.

'Here,' she said. 'He wants to say hello to the girl who stood up for his mam.'

Winnie cradled Lorcan with tears running down her cheeks. 'Sorry,' she kept saying. 'Sorry, I don't want to make a show of myself.'

Jacinta told her it was all right and that she understood. 'You won't upset him,' she said. 'He's very good.'

'You smell great,' Winnie said to Lorcan. 'I had a baby girl. She was as gorgeous as you, only they killed her.'

'Hush now,' said Jacinta. 'Don't go upsetting yourself, Winnie.'

'They wouldn't let me see her, either. Not until she was bundled up like a mummy and ready for the grave. They didn't want me to see how lovely she was.'

Lorcan remained quiet.

'They kill babies, you know. Just for spite.'

Jacinta sent a look of alarm to the nun in charge, who went to find Sister Agnes. She arrived five minutes later in a lather of indignation. By then, word was travelling around Carrigbrack. 'I hear Winnie's gone mad,' one of the girls in the laundry said. Patricia put down what she was doing and walked out. Faustina called after her, but she was wasting her breath.

When Patricia reached the nursery, Winnie was sitting beside the window with Lorcan in her arms. Sister Agnes was ordering her to hand him back to his mother.

'You're not the first girl to lose a baby and you won't be the last,' she said. 'I don't want to hear any more lies about anyone killing your daughter. Give that child back to his mother and go to your dormitory.'

Patricia watched as Winnie followed the nun's orders. Jacinta took Lorcan and kissed him on his placid head. Instead of going to the dormitory, however, Winnie walked to the corner of the room, faced the wall and slumped to the floor, where she rocked back and forth, sobbing and moaning. Her misery was all-pervading. It filled the room and seeped into every one of them. Sister Eunice, who'd also heard about the commotion in the nursery, tried to comfort her, as did one of the young nurses. Patricia joined them. They attempted to defuse the situation with soothing words and gestures. Agnes scowled, but didn't intervene. Winnie swayed to and fro. She was inconsolable, her speech little more than gibberish.

'Wanted to see her,' she said. 'Kiss her and smell her. Tell her I loved her.'

After ten minutes of coaxing, they convinced her to leave. Patricia wanted to bring her friend to the dormitory, but Agnes stepped in and ordered her back to work.

'It's okay,' whispered Eunice. 'Don't get yourself into trouble. I'll look after Winnie.'

It was as Patricia was returning to the laundry that she spotted Sister Sabina. Their old adversary was standing beside the door, drinking everything in as if it was a scene from a John B. Keane play.

Don't say anything, Patricia told herself. She's not worth it.

'Winnie's lost all of her backchat and cheek, I see,' said Sabina.

Don't say anything.

'Ah, and you've lost your voice too. It was about time you were both taught a lesson.'

Patricia couldn't stop herself. 'You're bitter because you were cruel to her, and she had the gumption to stand up for herself. A sixteen-year-old girl got the better of you, and your pride was hurt.'

'Well, she certainly paid for her insubordination.' Sabina stabbed a thin finger at Patricia. 'You, on the other hand, were let off far too lightly. You're indulged by Sister Agnes because you're better educated than some of the others. In my book, that makes your sin even more heinous.'

A black anger rose within Patricia. She wanted to strike out at the woman standing in front of her. That wasn't a realistic option, however. She was eight months pregnant, as wide as she was tall, and her right hand was stinging with pain. 'How is it that you have no charity or mercy?' she said 'Winnie is devastated by her loss, and you're here smirking at her and making snide remarks. What sort of Christian are you? Then again, I could ask the same of most of the nuns here. For the past two weeks, you've watched that poor girl fall apart and done nothing to support her.'

'Is that right? If you ask me, she has no one to blame but herself. I heard she refused to pray for the tortured souls in purgatory. She got what was coming to her.'

Carrigbrack could be a callous place, yet Patricia didn't

think she'd heard anything as stony-hearted as this. 'If you really believe what you've just said, I pity you. If there is a God, I'm sure he can see that Winnie's worth ten of you. No, a hundred of you. You're an evil bitch, and no mistake.'

Sabina smirked again. Patricia knew she had to walk away. When she turned, she saw Sister Agnes standing behind her. She'd been listening to every word.

'You can't say you weren't warned,' said Agnes as she brought the scissors close to Patricia's scalp. 'You were given chance after chance. I gave you permission to attend the burial, and you repaid me with a foul-mouthed attack on Sister Sabina.'

'I couldn't listen to her being mean about Winnie,' said Patricia, as she watched a hank of light brown hair tumble to the floor. 'She went too far, Sister.'

'It's not your place to tell Sister Sabina, a woman who's been a devoted servant to Carrigbrack, what she can or can't say. Imagine calling her evil! Everything she does is designed to help girls like you. Girls whose failures have got them into trouble. At this advanced stage in your pregnancy, I'm reluctant to discipline you further. But if necessary, I will. Now, close your mouth and take your punishment.'

Agnes continued until the floor was covered with hair. Finally, she declared her job done. 'Get a brush and sweep up that mess,' she said. Patricia put a hand to her head to feel the damage. She'd been left with an inch all round.

She found Winnie in their old hiding place: the

bathroom beside the dormitory. Her friend's reaction was as unexpected as it was wonderful. She lifted a hand to her mouth and said, 'Jeepers, she's made a shocking job of you.' Then she giggled.

'To tell the truth,' said Patricia, examining herself in the spotty mirror, 'it was never great-quality hair. With any luck, it'll grow back a bit thicker.'

'Or blonde.'

'Even Agnes can't work miracles.'

Winnie laughed again, a proper throaty laugh. 'St Agnes of Carrigbrack, patron saint of hairdressers.'

'Did I ever tell you,' said Patricia, 'that when the priest was driving me here, my mam and dad made me wear a wig? They were terrified for fear the neighbours caught sight of us. Perhaps I should dust it down and put it on.'

'A wig?' said Winnie, with another snort of laughter.

'Hmm. It's an awful-looking yoke, like something you'd see on a mannequin in a shop window.'

'I thought I'd heard it all, but that's something else.'

It was so wonderful to hear Winnie's laughter and to see the haunted look lift from her eyes that Patricia decided her haircut had been worth it.

'This is probably a stupid question,' she said as she lowered herself to the floor, 'but how are you? I was really worried earlier. We all were.'

Winnie slipped down beside her. 'Honestly? I don't know if I'm strong enough for Carrigbrack. Here I am surrounded by pregnant women and babies, knowing there was only one thing I had to do – deliver a healthy child – and I couldn't even get that right.'

'You can't think like that.'

'I keep asking myself, did I do something wrong? Did I kill her?'

'No, you didn't, Winnie. Those are bad thoughts. You've got to push them out of your head.'

Winnie played with the frayed hem of her skirt. 'When I was down in the nursery, I blamed the nuns, but I was only lashing out. I just wanted to point the finger at someone else. I'm rotten with anger and bitterness, and for as long as I'm here, that's not going to change.'

Patricia didn't feel equipped to deal with Winnie's fragility. Every single thing about Carrigbrack was designed to cut her open and rub bleach in her wounds; to tell her that she'd failed. Patricia's own baby moved, yet she was reluctant to say so. It would sound cruel.

After the evening rosary, she sought out Sister Eunice.

'I heard about the hair,' said Eunice. 'You didn't deserve it. I usually try to defend Sabina, but this time she went too far. I wish I knew why she's so hard. Maybe that's what a long time in an institution does to you.'

'I'll be grand,' said Patricia. 'Sure who's looking at me anyway? I'm very worried about Winnie, though. I'll miss her, but they've got to let her go. If she's forced to stay, she'll never recover. It'll only be a matter of time before she returns to the nursery, and the next mother mightn't be as reasonable as Jacinta.'

'I don't know what to do either. I asked Sister Agnes if there could be a dispensation for her. She said no. She claimed that ignoring the rules would send the wrong message to everyone else.'

'There's no way, is there, that Winnie's parents would be able to pay for her release?'

'As I understand it, they're in very bad circumstances. Winnie's the third eldest of ten, and the house doesn't have running water or an indoor toilet. A hundred pounds or a million pounds: it makes no difference to them. I doubt they could even afford her bus fare home.'

For the most part, Patricia viewed the nuns not as individuals but as enforcers of a regime. They recited the rules and warned about sinful behaviour. Eunice was the exception. In different circumstances, the two of them might have been friends. She wondered why Eunice had chosen religion. Or had she been given a choice? Although she allowed occasional glimpses into her life, she didn't reveal much. Patricia knew she had a sister and that she liked reading, but that was about all.

She said good night to Eunice and made her way to the dormitory. As she did so, her anger returned. She wanted to roar and howl. What sort of rancid system could treat a distressed girl like Winnie in such a shoddy way? How warped was their religion if someone like Sabina could come out with such poison and get away with it? The only positive Patricia could find was this: so consumed was she with the injustices of Carrigbrack that in more than a week, she'd barely given a thought to Mike or her parents.

*

Patricia was in the laundry, passing sheets through the calender and cursing her blistered hand, when an out-of-puff Sister Agnes pushed open the door.

'Has anyone here seen Winnie?' she asked.

The honest answer was no. A murmur to that effect travelled around the room.

'What about you, Patricia? When did you last see her?'

'This morning at breakfast, Sister. Is she not in the kitchen?'

Agnes looked at her like she was half-witted. 'If she was in the kitchen, I wouldn't be looking for her here, would I?'

'I suppose not.'

'Have you tried her baby's grave, Sister?' one of the others asked. 'She might have needed a few minutes with her little one.'

'We've already looked,' replied Agnes, glasses fogging up. 'Patricia, you're to come with me. The rest of you are to continue with your work.' She nodded at Faustina and ushered Patricia into the corridor.

'If you have any idea where Winnie has gone, I'm ordering you to tell me. Covering up for her would be a mistake. A serious mistake. If she's left the grounds, she'll be found and she'll be brought back. Do you hear me?' Such was her fury that she spat as she spoke. Patricia didn't dare wipe her face.

'I promise you, Sister, the last time I saw her was this morning. I haven't a clue where she is. In fact, I'm concerned about her. She's been finding life very difficult. Don't take this the wrong way, but I don't think you appreciate how vulnerable she is.'

Clearly, the possibility that Winnie might harm herself hadn't occurred to Agnes. She pursed her mouth before replying. 'What are you suggesting?'

'I ... I'm not sure. All I know is that she hasn't been herself. How could she be?'

'I see,' said Agnes, whose face had lost its colour.

'May I help you look for her?'

'That wouldn't be advisable.'

A dark feeling wrapped itself around Patricia. 'If Winnie's hiding somewhere, she might come out for me. She trusts me.' She scratched her hand. 'Please?'

'Very well, but you're not to go anywhere on your own. And before you do anything, you're to get a bandage for that hand. You shouldn't have allowed it to get into such a sorry state.'

For two hours, they looked everywhere. Then they looked again. They scoured the fields and outbuildings. The combed every hedge and thicket. They tried all the rooms and all the cupboards, every nook and crevice. They searched the church and the attic. Sister Agnes made enquiries in the nearby village.

Patricia did everything with a rising sense of panic. Winnie wasn't in the right frame of mind to escape. Even if she didn't intend to hurt herself, she wouldn't be able to cope on her own. She was a child grieving the loss of a child. Oh, and she was wearing that terrible uniform. Any sensible person would ask about her clothes and wonder where she'd come from. Plus, she was penniless. She couldn't afford to pay for a bus, not to mind spend a night in a bed and breakfast. The weather might be fine, but that wouldn't last, and she was in no condition to sleep in fields and barns.

Patricia realised she was trembling. Oh Winnie, she thought, where are you?

At ten o'clock, with the light fading, they gave up.

'She can't just have vanished,' everyone said. But it looked as if she had.

Agnes called the guards, who said that while they'd keep an eye out for Winnie, there'd been a bad car accident near Kilfenora and a robbery in Ennistymon. They were up to their tonsils, the officer explained, and a young girl who'd committed no crime wasn't their top priority.

'Girls go missing,' he said. 'That's what they do.'

Agnes was raging. She told him that Carrigbrack runaways had always taken precedence over minor incidents and that he'd regret his lack of respect. The policeman wasn't for turning. Or at least, that was how it sounded when Eunice relayed the news. Despite everything, Patricia smiled.

That night, she lay in her narrow bed, running through the possibilities, almost all of them troubling. Every inch of her body ached. After an hour or so, she turned over the thin pillow. There was an envelope underneath. It could only be from one person.

While the women weren't supposed to use the lavatory at night, a blind eye was turned to those in the final stages of pregnancy. Patricia tucked the envelope into the top of her knickers. Then, quiet as a shadow, she tiptoed to the bathroom. All the while, her mind was spinning. The letter hadn't been there earlier in the day; she was sure of it.

She didn't open the envelope until she was safely inside the cubicle. The note was short.

Dearest Patricia,
Hopefully by the time you read this, I'll be far away. I'm sorry I didn't say goodbye, but I decided it was safest this way. Had I been capable of staying, that's what I would have done. But the past few weeks have torn me in two, and I wasn't able to take any more.
Please don't worry about me. Just take care of yourself and your baby. Oh, and wish me well. Please wish me well.
I was very lucky that we became friends. Thank you! I hope we meet again one day. Even if we don't, I promise I'll never forget you.
With love,
Winnie

Patricia sat in the bathroom for as long as she dared. She was part relieved, part scared, part thrilled. Oh, and if she was being honest, she was disappointed. As much as she knew that Winnie had needed to flee, she couldn't imagine getting through the days in Carrigbrack without her. There were questions too: how had she escaped in the middle of the day without being spotted? She couldn't have left through the hole in the hedge. Anyone trying to get out that way would have been located within ten minutes. And where had she found writing paper and an envelope?

'Travel safely, my brave, brave friend,' whispered Patricia, as she unlocked the door and returned to her dormitory.

Chapter 18

Gary

Frank was there before him, in the corner of the bar, phone clamped to one ear, lolling with intent. Gary had chosen the Palace because he wanted a neutral venue where Dubliners enjoyed an afternoon pint and tourists took each other's pictures. In such a public place, they'd be forced to keep their tempers in check.

The search for his birth mother was at a standstill. Worried that too direct an approach would scare her, he'd written what he hoped was a cleverly worded letter to Gráinne Holland. In it, he described himself as an 'old friend' from 1971. *We last saw each other in north Clare*, he wrote. He wondered how life had been for her and expressed an interest in renewing contact. If she was the right woman, and he suspected she was, she would understand the letter's significance. If she wasn't, there was no harm done. She had yet to reply.

The other names on Katie's list were even harder to trace. Her original message board post had become a lengthy thread in which people spoke about Carrigbrack and traded tips. Some of the messages related to 1971 and '72. Others referred to earlier or later years. Every day, Gary checked the discussion. He'd also provided DNA samples to two ancestry websites. Spitting into the tube reminded him of the time an Ohio woman had claimed he was the father of her four-year-old son. Gary had been – almost – certain he'd never met the woman. On that occasion, he'd been glad to draw a blank. This time, he wanted a different outcome, but he wasn't getting his hopes up.

The more he learnt about Carrigbrack and the heartbreak behind its walls, the more he thought about his birth mother. Had she meekly accepted her lot, or had she stood up for herself? Had she been relieved to see her baby go, or had she fought to hold onto him? Was she musical? Was that where his talent had come from?

And what was she doing now? Had her life been blighted by what had happened to her? Or had she shucked off her early misfortune?

Frank bought him a pint and told a string of entertaining stories. One, involving a racehorse, a famous guitarist and a cheap flight to Thailand, was especially brilliant. Stories had always been his forte. Back when he'd first managed Black Iris, when they'd been four skinny young bucks without a penny to their names, he'd made them laugh until they'd keeled over. He'd made them believe in themselves too.

Frank's trip to Dublin was a fleeting one. He'd been in Los Angeles just two days earlier. The following morning, he would fly to New York, where he spent most of his time. He was still scouting bands, cutting deals, adding to his fortune. Nobody would ever have accused him of being handsome, but he looked well. Gary reckoned he'd had something done to his eyes. They both wore a uniform of sorts: factory-faded jeans and pricey suit jackets. They looked out of place.

Outside, the pre-Christmas mania was at full tilt, the streets crammed with shoppers and drinkers. Women wore cocktail dresses at two in the afternoon while young guys put on plastic antlers and pretended to drink a beer in twelve different bars. Stalls were laden with wrapping paper and tinsel, Conor McGregor posters and cheap make-up. People had more money; they were better groomed and better travelled. Yet in lots of ways, Dublin at Christmas was the city of Gary's childhood. It was glittering and tawdry, beautiful and dark. And he loved it for that.

Frank was there to soften him up. That was okay; he could handle it. He wouldn't be coerced or cajoled into something he didn't want. They'd already had several phone conversations. Ray and Liamo had been in touch too. Anton continued to do his talking through intermediaries. The reunion plans had been stepped up, and the guys were keen to go back into the studio. They'd been working on new tracks. They had ideas.

'So, then,' said Frank. 'What's the story? Are you in?'

Gary ran a finger down the side of his glass. 'It's not the right time for me.'

'So you say. I'm not sure I understand why, though.'

'Like I explained on the phone, I'm busy.'

'Nah you're not. You're messing around.'

'You're wide of the mark there, Frank. In case you weren't listening before, I'm committed to finding my birth mother. I've been putting in the work and I've narrowed the list down to three.'

Frank took a mouthful of Guinness. 'Did I ever tell you about where my ma grew up? Until she was ten, she lived in a tenement in the north inner city. Rotten kip of a place. Four sisters in one bed, and six families sharing a toilet. Vermin galore.'

'I'm sorry to hear that, but I don't know what it's got to do with me.'

'Yes, you do.'

Gary lifted one shoulder, as if to say, *Tell me, so.*

'What I'm saying, Gar, is that life in those days was tough and unfair. Everybody had it hard. No sooner had we got rid of the Brits than we handed the keys to the Vatican. But you can't let that control you. Your fixation isn't … healthy.' He gestured towards the door. 'Look at this city. There's building going on everywhere. All the cranes are back, like the bust never happened. There are thousands of tourists out there in Temple Bar, spending all their lovely dollars and pounds and yen and whatever you're having yourself. This is no time to hide away and become a recluse.'

'I want to find her, Frank. It's a need I have. I want to talk to her.'

'And then what?'

Gary stared at his pint. 'What do you mean?'

'What do you do after you've found her? That's *if* you find her. Are you allowed to restart your life? I mean, Jesus, man, you already have a family. Your folks are fine people. Compared to many kids, you had a peach of a childhood. Have you told them about this obsession of yours?'

Gary had mentioned the search to his parents but only in the most general of terms. They didn't know about Katie or Beth or the bracelets. Nor did they know that he'd been to Carrigbrack. It was hard to argue with Frank. His upbringing had been privileged. His father had taught at a private school, which had made it possible for Gary to attend on reduced fees. Alone among his friends, he'd been taken on foreign holidays. He'd never had to wear cheap chain-store jeans. His crooked teeth had been fixed.

'Yeah,' he said, 'we talk.'

'You see, what gets me is this: a couple of years back, you didn't know you were adopted, and your life was none the poorer. The people who raised you, Shay and Lillian, they're your parents. What can a stranger give you that you don't already have, huh?'

'I can't unknow what I've learnt, man. Simple as that.'

Frank slapped his knees. 'I reckon we need two more pints.'

Gary drained his glass. Beside him, two middle-aged men were discussing their cholesterol. Three Englishwomen, Christmas shopping pooled at their feet, were planning the hours ahead. He caught a whiff of perfume, and although it reminded him of someone, he couldn't remember who.

A recluse. Was that how people thought of him? A month back, he'd dipped a toe into the dating pool. He'd spent a few nights with a model he'd met through a friend of a friend. She'd been all right, if a little Instagram-obsessed. Did people really need to know what she wore to the cinema, aka her 'off-duty look'? Finally, she'd thrown a tantrum over his reluctance to pose for her page, and he'd realised that she was just a reheated version of his second wife, Carly McCall. Carly had been hot hot hot. She'd also been as mad as a bag of spiders.

On his return from the bar, Frank employed a familiar tactic. He began talking as if the previous twenty minutes hadn't happened. He restarted the conversation from a different angle.

'I met up with Anton,' he said.

Gary replied in his flattest voice. 'That's good.'

'He's keeping well. I don't know how the guy does it, but he looks like he's just walked out of 1992. Did you hear he's totally clean and sober? Twelve-step programme, the whole lot. He's raring to go.'

Gary's eyes roamed the ceiling. 'There's nothing stopping him.'

'That's not true.'

'Well, that's how it looks to me.'

'You said you were going to LA for the holidays? You might come across him yourself.'

'It's Los Angeles, Frank, not Stepaside. We're unlikely to bump into each other at Midnight Mass.'

'We want to do this reissue of *Overboard* in style.'

'I've already explained that now's not good for me.'

Frank rested a hand on Gary's arm. 'I'm not saying I don't know what your issue is … because I do. What I'm saying is, the time has come to sort it out. Obviously, we can do the reunion without you – and, believe me, if we have to, we will – but we'd prefer not to.'

Overboard was Gary's finest achievement. The bassline for the title song was his 'Under Pressure', his 'Dancing in the Moonlight', his 'Lust for Life'. The thought of some other guy, some glorified session-head, playing it on stage brought him actual physical pain.

And yet …

'Listen to me, Gar,' Frank was saying, 'music is your life. And, yeah, that sounds corny, but it's true. You and Anton are the core of the band. You can't stay away forever.'

Gary couldn't argue with the first part of that statement. Music had been his life. From the time he'd learnt 'Twinkle, Twinkle, Little Star' on the tin whistle, he'd known he was a musician. Yeah, he'd put in a lot of effort, but he'd been rewarded tenfold. He thought of it all: the exhilaration of a track coming together, every beat and every note; the buzz of the stage; the thunder of guitars; the roar as they played the opening notes of a favourite song. Black Iris had been everything he'd ever wanted. He recalled hearing a line about another musician: the thing that made him different had never made him happy. Gary had been convinced that didn't apply to him.

And yet …

The cholesterol men had abandoned their chat and were listening in. He didn't care. He wriggled his arm free of Frank's hand.

'Do you remember,' he said, 'back when we were starting out and shit used to go wrong? When the van broke down or an amp blew or a record company said "thanks but no thanks". You'd always say the same thing. "Nobody's dead, lads," you'd say. "Nobody's dead."'

Frank spoke slowly. 'I hear you.'

'I can't brush it all aside and pretend it didn't happen.'

'It's not like everyone else is cool with how things turned out.'

'Sometimes I wonder.'

'That's not fair.' Frank leant in. 'And remember, you were complicit, whether you choose to admit it or not.'

'I never said I wasn't,' replied Gary, before taking a deep drink of stout. 'She had a name, by the way. In case you've forgotten, her name was Shanna Ellis.'

It had been a long time since he'd said it out loud. It left a metallic taste in his mouth.

'I haven't forgotten her,' said Frank. 'None of us ever will.'

'Really? If you ask me, everyone wants to sail on like nothing happened.'

Whatever Frank said, however he protested, Shanna's

death couldn't have affected him in the same way. He'd been a bystander, a cleaner-upper. Gary had been part of the story, and he carried the guilt like a sackful of rocks.

'You know what you need?' said Frank. 'You need to go back to therapy. You sit here talking about your mother and about stuff that went on fifty years ago and how everyone's got to be brave and face up to that. But when it comes to your own life, you want to run away and hide.'

'Whoa there. You accuse me of being unfair? What do you think you're doing?'

'I'm being straight with you, that's all. You've got to move on.'

Gary got to his feet, prompting worried looks from cholesterol men and shopping ladies.

'Thanks for the pints,' he said, 'but I could do without the amateur psychology. Oh, and you've made up my mind for me. You'd better find a new bass player.'

Half an hour later, and he'd have missed it. The letter arrived as Gary was zipping up his case and preparing to leave for LA. Guessing it was from Gráinne, he paused and told himself that, either way, everything was good. If she wasn't his natural mother, he would redouble his efforts with the remaining names on Katie's list. He would work on and he would find her. It was all good.

Oh, who was he kidding?

He had a hundred reasons for wanting the news to be

positive, not all of them pure. Over the coming days, he'd be spending time with his four children, his ex-partner and his first ex-wife. He'd have to tell them that he was quitting Black Iris. 'You know that thing that keeps us all in high style?' he'd say. 'Well, it's no more. Or, rather, it carries on, but without me.' Breaking the news would be much easier if he had a distraction, a shiny bauble to display. He pictured his *ta-dah* moment where he told them all about his birth mother and his new life.

Four days had passed since his falling-out with Frank. He hadn't heard from Ray, Liamo or anyone else connected to the band. The fact that nothing had appeared in the press or online made him suspect that, so far, the manager had kept the news to himself.

He opened the envelope slowly and unfolded two sheets of lined paper. Gráinne wrote in small, round letters.

Please forgive the delay. Had I replied sooner, I might have written in anger, and that wouldn't have been fair. Despite its cryptic wording, I understood the meaning of your letter. I don't know how you found me, but you obviously have reason to believe that I'm your birth mother. It's a shame you didn't give more thought to the likely impact of your query.

To answer the question you appear to be asking: yes, I did give birth to a boy in Carrigbrack in August 1971. I was young and naïve, and my baby's father refused to accept his responsibility. I had no choice but to give my son up for adoption. Although it wasn't easy, I'm satisfied it was the best course of action. I had neither the money nor the support to raise a child.

Gradually, I got back on my feet and put what had happened behind me. I met a better man, we married and had three children. None of them knows about my fourth child, and I'd like to keep it that way.

Gary stopped and cursed his hubris. Why hadn't he given more thought to the possibility that she wouldn't want to reconnect?

The letter continued:

My children are in their late thirties and early forties. They're fine people, but I can't say how they'd react if I told them the truth. One thing's for sure, my marriage would be over. Think about it: how would you feel if your wife told you she'd been lying for more than forty years?

Gary felt a pain in his chest. This wasn't how it was supposed to be. The script called for an emotional yet joy-filled reunion. For tears and shared photos and unquestioning love. He read on.

For the avoidance of doubt, let me assure you: you're not my son. I can say this with certainty because my real son found me, through the adoption authorities, a number of years ago. We met once, I explained my situation, and he agreed not to contact me again. While this might sound hard, I don't think I'm a bad person. Rather, I'm a woman who's had to deal, in the best way she can, with what life gave her. I made my choice and I'm content with it. I have great respect for my first child, but my relationship with him could never match the love I have for my other children. Once ties are severed, they can't always be joined together again.

There are many of us out here living delicately balanced lives, fearing that a stray word could blow the house down. Not everyone can revisit the past.

Gary put the letter down. The pain in his chest had eased and was replaced by a dull sadness. Gráinne said she was content with her choice, but what a shadowy existence. Her life was built on lies. Did she really believe that telling the truth would drive her family away? His head was a mishmash of thoughts. He should be positive: her reply had brought him closer to solving the mystery. The list of names had been cut to two. Why, then, did he feel so low? There was, he realised, another possibility. Perhaps she was the right woman after all, and this was her way of giving him the brush-off.

Outside, a scattering of snow lay on the fields like desiccated coconut. The sky was marbled with grey. He ought to get moving. A sunnier place was waiting. First, though, he needed to talk.

*

While Katie didn't sound down, neither did she sound like her normal self. Her questions and answers lacked their usual precision.

'Ah well,' she said, 'that's one bracelet that's likely to remain in the box. I'm sorry things didn't work out the way you'd hoped, but you don't need me to tell you ...'

'... that there are only a couple of women left. Yeah, I just wish I felt more upbeat.'

'Tell me you're not judging Gráinne for what she's done.'

'I didn't say—'

'You've got to understand, Gary, that when we were growing up, everyone was more guarded. Nowadays, we're all expected to chat about every last element of our lives. And if we don't, we're labelled secretive or repressed. I heard Beth say that about someone the other day. "No, lovey," I said, "our generation are more reserved. And, whether you like it or not, that's our right. When we were young, we were told to keep our mouths closed because no one cared what we thought. And that's hard to shake off."'

'The silent generation,' said Gary.

'That's us.'

'How did Beth react?'

'She harrumphed a bit, but she's got a sound head on her, has Beth. My heart goes out to Gráinne. You can be sure that writing the letter wasn't easy.'

'I hope that if I do find my birth mother, she doesn't feel the same.'

'If she does,' said Katie, 'you'll have to accept her wishes.'

'I suppose.' He'd expected a more understanding response. And, yes, he was judging Gráinne. He didn't like the sound of her at all.

'Is everything else okay with you?' Katie said.

'Why do you ask?'

'Because you sound defeated. And you shouldn't. We've been through this before; you're making progress.'

'I know. I know.'

'There's something else, isn't there?'

Gary figured that Katie and Beth had spotted the media speculation about Black Iris. They were quite a pair.

'Aw,' he said, 'it's a band thing. It'll get sorted.' That wasn't true, but this wasn't the day for full disclosure. 'It's a long story. Maybe I'll tell you some time.'

'I'd like to think I'm a decent listener. Mind you, a few days ago, I made a right mess of a situation. A total hames.'

'Was it connected to one of the bracelets?'

'Yes. I'm afraid I wasn't gentle enough with someone. I should have known that he needed more time.'

Her weary tone made more sense now. Gary tried to come up with some reassuring words, but reassuring wasn't part of his repertoire.

Katie continued. 'I'm convinced that in the new year you'll find the woman you're looking for.'

'Fingers crossed you're right. I've got to get over Christmas first, mind.'

'That makes two of us,' she said.

Chapter 19

Katie

They drove west on Christmas Eve. Beth insisted on a meandering route.

'Come on,' said Katie. 'We've got to make an effort. Surely you're looking forward to seeing everybody?'

'The problem with this country,' replied Beth, 'is that Christmas is never-ending. It's a form of penance. Why can't we be more like the Americans? One day of family and overindulgence, and then you're back to work with no harm done.'

'That's what it was like when we were growing up. Well, without the overindulgence … and with a lot more religion.'

'You sound like Mam when she does her routine about how children were content with an orange and a new pair of socks.' Beth adopted Margo's clipped voice. 'Ask for more, and you'd get a good hiding.'

'Don't pay any heed to your mother. Mam and Dad never

said boo to her. Although what the pair of them would've made of Christmas nowadays, I don't know.'

Katie was trying to push her misgivings aside. She reminded herself that she was fortunate to have family who wanted to share their Christmas. The country was full of people who'd love to spend a few days in a large house of plenty. She did her best to think generous thoughts about her sister. It was too easy to dismiss Margo as a Central Casting social climber. True, her need to be seen as living a life of endless success was tedious, as was her mania for organising the lives of others. To be fair, though, she'd achieved a lot. Her six children were educated, productive members of society. She'd nurtured and loved them. Her house was spotless, her garden well tended. She was never over- or underdressed, and whoever tweaked her face was skilled at their craft. She was elegant and entertaining and tough as saddle leather.

She also lived in a world of post-recession excess, where Christmas trees were dressed according to a colour theme, spa weekends were a necessity, and weddings lasted for three days. But she had the money, and those were her choices. She'd grown up in a make-do-and-mend house where shop-bought cake was considered extravagant and the purchase of a new towel was viewed as a major event. Who was Katie to judge her?

They should have been close. In an era when families of six or more had been the norm, they'd had no other siblings. Yet Margo remained an enigma. Rarely combative, the sisters weren't affectionate either. Like a pair of parallel lines, they could carry on forever without connecting.

Christmas in the Linnane house was an elaborate affair. The rooms of the farmhouse were decorated in red, green and silver, while white lights twinkled on every tree. In the sitting room, there was a real Christmas tree, its pine scent prompting burst upon burst of nostalgia. The cupboards were full, the drink flowed, and the heating was cranked up to tropical levels. Even Ranzo the dog – part collie, part who-knew-what – wore a special velvet collar.

On Christmas Day, they all maintained a determined politeness. They went to ten o'clock Mass, the one ceremony of the year when a capacity crowd was guaranteed. Everyone wore their new Christmas scarf and mumbled along to 'Silent Night'. There was a kerfuffle over whether to put the family name on the envelope for the priest's collection. Margo claimed that to do so was vulgar. She also complained about the men who made a swift exit after communion and the altar girls who wore jeans and runners under their surplices. Whatever else had changed, Mass etiquette in Danganstown was still a delicate business. Afterwards, the parish priest waved at his flock but didn't stop to speak.

'We have to share him with Clonbreen and Lacken's Mills,' said Margo. 'The man barely has time to bless himself.'

During the afternoon, various brothers, wives and

children came and went until Katie lost track of who was who. There were presents galore. She was touched by her gifts from Beth. They included a voucher for a manicure (she had shocked her niece by announcing that she'd never had one) and a scarlet storage box.

'That old shoebox is in danger of falling apart,' said Beth, prompting a quizzical look from her mother.

Katie gave Beth an antique silver and enamel bracelet.

'What an inspired choice,' said Beth.

There were eleven of them for dinner: Margo, Con, Beth and Katie, plus two of Beth's brothers, Barra and Eoin, along with their wives and children. True to form, Margo insisted on doing almost everything herself. Even though Katie had never had much of a taste for turkey ('a horrible dry old bird', according to Johnny) or sprouts ('the filthy things smell like a fungal infection'), she had to admit the food was a triumph. It was a wonder the table didn't collapse under the weight of dishes. Along with the turkey, there was a Limerick ham, carrots, sprouts, peas, parsnips, three types of potatoes, stuffing, gravy and cranberry sauce. Afterwards, there was a choice of Christmas pudding or trifle. Margo had found the trifle recipe in the latest book by a popular TV chef. Con made the mistake of saying that his mother had made a lovely trifle. For the next five minutes, his wife sent withering looks in his direction. Eventually, he qualified his statement by saying that his mam's plum pudding had never been great, and her gravy had been too thin. Harmony was restored.

Only a careful listener would have caught the imbalance in the dinner table conversation. While the minutiae of the boys' domestic lives were discussed, Beth's personal life was ignored. She could talk about her job or the state of the nation, but anything else was taboo. While she wasn't subdued, she wasn't her usual witty, outspoken self either. Katie became irritated on her behalf. Not that she said anything. For the most part, she was quiet. If the loneliest sound was a couple having sex in the next room, the loneliest experience was Christmas in a full house when the person you most wanted was gone. Six months on from Johnny's death, Katie craved intimacy. By that, she didn't necessarily mean sex – though sex would be welcome – but the loaded glances, conspiratorial smiles and shared memories that made up a relationship; the countless subtle signs that said the two of you were together. The knowledge that all of this was gone, and wouldn't be back, filled her head.

If Johnny was still alive, she wouldn't be here. It wasn't that he hadn't liked Margo; more that they were very different people who'd struggled to find common ground. While her husband had made an effort to get on with most people, he'd rarely bothered with Katie's sister. 'That's just it, Kateser,' he'd said. 'She's family. I shouldn't have to spend every blessed minute on my best behaviour. It shouldn't feel like hard work.'

A couple of days earlier, Katie had left flowers at his grave. Although people still offered their sympathies and asked how she was getting on, she suspected they didn't want an honest answer. Other people's grief was tedious.

More than once, she'd wondered if her memories of Johnny were too golden-hued. It wasn't as if they'd never fallen out. There'd been times when she'd felt smothered by his overly protective behaviour. 'Be careful in town,' he'd say. 'There are fellows who'd steal the fillings from your teeth.' Or, 'I can't believe you walked home on your own. That was asking for trouble.' Then there'd been the way he'd insisted on talking to casual acquaintances whether they'd wanted to engage or not. He'd been particularly zealous on holiday, when it had felt as if every other couple in the hotel had been quizzed about where they were from and how their summer was going. Oh, and there'd been his mania for talking to the radio. 'What would you know, sonny boy?' he'd ask a presenter. Or, 'That's a lie if ever I heard one,' he'd tell a politician.

But these were petty complaints. Johnny and Katie could have annoyed each other fifty times a day, and it wouldn't have mattered. What mattered was the love they'd shared.

The bracelets were also ever-present in her thoughts. She remained annoyed with herself for falling out with Brandon. She'd toyed with the idea of contacting him, then decided to wait. As a fictional Irish American had famously said, tomorrow was another day.

The following morning, the dam broke. They were at the kitchen table eating breakfast. In the background, country music played on the local radio station.

'I'll get the news,' said Con, as he turned up the transistor, the oldest item in the room by a good two decades.

Katie smiled. She said the same thing, and it usually prompted a teasing reminder from Beth that the world had moved on. 'You can get the news on your phone any time you like,' she'd say, 'twenty-four hours a day, as much or as little as you want.' Katie would try to explain that, while she knew what was possible, a fifty-year habit was hard to break.

The muddy boots beside the door revealed that Con had already been at work. He farmed close on one hundred and fifty acres, and even at Christmas, there were jobs to tackle. Like his wife, he crammed a lot into the day.

The main story on the local news bulletin was about a three-car pile-up outside Kilmitten. One man had been killed, and two women were in hospital, both in a critical condition.

Beth put down her spoon. 'I hope no one belonging to Ailish was involved.'

'Who's Ailish?' asked Margo.

They could have ignored her. They could have lied. But Katie didn't want to. She'd had enough of ducking and dodging. She decided that, while this wasn't the time for full transparency, it was wrong to hide everything from Margo. Plus, if she was going to talk, it was safest to do so in the presence of Beth and Con. She steadied herself for the backlash.

'Ailish is a woman who's looking for her birth mother,' she said.

'What?'

'She was born in Carrigbrack,' added Beth, 'when Katie worked there.'

They told Con and Margo about the box of bracelets and about the work they'd been doing to reunite birth mothers and their children. After their outbreak of honesty, both tried to be diplomatic.

'We didn't tell you before,' said Beth, 'because we didn't want you thinking we were mad.' She looked at Katie. 'Because, let's face it, it is a bit of a mad scheme. But it's a great one too. You wouldn't believe the people we've met … like Gary Winters.'

Margo pressed her lips into a thin line before speaking. 'Should I be familiar with him?'

Con appeared more impressed. 'He's in that band, Black Iris. Tall fellow. Plays the guitar, is it?'

'Bass,' said Beth.

Margo fiddled with the sleeve of her green cashmere cardigan. As usual, she was immaculately turned out. In the way that expensive clothes often were, her cream silk T-shirt and black jeans were understated. Her ash-blonde hair was blow-dried to lightly tousled perfection. Katie sensed that she was casting around for objections.

Finally, she spoke. 'You're both grown women, and it's not my place to tell you what to do. But it doesn't sound like a particularly sensible plan. If a reunion goes wrong, you can be certain you'll get the blame.'

'You know, Mam,' said Beth, 'I reckon we'll jump that fence when we get to it.'

'What about you, Katie? Are you sure this is the wisest way to use your time?'

Katie, who'd been buttering a slice of soda bread, stopped and reflected on how much they'd achieved: the emails they'd received, the conversations they'd had, the tips passed on, the bracelets returned. It had taken over her life in a way she hadn't expected. Sometimes, the collision between past and present threatened to overwhelm her. At other times, it felt like she was trying to break through a wall of granite, one chip at a time. But what was the alternative? Sitting at home smelling Johnny's old shirts and allowing her loneliness to fester? She'd been given an opportunity to meet different people and to see life in different ways. She thought of the men and women who'd written to her as part of a mosaic: it was only when you brought their stories together that you had the full picture.

'I'm sure,' she said.

Later, when Con was outside and Beth upstairs, Margo was more vocal.

'For the life of me,' she said, 'I can't fathom what you're doing. I mean, I can see why Beth would view it as an interesting historical project. But you? You ought to have more sense.'

Katie examined the kitchen. There was something

intimidating about its glass, steel, stone and wood. Although Margo's home was only five miles from the house in which they'd grown up, it felt like another world. It was a world created by Margo, and she was its ruler. Katie twisted the gold band she still wore and reminded herself of her extra nine years. She was the senior party here.

'Please don't talk down to me,' she said. 'I've already told you that I'm satisfied we're doing the right thing.'

'And I don't believe you've thought it through. Is this bracelet business … is it some sort of delayed reaction to Johnny's death? Is it that you now feel free to … talk about those times?'

'I understand your concerns. Of course I do. But this isn't about you. We've made a lot of progress, and we're determined to continue. And Beth has been fantastic. She's really supportive and understanding.'

Their eyes locked. Margo went to say something, then drew back. She'd never enjoyed discussing the past. Despite being the one who'd stayed close to home, she rarely spoke about their parents. When she did, it was in the jokey way that Beth had mentioned in the car. She would ramp up her childhood poverty to *Angela's Ashes* levels and scold her sons and daughter for failing to appreciate their own good fortune.

Was this, Katie wondered, a genuine reflection on her childhood and teenage years? Did she recall her youth as unrelentingly bleak, or did she also have happier memories? It seemed to Katie that, when it came to families, memory was especially unreliable. Even among Johnny's contented clan, there had been disagreements. One family member would tell a story about their childhood only for another to say, 'That's not how it happened at all.'

'You've nothing to worry about,' she said, in what she hoped was a confident voice. 'You'll have to trust me on that.'

Margo played with her hair. 'Please don't belittle my concerns. Are you certain that Johnny's passing hasn't affected your judgement?'

'That's not fair.'

'It's a legitimate question.'

'I'm doing it,' said Katie, 'because I believe we can help people.'

'And what if I don't agree?'

Katie told herself to stay calm. While there was never a good day for an all-out row with Margo, this was definitely the worst possible time. If they raised their voices any further, Beth would hear. The atmosphere at the previous day's dinner still on her mind, she decided to change tack.

'I meant what I said about Beth. She's been brilliant. I couldn't have done anything without her. I know she's her own woman, but she's a credit to you.'

'She's her own woman all right.' The reply was heavy with meaning.

'Ah, Margo.'

'Don't "Ah, Margo" me. You don't know anything about our relationship.'

'I know she's upset about the way you're treating her.'

Margo put up a hand, as if to bat her away. 'I can't imagine what Beth has told you, but no doubt she's put her own slant on it.'

'I don't think that's fair. I'm telling you how it looks to me.'

'Listen, I'm not going to be the cartoon bigot here. If you had a daughter of your own, you'd understand.'

The words hit Katie like a slap from a wet towel. 'Let's not fall out,' she said. 'I wanted to tell you that you're a lucky woman to have such a fantastic daughter, that's all.'

Margo was still floundering when the kitchen door swung open and Beth came in. Katie worried that her niece had been listening. Thankfully, the jauntiness of her walk suggested she was unaware of their argument.

'Has someone new been in touch about Carrigbrack?' Katie asked.

'Nope. There's a sheepish email from Robyn, though, wishing you a happy Christmas. Funnily enough, she didn't mention Brandon.'

'Ah. I'd say we can assume that, as far as Eddie's concerned, they're not on the same page.'

'Poor Brandon.'

'You've changed your tune. I didn't expect you to have sympathy for him.'

Beth sat down. 'I wouldn't go that far, but there's something a bit sad about him. He's very uptight. When you were telling him about Eddie, he was so stiff he looked ready to be embalmed. Anyway, that wasn't what I wanted to say. I've got good news.'

Margo's words continued to sting. Katie told herself to focus on Beth. 'Go on,' she said.

'After we were talking, I messaged Ailish. Everything's grand. None of her family was involved in the crash. While I was thinking about her, I decided to do another trawl for Chrissie. The old man in Hackett's Cross said she'd gone to London, so I thought I'd see if there was any mention of her in the British records. I assumed that, like here, it'd be hard to get much information online. And in some ways, it is. There's an official site you can email, or there are several others where you have to sign up and become a member. But I also found a separate site where volunteers have posted images of original birth, death and marriage records. Just a line or two ... nothing overly revealing.'

'And?' Katie glanced at Margo. Despite what she'd said about the bracelets, her sister was following Beth's story. Who wasn't fascinated by other people's family secrets?

'I entered Chrissie's name, and I discovered that a Christine M. Culligan got married in west London in 1978.'

Katie did the sums. 'Our Chrissie would have been twenty or twenty-one then, so, yes, that's possible. And the middle initial is right too. Did it give you a name for her husband?'

Beth moved closer. 'Yes and no. Just a last name, Mulcahy. I was excited, but I thought, ah, no, it's too much to hope for. Either there'll be no other reference to her, or it'll become clear she's not the woman we're looking for. So I typed Chrissie Mulcahy into Google … and up she popped.'

'Is she the right Chrissie?' asked Katie, who already knew the answer. Nothing else could explain the beam of satisfaction on Beth's face.

'Uh huh. And wait until you see her.' Beth tapped her phone and showed the screen to Katie. 'She's absolutely one hundred per cent the right Chrissie. And she's amazing.'

Chapter 20

Ailish

When the text arrived, Ailish was pulling the last of the turkey meat from the carcass. She'd torn a recipe from a magazine she'd found in the hotel and planned on making a casserole. Keith was in the sitting room watching television. Stevie was out with his friends. Although it wasn't yet four o'clock, the dark was closing in. She'd lit the fire several hours before, and the afternoon had a sleepy post-Christmas feel. Tired from the previous day's festivities, she was looking forward to a rest.

Because Beth had already contacted her about the car crash, she was surprised to see a text message from Katie.

Can you talk? it said.

Not really. Ailish lowered the sound on her phone. If Keith heard the *bing-bong* of her message notifications, he'd ask questions.

Beth's about to send you an email. It's very important!!

Please tell me it's good news.

Yes!!

She'd never known Katie to use even one exclamation mark, not to mind four in the space of two lines.

Another text arrived: **When you've read the article, call me (if you can).**

Article? Did this mean that Katie and Beth were sending her a newspaper cutting about Carrigbrack? Was Chrissie mentioned? From the sitting room, Ailish heard a familiar snort. Keith was asleep.

Will do, she replied.

She washed the grease from her hands, put on her coat and climbed into her boots. Her heart thumped so loudly she worried her husband would hear. Slowly, stealthily, she opened the front door and closed it behind her. She slunk down the road like a fugitive and turned the corner onto Kennedy Crescent before risking a look at her email.

The article, from a London newspaper called *The Irish Herald*, was five years old. It was headlined 'The Woman Who Listens'.

She tapped to enlarge the image. She didn't have to see a caption or read a word. With one finger, she lightly traced the outline of Chrissie's face. The solemn eyes, the thin lips, even the gap between her front teeth: Ailish knew them all. They stared back at her from every mirror.

'It's you,' she said.

She sat down. That the footpath was wet didn't matter. She could have been sitting in the middle of a rushing river and she wouldn't have noticed. The article was far longer than expected. And it was entirely about Chrissie:

When Chrissie Mulcahy arrived in London at the age of sixteen, she'd already been through more than many people experience in a lifetime. Chrissie, who's originally from County Clare, was just thirteen when she became pregnant. She'd been raped by an elderly neighbour.

It was, she says, 'a different and distant world. We didn't use the word rape back then. Nor did we know words like paedophile or abuse. "Interfered with" was about as far as people would go.'

It was made clear to young Chrissie that she was a source of shame, not just for her family, but for the whole village. 'I don't think my parents fully understood what had been done to me,' she says.

'I was sent to a mother-and-baby home, a place called Carrigbrack, and I was terrified. Most of the girls were older than me, and at that age, even a year or two can feel like a generation. For the first month, all I could do was cry. I prayed that God would take me during the night.'

Sitting in her cosy kitchen in Shepherd's Bush, it's hard to reconcile the confident, accomplished woman Chrissie has become with the frightened teenager who wanted to die. Most of her memories of Carrigbrack are grim.

'It wouldn't be right to describe all the nuns as cruel,' she says. 'One was very kind to me. To this day, though, I believe that one or two of them were evil. And they were supported by a system that gave free rein to bad people. There was a poison in that system. A wickedness.'

At fourteen, Chrissie gave birth to a baby daughter. When the little girl was six months old, Chrissie was instructed to wash and dress her for a photograph. The photo was never taken. Instead, without her knowledge, the baby was driven away and adopted. That was the last time she saw her.

For the next two years, she toiled in the fields in Carrigbrack. 'It was back-breaking work,' she says with a rueful smile. 'All the same, I found it hard to leave. I didn't want to go home, and I feared what would happen to me in the outside world.'

Eventually, Chrissie agreed to accompany another young mother to London. By then, it was early 1974. For a girl who'd never even been to Dublin, London was quite a shock.

'I grew up in a parish of scarcely three hundred people,' she laughs, 'so you can imagine what I made of my new home. I remember arriving into Victoria coach station and thinking I wouldn't last a week. I saw more people that first morning than I'd seen in my entire life.'

Chrissie found work as a cleaner. Then, having

attended night classes in shorthand and typing, she got a job in an insurance office. It was there that she met Iggy Mulcahy, who's originally from Listowel in County Kerry. They married in 1978 and have three children: Donna, Kirsty and Diarmuid. The Mulcahys' kitchen is filled with photos of their grandchildren.

In those days, it wasn't unusual for women to hide the fact that they'd already had a baby. Chrissie chose to tell the truth. 'It wasn't an easy thing to do. I hoped Iggy would understand. If he didn't, then he wasn't the right man for me.'

Not only did he understand, he pledged to help Chrissie should she ever decide to track down her daughter. In the 1990s, she did try to find her, but wherever she turned, there were obstacles.

'I was told there was no record of us. It was like we never existed,' she says. 'At one stage, I was asked if I'd imagined giving birth.'

The memory brings a tear to her large grey eyes. 'I can only trust that my girl found a loving home, and that life has been good to her,' she says.

This failure to find her daughter prompted Chrissie to set up a support group for other Irish women who'd spent time in mother-and-baby homes or Magdalene laundries.

'Our children have had lives big and small,' she explains. 'They've had choices. The women I meet had no choice. They were treated shamefully. And there were boyfriends too who were given no say in what happened to their babies.'

Chrissie remembers someone giving her a statistic: in 1967, 97% of children born outside marriage in Ireland were placed for adoption. To begin with, she didn't believe the figure. It sounded too extreme. It turned out to be true.

As she talks about the survivors of the homes, Chrissie becomes more animated, and her west Clare origins come out in her voice. 'It's not every town that has a story,' she says. 'It's every village. Every street. It's the cousin who disappeared, the neighbour who was supposed to be helping an aunt, the friend who suddenly moved to Dublin. They were banished, and their lives were altered forever.

'When I was younger, I couldn't have articulated any of this. For years, I buried my anger, then it came bursting out. I had to do something, and that was how the support group came about.'

For almost twenty years, Chrissie Mulcahy has been a familiar face in London Irish circles. She campaigns for, and offers advice to, survivors of the homes.

'I've been very lucky,' she says, with characteristic modesty. 'Many others have had difficult, fractured lives. Some have felt the need to suffer in silence. Forty or fifty years on, they're still trying to cope with a stigma they never deserved.'

She talks of one woman whose baby died in a home and who never received an explanation. 'We live in a time when motherhood, in all its forms, is celebrated. Only the other day, this lady was in a shop. She picked up a magazine, and there was a celebrity on the cover saying that since she'd had a baby "the world shone with a different light". The poor woman ran out of the shop in tears. All these years later, the pain is still there.'

Through the support group, many of the women have become friends. Chrissie says they can talk more openly and honestly than with others. 'There's a bond there,' she says. 'It's like we went through a war together.'

This weekend, she will receive the Lifetime Achievement Award at the London Irish Centre. It's in recognition of the time she has spent lobbying and campaigning. But above everything else, it's for her willingness to listen to the stories of others.

'When I was a young girl, no one would listen to me,' she says. 'I know how much damage that can cause.'

As for her own story, Chrissie hopes that one day she'll be reunited with the daughter who was taken from her. In the meantime, she keeps a candle in the window for the girl she never got to know.

*

When she'd finished reading, Ailish sat and allowed the tears to run down her face. Her teeth chattered, not from cold but from shock and exhilaration and a hundred sensations she couldn't explain. She'd had this skewed notion that her birth mother would be a feeble God-help-us character, worn down by abuse. Instead, she was a heroine.

After a few minutes, she called Katie. Her fingers felt thick and awkward, as if they belonged to someone else.

'Well?' said Katie.

'Thank you,' replied Ailish. It was all she could say. 'Thank you.'

'It was Beth who did the work. All this time, Chrissie was ... what's that phrase? Hiding in plain sight, that's it. And she's been looking for you.'

'I can't believe I never came across the article. As soon as I saw the picture, I knew it was her.'

'She's the spitting image of you, right enough. To be fair, you only recently discovered the London connection, and you didn't know her married name. What do you make of her?'

'I'm ... I'm stunned. She's incredible, isn't she?'

'She surely is. Imagine having that much strength. And she's so articulate, too. She said everything I would have liked to say. What a fantastic person.'

'I know,' said Ailish, half laughing, half crying. 'I've gone back to feeling inadequate.'

'Now, Ailish Dwan, you're not to get silly on me. Do you hear?'

'Sorry. I'm not sure it's fully registered with me yet. Also, God love her, I'd guessed she might have been abused, but seeing it in black and white is awful.'

'It's a shocking tale. No wonder people in Hackett's Cross were reluctant to talk.'

Ailish was taken aback by how emotional Katie sounded. 'The one thing that concerns me is ...'

'... the fact that the article's five years old? There's no need to fret. Beth's been doing some more sleuthing. She found a London Irish Community Facebook page. There's a photo of Chrissie from earlier this year. You've got to remember she's only sixty-one. She's still a youngster.'

'Tell Beth I said thanks.'

'I will. She's practically gone into orbit, she's so happy. Oh, and she found a few other mentions of Chrissie too. There's a printer here, for the farm paperwork, and we're going to print everything out. We'll send it to you at the hotel. When are you back?'

'Tomorrow, unfortunately.'

'Ah, I see. Would it be possible for us to call in, do you think?'

'I don't see why not.'

After they'd hung up, Ailish remained on the kerb, allowing what she'd learnt about Chrissie to circle her brain. Night was falling fast, and the half-moon had been joined by a sprinkling of stars

She was jolted from her reverie by a neighbour and his daughter. The young girl was on a pink bicycle.

'How are you going on, Ailish?' said her neighbour. 'Are you all right down there?'

'Do you know, Lar, I'm the grandest,' Ailish said. 'Hello there, Saoirse. I see Santa Claus brought you a lovely new bike.'

'Yes,' said Saoirse, in her practical seven-year-old tones. 'It's been a very good Christmas.' She gave a smile as wide as a piano, albeit one with a few missing keys.

'It has indeed,' replied Ailish as she got to her feet.

All the while, happiness swelled inside her. Tomorrow she would try and find a phone number for Chrissie. In the meantime, she'd have to go home, make turkey casserole, iron her uniform and act as if everything was normal.

The three of them sat in Beth's car. Short of commandeering a hotel bedroom, it was the only place they could speak in private. Nearby, a bird sang: *twiss, twiss, twiss*.

'We've got some more news,' said Katie. 'Well, Beth does.'

'The centre where Chrissie's support group hold their meetings has a website. I had a poke around and I found a contact number. I'm pretty sure it's for Chrissie herself.'

Ailish clapped. 'No way!'

'Ordinarily,' added Katie, 'I wouldn't recommend calling out of the blue like this, but we know she's anxious to find you.'

'I've put the cuttings in here,' said Beth, handing over a

large brown envelope, 'and written the number on the back. There's an email address too, so you can try that first if you'd prefer.' She smiled. 'I never thought I'd be handing over brown envelopes in hotel car parks. This is what spending time with Katie Carroll has done to me.'

Ailish laughed, then stared at the envelope. 'I'm overwhelmed. I'll never be able to thank you enough.'

'In a way,' said Katie, 'you already have.'

'I don't follow you.'

'What's happened this week proves that trying to return the bracelets and pass on what I know is worthwhile.'

'Please don't ever doubt that,' said Ailish.

For a short while, they chatted about Christmas. Ailish talked about her grandchildren and showed them some photos. Katie spoke about her sister, Beth's mam. They'd told her about the bracelets. It sounded as though she didn't approve. This puzzled Ailish. Then again, who was she to talk about difficult families? She hadn't said a word to Keith about finding her birth mother. Neither Beth nor Katie mentioned him.

'We'll have to get going,' said Beth. 'When you've spoken to Chrissie, do get in touch.'

'I promise,' said Ailish, 'you'll be the first to know.'

She went straight to Room 215, the Dolmen Suite. Such an important call deserved the best room in the hotel. Ailish had spent most of her life preparing for this moment. She must have visualised it ten thousand times. That didn't make it any easier. She sat in one of the enormous red and white armchairs, counted to ten and prodded out the number.

After three rings, a man answered the phone. 'Hello?'

'Hello, is that Mr Mulcahy?'

'Yes, Iggy Mulcahy here. Can I help you?' He had an English-Irish accent, like the singer with the V-neck jumpers who'd been on the television when Ailish was a child.

'Hi, um, gosh. My … Sorry, I'm going to start that again. My name is Ailish Dwan, but my original name, back when I was born, was Jacqueline Culligan.'

A pause followed. 'I see … Oh … Really?'

'I've been trying to find my birth mother and … well, you obviously know who I am. I'm sorry to ring you at home, only I got the number and—'

'There's no cause to apologise. I'm shocked to hear from you, that's all. Where do you live, Ailish?'

'I'm in Clare. In Kilmitten. I didn't get very far.'

'There's no harm in that,' said Iggy, his voice warm. 'I have a million questions, and I know a woman who probably has a million more. She's not going to believe this.'

'If me making contact is too much of a shock for her, I can give you my number, and she can call me back. Oh, and I can send you a photo, so you know I'm not an imposter. We look alike.'

'Don't worry. You can talk to Chrissie about that.'

The background noise suggested Iggy was walking up the stairs. Then the sound became more muffled, like he'd placed a hand over the receiver. Finally, he returned.

'I'm going to hand you over to the woman herself,' he said.

A moment later, a hesitant voice came on the line. 'Hello. Is that Ailish?'

A tingling sensation took hold of Ailish. 'Hello, Chrissie,' she replied

There was a pause, as if Chrissie was collecting herself. Then she said, 'I've been waiting nearly fifty years to talk to you, but I still can't think what to say. Could you speak so I can listen to you? I'd love to hear you.'

Chrissie's voice was melodic. Although only a whisper of her Clare accent remained, she was unmistakably Irish.

'I'm the same as yourself,' said Ailish. 'I've been preparing for this for as long as I can remember, and now the moment is here, my mind's gone blank.'

'Tell me about yourself, my love. About where you are and what you do. Do you have a family? Where did you grow up? And how did you find me? I'd almost given up hope of us meeting again.'

Ailish surprised herself and spoke for a long time. Rathtuskert Manor could have dissolved into dust around her, and she wouldn't have noticed. She talked about her children and grandchildren, about Keith and her adoptive parents, about Kilmitten and her job. If nothing she said was untrue, neither did she give a completely accurate picture of her life. She hoped there would be other conversations where she could be more candid. She was conscious too that this was a once-in-a-lifetime moment. It was a little bit strange, a little bit awkward.

It was entirely wonderful.

The Chrissie she spoke to wasn't as talkative as the woman in the article. Her words came in fits and starts. Occasionally she fell into silence, then they'd both speak together. There was something slightly off about her voice, like she was lying down. It was the middle of the afternoon, though, so that didn't make sense.

Ailish told Chrissie about how she'd found her. About how a blend of chance and determination had guided her in the right direction.

'If it wasn't for Katie and Beth,' she said, 'I'd still be looking for you.'

She explained about Katie's notebook and the box of bracelets. Needless to say, she omitted the part about her own bracelet being reduced to ashes in a bedside glass. Chrissie had only vague memories of Katie, which was understandable. The two hadn't met in almost fifty years. Even then, Katie had been a professional woman, Chrissie a timid teenager.

While they spoke, the light began to dim. The phone in the hotel room rang twice. There was a danger the head housekeeper would come looking for her soon. For once, Ailish didn't care. No one, not even Keith, could spoil this day.

Chrissie spoke about her other children and grandchildren. She was amused to discover she was a great-grandmother.

'That's terrible,' she said with a chuckle. 'I'm far too young and glamorous to be anyone's great-grandmother.'

'I have so many photos of them all,' said Ailish. 'You wouldn't believe how many photos I have.'

'I'm sure I would. Hasn't the world gone crazy for taking pictures? My grandchildren think I'm lying when I tell them I've only got one photo of myself from before I came to London.' She paused. 'And I've never seen a photo of you.'

'If you give me your mobile number, I'll send you some as soon as we've finished speaking.'

'And would you be able to send a few of your lovely young men and women? I'm desperate to see them all.'

For the first time, Ailish realised that Chrissie was crying. 'I didn't mean to upset you,' she said.

'Oh, my love, how could I not cry? This is one of the best days of my life.'

'Mine too. And would you send me some pictures? I'm dying to see everyone.'

'That'll be no trouble. Wait until they hear you've turned up. They'll be very excited.' Another pause, this time a lengthy one. 'Will it be possible for you to come and see me, do you think?'

Ailish had been hoping to hear this question. At the same time, she'd been dreading it. Chrissie's husband appeared to be in every way supportive, whereas Ailish was on her own. Once upon a time, she'd fooled herself that if she could only locate her birth mother, Keith would come around. A successful reunion would pacify him, she'd thought. The past couple of months had taught her that this probably wasn't true.

She longed to meet Chrissie. She needed to kiss her and hold her hand and tell her how proud she was to have such an amazing woman as her birth mother. They would have to meet in secret, though, and the only way this could happen would be for Chrissie to travel to Ireland.

'I was hoping,' she said, 'that you might be able to come over this way.'

'If money's an issue …?'

'No,' replied Ailish, a touch too quickly. 'No, not at all.' While she didn't have much spare cash, she could raid Stevie's college fund.

A sigh fluttered over the line. When Chrissie spoke again, there was a tremor in her voice. 'I didn't mention this because I didn't want to ruin such a fantastic day. What it is … I'm afraid I've been unwell over the past while.'

Ailish closed her eyes. She should have guessed. The clues had been there.

'There's no cause for alarm,' continued Chrissie. 'There's plenty of fight in me yet. I was diagnosed with breast cancer earlier in the year. I had a mastectomy, and then I needed chemo. Thankfully, that finished before Christmas. Now I'm due to have radiotherapy, so unfortunately I've got to stick around.'

'I'm sorry,' said Ailish. 'I had no idea.'

'Of course you didn't. It's just … like I say, at the minute, I can't travel. To be straight with you, I've been a bit depressed.

Well, the chemo does that to you, doesn't it? But getting your call ... it's like I'm being compensated for the past few months. Oh, and for fear you're worried, my cancer isn't the hereditary kind. I made sure to ask.'

Ailish's mind shifted in all directions. She would have to go to London, but even if she managed to fly there and back in one day, Keith would find out. You would have to be stupid not to, and whatever his failings, stupidity wasn't among them. The thought of telling him, of admitting she'd gone back on her promise to abandon the search, brought bile to her throat. She feared what the consequences might be. Since the day he'd destroyed her bracelet, she'd been preparing herself for his next eruption.

She realised Chrissie was waiting for an answer. 'I'd love to come and see you,' she said. 'When would be best?'

Chapter 21

Then, Patricia

For a week or more, they all believed Winnie would be found. Disappearing wasn't possible. As Sister Agnes was fond of saying, no one escaped from Carrigbrack, and on the rare occasion they did, they were hauled back and disciplined.

Every day, Patricia expected to see her friend. More than once, she imagined she had. She thought she spotted her at Mass or in the refectory. Wasn't that her shorn head? Wasn't that her striding walk? It was always someone else.

Everyone had a theory about Winnie, some plausible, some outlandish. One woman claimed she'd escaped through the hole in the hedge and joined up with a group of Travellers. Another maintained she hadn't left at all but was hiding in the attic. A third was adamant she was dead. Sister Sabina had killed her, she insisted, and buried her in the potato field. That this was accepted by several others said a lot about the general perception of Sabina.

Mother Majella gave a speech about aiding and abetting sinful behaviour, while Sister Agnes summoned everyone who'd been friendly with Winnie to her office. All insisted they knew nothing.

Patricia stayed quiet about the letter, which she'd hidden in the lining of her suitcase. While doing so, she'd got a surprise. The wig was missing. Wherever Winnie was, it was likely she'd gone there with black plastic hair. Patricia was grateful she'd never have to wear the cursed thing again.

Gradually, a possible explanation took hold. One of the nurses, a clodhopper of a Galway woman named Rita Farragher, had a car. On the day of Winnie's disappearance, she'd driven into Ennis to buy new sandals. No one, not even Agnes or Sabina, suspected that Rita would willingly have helped. She was an enthusiastic rule-follower. What was more likely was that Winnie had somehow stowed away in the boot of her old Ford Anglia. How she'd been able to get out, and where she went next, no one knew.

As the days turned into weeks and July faded into August, it became clear that Winnie wasn't coming back. Patricia wasn't sure she believed in God. If He did exist, what did He think of the cruelty inflicted in His name? She was forced to spend a lot of time on her knees, however, so she might as well pray for something. She prayed that Winnie was safe, that her own baby was born healthy and that Sister Sabina got a vicious dose of something painful. She found it hard to be civil to the people who annoyed her, not just Faustina and

Sabina but also the nurse who'd been there when Winnie's baby had died.

At some point, the weather changed. While the heat continued, the blue skies were replaced by heavy cloud. It felt as if a thousand miles of sky were pressing down on them. At night, lightning crackled and thunder roared.

More and more, Patricia thought about her baby; about who they were and what they'd look like. She decided that if the baby was a girl, she'd call her after her friend. Not Winnie, but Gretta. That was her real name.

She also thought about Mike. She wondered if his other baby had arrived. How bizarre was it that her boy or girl would have a sibling who was almost the same age? While she didn't want to be with Mike, this didn't stop her from resenting his decision to stay with Vera. It would be easier if she could belittle his wife, if she could dismiss her as grasping or ugly or dumb, but, hand on heart, Patricia had never heard an unsympathetic word about the woman.

Her mother continued to send drab letters in which the only people mentioned were ill or dead. There was considerable detail about the funerals, all of which had attracted big crowds. At the rate people were dying, there'd be no one left in the village. Patricia felt bad about letting her parents down, but not so bad that she wanted to live under their roof again. When she left Carrigbrack, she would have to create her own life. She would like to live in a city where no one knew who she was. She didn't want to be followed by the swish of gossip. She couldn't bear the thought of her behaviour being monitored, either by her parents or by the local rumour-mongers.

Sleep was hard to come by, and when she did drop off, she had long, violent dreams, populated by unfamiliar people. She was always running or falling and sometimes she called out in panic. This usually prompted an ill-tempered *shh* from the woman in the next bed. Patricia would wake up feeling as if her mind and nerve endings were on fire. At other times, she forgot where she was. For a moment, she'd be back at home. She saw herself with more detachment now. She hadn't had a lot of freedom, certainly not as much as the women in books and films, but she'd had some. She worried that she'd never be free again.

What would Mike make of what she'd become? Here she was, without lipstick or perfume. Without hair. She had no conversation to offer. No insights or quips. Being discarded was hard. Every day, it chipped away at her. Mike was the only man she had slept with. What if there were no others? What if her parents were right and no one else was interested in her?

One morning, she peeled away from the band of women going to the laundry and went to Diane's grave. Briefly, she considered the risk she was taking. Her baby was due within the next couple of weeks, however, and the range of available punishments was limited. It was unlikely that Winnie would ever return to her daughter's resting place. It was even more unlikely that anyone else would visit. Soon, the grass would grow over the earth, and no one would know that a little girl was buried there.

No sooner had she reached the right spot than the rain started. Great drops the size of rose petals fell, slowly at first, then gathering pace until the water was running in rivulets down Patricia's face, and what was left of her hair was glued to her scalp. The ground gave off the beautiful earthy smell of rain falling on dry soil. By the time she thought of moving, it was too late. She was drenched to the core, her uniform sodden and plastered to her body.

Agnes found her. 'I despair of you,' she said.

'I'm doing no harm, Sister.'

'Let me be the judge of that,' said the nun, before ordering her back inside.

That evening, after the rosary, Agnes announced that all discussion of Winnie was banned.

The following day, Jacinta's baby was taken for adoption. Only six weeks old, Lorcan was a premium child, born to a healthy young woman from a prosperous family. That explained why he was snapped up like a bargain in the January sales when the children of poorer women were left behind. Some were two or three years old before they were adopted. There was, thought Patricia, a contradiction in how their babies were treated. In one way, they were seen as lesser. They weren't as important as the sons and daughters of married women. Or as worthy of love. But in another way, they were valuable commodities. When Lorcan left, Jacinta whimpered like a puppy. One of the others tried to comfort her, and got a swift rebuke from Agnes. Jacinta left two days later. Her parents had the money to pay for her release. A group gathered to say goodbye, but were ordered back to work by Sabina.

Another baby was adopted that week. Her mother, seventeen and skinny as a drainpipe, was glad to see her go.

'Her father's an awful dose,' she said. 'I'm lucky not to get tied to him. I hope her new family have pots of money and give her all the things I didn't have.'

Every morning, Patricia wondered if this was the day her own little boy or girl would arrive. Work in the laundry was a hard grind. She was too big to be cooped up in a hot room. Her burnt hand healed slowly. She resolved that when she had a life of her own, she'd get the best washing machine money could buy. She'd rather go hungry than endure any more drudgery.

In the main, Agnes's diktat about Winnie was obeyed. It was as if she'd never existed. Patricia said as much one night when she met Sister Eunice in the corridor.

'It's probably for the best,' said Eunice. 'The speculation was getting out of hand.'

'You mean Sister Sabina didn't kill her and bury her among the spuds?'

Eunice laughed, then put a hand over her mouth. 'That's a desperate thing to say.' She winked. 'There's no way Sabina would endanger the potatoes. I'd say the cabbage field is a far better bet.'

'Oh, listen to us,' said Patricia. 'Here we are laughing and joking about Winnie when she could be sleeping by the side of the road – or somewhere worse.'

'Do you worry about her?'

'I do.'

Eunice gave a quick look around. 'You really don't need to,' she said, her voice scarcely louder than a whisper.

'What do you mean?'

'That's all I can say, but trust me, you shouldn't fret about her.'

With that, Eunice smiled and continued her walk down the corridor towards the nursery.

Chapter 22

Brandon

Christmas was frosty. When they weren't arguing, they were recovering from the last row or preparing for the next. Long silences were punctuated by tart remarks. Brandon had hoped that, given time, Robyn would accept his decision. Instead, she became more entrenched in her views. She never missed an opportunity to let him know he'd mishandled the conversation with Katie Carroll.

He conceded that some of the blame was his. He'd become too prickly too quickly. But he'd been ambushed. Who wouldn't recoil from such misery? And why did both Robyn and Katie keep telling him how he should react? It was as though there was a spectrum of appropriate responses and he'd fallen off the edge.

The Carrigbrack described by Katie was even worse than he'd anticipated. Who needed dystopian novels and TV shows when, in the recent past, those homes had existed?

What baffled him was why Katie had stayed working there. One thing was for sure: he'd been lucky to escape a country where that kind of behaviour was the norm. How many people had ended up spending years in therapy because of what had been done to them? Brandon guessed psychiatry must be a lucrative business in Ireland.

Over and again he told himself that his real and lasting bond was with his parents, Art and Ellen. They were the people who'd chosen, raised and cared for him. He'd also worked hard at shaping his own life. As far as he was concerned, that was what mattered. To use a modern phrase, that was his identity.

In the immediate aftermath of the conversation with Katie, he'd again been tempted to throw the bracelets away. Their presence dragged him down. The only thing that stopped him was fear of Robyn's reaction.

Ordinarily, Brandon avoided arguments. They were corrosive and pointless. He'd long been skilled at finding the right emollient words, at reaching an appropriate level of compromise. Nobody could change the subject more smoothly or walk away more calmly. Until now, he hadn't thought that Robyn was given to confrontation either. How wrong he'd been. She took to pacing the house like a caged animal, listing all the reasons why he should trace Eddie and Linda.

'You're assuming they can be found,' he said. 'If there was one thing Katie made clear, it was that tracking people down is difficult.'

'Difficult, but not impossible.'

'What I can't understand is why it matters so much to you.'

'What *I* can't understand,' she replied, 'is why it doesn't matter more to *you*.'

'That's unfair. I'm not saying I'll never look for them. I'm just saying not right now.'

Around and around they went, having the same circular argument until one of them – usually him – found a way to defuse it. Every day, he felt as if he was carrying explosives over cobblestones; one misstep and – *boom!* – everything he valued would be gone. All his certainties were cracking and shifting.

In early January, on a day when Boston was shivering under the sideswipe of a storm, he came home from work to find Robyn in the bedroom. Her black case sat in the middle of the bed surrounded by neatly folded T-shirts. He'd always admired her packing skills.

'I'm going to see Zinzi,' she said. 'I need a break.'

Zinzi was an old college friend who worked as a TV news anchor in Miami.

'Why didn't you tell me? Were you going to leave without saying anything?' The unspoken question: are you leaving for good?

She placed a fuchsia-pink top into the case. 'I only made my mind up this morning, so they agreed to rearrange some stuff at work. And no, of course I wouldn't have gone without saying goodbye.'

Brandon wondered what she'd said at work. January was the busiest time of year for personal trainers. There were fortunes to be earned from the 'new year, new you' crowd. He trusted she hadn't told the truth.

'If you'd given me some notice,' he said, 'I could've come too. I've got vacation time left from last year, and while it wouldn't be easy, I could probably have—'

'That wouldn't have been a smart idea. I'm going to Florida for fun, not to argue.'

'I wouldn't have argued. You're the one who insists on falling out. I just want a quiet life. I mean, come on, Robyn, we're *married*. You can't go on vacation on your own.' Brandon was babbling, like a child who wanted to play with the big boys and girls.

She folded a blue gingham dress, his favourite, and put it in the case. It was followed by a pair of white pants, a red sweater and a pink scarf. She was taking a lot of clothes. How long was she planning on spending in Florida? Not for the first time, he was hit by the feeling that Robyn belonged elsewhere with someone who was more like her.

Two years into their marriage, there were still times when he found it difficult to believe that she was his wife. Everything else in his life had entailed hard work and sacrifice. Meeting Robyn at a client's party had been sheer luck. That she had fallen for him had been little short of miraculous. Prior to her, there had, of course, been other women, but no lasting commitments, no one to ruffle his orderly existence.

'Maybe,' she said, 'you've put your finger on the problem. I don't want a quiet life.'

'I'm older than you. My priorities are different. I thought you were cool with that.'

She placed two pairs of sandals on top of her clothes and began zipping up the case. 'It's nothing to do with being older, so don't use that excuse. I've tried to see everything from your point of view. Believe me, I have. But I can't process the fact that you have a twin brother out there, not to mention a birth mother who went through a horrendous time, and you don't want to find them. It's just not ...'

'It's not what?'

'Nah, forget it.'

'No. What were you going to say?'

'I was going to say it's not human.'

His stomach twisted. 'Jesus, that's a cruel thing to say.'

'I'm sorry, Brandon. It's how I feel. I've done my best to see where you're coming from, but I can't. Even at the most basic level, your lack of curiosity bugs me.'

'Are you saying you don't love me any more?'

Robyn pinched the bridge of her nose. Her perfect nose in her perfect face. 'No. I ... I'm saying that perhaps I got you wrong. I thought I'd married this big-hearted guy who valued family and hard work and loyalty and all the good stuff. Compared to other men, you seemed so solid, so generous. So kind. But, faced with a challenge, you've chosen to run away and turn your back on your family. On people who might need you.'

Brandon had always said that he'd walk barefoot to New York for Robyn. And he would. That would be different, though. That would be his choice. Trailing around a foreign country looking for people who might no longer exist *wasn't* his choice. If he gave in ... Well, that was it, he would be giving in. He'd be getting involved in a messy situation that wasn't of his choosing. He had to make her see that he was doing the right thing.

'They're not my family. Mom and Dad are. And you are. Or at least I thought you were.'

'Don't bring Art and Ellen into this. They've no issue with you looking for Linda and Eddie. They said as much over the holidays. If you ask me, Ellen *wants* you to try and find them.'

There was more than a splinter of truth in what she said. Taken aback to discover that Brandon was a twin, both parents had urged him to trace Eddie and Linda. Again, he'd felt like he was being railroaded. He hadn't spoken to them in four days, which for the Bennetts was a lifetime.

Robyn went to lift her suitcase from the bed. Brandon tried to help, but she batted him away.

'I'm going to raise something I've shied away from,' she said. 'Do you have an issue with Eddie's disability?'

'Aw, Robyn. What do you think I am?'

He'd tried to inform himself about cerebral palsy. It turned out that much of what he thought he knew wasn't true. Katie had been right: usually, the causes were related to the woman's pregnancy rather than the birth. Some people with CP lived regular adult lives. Others had trouble not just with movement but with speaking, eating and sleeping. They suffered pain and became depressed. There was one fact that nagged at him. Early intervention was vital. Without it, children were in danger of becoming passive and uncommunicative. Their lives were diminished far more than they should be. It was impossible to imagine that Eddie, stranded in Carrigbrack, had received much intervention or support.

Robyn's voice cut through his thoughts. 'Okay,' she was saying, 'let me phrase it another way. Does Eddie's level of disability matter to you? Like, if you found out he was only mildly disabled, and that you could go for a beer with him after all, would that change your view?'

'I don't follow you.'

'It strikes me that if you were sure your brother could bring something to your life, you might want to meet him. The same goes for Linda. Only you're worried she never recovered from what was done to her.'

'Please,' he said, 'you can't see it like that. You can't see *me* like that.' Brandon was annoyed by how congested he sounded. Getting emotional wouldn't help. He touched Robyn's wrist. Even her wrists were perfect.

She pulled away. 'I need to get going. My flight's at eight.'

'I'll take you to the airport.'

'I've booked a cab. It'll be here in a minute.'

'Christ, Robyn,' he said, 'you can't go like this.'

'I'm sorry.' She shifted her gaze so she was looking anywhere but at him. 'It's what I need to do.'

After she'd gone, Brandon leant back against the bedroom wall and slid down until he slumped onto the floor. She hadn't said when she'd be back, or even *if* she'd be back. She was young. She could get a job anywhere. If she didn't want to be with him, there was nothing to keep her in Boston. Everything he'd worked for was unravelling. His luck was running dry.

Once, he'd been content on his own. He'd read that, contrary to popular belief, most bees didn't live in hives. Many were solitary creatures. He remembered finding solace in that. But those days were behind him, and he'd mapped out a future with Robyn: a baby, ideally two; a bigger house, or a place near the coast. There wasn't space for a dark backstory or damaged family members.

As much as he hated to admit it, some of his wife's accusations had been accurate. He was turning his back on people who might need him. But there was more to it than that. He was the man who'd walked away from the plane crash, the man who'd jumped clear of the burning building. His survival, once a source of comfort, now filled him with guilt. Why couldn't Robyn see that? To him, it was as plain as a rash.

Chapter 23

Ailish

'Would I like to come to London with you?' said Katie, her voice brimming with happiness. 'Of course I would. I'd swim the Irish Sea if I had to.'

Beth was equally enthusiastic. 'We won't make a nuisance of ourselves. We'll hide in the corner and pretend we're not there. Unless you need us … which you won't.' Then she laughed. 'Sorry, Ailish, I'm rambling. But it's all so exciting.'

Ailish assured her that rambling was entirely acceptable. Her own head was in fifty different places at once. The previous day, she'd tried to shine a mirror with toothpaste and clean a bath with bleach.

The three would leave Dublin on an early flight and return that evening. Ailish would stay in Drumcondra the night before. She booked two days off work and confirmed her plans with Chrissie. Despite her birth mother's illness, she felt a pleasure she hadn't experienced in years. Everything was in place. Everything was great.

Except it wasn't.

She'd had several conversations with Chrissie. They'd swapped snippets of information about their lives and families. She'd learnt more about her half-sisters and brother and about her birth mother's life after she'd left Carrigbrack. In return, she'd told stories about her own children and grandchildren. She'd done her best to talk warmly about her adoptive parents. Negativity wouldn't be fair, either to them or to Chrissie. The problem was Keith. When it came to her husband, Ailish had lied. He was delighted for her, she'd said. He wouldn't be travelling to London, but only because he was busy at work. Mostly, she guided the conversation in another direction.

In truth, she still hadn't said anything to Keith about Chrissie or London. She knew she'd have to tell him. She couldn't disappear, then reappear two days later with stories of her travels. The trouble was, even thinking about it brought a tightness to her chest and a tremor to her hands. She'd rehearsed several options, but the right words escaped her. The thought of Chrissie, and the gutsy way she'd risen above her rape and incarceration, made her feel worse. She was letting her birth mother down.

For a while, she didn't say anything to the children. She was scared that, however unwittingly, one of them would let something slip. Eventually, she had a coffee with Jodie. Then she called Lee in Kerry and Lorraine in Limerick. They bombarded her with questions.

'What does Dad make of your news?' they all asked.

'I wanted to tell you first,' she replied. 'After all, Chrissie is your grandmother. Do me a favour and keep it to yourself until I get a chance to talk to him.'

Although they must have been sceptical, none of the three challenged her. Jodie, always the plain speaker, came closest.

'Holy moly, Mam,' she said. 'If it was me, I wouldn't have been able to stop talking about her. I can't believe you've kept it all to yourself.'

'I'll tell him tonight,' promised Ailish.

She meant it. Sort of. Her hopes, such as they were, hinged on getting Keith into a good mood, then convincing him that Katie had done the legwork. 'Everything was arranged before I knew where I was,' she would claim. His attitude had been coloured by the belief that Chrissie would be impossible to find. Now that those fears had proven groundless, his objections would wither away. Wouldn't they?

Then she told herself to stop being stupid. Obviously Keith wouldn't agree to her meeting Chrissie. She would have to work her way around his disapproval.

First, she needed to speak to Stevie. Even though she still referred to him as her baby, Ailish was the smaller of the two by almost a foot. There were times when she questioned whether she'd really given birth to this broad-shouldered, curly-haired giant. Her first three children had grown up gradually. Stevie was different. In a finger click, he'd morphed from a rosy-cheeked kid to an adult who looked at her with benign confusion. At seventeen, he had a pink-haired girlfriend, a passion for something called grime and a habit of smoking Marlboros out of his bedroom window.

She would never admit it, but he'd always been her favourite. Right from the start, he'd been easy to love. Not only was he clever, he was sunny-natured. Ailish recognised her double standards. Behaviour for which she'd scolded the others – traipsing through the house in muddy shoes, drinking milk from the carton, spending half of Saturday in bed – now went over her head. She was relieved that he'd finally chosen a college course. He wanted to study data science. She pretended to understand.

When Stevie got back from school, Ailish was in the kitchen peeling potatoes. Her kitchen was weighed down with the accumulation of almost three decades of family life. There were saucepans and bowls, outdated utensils and recipe books. In among the books were bills and letters and pieces of paper she'd never got around to filing away. The kitchen was her place, and she liked it there. She especially liked the days when her son joined her before starting his homework.

'There's something I've been meaning to tell you,' she said.

He responded to the news with enthusiasm, giving her a bone-crushing hug then demanding to see every photo Chrissie had sent.

'This is amazing,' he said as he swiped through the pictures on Ailish's phone. 'She can't deny you, anyway.

You're the absolute spit of each other.'

'It's great, isn't it? As you can see, her other children all take after their father.'

Stevie read the newspaper article too.

'That's crazy,' he kept saying. 'I assume the old guy who raped her got away with it?'

'No doubt.'

'Does Dad know about this?'

'I was hoping to tell him this evening.'

Stevie handed back her phone. 'But you probably won't.'

'What do you mean?'

'Don't take this the wrong way, but we both know what'll happen. He'll come home in bad form, and you'll say to yourself, "Nah, I can't risk it tonight. I'll leave him be."'

How well you know us, thought Ailish. 'I have to tell him. I'm going to London on Monday.'

'Like, four days from now?'

'Yep.'

'I can't understand his problem with you finding your birth mother.' He held up a hand, as if making a stop sign. 'And don't say he doesn't, because I've heard him banging on about it. Is that what the row before Christmas was about?'

'Yes. I'm sorry about that.'

'Ah, Mam. Don't you be saying sorry when you've nothing to apologise for.'

'Okay, okay. You go and do your homework. I'll give you a shout when dinner's ready.'

Ailish hadn't expected Stevie to be so outspoken, and as

the three of them sat down for their evening meal, she was more uptight than ever. She chewed slowly. Without the help of a mouthful of water, swallowing was impossible. Even mashed potato was tricky. Her grip was unsteady, and she worried the knife and fork would fall from her hands. Stevie was no better. He examined his fish fillet like he'd never seen food before and wasn't sure what to do with it.

Keith complained about work. Stevie told an anecdote about an eccentric teacher. Ailish spoke about a well-known couple who'd stayed in the hotel and left the room looking like a tornado had passed through. When the conversation stalled, she knew she had to speak. Still she hesitated. Stevie fixed her with a questioning look, which was noticed by Keith.

'What's the story?' he said.

Neither of them replied.

He turned to Stevie. 'What have you done?'

'Nothing.'

'Is anybody going to put me in the picture here? Ailish?'

Maybe, she decided, it wasn't too late to back out of the London visit. She could come up with an excuse and go another time when she'd found the strength to talk to Keith. Katie would be annoyed, but she'd forgiven her for the bracelet, so she'd probably forgive this.

'Ailish?' he repeated.

'If you're not going to tell him,' said Stevie, 'I am.'

'I …' she started.

Keith put down his cutlery with a clang. 'Sweet suffering Jesus, will one of you talk to me?'

Ailish had dreaded this moment, but now that it was here, she had to get on with it. 'It's my biological mother,' she said. 'I've found her.'

'Hold on a minute. I thought we'd agreed you were going to let that business rest.'

She did her best to explain what Katie and Beth had done.

'Aren't they the right pair of busybodies? Have you approached this woman?'

'Yes. Her name's Chrissie. She's lovely. She wants to meet.'

'And where is she, this Chrissie?'

Ailish couldn't look at her husband. Instead, she focused on a stain on the wall, created years before when Lorraine and Stevie had gone through a phase of flicking cornflakes at each other. 'She's in London.'

'I see. Whereabouts in London?'

'Shepherd's Bush.'

'That's a fine spot, isn't it?'

'I think so, yes.'

'She must be fierce disappointed in you. Living in a poky house in Kilmitten, your days devoted to clearing up other people's filth.'

Stevie tipped forward. 'Don't speak to her like that.'

'I can't remember asking for your view,' said Keith. 'Eat your dinner or go upstairs and do your homework. When you're old enough to have an opinion, I might listen to it.'

Ailish started telling Chrissie's story. If he knew what a heroine she was, it might soften his attitude. She took her phone from her bag and showed him the photos. He held the phone in front of him and raced through the pictures in a way that suggested he wasn't particularly impressed.

'Why didn't you tell me before?' he said.

'I was nervous. We haven't always seen eye to eye on this, and I didn't know how you'd react.'

Keith tilted his head to one side. 'At least you admit you've behaved badly. What kind of marriage is it where you promise not to do something then lash ahead and do it anyway, huh?'

Stevie, who'd been slumped in front of his dinner, straightened his back. 'Why can't you be happy for her?'

'I told you to mind your own business. This is between me and your mother. Go upstairs, would you? You see, Ailish, this is what happens when you spoil a child. They get all mouthy.'

'I'm not going anywhere.'

'You'll do as you're told. When I was your age, I was out earning a living, not dossing around in a classroom learning Shakespeare and French and other crap that's of no use to any man. Mind you, if I'd spoken to my father like you speak to me, I'd have felt the back of his hand.'

'I'm staying here while you listen to what Mam's got to say.'

'Oh, there's more, is there?'

Ailish clasped her hands together. Her mouth was dry, as if she'd been gargling vinegar. 'I'm going to London to see her.'

Hardly had the words cleared her lips than Keith snapped back, 'Like fuck you are.'

'She's not well. She's got breast cancer, and I'm going to see her.'

'Where's the money coming from?'

'You know I've a little bit put by.'

Keith laughed. 'There you are, Stevie boy. For all her talk about your college fund, she's quick enough to spend the money on herself.'

'Don't worry about me,' said Stevie, his voice low. 'I want Mam to go to London.'

'What's that? Speak up there.'

'I said I want Mam to go to London. What sort of person wouldn't want her to meet her mother?'

Keith switched the phone from one hand to the other and back again. Save for the tick of the kitchen clock, the room was quiet. 'She lied to me. She lied and kept on lying. That's the reason she's not going. And while I pay the bills, my word is more important than yours. Isn't that right, Ailish?'

She didn't answer.

'I said, isn't that right, Ailish?'

There was a cold anger to his words. She ought to back down. Backing down was what she knew best, but she'd spent long enough with her nose pressed against the window, gazing on while others did what they wanted. She looked from her husband to her son and back again. They had the same eyes, but Stevie's were keener, more alert. If Stevie was drawn with a sharp pencil, Keith was more of a charcoal smudge.

'I'm going to London,' she said. 'My mother's unwell, and you can't stop me from seeing her.'

'Come again?'

'You heard me. I'm going to London.'

Keith tightened his grip on the phone and hurled it hard against the far wall. It fell asunder and the parts clattered across the floor. 'And I said you're not.'

Although Ailish's left eyelid twitched, she was unusually clear-headed. Before she could reply, Stevie intervened.

'What's wrong with you?' he said to Keith. 'Why do you have to behave like this?'

'For the final time, go to your room and study your precious fucking books.'

Ailish could hear Stevie's breath shaking.

'No,' he said. 'You've pushed everybody around for long enough. Did you ever wonder why the other three left as soon as they could? Why they practically ran out of the house? It was because of you and your roaring and your bullying. Lee says he'd rather sleep rough than come back here. Did you know that?'

Ailish gasped. It was a feeble sound and she hoped the others hadn't heard. Lee had often clashed with his father. She'd had no idea, though, that he'd been so badly affected.

She should have done more to protect him. And the girls: her sweet, funny girls. Had they too had miserable childhoods? They'd never said as much. Oh, she'd known that life with Keith was far from ideal, but she'd done everything she could to shield the children. When he'd been in bad humour, she'd shooed them out of the house. They'd never seen her cry. She'd tried to be upbeat. Why hadn't they told her that she'd got it all wrong?

Keith rose from his chair and grasped the shoulder of Stevie's hoodie. 'You little bastard. Go. Up. Stairs.'

Stevie stood and shook off his father's hand. 'No. We spend all our time in this house pretending that everything's okay. That we're normal. I've had enough of it.'

'Please, love …' started Ailish.

Stevie looked at her. 'And you're the worst. You pretend he doesn't hit you when we all know he does.'

A long beat of silence followed. Ailish felt something inside her shrivel. She'd been careful to camouflage her injuries. And some of what Keith had done to her had barely left a mark. The pinches, the pokes, the pulled hair: how could Stevie know about those?

Keith's eyes narrowed. 'I've never touched your mother.'

'You mightn't have given her a black eye or a swollen lip, but you've done everything else. I've heard her squeal. And I've seen the bruises on her arms.'

'Ailish, tell him he's wrong.'

Stevie glanced at her. 'Don't lie for him.'

Ailish stayed quiet. For the first time, she noticed that

Stevie was the taller of the two. Keith attempted to shove his son. 'I've had more than enough of your lip. You reckon you're better than me, don't you? With your loud music and your slut of a girlfriend and your college notions. Now, if you don't move, you're going to be very, very sorry.'

Stevie stood, still as stone.

'Please,' said Ailish. 'Please can we take a step back? There's no need for any of this.' Everything felt fragile, as if she was surrounded by tripwires and there was no safe way to escape.

'I won't be ordered around,' said Keith. 'Not by you, and definitely not by him.'

Stevie's face had turned egg-carton grey. He shrugged. 'I'm staying right here.'

Keith's shoulders dropped slightly, almost as if he was giving in. Ailish knew better. She recognised it as a preparatory move. Before she could shout a warning, before she could even open her mouth, she heard the crunch of his fist against Stevie's jaw. Stevie stumbled back. His head cracked against the jamb of the door and he hit the ground.

'I warned you,' said Keith. 'Now get up off the floor.'

Stevie was motionless.

It took Ailish a second to realise that the piercing sound was her own scream.

Chapter 24

Katie

The new year brought a flurry of enquiries. The Carrigbrack Nurse inbox was inundated with queries from people who'd resolved that this would be the year they found their birth parents. In the first ten days of January, Katie sent out three bracelets. She was waiting for further information before posting another three. Replying to those she couldn't help was tough. Their emails usually started with an apology for asking about a birth outside her time frame. Always polite, sometimes intense, they filled her with tenderness. She told herself not to get involved. The people who'd been born while she worked in the home were her priority.

As usual, Saturday saw them reviewing the week's correspondence. Sunlight was falling through the kitchen window. It was one of those crisp January days that caught you off guard with their beauty.

Beth leant forward on her elbows. 'We're good at this,'

she said, 'and we're learning all the while. Ailish is proof of that.'

Katie put down her pen and removed her glasses. 'You know she's vanished again? I've been ringing, but her phone's permanently switched off. She's a terrible woman for disappearing.'

'Don't worry about her. I mean, everything's far from ideal, but she always struggles through in the end. Anyway, what I was saying was that if you look at the emails we're getting, and at the posts on the message board, it's extraordinary. I'm stunned by how many people are talking about Carrigbrack.'

'There were worse places, you know.'

'That's the point. What we're doing – no, what you're doing – is opening up the discussion about one of the homes. Others are bound to follow.'

Three weeks had passed since Katie had last read the message board. She couldn't do it any more. The debate had taken off in too many directions, and in some cases the anguish was overwhelming. There was too much honesty, and it scared her. She didn't want this complication. As much as she admired Chrissie and other campaigners, it wasn't a path she wished to follow. She'd set out to complete a task and, day by day, she was getting there.

'What are you suggesting?' she said.

'I suppose what I'm asking is whether we can do more to help people who were born before or after your time in Carrigbrack. Plus, there must be women in a similar situation to yourself; women who worked in homes and have information that could nudge someone in the right direction.'

Reluctant to discuss her reservations, Katie tried a conciliatory approach. 'I hear what you're saying, lovey, but I want to concentrate on the people in here.' She patted the lid of her new red box. 'That's enough work for me.'

'You wouldn't be on your own.'

'You're already doing more than your fair share. You have a job … and a life to live.'

'Work's fine, but I get more of a buzz from this. There are some heartbreaking stories on the forum, most of them from before your time. Like, there's this one message from a guy who reckons his birth mother was from Limerick. His health is poor, and it sounds as though he'd like to find her before he dies. Wouldn't it be brilliant if we could help him?'

'But we can't. We don't know anything about him or his birth mother.'

'Are there not ways of finding out?'

Katie touched Beth's arm. 'You've very good, really you are. And I'm not saying we should never look at these other cases, but for the moment, why don't we focus on the people we know we can help?'

'Okay,' said Beth, finally, her tone suggesting she'd be revisiting the subject. 'I meant what I said about Ailish, by the way. You shouldn't worry. By now, she must have told Keith about finding Chrissie.'

'That's exactly what worries me.'

'If there was a serious problem, she'd have been in touch. We're going to London in two days' time. She can't just disappear.'

'I hope you're right.'

Katie assumed that if there was bother, Keith was the cause of it. The man was as slippery as black ice and twice as dangerous. The only other possibility was that Chrissie was in poorer health than Ailish had indicated. The nurse in her knew that these days most breast cancers were highly treatable, but it was only six months since stomach cancer had claimed her husband, and the word put her on edge.

'Oh, I forgot to tell you,' said Beth. 'Mam says hello.'

'Does she indeed?'

Beth grinned. 'It was a very cordial conversation, actually. You'd swear we were best buds. She asked about Ailish, and I told her we were off to London. I can tell she's still iffy about the bracelets, but at least she wasn't hostile.'

Since their Christmas skirmish, Katie hadn't spoken to her sister. While she didn't regret what she'd said about Beth or the bracelets, she'd no desire to get into a protracted row. By the sounds of things, Margo was keeping tabs on her through Beth.

Earlier, she'd received an email from Gary, who'd returned from Los Angeles. He'd attached some photos. One was of his three sons, each as dark and gangly as their father. Another was of Allegra and her mother. What beauties they were, and what a shame he didn't see more of them. The big news was that he believed he'd found Noreen Nestor, one of the two women who remained on his list. Her married name was O'Callaghan, and she lived in Galway.

To Katie's surprise, she'd also received an email from Brandon. The snag was, it didn't say anything of any significance. He wished her a happy new year and thanked her for her help. He didn't apologise for his crabby behaviour on the day of their phone call. Neither did he mention Robyn. Brandon, Linda and Eddie continued to nibble at Katie's brain. She suspected Eddie might be easier to locate than some of the other Carrigbrack babies. All the same, she was wary. Would it be right to try and trace him without Brandon's approval? Would she be crossing an ethical line? Her queasiness didn't end there. To find him, she'd have to reach out to others who'd been in the home, and she wasn't sure she wanted to do that.

At least Brandon was safe, with a thoughtful, supportive spouse. Others weren't so fortunate. Throughout the day, she fretted about Ailish. By eight o'clock, she was in a lather of nerves. Finally, a text arrived:

> **Sorry for not being in touch. Stevie hasn't been well and my phone was broken. Have a new phone now. Looking forward to seeing you tomorrow night and jetting off to London on Monday xxx**

Yes, phones broke and teenagers got sick. Yes, Ailish was a busy woman with a full-time job and a demanding husband. Yet something about the message troubled Katie. She prodded out a reply:

Beth and I are excited about the trip. Hopefully
you'll be able to get here at a reasonable hour, so
we can go out for a bite to eat. Is Stevie okay? Are
you okay?

Several minutes passed before she heard another ping:

All okay. Sometimes things get complicated, but
you know that. Don't worry about me. And for
fear I've never said this properly, I'm grateful for
everything you've done. I feel very lucky.

Katie wasn't reassured. She'd have consulted Beth, only
her niece had gone out.

Her thoughts returned to Chrissie in Carrigbrack.
How clearly she remembered her pinched face and air of
confusion. She was fascinated by everything Chrissie had
done yet nervous about meeting her again. She thought of
others, too, especially Linda. The bright, spirited women
had suffered terribly. Sister Agnes had seen herself as a
custodian of the old ways, and any woman who protested
had received a robust response. Linda had known she was
being mistreated yet had been powerless to do anything
about it.

There was a prickling at the back of Katie's eyes, an anger
in her chest. If Linda was still out there, she deserved to
know that one of her twins had been sent to America and
that he'd made a success of his life.

She went upstairs and after some rummaging found an old
black-covered address book. A few weeks before, Beth had
informed her that people no longer carried address books.

Everything was 'in the cloud', apparently. Although it didn't take Katie long to find what she was looking for, she wasn't optimistic. Landlines were on the same road to extinction as address books. When she tapped out the number, her doubts were confirmed. All she got in return was a hurried series of beeps. Then it hit her: she was missing a digit. Even in rural areas, numbers now had an extra digit. But which one, and where to place it?

An internet search told her that she needed to put a 3 before the old number. She tried again, and – hey presto! – it connected. It rang five, six, seven times. She was about to hang up when a woman's voice said, 'Hello?'

'Er, hello. I'm not sure if I've got the right person or the right place. If I have, I hope you can help. This is Katie Carroll. You might remember me from Carrigbrack. Well, I was Katie O'Dea in those days.'

She heard a quick breath.

'Oh yes,' said the woman. 'I remember you.'

Chapter 25

Then, Patricia

She would never admit it, but Sister Faustina had been chastened by the death of Winnie's baby. Afterwards, girls with burns were given more time to dunk their hands in cold water, and pains were taken seriously.

There was no sign of the others softening. If anything, they became more authoritarian. As far as Sister Agnes was concerned, one girl's escape meant they were all in need of a hell-and-damnation tutorial. She gave several sermons about the sixth and ninth commandments, the gist being that while you could probably get away with breaking some of the others, six and nine were mortal-sin territory. Sister Sabina told a simple young girl from County Galway that she was ruined and would be lucky to get work cleaning lavatories. An older girl protested and had her hair chopped off. Sister Eunice said no more about Winnie, and when Patricia asked, she just smiled like a ruddy-cheeked Mona Lisa.

On the day her baby started to push its way into the world, Patricia was in the laundry, ironing a mountain of pillowcases. It was one of the less arduous jobs, but even so, it was difficult. She was too big, too ungainly. She remembered how Winnie had joked about her having twins, and felt a flutter of panic. For a while, she said nothing. When, at last, she couldn't continue, she approached Faustina and asked to be excused. Her calm appearance belied her fear. She was scared of all the usual things: pain and infection and her own inadequacies. Most of all, she was scared that what had happened to Diane would happen to her baby. Winnie had claimed that women were better off being stupid because that way they didn't know what could go wrong. Patricia could see the wisdom in her words.

Over the following hours, time became distorted. There were stretches when she thought pain would defeat her. Then a respite would come, and she'd tell herself she could cope. As soon as she began to accept this, the agony would return. She'd sworn she wouldn't shout, not out of any deference to the rules, but because she wanted to be strong and dignified. It turned out this was impossible. She shrieked and roared until the nurse warned that if she didn't quieten down, she'd be punished. She'd been relieved to see Rita Farragher in the delivery room. The midwife was too aloof, and however irrational it might be, Patricia still believed the other nurse could have done more to save Winnie's daughter.

Twenty-two hours later, when she reckoned she couldn't take another minute of torture, her baby arrived. He had soft dark hair and a nose so small it was practically transparent. He was red and noisy – and huge.

I have a baby, she thought, a gorgeous, living, breathing person.

'Ten pounds four ounces,' said the nurse, in a tone that suggested she was weighing potatoes.

Nobody congratulated Patricia on her son's safe delivery. There were no smiles or celebrations. The nurse wrote down his particulars, then asked what she wanted to call him.

'Graham,' she replied.

'I don't think that's allowed. It sounds very Protestant. Is there a St Graham?'

Sister Sabina stalked over. 'No. We can't allow that. Pick something else. Paul or John, maybe.'

That summer, there was a glut of Johns and Pauls in Carrigbrack. There was a George, too. Unfortunately, until the Pope canonised a Ringo, the band would be incomplete.

'I think Graham's a lovely name,' said Patricia, 'and that's what I'm calling him.'

'Put down Paul,' said Sabina to the nurse. 'His parents will probably give him a different name anyway.'

Rita added Paul to her notes before transcribing the details onto a thin strip of paper. 'I'll put this on his wrist,' she said.

'May I hold him?' asked Patricia.

Sabina shook her head. 'You most certainly may not. You'll be shown how to feed and wash him, and that'll be enough for you. If you'd wanted to moon over a baby, you should have got married first.'

'What's wrong with holding him? Doesn't he deserve to be welcomed into the world the same as any other baby?'

'There'll be time for that when he's with people who are fit to look after him.'

Patricia decided not to argue further. She was sore and weak. What was important was that Paul was alive and healthy. She didn't care what Sabina said: he was her child, and he was entitled to know that she loved him.

After the first frantic days, life took on a pattern. She was forced back to work in the laundry, something she found exhausting and frustrating. As Sabina had warned, her contact with Paul was limited to feeding, bathing and the occasional nappy change. Some days, it felt like he was made of right angles. At other times, he wriggled and thrashed. He wasn't a fretful baby, though. Right from the start, he seemed satisfied with life and keen to find out more. When no one was looking, Patricia would kiss his feathery hair and tell him how handsome he was.

On several occasions, when she should have been asleep, she crept out of the dormitory and went to see him. No matter that she was shattered from her day's work, ten minutes in the nursery brought solace.

The babies slept in steel cots, lined up in military-style rows. At night, two young mothers took care of them. One,

Imelda, was a chatterbox. Her own baby, a girl, had already been taken for adoption, and she must have found her job difficult. Nevertheless, she did it with grace and generosity.

'I'll be free to go in a couple of months,' she whispered to Patricia, 'which is great. Only to be honest with you, I'll miss these little ones. I used to think that all babies were the same, but even the tiniest tots in here have their own personality.'

'You're very good with them. Did you ever consider becoming a nurse?'

'I can't see anyone giving me a chance. Sister Sabina says I'm damaged goods, and that you'd only have to look at me to know that.'

'That's pure rubbish,' said Patricia. 'I'd say any hospital would be lucky to have you.' Although the light was dim, she could see Imelda was blushing.

A fortnight after Paul's birth, Patricia received a letter from home. Her parents told her that a girl down the street had done well in the Leaving Cert, a man out the road had been injured in a farming accident, and one of Father Cusack's sisters had died. There was no acknowledgement of the birth of their grandson. There was no reference to her pregnancy at all. Patricia's parents were not bad people. When she was a child, her mother had given her the cream from the top of the milk and gently brushed the tangles from her hair. Her father had held her hand as she'd crossed the road and taught her how to tie her laces. What was more, her mam had doted on the babies of others, tickling their chins and admiring their minuscule nails and asking who they took after. What was it, then, that caused them to be so hard-hearted now? They must have known that Paul had been born. How could they have no interest in him?

As she became more attuned to the ways of the nursery, Patricia realised that a handful of women felt no connection to their children. The saddest case was a woman in her mid twenties called Nancy. Nancy's arms and legs weren't much thicker than the bones beneath, and her hair was so thin her scalp shone through. She held her son in an awkward, detached way, as though there was something distasteful about him. When he was at her breast, she cried, not from physical pain but from unhappiness. The baby, too, appeared stringy and malnourished. Echoing the way Winnie had been regarded, some of the others saw Nancy as a latter-day Typhoid Mary. They swerved around her and turned their backs. Patricia wanted to find out what was wrong, but every time she attempted to have a chat, a nun zoomed in and ordered her to stop.

Finally, Imelda filled her in. According to rumour, she said, Nancy's own father was also the father of her baby. 'I didn't think such a thing was possible,' she added. 'There was a lot I didn't know until I came here, mind.'

'That makes two of us,' said Patricia. From pregnant children to the unexplained deaths of infants, Carrigbrack had introduced her to a catalogue of horrors.

The next morning, she asked Eunice if anything could be done to help Nancy.

'The problem,' said Eunice, 'is that she's better off here than at home. The moment she goes back, her father will interfere with her again. Apparently her mother pretends it isn't happening. And you've seen the state of the girl; she wouldn't survive in the outside world.'

Grim as this sounded, it was probably true. Afterwards, Patricia tried to be kind to Nancy. She made a point of sitting beside her and offering to share her food. She tried to engage her in conversation about the habits of small babies and the foibles of elderly nuns. She was wasting her time. Nancy was barely conscious of her surroundings. Having a proper chat was beyond her.

The weeks whipped past. New girls arrived. Others were allowed to leave. Babies were born. Others disappeared. There was no logic to how their departures were handled. Some mothers were given a chance to say goodbye, while more were only informed when their child was already gone.

The longer she spent with Paul, the more certain Patricia was that she wanted to keep him. If she didn't fool herself that this would be easy, neither could she believe it was impossible. Remembering what Agnes had said about silly young girls not being able to take care of children, she set out to prove her maturity. She increased her work rate in the laundry and ignored Sabina's goading. She never asked for more food or moaned about getting up for early Mass. Although her hair was growing back in uneven hanks and whorls and her burnt hand still throbbed, she didn't complain. She was a model penitent. When she had time to think about it, she was uncomfortable at collaborating with the Carrigbrack regime. She didn't like pretending that everything was normal. But she was desperate, and if she had to play Agnes's game, so be it.

Despite everything, there were days when her head hummed with contentment. Insofar as it was possible for a prisoner to be happy, Patricia was.

Her new-found obedience didn't prevent her from sneaking in to see Paul. She did, however, ration her visits. She tried to convince herself that in the long run her sacrifice would be worthwhile.

One late October night, with a full moon throwing pale yellow light into the dormitory, she padded out to the nursery. First, she apologised to Imelda, who was on her own. It was unfair to wake a sleeping baby. The glorious thing about Paul was that he never grizzled. He nuzzled into her and clamped his fat fist around her index finger. Then he gurgled, as if to say, *Ah, it's you.* This was followed by a muted whimper, which she took to mean, *If there was a feed available, I wouldn't say no.* Bless him, he was a hungry child. He was also Patricia's confidant. Winnie's departure had left her without a close friend, and while Paul didn't have much to contribute to the conversation, he was a good listener. He would look at her with his bright eyes, and she'd be convinced he understood every word.

No sooner had she sat down to feed him than she heard a

grunting sound from one of the cots. This was followed by a prolonged wheeze, then another grunt. Patricia returned Paul to his own bed.

'I'll be back in a sec,' she said.

He let out a howl of impatience, which was repeated by another baby. She ignored them. The wheezing sound was being made by Nancy's son.

'Has he been unwell for long?' she asked Imelda.

Because Nancy never spoke, Patricia couldn't remember her baby's name. Something with a J, she thought. Was he one of the Johns, perhaps? Or was he a Jerry?

Imelda nodded. 'He had a temperature earlier. I thought he was fierce hot, but Sister Agnes was doing her rounds and she told me not to be making a fuss over nothing. It was only a sniffle, she said. Is there something wrong with him, do you think?'

Nancy's baby wheezed again. This time, the sound was more disturbing, like he was fighting for breath.

Patricia bent and picked him up. Even in the half-light, she could see that his lips and hands were tinged with blue. His face felt clammy. Once more, he tried to breathe, but the air wasn't making it as far as his lungs.

'Is he all right?' asked Imelda.

Instead of replying, Patricia urged the baby to breathe. 'Come on, little chap,' she said. 'Come on.'

The muscles in his neck appeared to move and his chest sank. He gasped. The baby in the adjacent cot began singing, 'Ba, ba, ba,' as though it was all great fun. Another joined in, chirruping away for all she was worth.

Patricia turned to Imelda. 'You should go and get one of the nurses.'

'But if they find you here, they'll—'

'Go. Please go.'

The sudden rise in the pitch of her voice disturbed another baby, who squealed. Imelda didn't move. All the while, the child in Patricia's arms struggled to breathe.

'If you don't go,' she said, 'I will. Then we'll both be in serious trouble. If he doesn't breathe soon, he might die, and I don't know what to do. Please, Imelda, I'm not making this up.'

Imelda hesitated for another second, and then, at last, she took off like one of the young hares that loped along the nearby lane.

Sister Agnes peered over the top of her glasses.

'So here you are,' she said, 'in trouble again.'

Patricia, standing at the other side of the mahogany desk, fiddled with the sleeve of her uniform. 'I did my best for the baby, Sister.'

'That's not in dispute. I hope that any good Christian would have done the same. The fact remains: you shouldn't have been in the nursery. Do you think that your baby is more important than the others, is that it?'

'No, Sister.'

In that moment, Patricia felt an intense dislike for Agnes. She couldn't let it get the better of her, though. She had to try and use the situation to her advantage. 'How's Nancy's baby this morning, do you know?'

'I gather the child, James, is doing well. According to Nurse Farragher, his respiratory distress has passed, and his temperature has eased.'

'That's good. I was very concerned. He's a delicate boy, and his mother ... well, his mother isn't as sturdy as the rest of us either.'

During the night, she had mulled over her intervention. Had she made the right decision? The signs were that, far from loving him, Nancy could barely tolerate her son's presence. He was a sickly child, listless and prone to infection. That wasn't all: Patricia had heard that the children of incest victims had all sorts of mental challenges. There was a danger that no couple would want him. Maybe she should have ignored his distress. Maybe she should have pretended she didn't understand what was happening. Immediately, she rounded on herself. Of course she couldn't have let a baby die. All the same, she couldn't help but wonder: what if she'd spent years here and had been ground down and hardened by suffering? Would she have made a different choice? She'd lain awake for hours, fretting about the ways in which her mind had already been distorted by the misery around her.

Sister Agnes had fallen silent, and Patricia feared she was choosing her punishment. When she spoke again, her tone was brusque. 'Apart from reporting on the baby's condition, Nurse Farragher also said that, if it hadn't been for your intervention, James mightn't have survived. I'm not condoning your misbehaviour. Indeed, any repeat will be regarded most seriously. However, it seems your responsible attitude was important last night.'

Patricia had to stop herself from smiling. She liked the sound of the word 'responsible'.

'Thank you, Sister,' she said.

Chapter 26

Ailish

In the air, Ailish attempted to relax. Below, Dublin's houses and factories were giving way to a patchwork of fields. She was on her way to see the woman she'd spent most of her life thinking about. She told herself to focus on the day. To savour every second.

If only it was that simple.

At the airport, she'd tried not to see herself in the bathroom mirror. Even though she was wearing her favourite blue jacket and a month's worth of make-up, she looked wrung out. Her cheeks were hollow, her skin yellow-grey.

So far, she'd managed to avoid an honest conversation with Beth and Katie. Not that fooling them was easy. Beth was smart and quick-witted, and Katie was experienced. She had an old-fashioned intuition that Ailish respected. They'd peppered her with questions about Keith's attitude to their visit, and she'd done her best to slip-slide around the answers.

She was grateful that Katie was preoccupied. Uptight, almost. She supposed this shouldn't be a surprise. Katie was also revisiting a difficult part of her life.

There'd been a funny moment in the taxi. The driver had been listening to a classic rock station, and as they reached the airport turn-off, 'Overboard' had come on.

Beth had said, 'There's Gary earning another five cents.'

Ailish had laughed. 'How's his search going?'

'He's making progress,' Katie had replied. 'As I keep telling him, he's getting closer every day.'

Ailish had been pleased to hear this, if not for his sake, then for his natural mother's. She deserved to know what he'd achieved.

'Overboard' was her favourite Black Iris song. She knew it wasn't poetic or profound, but the lyrics and melody lingered in her head, exciting her and soothing her. Like all the best music, it enhanced the good times and made the bad times more bearable:

> *I thought I was safe, I stayed close to shore,*
> *But the dangers were there,*
> *Unheeded, ignored.*
> *You ripped up the sail and burnt both our oars,*
> *I'm a long way from safety,*
> *I'm lost overboard.*

As they glided over the petrol blue of the Irish Sea, Ailish ordered a coffee and flicked through the in-flight magazine.

She looked at pictures of Toulouse and Connemara, rugby players and chefs, but couldn't get any purchase on the words. Her thoughts kept skittering back to Kilmitten. For the ten thousandth time, she asked herself if she should be here at all. Should she not be at home, safeguarding Stevie and tackling Keith? The day after the fight, she'd resolved to cancel the trip. Oh, listen to her, calling it a fight. It had been an assault. Her husband had assaulted her son, and she'd done nothing to stop him. It had been Stevie who'd insisted she stick with her plans. 'If you don't go,' he'd said, 'you'll only be giving him what he wants. For everyone's sake, you need to get on that plane and meet Chrissie.'

She'd left Kilmitten the previous evening without saying anything to Keith. He hadn't tried to stop her. Neither had he made any attempt to wish her well.

She would never forget Thursday night. For a long two minutes, she'd thought her son was dead. She'd screamed, and then when Keith had bent down and touched him, she'd screamed again. She'd heard about similar incidents. They'd been on the news. People thought that one punch couldn't kill you, but fall the wrong way and it could. Gradually, Stevie came round. He was groggy and his head was bleeding. She wanted to call an ambulance. Failing that, she'd drive him to hospital in Limerick. He needed tests. He might be seriously hurt. She spoke too about calling the guards and having Keith removed from the house. Throughout, her voice quivered with hysteria.

She didn't know which was more unsettling: Keith's attack

on his son or the way he attempted to deflect responsibility. He moved smoothly from shock to mild contrition to blaming everyone else. 'I'm under pressure,' he said. 'I was provoked.'

Irritated as she was by his excuses, she needed to focus on Stevie, who was adamant that he'd be fine. She fussed and nagged until he snapped. He was off to bed, he said, and would think about everything in the morning. Keith stayed put. Ailish didn't call the police. She spent the night in the girls' old room, shivering and staring at dog-eared posters of Katy Perry and the Kings of Leon.

In the morning, Keith left early for work. Although Stevie maintained his head wasn't troubling him, he didn't look well. Eventually, he gave in and went to the doctor, who cleaned his wound, asked a string of questions and told Ailish to take him to hospital. He also had a quiet word with her.

'There are people you can talk to,' he said. 'They can give you advice.'

'Honestly,' she replied, 'it was an accident. Sure you know how clumsy teenage lads are.'

After a six-hour wait in the regional hospital, Stevie was examined. The doctor decided his injuries weren't serious. It was then that he told her he wouldn't be coming home. He'd called Jodie and, for the time being, would be staying with her.

'You can't expect me to sleep in the same house as that man,' he said. 'I'm amazed you've let him stay.'

Pummelled by the force of her son's words, Ailish went to hug him. He squirmed away, not because he was embarrassed, but because she'd betrayed him. She'd betrayed all four children. She hadn't been malicious or neglectful, but she'd been wilfully blind, and the result was the same. The greatest gift you could give someone was a happy childhood. She'd had the chance – and she'd failed.

As they made their descent through gauzy cloud and landed at Heathrow, as they bought their train tickets and threaded their way to the platform, her failures were all she could think about.

Number 32 Annaville Street was a red-brick terraced house with a turquoise door and a deep green creeper. Katie and Beth had offered to wait in a nearby coffee shop, but Ailish was nervous and wanted them to accompany her.

'Just drop in and say hello,' she said. 'Please? I'll find it a lot easier if you're there.'

'We've been amateur detectives for a while,' said Beth with an encouraging smile. 'We might as well be amateur social workers too.'

Ailish hadn't known what to expect. She'd fretted that Chrissie would be too weak for anything other than a short chat. Her fears were misplaced. The woman who greeted them was thin, her hair sparse, but she hugged with such ferocity that Ailish worried they'd squeeze the life out of each other. It was a good job Beth was holding the flowers they'd brought as a gift.

'My beautiful girl,' said Chrissie. 'My beautiful girl.'

As often as Ailish had imagined this moment, she wasn't prepared. The woman embracing her was a ghost made flesh. Sensible words wouldn't come, and all she could say was 'Thank you.'

She wanted to hold this moment in her hand. To make sure she would remember every second and every detail. Even if they never met again, this was perfect.

Chrissie was wearing a navy dress, a crimson scarf and silver earrings in the shape of stars. Despite her physical frailty, she twinkled with joy. Her perfume smelt like freshly cut grass.

When they disentangled, Iggy stepped forward. He was a trim man with an intelligent face and corrugated grey hair. He hugged Ailish, then ushered them all into the front room. Despite more than forty years in London, he walked like he was herding cattle.

The room they entered was pale green, cream and brown; the fireplace a shiny black. The walls were dotted with prints, some old-fashioned, others more contemporary, as if they'd been chosen by a child or grandchild. Her years in Rathtuskert Manor had taught Ailish well, and she appreciated the quality of Chrissie's furniture. She was happy to see that her birth mother was surrounded by nice things, though, truth to tell, they could have been sitting on upturned crates with old fertiliser bags for curtains and it wouldn't have mattered. Her eye was drawn towards the family photos on top of the bookcase, some of which she hadn't seen before. These were her children's aunts, uncles and cousins. This was her family.

Her thoughts swung back to Stevie. Jodie was great, but she was a student with a husband and two small children. She had no space in her life for a seventeen-year-old. And what about Stevie's exams? How could he study in such a noisy house?

For a minute or so, the five of them sat in silence, grinning at each other. Strangely, Ailish felt no compulsion to speak. She had a thousand questions, but if they went unasked, so be it. Although she'd seen many photos of Chrissie, meeting her was mesmerising. She kept spotting small similarities: the point of her chin, her unexpectedly broad wrists, her child-sized feet.

'You have a lovely house,' she said.

'Thank you,' replied Chrissie. 'We were lucky. Back in the early eighties it was possible for regular people to buy on a street like this. I can tell you, it wouldn't happen today.'

'It's the same in Dublin,' said Katie. 'I don't know how Beth's generation are supposed to live at all.'

'We rely on kindly aunts,' said Beth.

Chrissie told them that her treatment was going well, and fingers crossed her prospects were good.

'At least my hair's still red,' she added. 'I was worried that when it grew back it'd be grey. But it's strong stuff, red hair. None of your children are redheads, are they, Ailish?'

'No, they all take after Keith.' As the words left her mouth, she found herself hoping they weren't true. She didn't like to think of her children inheriting any part of their father.

Chrissie touched her scalp. 'I've always been glad of it. Of course, the English insist on saying "ginger". "Ginger's for cats and cake," I tell them. "My hair is red."'

Iggy was on catering duty and, having confirmed that they'd all prefer coffee to tea, he went out to the kitchen. Slowly, the conversation moved to more personal matters. Katie and Beth offered to leave, but Chrissie insisted they stay.

'It's funny,' she said, 'how even well-meaning people expected me to forget about my daughter – and about Carrigbrack. I've tried to be open, but I couldn't tell you how many times I've heard things like "You were only a child yourself. At least you were able to move on." And in some ways, I did, but I could no more have forgotten my girl than I could have forgotten an arm or a leg.' She bent her head towards Ailish. 'I wish there'd been some way of knowing how you were getting on. Even brief updates would have helped. No matter what else was happening, I thought about you every day.'

'It was the same for me, except because I had no memories of you, I had to invent you. I called you my other mammy, and I'd walk down the street thinking, could that woman be my other mammy ... or what about that woman? Then I'd get it into my head that you were in Dublin and I'd find you there.'

'Why Dublin?'

'Because it was about as exotic a place as I could imagine.'

'Bless you. For me, the worst day of the year was the tenth of November.'

Ailish smiled, and a tear dribbled down her cheek. 'My birthday.'

'I'd do nothing but think about you. I'd be wondering where you were and what you were doing and if you were having a party.' She looked at Katie and Beth. 'I'm so grateful, more grateful than you can imagine.'

Katie's eyes were also damp. 'I should have done this years ago. I regret that I didn't. It's not too late for the two of you, but I'm afraid it might be for others.'

'What matters is that you're doing it now.'

Katie took a handkerchief from her pocket. 'Sorry, I feel like a right eejit.'

'Well, you shouldn't,' said Chrissie, her voice firm. 'I've often cried at other people's reunions. I just never thought I'd get to experience it myself. I remember you more clearly now, by the way. Didn't you leave Carrigbrack while I was there?'

'Yes, in late '72. There were two other nurses there at the time.'

'That's right. There was an older woman, and then there was another nurse who also seemed ancient to me. Looking back, though, she can't have been more than twenty-five or six. Rita, was it? She was still there when I left.'

'Rita Farragher's her name. You won't believe this, but I was talking to her only the other day. I had a feeling she might know what happened to one of the babies. Do you remember the twins?'

'Yes,' said Chrissie, 'I do. They were little dotes. One of them was ... we said handicapped back then, but I'm sure there's a better word.'

'Eddie had cerebral palsy.'

Iggy came in with a clanking tray of mugs. The smell of coffee filled the room. 'I don't know,' he said. 'I turn my back for five minutes, and you're all crying.'

Chrissie handed round the mugs. 'Forgive my husband,' she said. 'He's a terrible messer.'

'Yes, but I'm the messer with the cake. I'll be back in a moment.'

Beth leant forward. 'Do you mind me asking, Chrissie: have you come across other Carrigbrack women? Through the support group, I mean?'

'That's a good question. I know a couple of ladies who were there in earlier years, and there are three or four from after I'd left. There's only one woman from my time, though. Tina Dennison's her name. Let me see, she would have been ... Tina McNulty back then.'

Katie and Beth exchanged a glance.

'Was she originally from County Kerry, by any chance?' asked Beth.

'Yes, I always remember the Kerry women, on account of them being Iggy's county folk.'

'And did she have a son?' said Katie.

'She did. He tracked her down too, only the reunion

didn't go well. Tina's a bit … scattered, shall we say … and her son's wife didn't take to her. It's a shame when that happens.'

Ailish thought of her own family troubles and closed her eyes.

'Why are you interested in Tina?' asked Chrissie.

When Katie answered, her voice was so bright it practically bounced off the magnolia walls. 'We've been trying to help a man called Gary, only he doesn't have a correct date of birth. He's narrowed the list of likely birth mothers down to two.'

'And Tina McNulty is one of them,' continued Beth. 'So if Tina has already found her son, then fingers crossed, the other woman on his list – Noreen, is it?' Katie nodded. 'Noreen must be the right one.'

'Isn't that fantastic news?' said Chrissie, her smile as wide as the Shannon. 'Fantastic news altogether.'

When Iggy returned with a plate of sandwiches and the promised cake, she filled him in.

'That's a gas one,' he said. 'Dig in there, ladies. You must be hungry after your early flight.'

Ailish noticed that the longer he spent with them, the more Irish his accent became. By the time they left, he'd probably sound more Irish than her own children. She couldn't stop thinking about them – and about Stevie in particular. She shouldn't have come here today. What if, safe in the knowledge that she was out of the country, Keith decided to have another go at him?

While they ate, Chrissie spoke about Carrigbrack.

'Say what you like about Sister Sabina,' she said, 'but at least she was a straightforward bitch. With Agnes, you were never quite sure. Sometimes, she'd turn on the "I care about you" charm, and you wouldn't know what to think. She used to give these homilies where she'd brainwash us into thinking we were worse than useless. "I gather," she'd say, "some of you think you're capable of rearing your child. Well, let me put you straight about that: you're not." She used to make it sound like we'd all be out in the town, and our children would spend their lives in pubs and dance halls.'

'Were any women allowed to keep their babies?' asked Ailish.

'I've heard of one or two,' said Chrissie, 'but no more than that.' She sipped her coffee. 'I remember the day I left. I was sixteen by then and I'd paid my dues. They couldn't force me to stay. The bold Agnes called me into her office, and you know what she said? "You've made a lot of progress while you've been here, Hanora." She insisted on using my home name. "I trust you can keep that up."'

'The miserable cow,' said Beth.

Chrissie's eyes rose to the heavens. 'Wasn't she something else? You'd swear I had sins to atone for.'

'Were the nuns not able to think for themselves? They can't have believed everything they came out with.'

'No doubt Agnes thought she was fulfilling her duty,' said Katie. 'She was big on duty.'

'I had the last laugh,' said Chrissie. 'She put me on the bus, but instead of getting off at Hackett's Cross, I went as far as Limerick. Then I got another bus to Dublin and the ferry to Holyhead.'

'You did go back, though,' said Ailish. 'Didn't you? I saw the gravestone. And I ... I assumed you must have paid for it.'

Iggy touched his wife's hand.

'Yes, I returned for Mam's funeral and for my brother's. Perhaps I should have made more of an effort to see them before they died, but going back was difficult. A lot of people in the village knew the real story, only no one would admit it. Some of them were cool towards me. I held my head high, but it was hard.' With her free hand, Chrissie dabbed at her eyes.

'You don't have to talk about it. I don't want to upset you.'

'No, love. You deserve to know. It's important that these things are spoken about. If I've learnt nothing else, I've learnt that.' She paused. 'Mammy died in the spring of 1985, and I got it into my head that I had to attend the funeral. I don't know why I felt that way when I hadn't gone back for Daddy. I suppose I hadn't wanted to face either of them while they were alive. They'd given me no support. No understanding. I can see now that they weren't evil people. They were products of their time. Simple as that.'

'When your parents found out you were pregnant,' said Beth, 'did they not consider calling the guards?'

'If they did, they didn't mention it to me. Mind you, nobody said much of anything to me. And say they had contacted the police? You can be certain the man who abused me would have denied all knowledge. Either that or he'd have claimed I led him on.'

'You were *thirteen*.'

'I hear what you're saying, only who do you think the guards would have believed? A scrappy girl with holes in her pinafore or a big landowner … because that's what he was? The other thing is, and this might sound mad, I wasn't certain what he'd done to me. In my innocence, I wondered if this was the sex that people talked about – or was it something else. He raped me four or five times before I found the courage to run away from him.'

'I'm so angry for little you.'

'Thanks, Beth. These days, a child would be taken seriously. Or, at least, I hope they would. Now, where was I?'

'You were talking about the funeral,' said Ailish.

'Yes. Iggy came with me, of course. We'd been married for several years by then. We had the two girls, and Diarmuid was on the way. So there we were, at the top of the church, and who turned up but him.' Chrissie breathed out heavily. 'I hate to refer to him as your father, Ailish, but biologically speaking, that's what he was. His name was Manus Sheedy. Like I say, he was a farmer. Not only did he have a big farm of land, he had a wife and a tribe of kids. He's dead, but to the best of my knowledge some of his family are still there.

'He stood in front of me and offered his hand. I was so shocked I nearly took it too. Thankfully, I pulled myself together in time and declined the offer. "Sorry for your trouble, ma'am," he said, as though he'd never seen me before. "It's fifteen years too late for that," I said, "and if you don't make yourself scarce, I'll start talking about how you raped me when I was a child." Well, you've never seen a man scuttle out of a church so quickly. You'd have thought the place was on fire.'

'Fair play to you,' said Ailish. 'You were very young to take control of the situation like that. And at your mother's funeral too.'

'With everything that had gone on, I was an adult by the age of fifteen. I'd had no choice.'

'My late husband, Johnny, used to say that once you've grown up, you can't grow back down again,' said Katie. 'That seems to be true for all the girls who were sent to Carrigbrack.'

The pride with which she spoke about Johnny, and the love between Iggy and Chrissie, brought a rush of sadness to Ailish. It didn't feel appropriate, and she tried to will it away. 'This is an awkward question,' she said, 'but am I not a reminder of what Sheedy did to you?'

'Oh, Ailish, love, you can't talk like that.'

'I promise you,' said Iggy, 'for as long as I've known Chrissie, she's wanted to find you. You're not to blame for that man's crimes.'

'Do you know,' said Chrissie, 'I often think of Hackett's

Cross, and not in a melancholy way. It's spectacular around there, especially in the summer. I only wish I'd been allowed a proper childhood to enjoy it.'

Katie looked at her watch. 'Come on, missus,' she said to Beth, 'we ought to leave these people in peace for a couple of hours.'

'And we'd better ring Gary so we can pass on the news.'

Before they left, Beth took some photos. Ailish tried to mask her face with her hand, like the accused going into court. Why, on this day of all days, did she have to feel so awful? Afterwards, Iggy drifted away. He had calls to make, he said. Chrissie rose from her armchair and moved to the sofa beside Ailish. 'I want to show you around the house, and I have a million pictures you might like to see. But before I do ...'

Ailish took her hand. 'Is everything all right?'

'Everything's great with me. I'm on the mend, and my long-lost daughter is here.' She hesitated. 'I don't want to be a nuisance, but over the years I've developed a nose for unhappiness. Iggy says it's my greatest talent. There's something wrong, isn't there?'

Chapter 27

Gary

'Come in, come in,' said Katie. 'We're only just back ourselves. It's great you could drop over.'

Gary stepped into the warm hall and removed his overcoat. It was a typical January night, blustery with flecks of rain in the wind.

Katie had called from London. 'Gary, you are not going to believe this,' she'd said before outlining the information they'd received, and just like that, his search was almost complete. 'I'd better give you the bracelet belonging to Noreen's baby,' she'd added. 'You must have been Paul.' In a moment of giddy relief, he'd agreed to drive to her house and collect it. She'd explained that Ailish would be there, and he was cool with that. The idea of meeting someone who'd spent the first months of her life in the same place as him was appealing. He was excited, too; although she hadn't replied to his letter, he was almost certain he'd located the right Noreen.

To be honest, there was another reason for accepting the invitation. Embarrassing as it sounded, he could do with an hour of regular company. Straightforward, undemanding company. He'd taken one piece of advice from Frank and returned to therapy. He was seeing a counselling psychologist, a young guy who spoke a lot about tools and techniques and appropriate responses. Actually, he was pretty helpful, but when the only person you'd talked to in three days was charging by the hour, you'd got to wonder about your life.

That Gary didn't spend more time with his family wasn't a reflection on them. He was avoiding them because he wasn't sure how much to say. From the start, he'd worried they would consider him disloyal. He swore that when he met Noreen, they'd be first to know. Well, second. He'd have to tell Katie and Beth first. In the meantime, there was no point in stirring up unnecessary trouble. He'd had enough of that.

If there was one thing he had learnt from Black Iris, it was this: early fame meant you spent the rest of your days checking behind you. You worried constantly about being supplanted by the next generation. You fretted that the younger, hotter, more relevant guys were biting at your heels. Eventually, the day came when you saw that your fears had been premature, but by then you really were past it. Gary Winters, a man who'd once believed that every night needed nudity and epic drunkenness, was looking forward to a cup of tea with three women: one in her late sixties, another a grandmother and the third a lesbian. Hail! Hail! Rock 'n' Roll!

The women were drinking wine.

'I'd better not,' he said, refusing Katie's offer, 'what with the DUI laws being the way they are.'

She gave him an enquiring look.

'He means drink-driving laws,' explained Beth.

'You're back in Ireland, Gary,' said Katie, in the voice that always made him feel like a ten-year-old whose football had shattered the kitchen window. 'Will you have a cup of tea?'

Her house was like his parents' place: old-fashioned but not excessively so. There was a dusky-pink three-piece suite, a pine coffee table, an ageing television, a CD player, a standard lamp with a low-watt bulb and plants galore. Oh, and there were several photos of her late husband, including one of those early seventies wedding pictures where everyone looked pale and surprised. While he acknowledged that rating people on their physical appearance was wrong, any fair observer would say that Johnny Carroll had done well for himself.

Katie bustled about supplying snacks and drinks and offering snippets of conversation. Beth chatted away, droll one minute, earnest the next. Ailish was quiet. Knowing she was a Black Iris fan, Gary initially assumed she was tongue-tied by his presence. He quickly realised that he was kidding himself. She'd been through an extraordinary day. Her mind was elsewhere.

'I liked your message board post,' he said.

'How did you ...' she started before tapping herself on

the side of the head. 'Of course you guessed it was me. Thanks.'

'It's good to give people hope, y'know.'

'What's this about?' said Katie, as she sat down and placed a red box on the floor beside her.

'Last night,' said Ailish, 'I wrote a few lines on the message board to say I was about to meet my birth mother, and that it wouldn't have happened without your help. I didn't give my real name, but …'

'As soon as I saw it, I guessed,' said Gary, 'and then when Katie called from London, my hunch was confirmed.'

'That's lovely,' said Katie. 'Thank you, Ailish. With one thing and another, I haven't had much time for the message board lately.'

'I thought I'd let people know what was happening, because sometimes it feels like no one's making progress.' A smile danced across Ailish's face. 'And the truth is that some of us are.'

'Speaking of which,' said Katie, picking up the red box, 'I have baby Paul's bracelet in here.' For some seconds, she was quiet. Then she removed the lid from the box. 'Chrissie remembered Noreen and Paul a lot more clearly than I did. Her recollections jogged my memory.'

'Really?' said Gary.

'Yes. I can see her now. She wasn't particularly tall or dark, so you must have got your looks from your biological father. She got into a couple of scrapes in Carrigbrack, but then again, quite a few girls did.'

Katie took her notebook from the box. Gary was pleased to see she was using the cover he'd given her. Then she produced a thin piece of paper. She peered at it as though seeing it for the first time.

'She guards that box very carefully,' said Beth. 'She's got nuclear codes and all sorts in there.'

'Here we are,' said Katie. 'According to this, you were born on the seventh of August 1971.'

She passed the bracelet to him. Even though Gary had done nothing, he felt a sense of achievement. He was part of the inner circle; one of the people who had either found their birth mother or were just a step away. He couldn't remember his own children ever being small enough to wear such a tiny band. Chances were he hadn't paid sufficient attention. He'd been on the road when Clark and Sam were born. Angus's mother hadn't wanted him there ('You're only a glorified sperm donor' had been her exact phrase). And while physically he'd been present for Allegra's birth, mentally he'd been in the studio with the rest of the band.

His daughter was growing so quickly that Gary had been tempted to extend his stay in Los Angeles. The day before he'd left, she'd said, 'It's more fun when you're here.' He'd almost cartwheeled with delight. Then the truth had hit: it was a criticism not a compliment. He needed to spend more time with her.

During his three weeks in LA, he'd stumbled around giving vague answers about the band and what he was up to in Ireland. Although he'd managed to avoid Anton, he'd met up with Ray. He missed Ray and Liamo. 'We're firing ahead with our plans,' his old buddy had said. 'It's not too late to change your mind.' They'd talked about Shanna, they'd talked about Anton, but ... Gary realised that Katie had asked him a question. Beth had said something too.

'Sorry,' he said. 'What was that?'

'We were wondering what you're going to do now,' said Beth.

'Step up my efforts with Noreen, I suppose.'

There was a lull in the conversation. Katie's thoughts appeared to be elsewhere, while for once, Beth didn't have much to say. He guessed they were tired.

It was Ailish who spoke. 'This morning, when we were in the taxi, "Overboard" came on the radio. It was funny. Well, not funny exactly, but you know ...'

'Yeah, I do.' Gary was still holding the bracelet. He needed to find somewhere safe for it.

'I probably shouldn't ask, but is it true you're not going on tour with the band? I mean, that's what it said in the paper, only ... it wouldn't be the same without you.'

'That's my plan at the minute all right.'

'Is everything okay?' said Katie who appeared to have returned to the present. 'Beth and I had the feeling that something was bothering you.'

'Not that we want to pry,' added Beth, 'only we read about the tour, and we thought it was a shame you wouldn't be there.'

'But, like Beth says, we wouldn't want to be nosy.'

He could choose to say nothing. He could allow the story to emerge, drip by corrosive drip. Or he could go ahead and tell the truth. Talking wasn't the easiest option. It probably wasn't the wisest, either. But if he didn't tell them, they'd keep on wondering. They'd keep on asking. They were looking at him, faces upturned like birds waiting for a worm. Besides, learning about Noreen had put him in a reflective mood. And he owed Katie more than a cheap piece of leather.

First things first, though. He held up the bracelet. 'Would you have a bag I could put this in? Oh, and I've changed my mind. I'll have a glass of wine after all.'

Two minutes later, with the bracelet in a plastic bag and a glass of white in hand, Gary began a rarely told tale. There was no good way of telling it, and he'd have to edit along the way, but so be it.

'I need to go back almost four years,' he said. 'We were touring the US on the back of a mediocre album.'

'*Sands of Time*,' said Katie.

Jesus, she was something else. She must have memorised their entire back catalogue. She probably knew how the album had been rated, too: three stars from *Rolling Stone* and *NME*; a pathetic 4.2 out of ten from *Pitchfork*. Not that he could complain. For several years, they'd been trying to pass stones off as diamonds. They'd finally been found out.

'Yeah,' he said, 'even the title was crap. It made us sound like a metal band from 1985. The tour wasn't happy, either. Too many egos, too little energy. And most of the time, Anton was off his head. Up until then, wasted or not, he'd put on a show. It's that special front-man thing: even when we were in the world's dreariest city, he'd make the audience believe we were having the wildest time ever. Nobody could do intense like Anton. On that tour, he lost it. Sometimes, he forgot half the lyrics.'

'What was he taking?' asked Beth.

'Heroin.'

'Shit.'

'You said it. As you can imagine, it led to a hell of a lot of friction. Whatever else I've done, I've had the sense to avoid smack. You come from this city, you know its power to screw you up. For years, Anton had been the same. He was convinced it was a mistake he'd never make – and then he did.'

'What about the others?' said Katie.

'Liamo had fought his own battles with drink. By that stage, though, he was sober. Ray had always been a clean-living guy. He'd had a rough childhood, and out of the four of us, he probably had the greatest appreciation of what we'd achieved. What you've got to bear in mind is that we were surrounded by enablers. When you reach a certain level of success, there are lots of people there to tell you you're right – and that you can have whatever you want. It's a power thing. And, yeah, it's a money thing too.'

Gary stopped and took a long drink. Although in some ways his story was about wealth and fame, it was also pretty basic. That was something else he'd learnt: how basic most people were. And how a handful of decisions could shape your life.

'Anyhow,' he said, 'at some point, a woman drifted into our orbit. Shanna was her name. Shanna Ellis. She was a friend of one of the crew. And she was just … there. I'm probably making her sound like a groupie. Y'know, a girl who—'

'We know what a groupie is,' said Katie. 'I'm fairly sure they originated with my generation.'

Beth and Ailish smiled.

'Right,' he said. 'Anyway, Shanna wasn't like that. She wanted an adventure. She came from a well-to-do family in LA. Her father was – still is – a scriptwriter, and her mother's one of those underfed, overdressed types you meet everywhere. I won't pretend Shanna wasn't beautiful, because she was. She was a blonde, blue-eyed California girl. So far, so generic. But there was more to her. You get accustomed to everybody being jaded and blasé. Shanna was the opposite. She was an enthusiast.'

Beth swooped in. 'Did she do anything? Like, did she have a job?'

'No, not really. She was seeing America.'

Before Beth could say anything else, Katie gave her a gentle look that said, *Let the man tell his story, will you?*

Gary took another drink and continued. 'I'd split up with Posy, Allegra's mother, and I was on my own. And, well, it wasn't long before Shanna and I were together. I would've been happy for us to be properly together, but she was more laid-back about the relationship. Some nights she disappeared, which, of course, made her all the more appealing.'

He paused and drank the last of his wine. He was waltzing around the truth. When it came to Shanna, he always had.

'How old was she?' asked Beth.

'Twenty-three,' he replied, wishing the answer sounded less sleazy. 'So, yeah, she was a bit younger than me.' To be precise, twenty-one years younger, only slightly older than his eldest son. When Shanna had been born, Black Iris had already made the move to America. They'd already been adults. 'It was cool to see everything through the eyes of someone who hadn't seen it all before. The tour was a long one, filled with cities like Tulsa and Glendale and Newark; places I'd been to fifty times but still wouldn't recognise. She gave everything a different perspective. She was a reminder that I'd once loved being in the band. That every day had been a thrill. After I hooked up with Shanna, the tour became bearable, and, foolish as it sounds, I loved her for that.'

'Hold that thought,' said Katie. 'We need more wine.'

'I'll get it,' said Beth.

She returned a minute later with another bottle of Sauvignon Blanc and another question. 'You mentioned that Shanna sometimes disappeared. Where did she go?'

Gary put down his glass and pressed his fingers against his temples. 'Part of her appeal was her edge, if you know what I mean. She alluded to stuff in her background, like how at university she'd been part of a hard-core scene with a lot of drugs. Her stories were entertaining, though, and I didn't read much into them. I suppose I should have seen what was happening, but I didn't.'

'You haven't—'

'She was with Anton,' he said, picking up his glass. 'I wasn't enough for her. The problem was, Anton wasn't capable of having a proper relationship. The other problem was that his wife, who was back home in LA, was pregnant.'

Beth rolled her eyes. 'The poor woman.'

'How did you find out?' asked Katie.

'In the old-fashioned way. I walked in on them. After I got over the immediate shock, I called her all the names I could think of, which was quite a few. We were in Orlando – Mickey Mouse country – and that night on stage, the atmosphere was toxic. Nah, toxic doesn't do it justice. I'd happily have killed him. And yeah, I know that's a phrase everyone uses, only in this case it was true.'

'Was she … was Shanna taking drugs with Anton?'

'I assumed so. Later, it turned out I was wrong. In an odd way, it might have been better if she had been shooting up.'

Both Katie and Ailish frowned.

'Bear with me and you'll understand. I couldn't find her that night, but the following morning she found me. I'm not certain what I expected; some kind of apology maybe. What I knew was that I still wanted her and that I didn't think she should be fooling around with a married smackhead. She got all high and mighty, saying we'd had fun, but she was young and couldn't handle being tied down. Now, I can see what an idiot I was. I was trying to recapture my twenties, but in the safest possible way. An actual twenty-something was going to hanker after a different life. She wanted all the euphoria and the angst and the craziness. I'd had that, and I couldn't go back. I wanted a sanitised middle-aged version.'

He stopped and swallowed some wine. He could still see Shanna. She'd been wearing a bright green floral dress, a tiny thing that had barely covered the tops of her thighs. Her hair had been braided on top of her head, like an untidy milkmaid. The morning was sunny – they were in Florida, after all – and she'd appeared to shimmer in and out of the room.

He saw Anton too. Anton in his heyday, light brown hair flopping into his clear blue eyes. Anton with his disdain for mediocrity and his knack of turning humdrum days into adventures. Anton with the voice that soared over every venue and the strut that belied his suburban insecurities.

'I'll always regret what happened next,' said Gary. 'Always. But I felt as if I'd been taken for a fool, when in reality, she was the one being conned. I asked her if she knew Anton was married. "Yeah," she said, "except I'm not looking to become his wife. I'm looking for fun. Anyway, they have an open relationship." I couldn't believe she'd fallen for the corniest line in rock. So I told her. "That'll be news to Aimee," I said. "Especially as she's due to go into labour at any time." I could tell Shanna was surprised, but she pretended she was okay. "And the twins," I said, "poor

mites. Only two years old. What kind of childhood are they
going to have, huh? Not only is their father whacked out of
his skull, he's spent the last six months screwing anything
with a pulse." She asked what I meant, and I told her there'd
been at least three or four others like her on the tour.'

'Was that bit true?' asked Beth.

'Not as far as I'm aware. But I loved her, and she was
never going to love me. I felt the need to punish her. It was
clear she was grappling with what I'd said about Anton, so I
could have left it there. I was angry and humiliated, though,
and I kept on turning the knife.'

He went to take another drink, then noticed his glass was
empty. Katie refilled it.

'Thanks,' he said. 'So, I told Shanna she wasn't wanted
on the tour. She said I couldn't force her out if Anton liked
having her around. I pointed out that Anton had far more
reasons to be loyal to me than to her, and that all I had to
do was click my fingers and she'd be gone. By that stage, she
was fairly chastened, but I didn't stop. I told her that if she
had any heart or humanity, she'd run back home to Mommy
and Daddy in Beverly Hills.'

The more Gary spoke, the clearer his memories became.
He saw Shanna in sharp detail: the short green dress, the
messy blonde hair, the tears carving tracks through her
make-up. He'd wanted her to feel as low as he did. The
difference was, he'd been a twice-married father of four,
with decades of living behind him. She'd been a naïve kid.

A gorgeous, funny kid who should have gone on to have a great life. She should have been allowed to make mistakes.

'After that,' he said, 'I left. I had a tour bus to catch. We were moving on to Tampa. That was the last time I saw her. Well, no, that's not quite true.' He hesitated. 'Sorry, I need a minute.'

The silence was broken by Katie. 'You don't have to say anything else.'

'Nah, you should know the rest.' Gary's knee was jiggling. He tried to make it stop, but it had a mind of its own. 'We played the next couple of dates. Anton and I weren't speaking. There was no sign of Shanna. She was on my conscience, so I called her. When I didn't get an answer, I kept on calling. Don't ask me how, but I knew.'

Gary's right hand shook. This was hard.

'The last time I called, a cop answered. They'd found her body in a motel, one of the scummiest places in Orlando. She'd OD'd. The works were beside her. She'd been a user in the past, apparently, only she'd been clean for some time. She took a large dose, and when your body's no longer accustomed to the drug, that's what happens. It kills you.'

He wanted to add, *But the heroin didn't kill her, I did.*

All this time later, he could still feel the sweltering heat of the Florida morning, smell the bougainvillea, hear the hum of city traffic. He remembered how the initial flash of panic had morphed into a deeper sense of fear. Almost immediately, he'd realised that this wasn't something Frank or one of his flunkeys could magic away. There was no safe harbour. They might smooth over the cracks, but they couldn't bring someone back from the dead.

'Jesus, that's awful,' said Beth. 'What did you do?'

'The police asked if I'd identify her body. I agreed. Somehow, we got through it all without attracting any media attention. There were a few coded items online, some nudges and whispers, but nothing significant. Shanna's parents were devastated. Thankfully, they weren't aware of what I'd said to her. I planned on going to the funeral. They told me to stay away. They worried it'd become a circus.

'We blundered on to the end of the tour. It was only afterwards that it really, truly hit me, and I thought, I'm out. I can't do this any more. I never made it official. I didn't have to; we all knew we needed a break. I wondered if over time I'd be able to forgive Anton – not just for sleeping with Shanna but for souring everything by allowing his life to become such a mess. I also wondered if I'd be able to forgive myself. The answer, it seems, is no. I haven't spoken to him in more than three years. If anything, it's become harder to make peace. Cheesy as it sounds, I look at Allegra and I'm scared guys will treat her the same way.'

Katie crossed her legs. 'How's Anton these days?'

'As far as I know, he's good. It took him another couple of years, but everyone says he's clean and keen to begin working again.'

'And you're not?'

'It doesn't feel right. I can't pretend that Shanna never existed. I loved someone and I killed her.'

For most of the night, Ailish had said little. To begin with, Gary suspected she wasn't listening. Later, he noticed this wasn't true. She was drinking in every word but choosing not to interrupt. It was a rare gift, not speaking unless you had something to say.

Now she leant forward. 'You didn't.'

'Sorry?' he replied.

'You didn't kill her. Anton didn't either. Just because you treated her badly, it doesn't mean you were responsible for her death. I mean, you both abused your position and you're right to regret that. But she made bad decisions too. You didn't fill the syringe and stick it in her arm.'

'That's how it feels.'

'Well, if you don't mind me saying so, you're being a bit self-indulgent.' Ailish pushed her hair back from her face. She had a small face and large eyes, like a rare marsupial. Despite the wine, those eyes were focused. 'Sorry, that might have sounded harsh. I don't want to be harsh. But it seems to me that you've got into a bad way of thinking. We all do it. I'm worse than anyone.'

'I don't—' began Gary, part irritated, part fascinated.

'Answer me this: do you hate Anton?'

'No. I could never hate him. I had some of the best days of my life with the guy. We met when we were kids, and no matter what happened later, I'll always be glad we were friends.'

'Then you need to make your peace with him. I know it's easier to sort out other people's lives. I mean, you probably think I haven't a clue what I'm talking about. That I'm just a nobody from the back end of nowhere who can't understand how you feel. I do, though. Believe me, I know all about the stupid things we do to each other – and to ourselves. You're really talented, and you've brought a huge amount of joy to people's lives. You can't walk away because of one bad decision.'

Perhaps it was the alcohol, perhaps it was the release of telling his story, but Gary was touched by the force of her words. 'I hear you,' he said.

She nodded. 'You want to know what happened in my house the other day? And, Katie and Beth, please forgive me for not telling you before, but I was ashamed. My husband hit my son, Stevie, so hard he knocked him out.'

'Oh, Ailish, love,' said Katie, 'please don't be ashamed.'

'Well, I am. Today should have been brilliant. It should have been about Chrissie, this fantastic woman who's been through so much but managed to rise above it all. Instead, I spent an hour sobbing on her shoulder and telling her what a mess I've made of everything. Afterwards, I realised something: I hate Keith. I don't think I can ever stop hating him. But I'm too much of a coward to do anything about it.'

Chapter 28

Katie

Katie paced the kitchen, willing Beth to get up. She was pleased her niece had decided to take another day off work. They had a lot to talk about. Unfortunately, Beth slept like an elderly cat, and even though it was almost midday, she remained in bed. Ailish and Gary had left a couple of hours earlier. Ailish had spent the night in the spare room, and he'd slept on the sofa. 'I've bunked down in far worse places,' he'd said. She didn't doubt him.

What a night.

Katie couldn't stop thinking about what both of them had said. She couldn't decide which had shocked her more. Despite knowing what Keith was capable of, she was taken aback by the fact that he'd knocked his son to the ground yet wanted to carry on as if nothing had changed. The man must have the hardest neck in Ireland. She worried about Ailish's safety. She'd said as much, but Ailish had shrugged off her concerns. No matter that she'd stopped making excuses for him, she was still living under the same roof, while Stevie had moved out.

In the end, Katie had asked her directly. 'Does Keith hit you?'

'Yes,' she'd replied, 'but never in the way he assaulted Stevie. He's never broken a bone or punched my face.'

Oh, Ailish.

Then there was Gary. It occurred to Katie that somewhere along the line, she'd stopped seeing him as a rock star and had been lulled into thinking of him as a regular person. Now, she was forced to re-evaluate. In reality, he had very little in common with her or anyone she knew. And yet Ailish had spoken to him as if he was a friend in need of robust advice. What was more, he'd listened.

While Katie waited for Beth, there were things she could do. Well, one thing in particular. Her hand hovered over her phone. It was early in Boston. She would catch Brandon before he started work. Then she decided she'd do it later. The snag was, she'd been saying that for days.

She turned on the radio. People were complaining about bad driving, poor internet access and the price of beef. She turned it off and did another loop of the kitchen.

She was looking forward to Beth's take on Gary and Ailish. They hadn't had the chance to speak the night before. Not only had they both been mangled with tiredness, they'd been scared their words would be overheard. All they'd managed were a few furtive whispers, like schoolgirls after lights-out.

She wanted to talk about Chrissie, too. Seeing her again had brought back more memories of Carrigbrack. She recalled how the place had stripped beautiful young women of their lustre, making them grey and crumpled before their time. Despite everything, including her illness, Chrissie still shone. How had she done it? Katie could no more answer that question than she could explain why Ailish stayed with her violent oaf of a husband or why Gary was determined to abandon what he loved. Why should she understand others when half of the time she couldn't understand herself?

When this was all over, and they'd distributed as many bracelets as possible, Katie wondered if she would remain close to Beth. Margo's jibe about not having children had lodged in her mind. Over the months, Beth had become a surrogate daughter. Katie had grown accustomed to her clutter, her obsessions and complaints. To unfamiliar music on the radio, Netflix on the TV and a fridge full of exotic juices. She'd begun to like Thai food, horror films and strong coffee. She still missed Johnny, but her grief was less of a stabbing pain, more of a blunt ache.

She reminded herself that the arrangement with Beth was temporary. Her niece would move on, and she had to be prepared for that.

It didn't end there. Gary, Ailish, Brandon and the rest wouldn't be part of her life indefinitely. They would drift away, and she would miss them. Already, the bracelet box was looking depleted. Briefly, she'd considered caving in and broadening the list of those they were trying to help. But no, that would be a mistake.

Although she should have spoken to her friends about the task, something kept stopping her. The easy explanation was that she'd been too busy. The truth, as always, was more complex: the bracelets were her secret, and she'd never been one for sharing secrets.

When Beth finally surfaced, still in her navy dressing gown, hair straggling in every direction, Katie was peeling the potatoes for dinner. There was no harm in being organised.

'You're a terrible woman,' said Beth. 'Could you not have had a lie-in?'

Katie filled the saucepan with water and threw the peelings into the brown bin. 'I had to say goodbye to our guests. To tell you the truth, though, I couldn't sleep anyway. There was too much going on in my head.'

'That I can understand. Sit down there, and I'll make us a coffee.'

'So,' said Katie.

'So …'

'So, where do you want to start?'

'I don't know,' said Beth, as she put two slices of bread into the toaster. 'I was thinking of Ailish. What a mad day. There she was, finally meeting Chrissie, all the while knowing that Keith was back home resenting her happiness. Imagine hitting your own son so hard he ended up in hospital? I hope she's safe,'

'Me too. What did you make of Gary?'

'No wonder he's a bit strange. That's one bleak story.'

'Yes,' said Katie, 'only if you ask me, Ailish was right. He's doing himself no favours by staying over here and brooding about what he and Anton should have done differently.'

'Wasn't Ailish something else? She said far more than I was prepared to. And you know what? Fair play to her.'

Katie poured milk into her coffee. 'I don't think she'd have told us about Keith if Gary hadn't opened up first.'

'Yeah, how bizarre for her. She meets one of her heroes and practically the first thing he says is, "Actually, I killed a woman." It'd be like if you met – who did you idolise growing up? Perry Como? Frank Sinatra? – and that was how the conversation started.'

Katie snorted. 'Beth Linnane! How old do you think I am?'

'Sorry,' said Beth as she buttered her toast. 'I obviously got the wrong era. But you know what I mean.'

'I do.'

'Besides, I know how old you are. You're seventy in March.'

'How …?'

'Mam asked if you'd like a party.'

'Lord Almighty, no.'

Beth laughed. 'I guessed that'd be the answer. You'd want to be careful, or you'll end up with a monster of a cake and a marquee in the back garden.'

'What brought that on?' asked Katie. There were several possibilities. Margo might be feeling guilty about what she'd said at Christmas. If so, the offer could be an attempt to

salve her conscience. Or she might be looking for an excuse
to show off her lovely house and cute grandchildren. Or she
might be genuine in her desire to mark her sister's birthday.
It was possible the latter was true. Possible but unlikely.
Stop it, Katie thought. You're being mean-spirited. Why
can't you see the offer as a kind one?

'I haven't a notion why she wants a big do,' said Beth.
'You can relax, though. I'll tell her you don't want any fuss.'

'Thanks. If it helps, you can say I think it would be too
soon after Johnny's death.' Katie had never been one for
parties. She preferred to keep everything low-key. It was one
of the reasons she'd taken to Dublin. After Danganstown,
where everybody knew everything about you, and had an
opinion on where you were going wrong, she treasured the
anonymity of the city.

Beth sipped her coffee. 'Are you all right?' she asked.
'You're very thoughtful.'

'There's plenty to think about.'

'Including Linda and Eddie?'

'Yes.'

'Why don't you ring Brandon?'

Katie looked at her watch. 'It's too late. He'll be at work.'

'He's not a teenager in a minimum-wage job. I'm sure
he's allowed personal calls. If he's not interested, that's his
lookout. He's had lots of time to think it all through. And
you've put in a huge amount of work.'

Although it hurt Katie to think that Brandon might not
want to meet his twin, the choice was his to make. He had

a supportive wife and loving parents, and maybe they were enough. Still, Beth was right. He was entitled to know what she'd learnt. She counted to ten, then dialled his number. He answered almost immediately.

For a minute, they exchanged stilted greetings. Then, steeling herself for rejection, Katie began. 'We didn't get off to the best of starts, and I blame myself for that. But I've found out a little more about your brother, and while it's up to you ... obviously it's up to you ... I think it might be possible to track him down.'

There was a delay before Brandon replied, not a transatlantic phone line delay, but one that suggested he was weighing up his response. She feared he'd get angry. After all, she'd gone ahead and made enquiries about his family without seeking permission. She'd interfered when she should have let matters rest.

To her surprise, he sounded conciliatory. Conciliatory and hesitant. 'You're okay,' he said. 'I shouldn't have got annoyed with you. It's just that ... well, this has all become more complicated than I wanted or expected. But ...'

His words came to a halt, leaving Katie to fill the silence.

'If you'd like to discuss it with Robyn,' she said, 'you can call me back. Or you can take a few days. I don't want to put any pressure on you. Take as much time as you like.'

'No. You've gone to the trouble of finding out more about Eddie and Linda. The least I can do is listen. Robyn ...'

Again, his sentence ran dry, and Katie wondered what he'd been about to say.

'If you're sure,' she said.

'I'm sure.'

Relief washed over her. She gave a thumbs-up to Beth. 'It's a long story,' she said, 'but when I was working in Carrigbrack, there was a young nun called Sister Eunice ...'

Chapter 29

Then, Patricia

At five months old, Paul was a solid little fellow, fascinated by the world around him. Although the nuns insisted that 'ma-ma-ma' was meaningless babble, Patricia was convinced he was talking to her. What did they know? Not that she challenged them. As part of the campaign to keep her son, she continued to obey the rules and behave like a responsible person. She'd even broken up a fight between two girls who'd been kicking and hair-pulling after one had claimed the other's baby had a plain head. Winnie would have laughed at how compliant she'd become. It was six months since Winnie's disappearance, and Patricia still missed her. The grass had grown over Diane's grave. It was unmarked and uncared for.

Not only had Patricia become more dutiful, she took every opportunity to emphasise Paul's superiority. Surely, having the brightest, healthiest baby must count for something? And yes, she was biased, but even Sister Agnes admitted he was a well-behaved child. Sabina had no such generosity. More than once, she'd remarked on his dark hair and asked if his father might be foreign. She said the word with studied distaste.

Often, Patricia would lapse into a daydream where, freed from Carrigbrack, she went to work while Paul stayed with a friendly – yet affordable – childminder. They lived in a lovely bright flat, and in the evenings, they played and read stories. After a while, she met a man who was unfazed by her already being a mother. He loved Paul as much as she did, and they became a proper family. Then she'd snap out of her trance. She had to be sensible. If she was going to hold on to her boy, she needed more than a romantic fantasy. She needed a practical plan. And that was what she was trying to put together.

One dank evening in late January, she made her way to the nursery. At this time of year, the laundry was a prized workplace. Unlike most of Carrigbrack's other residents, the women there enjoyed a few hours of warmth. The main building was a draughty old place, with more holes than a colander. At night, you could see your breath, and in the mornings, there were slivers of ice on the insides of the windows.

That Paul wasn't in his cot didn't worry her. She was late, and one of the women who worked in the nursery was probably giving him his bath. Patricia would find them and take over. Bathtime was her favourite part of the day.

She walked to the far side of the room, where the babies, some keener than others, were having their evening wash. Each was in a neat tin tub. One of the girls looked up then quickly glanced away.

'Do you know where Paul is?' asked Patricia. 'I can't see him.'

The girl didn't reply. Nor did any of the others. They stood in line, each as mute as the next. A baby squealed. Another splashed with pleasure. Paul liked splashing.

'Has anyone seen Paul?' she asked again.

The silence continued.

She spotted Sister Eunice walking towards her, head bowed, hands clasped as if at prayer.

Eunice raised her face. 'Sister Agnes will be along in a minute.'

'What's wrong?' asked Patricia, heart pumping like a steam engine. 'Has something happened to him?'

'Sister Agnes will explain.'

A realisation crept over her. 'Is he gone?'

Eunice's cheek twitched. Otherwise, she was impassive. 'Yes.'

'That can't be right. I didn't give my permission. You've got to bring him back. You've got to tell whoever took him that there's been a mistake.'

'I'm afraid—'

Patricia grabbed Eunice by the shoulders. 'I don't want to hear any gobbledygook about the rules. Paul is my son, and I didn't agree to give him away.' By now, her voice had risen to its highest pitch. A baby began to cry. 'How could you let this happen? I thought you were my friend.'

The young nun said nothing.

Patricia was about to speak again when Agnes came pounding in, skirt rustling, face the colour of smashed plums.

'What's all this commotion about?' she said. 'Patricia, let go of Sister Eunice this minute.'

Patricia didn't move.

'I'm ordering you to let go of Sister Eunice. Do you understand me?'

She removed her hands from Eunice's shoulders then took a step towards Agnes. 'Did you steal my baby?'

'Of course not. If you'll accompany me to the office, we can talk about this without an audience.'

'If you didn't steal him, where is he?'

'Nobody stole anything. The child has gone to his permanent home.'

Patricia felt as if the ground had given way beneath her and she was falling. Down, down, down she went, through the floor, through the basement and on to the centre of the earth.

'Why my son?' she said. 'There are children here whose mothers would be happy to see them go. And, let's be straight, there are women here who couldn't be trusted with a cat, not to mind a child. Why not take one of their babies?'

'That's a lie,' shouted one of the girls.

'Take that back, you snobby cow,' said another.

Patricia ignored them. 'You haven't answered my question.'

Agnes grabbed her arm and shoved her towards the door. 'Because I won't entertain such nonsense. You're coming with me. We can discuss the child's adoption in my office.'

'Don't call him "the child". He has a name. His name is Paul.'

'Very well. We'll discuss Paul's adoption in the office.'

As they left the nursery, a grumble of voices behind them, Patricia noticed that Eunice was crying. Good. Despite her honeyed words, she was no better than the rest. She could cry for the next six months for all Patricia cared. She was finding it hard to think. She'd played Agnes's game. She'd followed all the rules. This wasn't supposed to happen. They couldn't just take Paul, could they?

In the office, Agnes made the unusual move of allowing her to sit down. Almost immediately, she began speaking. Her words were careful yet fluent, and Patricia suspected she had rehearsed them.

'Paul went to his new home this afternoon. Let me assure you that it's a very fine home with a lovely Catholic couple. Not only are they people of good character, they're comfortably off and can give him the best possible start in life. They have two other children, who are looking forward to meeting their brother.'

'He's not their brother. He belongs to me.'

'That's where you're wrong. He was conceived in

unfortunate circumstances, and we rescued him. He'll have the same advantages as any legitimate child.'

Patricia attempted to speak, but her throat was paper dry, and the words wouldn't come.

Agnes continued. 'When will you realise that this isn't about you? It's the baby who matters. He deserves better than a woman who committed adultery. When your time comes, you can leave here and begin again. You're only twenty years old. If you can stay quiet about your past shame, there's every chance you'll find a husband. Then, God willing, you can have other children. Paul will be just a distant memory.'

Patricia found her voice. 'No, he won't. I want him back. I was supposed to sign a form giving my permission for his adoption. I never saw a form and I certainly didn't sign one.'

'You'd become too close to him. That's never a positive development. I consulted your parents. They said to do whatever I felt was best.'

'We're not living in the Middle Ages. I have rights. I agreed to nothing and I want my son back.'

'Please don't give me any fraudulent modern ideas about rights. What are you proposing to do: call the guards and tell them your illegitimate child has been taken in by a loving family?'

'But—'

Agnes fluttered her hands. 'But nothing. Your mother and father sent you here after you'd disgraced yourself. I asked for their guidance on Paul's care, and they made a wise decision.'

With every second that passed, Patricia grew more scared. She might as well have no voice. What she valued most had been taken, and she had no power to change that. There was nobody on her side. 'Please, Sister Agnes, I could give him everything he needs. I promise you, nobody else will love him as much as I do.'

'What does a girl like you know about love? Now, I've said all I intend to say. Get up and go to your dormitory. Mind you, I can't imagine the penitents you so grievously insulted will have much of a welcome for you.'

'I didn't mean what I said. I was upset, that's all.'

'Well, you'd better apologise to them. Pride is a terrible sin and it's one of your deepest failings. Tomorrow, you'll be excused from your duties in the laundry. I want you to spend the day in silent prayer and reflection. You've got a lot to learn about humility.'

'Why didn't you allow me to say goodbye? What would have been wrong with letting me give him one more kiss?'

Agnes rose from her chair. 'You're too immature to understand now, but with the grace of God, you'll come to your senses. Believe me, one day you'll be grateful for the guidance and support you've received here.'

As the weeks went by, everything became more difficult. Sometimes, Patricia missed Paul so much she found it hard to breathe. She worried that he missed her. She worried that the new people wouldn't know what he liked. How would they know that he enjoyed lying on his tummy? How would they know what made him giggle and what made him cross?

She could have told them, if only she'd been asked.

He was constantly on her mind. She would think she was coping, then out of nowhere she'd be ambushed by longing for him, for his gorgeous smell and his small, squishy body. It was as if part of her had been amputated. She'd still been breastfeeding, and for a while the milk continued to build up in her breasts. The pain was raw, like a physical manifestation of the torment in her head.

She was a disaster at work, scorching holes in sheets and putting a red towel in a white wash. She refused to go to the nursery. Even the thought of the other babies was upsetting. Sister Faustina yelled at her, but what did she care? For months, she'd obeyed every rule, and it hadn't made a whit of difference.

Food tasted peculiar. She would chew and chew, but nothing cleared her throat. Her legs were heavy, her brain filled with ragged, incomplete thoughts. She wished she could slip into a deep, dreamless sleep, but sleep eluded her. On the worst days, she prayed her heart would stop.

The others hadn't forgiven her outburst in the nursery. The one person who wasn't cool towards her was poor Nancy, who still credited her with saving her baby's life. Although her parents wrote, Patricia threw away the letters without reading them. She had no interest in their catalogue of the ill and the dying, still less in their 'whatever you say, say nothing' approach to Paul.

Frequently, she thought about escaping. One afternoon, she stood near a window at the front of the building. An aeroplane ploughed a furrow through the sky. Assuming it was bound for America, she imagined being on board. Then reality hit. Even if she managed to get beyond Carrigbrack's walls, she had nowhere to go and no one to support her. Her friends must have wondered about her disappearance, but it had been almost a year since she'd seen them. She doubted any of them would be able to help.

She didn't hear Eunice sidle up behind her. They hadn't spoken since the day Paul was taken. They went to the bathroom where once they'd hidden with Winnie. As before, they sat on the floor.

'I don't want your excuses,' said Patricia. 'You could have warned me they were about to take him, only you decided not to.'

Eunice's brow crinkled. 'Sister Agnes instructed me to remain quiet, and I've got to try and be obedient. I'm not sure if you can understand that.'

'What I understand is that you could have behaved like a human being, and you chose not to.'

'I'm very sorry. I wish I'd told you.'

'Well, that's no good to me or to Paul.' Patricia attempted to stand up. Her legs felt like they were encased in concrete. 'There's no point in having this discussion. What's done is done.'

'Please stay,' said Eunice, 'just for a moment. I'm concerned about you. You don't speak to anybody.'

'What's there to say?'

'You can talk about Paul.'

'It's best if I don't.'

'Why?'

'Because I'll only start to cry. You don't get it, do you? He loved me but he won't remember me. He'll love other people and he'll never know about me. He won't know how much I cared about him.'

'You don't know that.'

'Yes, I do. He'll have a new name and a new life. Maybe the people who took him won't tell him he was adopted.'

'That would be wrong,' said Eunice, her voice low.

'That doesn't make any difference. It's what happens.' At last, Patricia got to her feet. 'I'm sorry. Like I say, I'm not able to talk about it. I've got work to do. I think you're a good person, Eunice. If you want my advice, though, you'll leave this place before it hardens you any further.'

As she left, the truth slammed into her. Paul wasn't coming back. It was unlikely she would ever see him again. She dropped to her knees, lay down on the floor of the dormitory and howled with pain.

Chapter 30

Gary

Gary hesitated before leaving the car. It was three weeks since he'd received the bracelet, more than a month since he'd sent his letter, and he'd yet to hear from Noreen. He'd considered writing again, then decided that visiting would be smarter. If he turned up, she'd have to talk to him, wouldn't she?

So here he was, parked outside a suburban Galway house, chest tight, head filled with questions. He hadn't told anyone about his journey. Katie wouldn't approve, that was for sure.

He spoke to her all the time. He'd also stayed in touch with Ailish. Well, it was just the occasional text message really. Initially, he'd been stunned by the way she'd confronted him, but the more time passed, the more he admired how candid she'd been. He also gleaned hope from her reunion with Chrissie. What he couldn't understand was why she stayed with a man who assaulted and bullied her. The guy deserved to be shown the door. As she said herself, though, other people's lives were always easier to fix.

The morning after his confession, Gary had regretted how much he'd said. While Katie's immediate reaction had been mild, sympathetic even, he was convinced that would change. She would consider the seedy circumstances in which a young life had ended, and relations would cool. What actually happened was that she badgered him to call Anton. 'Even if you don't stay with the band, you ought to talk,' she'd said. 'You can't bring Shanna back, but you can resurrect your friendship.' Then she'd pledged that if he did tour with Black Iris, she'd go and see them. 'Don't tell me I'm too old, either. I've looked it up: I'm the same age as Bruce Springsteen and six years younger than Mick Jagger. And if you'll forgive me for saying so, I'm in much better shape than Mick.'

She cracked him up, that woman.

He could never have imagined that talking to Katie, Beth and Ailish would assist him, but somehow their conversation had cleared his mind. Or maybe it had helped to crystallise the ragtag thoughts already there. One thing was certain: he couldn't spend the rest of his life hiding away in Wicklow, compiling lists of the mistakes he'd made.

He'd considered attempting to join another band, but figured he was too old. What else was there? Writing? Production? He'd played around with both, but when it came to music, he was a collaborative sort of guy; he wasn't equipped to work on his own or be the boss. He had no other skills, and one year of a UCD arts degree hardly counted as a qualification.

Number 19 Collins Drive was coated in tired pebble-dash. Its garden was bare, its door in need of a coat of paint. The woman who answered that door had shoulder-length brown hair threaded with white. There were dark half-moons beneath her eyes and drawstring lines around her mouth. She was an old sixty-seven.

Although Gary had prepared a speech, his words were garbled. Her face said little, but she didn't turn him away. She confirmed that she was Noreen O'Callaghan, formerly Nestor, and that she'd received his letter. There was no sense that she was greeting a long-lost son – or that she was aware of his fame.

Confused, he made another attempt at his introduction. 'So I suppose,' he said finally, 'I've been wondering if you're my birth mother.'

'You'd better come in,' she replied. There was a croak in her voice, as if it had been a while since she'd spoken.

'I don't want to interrupt. I can come back, if you'd prefer.'

'No, not at all. You're here now.'

Gary followed her into the hall. He carried the bracelet in a paper bag.

The house was neat but faded. There were few personal touches and no photographs. He sat on a sagging brown sofa while she rummaged through a sideboard. In the 1980s, his parents had owned a similar model. What was she searching for? An old document that proved the link between them? A black-and-white photo? Eventually, she located a slim beige folder and sat down.

'I should have replied to you,' she said. 'I was taken aback by your letter and I didn't know what to say.' She removed a newspaper cutting from the folder and passed it to him. He put on his glasses. From the sports pages of a local freesheet, the article told him that a man called Fergus Keating had become captain of a golf club. The article was accompanied by a picture of a beaming Fergus. His pink V-neck sweater matched his round face. Beside him was a starched blonde in a white jacket and heavy gold jewellery. Gary looked from the photo to Noreen and back to the photo. Her blue-veined hands were shaking.

'That's my son,' she said. 'I called him Paul, but he's Fergus now. He lives about twenty miles away.'

'I see.' Gary handed back the cutting.

'He contacted me ten years ago. I haven't seen him in seven – no, eight – years. I've rung a few times, but he doesn't reply. If he doesn't want to see me again, that's all right. But I'd like to meet his children. No doubt he grew up dreaming that his biological mother was exciting or glamorous. And as you can see, I'm neither.' She glanced down at her grey polyester skirt and matted brown slippers. 'I'm sorry you've had a wasted journey. You seem like a nice man, and I wish I was your birth mother. But you've got the wrong woman.'

This was no artful stonewalling. Noreen was telling the

truth. Gary's disappointment was joined by a sense that he was intruding on her grief.

'No, I'm sorry for making a nuisance of myself,' he said. 'And I'm sorry things didn't work out with your son. I gather it's not uncommon. Sometimes, people just need to get the answers to their questions, and then they disappear again.'

'It's hard, though, when you've built up your hopes, and your child decides you're not enough.' She handed him a blurred picture of a young woman with large eyes and a shy smile. 'That was me, a couple of years after I'd left Carrigbrack.'

'It's a lovely photo.' He took the baby bracelet from the bag and explained the story behind it. 'It's yours if you want it.'

'Thank you. I'd like that. I don't have many mementos. When my time comes, I'll leave no trace at all.' She patted her cheeks. 'Oh, what am I like? Please pay no heed.' She put the bracelet on a small table beside her. 'I remember Katie, the nurse you're talking about. She was a similar age to many of the mothers, so it must have been hard for her. She always looked like she was under a lot of pressure.'

Gary steered the conversation around to the question that had been bothering him. 'And your husband? Is he still alive?'

'As far as I know, he's in England. We haven't seen each other in more than forty years. We never divorced, mind. It wasn't possible in those days.'

He moved slightly, prompting a loud creak from the sofa. 'My apologies, Noreen. I'm asking questions that aren't mine to ask. I should learn to keep my nose out of what doesn't concern me.'

'You're grand. I didn't tell him about Paul or Carrigbrack, you see. And then, well … I wasn't easy to live with. I don't think any of us ever left that home behind. I used to dream about it all the time. In the end, I decided to confide in him and … he didn't take the news well. He said he'd never be able to trust me again, that I was a fraud and he was entitled to an annulment. After that, he disappeared. It's hard to fathom today, but that was how things were. Most folks would have said it was my own fault, that I should have confessed before we got married. Thankfully, we didn't have any children of our own.'

Her words were all the more powerful because she spoke in such a quiet, matter-of-fact way. Not that long ago, Gary had read something about the secrets of one generation becoming the traumas of the next. In truth, the pain was still being borne by the women whose children had been taken. The women who hadn't been allowed to speak. As a youngster, he'd been scornful of people like Noreen. They were quiet, unassuming, anxious not to take up too much space. They moved lightly through life, wearing dowdy clothes and becoming old before their time. Their default position was apologetic. He'd never paused to think about the forces that had made them that way.

He asked what she knew about the other young mothers. Perhaps she might have information that could point him in the right direction. She said her memories weren't reliable.

Besides, in most cases she'd only known the women by their pseudonyms.

She took back the photo and smiled. Her face lifted, and the young woman in the picture came to life again.

'Please stay for a cup of tea,' she said. 'I don't have cake or anything fancy, but I have a few biscuits.'

Gary agreed. She didn't, he suspected, get many visitors. There was something gentle, almost other-worldly, about her. His mother, Lillian, would have called her a lady.

He accompanied her to the kitchen, which looked as though it hadn't been updated since the 1970s.

'I like your tattoos,' she said, as she poured milk into a china jug. 'Did they hurt?'

'Yes, to be honest. I was young, though. I'm not sure I'd be able to handle the pain these days.'

'You don't strike me as a man who plays golf.'

Gary smiled. 'You're spot on. It wouldn't exactly be my thing.'

'And I'd say you'd spent a while in America, would I be right?'

'You would.'

'What do you do in Wicklow, if you don't mind me asking?'

'That,' he said, 'is a good question.'

It was only after he'd left that Gary was able to digest the implications of their conversation. He parked near the harbour and walked along the riverbank. Beside him, the water surged and roared. He'd been convinced that Noreen was the one. He'd thought the same about Tina, Gráinne, Olivia and Edel. In every case, he'd been wrong. 'I wish I was your birth mother,' she'd said. He wished he was her son. He should have told her that.

Fuck you, Fergus, he thought. May your next round be fifty over par.

Then again, he wasn't best placed to throw stones. How many times had his parents met Allegra? Nine or ten, at most. The figures for his sons weren't much better.

He paused to assess his options. On the opposite bank, a haughty black bird, a cormorant perhaps, took up position on the roof of a stone building. Beside him, he noticed a yellow lifebuoy and a contact number for the Samaritans. Such was the power of the river, he could see why the desperate would come here. A step too close, and – *whoosh* – even the strongest swimmer would be swept away.

He had reached a dead end and he didn't know what to do. He could go back to Katie and see if there were other possibilities. If he hadn't been born in July or August '71, when had he arrived? He remembered her saying there'd been no male births in September, so maybe he should try October. Or June. These were long shots, though, and he didn't want to spend another year scouring records and writing speculative letters. Part of him clung to the belief that Gráinne had been the right woman after all. She'd rejected his approach, however, and he was powerless to do anything about it.

He was missing something – but what? All the old questions returned: why had there been an extra layer of secrecy about his birth? Why had his parents been reluctant to tell the truth?

And if he wasn't Paul, who was he?

Chapter 31

Ailish

When Gary called, Ailish was cleaning the Dolmen Suite. Her new phone had a more sober ringtone, and Stevie wasn't around to change it. She tried not to sound flustered. She imagined the conversation with her colleagues: 'Mmm, it was a regular day. The towels in Number 25 were streaked with fake tan. The hoover went on the blink. Oh, and the bass player in Black Iris rang for a chat.'

It turned out that Noreen wasn't his birth mother, and his background remained a mystery.

'Anyhow,' he said, 'the reason I'm calling is to let you know that I took your advice. I had a word with our manager, Frank. And he told me that while they'd approached a different bass player, the arrangement's a loose one.'

'The door's still open for you, then?'

'Uh huh.'

'So you're going on tour after all?'

'If they'll have me, I guess I am.' There was a lightness in his voice that suggested he'd surprised himself.

Ailish fell back on the newly made bed. 'I'll have to go and see you.'

He laughed. 'I'd say I'll be able to find a spare ticket. I haven't spoken to Anton yet, mind. But I will.'

He didn't add, *If I can make a difficult call, so can you.* He was too clever for that. It was what he meant, though. Three weeks on from that strange night in Katie's house, and Ailish still cringed at how open she'd been. The one thing that tempered her embarrassment was the knowledge that Gary had said far more.

She asked what he was going to do about his birth mother. He said he wasn't sure and that he might have to put his search on hold. She wished him luck. He told her to take care.

That was what everyone said: 'Take care of yourself.' Despite everything, Ailish remained in the house with Keith, while Stevie stayed with his sister. If she said little, her husband said less. Apart from the occasional cranky comment about work, he was silent. She continued to sleep in the girls' room. Both knew the situation couldn't continue. Neither was willing to make the first move.

Every day was a struggle. In books and films, people made decisions, then followed through. Her life wasn't like that. A step forward was immediately followed by two steps back. It wasn't just that she was scared. Ending her marriage would feel like discarding a large part of her life.

She thought about the advice she'd always given others. Persevere, she'd said. Play the hand you've been dealt. Wasn't that what she should do? Then her thoughts would flip, and she'd be disgusted by her cowardice.

She was going to London again soon to meet her half-sisters and brother. Despite her protestations, Chrissie and Iggy had bought the ticket. When Chrissie was feeling stronger, she planned on coming to Ireland to see her grandchildren. Although she hadn't said, 'I trust Keith will be gone by then,' this was what she wanted.

Oh, Ailish knew what everyone thought of her. She was too accommodating. Too timid. She was convinced that Beth considered her a hopeless case. Beth was gutsy. All the girls were these days.

No sooner had she said goodbye to Gary than her phone rang again. The number was local but not familiar.

'Mrs Dwan?' said a careful voice. 'It's Sorcha Hession here, the principal at St Ursula's. Have you got a few minutes?'

Every part of Ailish's body tightened. She rose from the bed. 'Is everything okay? Is Stevie okay?'

'The honest answer is yes and no. There's no cause for alarm, but we'd noticed that Stevie had been out of sorts in recent weeks. A couple of his teachers had mentioned it to me. And then this afternoon there was an incident with another boy. Some name-calling got out of hand and … well, there was an altercation and—'

Oh Jesus. 'Was he hurt?'

'No, he's fine. The fight was broken up before any damage was done.'

'What was it about?'

'As far as I'm aware, the other boy was giving Stevie a hard time about the fact that he's not living at home.'

Oh hell. 'I see.'

'I took the opportunity to have a chat with Stevie. I try not to pry; however, if there's a sudden deterioration in a student's performance or behaviour, we need to know what's behind it. He told me about the, er, situation.'

Ailish pictured Mrs – or was it Ms? – Hession. They were completely different, these modern teachers. The grey conformity of Ailish's youth had been replaced by beads and bangles and uplifting speeches. 'What did he say to you?' she asked.

The principal ran through what Stevie had told her, which was almost everything, including the fact that Keith had knocked him out. Hearing it from the mouth of another made Ailish want to crawl under the bed.

'Obviously,' continued Mrs Hession, 'I don't want to make a sensitive situation worse, but I do have a duty of care to my students. The days when we could look the other way while young people suffered are gone.'

'I appreciate that.'

There was a slight pause before the teacher spoke again. 'This is awkward, Mrs Dwan. What you've got to understand is that I'm not talking simply about a change in attitudes. There are child protection laws, and we have to follow

them. If I suspect one of our students is in danger, I must
intervene. Child welfare is paramount.'

Ailish, who'd been walking around the room, came to an
abrupt halt. Was the woman suggesting she wasn't fit to take
care of Stevie? 'Do you mean you might tell the guards?' she
said. 'I never thought ... Please don't do that. I promise I'll
sort it out. I promise.'

'I know you have a full-time job. I was wondering, however,
if you and I could have a proper chat. Stevie is one of our
brightest students, and I'm worried that if his circumstances
don't improve, his results won't match his capabilities. You
don't need me to tell you that this is an extremely important
year. I don't want to see his opportunities drifting away.'

Ailish wasn't certain the words were intended as a
reprimand, but for a moment, they hung there, a reminder
of her failures. 'I'm not a bad mother,' she said.

'I'm not saying you are. I'm not blaming you at all.
Frankly, I'm concerned for your welfare too.'

'I can be with you in half an hour, if that's all right.'

'That would be good.'

'And Stevie?'

'He's in the staffroom. I didn't think he should return
to class; however, there wasn't anywhere else for him to go.'

Ailish couldn't think clearly. Her limbs moved, but only
because they knew what to do. With her free hand, she
picked up her cloth and polish and placed them back on the
trolley. Somebody else would have to finish the room.

*

After she'd met the principal and learnt to call her Sorcha, after she'd rebuffed an offer of professional help and pledged to stay in touch, Ailish collected Stevie from the staffroom. Whatever else had changed, the smell of St Ursula's was constant. How well she knew the blend of socks and sweat and stale milk, hormones and spot cream and fear. She thought of all the parent–teacher meetings she'd attended. With Lorraine, Jodie and Lee, she'd never been sure what she'd hear. With Stevie, everything had been straightforward. In fact, she'd often felt a smug sympathy for other parents. She'd looked at their despondent faces and been grateful for her youngest child.

'I'm sorry,' she said.

Stevie shrugged. 'I shouldn't have given him a dig. Evan O'Gara, I mean. But I'd heard enough.'

'It's not your fault. What did he say to you?'

'Do you really want to know?'

Ailish gripped the steering wheel. 'I do.'

'He was slagging me off for living with Jodie. He claimed you'd thrown me out. Then he started going on about college and that. He said the only hope I had was an access programme.'

'What's an access programme?'

'It's like a special scheme for people whose folks don't have any money.'

'Did you—?'

'It's all rubbish, Mam. Don't pay any attention to the

likes of him.' He pulled at the sleeve of his jacket. 'Are you mad at me for being a snitch?'

Suddenly, he wasn't a handsome six-footer. He wasn't smart, capable, funny Stevie, with a university application list she couldn't understand. Nor was he the young adult who'd taken control of his life because his mother wasn't strong enough to look after him. He was a child, hunched over in the passenger seat of her car, too many troubles bearing down on him. She had to stop letting him down. He deserved better. They all did.

'You did the right thing,' said Ailish. 'Will you come home?'

'I can't.'

'If I get your father to leave?'

'But will you? You've had plenty of opportunities and you've done nothing. Why should this time be any different?'

His scepticism tore at her, the pain all the sharper because his doubts were justified. 'I promise,' she said.

'You know the deal. I'll come back when he's gone.'

Keith was home before her, sitting at the kitchen table with a mug of tea. Outside, night was closing in, bringing with it a stinging frost.

'There you are,' he said. 'You'd want to get moving on the dinner.'

She put down her bag and leant against the counter for support. She needed to silence the voice that told her she wasn't good enough. Then she needed to put one word after another until Keith accepted he had to go.

'I want you to leave,' she said.

He didn't bother to look up. 'What's brought this on?'

'A million things, including what you did to Stevie.'

'That was almost a month ago. Why get into a flap about it now?'

'Because it's affecting his schoolwork, and he won't come home while you're here.'

'Great, so a child gets to decide where I live.'

Ailish dug her nails into the fleshy part of her palms. Keith's act was well practised. He planned on wearing her down by acting as though her complaints were unreasonable. 'I want you to go,' she said. 'Not just for Stevie's sake, but for mine too. What we're doing is ridiculous. We're both miserable.'

At last, he looked at her. 'I'm confused here, so you'll have to help me out. Do you want a divorce or do you want me to lie low for a couple of months so the boy wonder can do his homework?'

'In the longer term, I want a divorce. In the short term, as in tomorrow, I want you to leave the house. I want Stevie to come home where he belongs, and I want to live my life in peace.'

Ailish watched Keith's face harden.

'And where am I supposed to go?' he said.

'I don't know. Your mother's place? One of your sisters? That's not my concern.'

'"That's not my concern",' he said, mocking her voice. 'They're messing with your head, aren't they? Your new friends in Dublin and London? I can hear them urging you to throw me out. I'll bet they think I'm not good enough.'

'You weren't always like this,' she said.

That wasn't true. Keith's capacity for cruelty wasn't new, but she'd chosen to ignore it. She'd been the champion of looking the other way, the queen of self-delusion.

'No, Ailish, that's where you're wrong. I'm the same old, same old. You're the one who's changed.'

He was right. Finding Chrissie had changed her, but in ways he could never understand. Trying to explain was pointless. It was only now, when challenged, that she realised it herself.

'You've got to leave,' she said

Keith stood up. 'And what if I don't? What'll you do then?'

'You've got to leave.'

'If you're so keen for us to split up, why don't you go? I'm all right here.'

For five minutes, they tossed arguments back and forth. Lobbing and volleying. Then he pounced, throwing in something she hadn't expected. It was a skill of his, the ability to reveal information if and when needed.

'Who's Gary W?' he asked.

'I'm not with you.'

'Don't lie. The pair of you have been texting each other. At least that's the name on your phone. Who is he?'

For a moment, she froze. It hadn't occurred to her that Keith would go through her phone. She tried to recall what the messages said. 'Why were you snooping on me?'

'Because I suspected you were about to go flitting off to London again – and I was right. Anyway, you haven't answered my question. Who's Gary W?'

She explained that he'd also been born in Carrigbrack and that he was searching for his biological parents.

'There's more to it than that,' said Keith, taking a step towards her. As he moved, she felt as if air was leaching from the room.

'I swear to you there's not.'

'Well, surprise, surprise, I don't believe you. If all you were doing was comparing adoption notes, what was the other stuff about? Why was he telling you to "be brave" and "do the right thing"? Were you talking to him about us?'

'No,' said Ailish, her voice splintering.

'Is there something going on between you and this Gary W character?'

The temptation to say, 'Yeah, in a parallel universe' was strong. She managed to resist. 'You've got it wrong. It's not like that.'

Another step. 'I've told you before, Ailish, your trouble is that you're a liar, and a lousy one at that. Not only was your friend Gary texting you, Katie and Chrissie were too. What sort of tales have you been spinning to them?'

Bluffing was futile. If she didn't own up, they'd be stuck in this pattern for hours. 'Okay,' she said, 'I told them what you'd done to Stevie. And to me. Oh, and you're right, I also spoke to Gary. They were worried about me. They still are.'

Keith took a further step. He was an arm's length away. She could see the curl of his mouth, the veins in his eyes, the pores on his nose.

'You're some bitch.'

'Chrissie's my mother. For some warped reason, you don't want to accept that, but she is. I'll tell her whatever I want.'

Before she could say anything else, Keith's right fist flew through the air. The move was too quick for her, and the punch hit hard under her eye. As his knuckles connected with the bone, pain exploded across her face, and for a second or two the world turned crimson.

'There's only so much I can put up with,' he said. 'No normal wife would behave like you, running off behind my back, telling your miserable little story to anyone who'll listen. You're pathetic. I always said you needed psychiatric help.'

Ailish found herself unable to speak. Her breath was ragged. Her skin burnt. She brushed her fingertips against her cheekbone, releasing a flare of pain. Her first impulse was to run. What if he hit her again? He'd never struck her across the face before, but what if he lost control?

Then Stevie entered her thoughts. If she wanted him home, she had to persevere. Although Sorcha Hession had outlined the law, Ailish had been in such a state that most of it had slid past her ears. What she lacked in detail, she'd have to make up for in attitude.

Eventually, she spoke. 'You ought to know that I met the principal of St Ursula's this afternoon. We discussed what you'd done to your son. She said that if Stevie was in danger, social services would have to get involved.'

'For fuck's sake, is there anyone you haven't blabbed to? Why not go on local radio or take out an ad in the paper?'

Keith's words might have been dismissive, but for the first time, Ailish noticed a flicker of anxiety. 'I didn't contact Mrs Hession. She rang me because she was worried about Stevie.'

'If either of you accuse me of anything, I'll deny it.'

'That won't work. The day after you hit him, we went to the doctor. There's a record of his injuries.'

'Aren't you the sneaky one?'

'At the time, being sneaky was the last thing on my mind. I was terrified he was seriously hurt.' Pain radiated from her cheek, and her eye was watering. Although every word required enormous effort, she had to continue. Just breathe, she thought. Just breathe and talk. 'We've come to the end of the road, Keith. You know that; you just don't want to admit it.'

'What I know is, you're fooling yourself if you reckon I want to stay married to you.'

'Good. I want you to go. Now. If you don't, I'll call the guards. They'll see what you've done to me. And be assured that everyone in the village will hear about it too.'

For an agonising moment, Ailish worried he would strike her again.

Instead, he took a step back.

'If you think I'm going to make this easy for you,' he said, 'you're wrong. But it's been years since I had any interest in you. I should have moved on a long time ago. That's what most men would have done.' His voice cracked through the room like a whip.

And then, before Ailish could absorb what was happening, he was gone.

Chapter 32

Katie

Katie should have been working her way down her to-do list. Tomorrow was an important day. Instead, she was sitting on her bed sorting through the box. The number of queries had slowed, and more than a week had passed since their last significant email. Unusually, it had been from a woman who'd given birth in Carrigbrack. She was going through the official process and hoped to be reunited with her daughter.

Having avoided the board for several weeks, Katie risked a peek. Her post about the bracelets had been the catalyst for dozens of others to open up about their experience in Carrigbrack or their search for long-lost family. Some posts pulsed with anger. More were filled with disappointment and longing. Others were reassuring. *Please don't despair*, one woman wrote. *It took fifteen years of asking questions, but I found my natural mother in the end.*

Ailish's post about Chrissie was there, as were a number of others from people who'd received bracelets. After five minutes, Katie put down her phone. There was only so much she could read without getting emotional, and this wasn't the time for tears. If Beth was home, they could talk about it, but she was out with Iona, her new girlfriend.

The day before, Margo had called. 'Are you sure you don't want a birthday party?' she'd said. 'My offer still stands, you know.'

'You're very good,' Katie had replied, 'but I'm one hundred per cent certain. Seventy's not a big deal for me.'

Her sister had segued into a question about the bracelets, and soon they were bickering about the wisdom of the exercise. The row had only been brought to a close by Katie pretending that Beth had entered the room.

When she protested that turning seventy was of no significance, she was lying. She remembered how Johnny had seen 'three score years and ten' as a landmark birthday. 'After that, you're trespassing, Kateser,' he'd claimed. She told herself that this was no longer the case. These days, seventy was nothing. There was every chance Beth would live to be a hundred.

Sometimes, she felt that age was catching up with her. Take what had happened earlier in the day. She'd gone into town for a few bits and pieces, and while she'd expected her first destination, Penneys, to be busy, it had been frantic. Girls had swished past with armfuls of clothes and cosmetics. Katie had made the mistake of standing still for a moment and had been rewarded with a bony elbow into the side. Elsewhere, she'd found fault with everything. She'd tut-tutted over a handbag described as 'vegan'. 'Why can't they be honest and call it plastic?' she said to the slack-mouthed shop assistant. That was one of the problems with getting older: no one took you seriously. Complain, and you were dismissed as either cranky or confused. The best you could hope for was to be labelled 'feisty'. Katie hated that word.

Afterwards, she went for lunch. In a café, she ordered a cheese sandwich, only to be told this wasn't possible. 'What about hummus, pesto and beetroot?' suggested the shiny-faced young man behind the counter. 'Or bacon, coriander and Brie?' She settled for a scone and a strong cup of tea. As she was finishing her tea, a nearby mobile phone sprang to life. Johnny had used the same ringtone, and for one haunting moment, she was convinced the phone was his. She couldn't stop thinking about what had been and wouldn't be again. Exhausted and empty-handed, she got the bus back to Griffin Road.

Now, she counted the bracelets. There were twelve left. At least two, those belonging to the sons of Tina McNulty and Gráinne Holland, seemed destined to stay in the box. She was disappointed for Gary. He was back in LA, writing new music. Relations with Anton would never be quite the same, he said, but they'd shaken hands and were trying to write together. She could tell he was happy to have returned to the life he'd once loved. He pledged to keep in touch, but she feared that he wouldn't.

Lately, she'd been thinking a lot about forgiveness. It was funny how forgiving yourself could be more difficult than forgiving others. It certainly had been for Gary.

She continued to receive regular messages from Ailish. Keith might be gone from the house, but she remained uneasy. *What'll I do when Stevie leaves for college?* she asked. I *can't live here on my own.* If you asked Katie, she needed to go to the guards and apply for a barring order. Beth agreed. The decision wasn't theirs to make, however, and Ailish was under enough pressure without them adding to it. They did their best to reassure her that she'd done the right thing and that life would get better.

For a short while, Katie stayed where she was, reading and rereading the names on the bracelets. She knew every name, every date of birth. Finally, she placed the lid back on the box and returned it to the wardrobe. It really was time she got down to work. In less than twenty-four hours, their American visitors were due to arrive.

Chapter 33

Then, Patricia

Patricia thought she'd let out all the pain on the day she'd lain on the floor and cried. She was wrong. There was always more. Her grief didn't go away; it just changed shape. She would think she was coping without Paul. Then something simple – a baby's squeal or the smell of fresh linen – would spark a memory, and she'd have to fight for breath. She wished there was a way of communicating with her son. She wanted to be the voice in his head. Sometimes, she imagined she was.

What are you doing now?

Have you started to crawl?

Are you happy?

Do your new parents love you enough?

That she would never hear the answers to her questions didn't stop them from coming.

Spring arrived early, and Patricia visualised taking Paul

for a walk. He'd have a smart pram, the best she could afford. Not a smelly old hand-me-down like many babies. Women would stop to admire him. 'Isn't he the fine fellow,' they'd say. 'Who does he take after?'

Her mother would get out the knitting needles and make him a matinee jacket. Maybe Patricia would take up knitting herself.

Then she'd return to the real world. Sister Faustina would whine at her over some minor mistake ('For an educated young woman, you're very slow'), or Sabina would chastise her for not eating ('When half the world is starving, it's a sin to refuse nutritious food'), or one of the other mothers would lose patience with her ('The face on you. You'd swear you were the only one who's been badly treated').

Patricia had come to hate Carrigbrack. She hated the walls, the statues, the sounds and smells. She hated every rancid thing about the place. She disliked the nurses, with their subtle ways of reminding her of their superiority, and she loathed the nuns, especially Sabina. She no longer spoke to Eunice. Why should she? Eunice had let her down. She'd also colluded in Winnie's escape, yet refused to reveal anything about where she was or how she was getting on.

Patricia tried to block memories of her early months in the home. Unbidden, unwanted, they returned. She remembered the singing protest, and how they'd all stood together. She remembered how they'd fantasised about what they'd do when they were released. She'd been a different person then. A better one. Lurking within, though, had been a seam of inadequacy, a latent flaw that prevented her from handling adversity. She was surrounded by women who'd suffered more, yet they struggled on, squeezing moments of joy from their regimented days. Even Nancy, poor abused Nancy, had become more open.

By comparison, Patricia felt suffocated by sadness. For no reason, tears would collect at the back of her eyes. Usually, but not always, she was able to hold them back. Sister Agnes had told her that she knew nothing about love, but she loved Paul. She couldn't imagine that his loss would ever become easier.

In early April, she decided she couldn't stay. She talked to Sister Agnes, who quickly put her right.

'You know the rules,' she said. 'You'll have to work here until you've paid off your debt.'

Patricia recalled something her mother had said on the night Father Cusack had taken her away. 'Please God, we'll see you later in the year.' What if her mam had never intended her to stay this long? What if her parents could be convinced to hand over the one hundred pounds that would secure her release? Actually, given that she'd already contributed several months of work, the debt was likely to be less than that. Because Patricia wasn't allowed to write to her family, she asked Sister Agnes to intercede on her behalf.

Their answer came the following week. *No,* her father wrote, in neat, narrow letters, *we don't have that sort of money, and even if we did, it wouldn't be appropriate for us to spend it. You need to pay for your mistakes.*

Patricia could picture him writing the letter, his face as pinched as his penmanship. She should have foreseen his response. After all, one of his favourite sayings was 'Neither a borrower nor a lender be.' Frugality was a virtue in Patricia's house. Her mother collected Green Shield stamps, made soup from leftovers and darned socks until the toes were a hotchpotch of stitches. Her father travelled everywhere on a battered High Nelly bicycle and still wore his wedding suit. None of this was unusual. Patricia must have known fifty families whose lives were no better than basic. Far less common was the house where money was spent freely.

The anger she'd once felt towards her mam and dad was gone. In its place was shame. Theirs was a hard life. Both came from large families where most of the children had emigrated. They didn't deserve the stigma she'd brought to their door. Regret flowed through her body like poison.

That month, her period was extremely painful. The usual dull weight was accompanied by a drawerful of hot knives. They stabbed and twisted until she thought she would faint. Although pain relief was hard to come by, the nurses had a range of pills in their office, and sometimes they could be persuaded to dispense one or two. Pretending she needed to go to the lavatory, Patricia slipped away from dinner. By then, she felt as if all her internal organs were in revolt.

The younger nurse, the one who'd been there when Diane died, answered the door. She listened to Patricia's request, then shook her head.

'I can't,' she said. 'It's against the rules.'

Patricia could tell from the nurse's narrow vowels that she was local. There was a jumpiness about her too. Patricia supposed she should try wheedling and cajoling, but she didn't have it in her. Besides, she was practically crumpled over with pain.

'I'm begging you to help me,' she said. 'It's never been this bad before.'

The nurse looked like she was going to repeat her mantra about the rules. Then she hesitated and pressed her lips together. Finally, she spoke. 'I can't give you anything. But I'm about to go and check on a baby, and if, by any chance, one tablet from the top shelf was to go missing,' she looked at the shelf behind her, 'there's a chance I might be too busy to notice.'

'Ah, I see.'

'That's *one* tablet,' repeated the nurse. 'If any more were unaccounted for, Sister Agnes would have to be told.'

'I understand.'

After the nurse had left, Patricia filled a glass of water from the sink in the corner. Then she took down the brown glass bottle. It was full. Figuring that one tablet was hardly worth her while, she shook out three and swallowed them. The label warned of drowsiness. That was exactly what she wanted: drowsiness followed by a deep, dreamless sleep. She swallowed a further two tablets. Then another handful. She would be in trouble when her theft was discovered, but so what? The worst had already happened; what more could they do to her? There was something pleasing about swallowing the pills. Something liberating. She took four – no, five – more before returning the bottle to the shelf.

The dormitory was empty. Everybody was in the refectory or the nursery. Outside, the blue-grey of dusk was closing in. Patricia lifted her mattress by an inch or so and took out her one tangible connection to Paul, his paper identity band. It was all she had left of him. She lay on her back, the bracelet in one hand, and allowed the tears to run down her cheeks. Within a few minutes, the pain started to lift, and she felt more peaceful.

Gradually, she was overcome by tiredness. She tried to focus, but no sooner had an idea entered her head than it galloped away again. Her thoughts were wild, freewheeling. Was it her imagination or was the room running out of air? What went through her mind in those moments? A tangle of memories, of Mike and her parents and Paul; of the whitewashed building where she'd attended national school and the boys and girls in her class; of the day Diane was buried and the day Paul disappeared. They danced in front of her closed eyes, blending together and forming patterns like the images in a kaleidoscope. Bit by bit, the pictures fractured and faded until everything was black.

Patricia was being tugged towards sleep, a long, dark sleep without memories, troubles or sadness. It was what she had longed for, and she was ready.

Chapter 34

Brandon

From above, Ireland was untidy. The fields were divided into irregular shapes, like a jigsaw made entirely of different shades of green. As the plane approached Dublin, the grass was replaced by a sprawl of roads, factories and houses. Forty-six years after he'd been bundled up and sent to America, Brandon was back. He didn't know what to call this country. It wasn't home, but it was where his mother had lived and where his twin still lived.

Beside him, Robyn was waking. She'd slept all the way across the Atlantic. Brandon's rest had been more fitful. He'd started watching three different films, but couldn't concentrate.

'Here we are,' she whispered, as the plane bumped onto the runway. 'Your other home.'

He decided he could go with that. His other home.

He kept expecting things to go wrong, for the weather

to be foul or their luggage to have been left behind in Boston. The morning was fine, and their bags were first on the carousel. He worried that Katie wouldn't be there. Then he decided it might be easier if she left them to their own devices. He recognised Katie and Beth immediately, the younger woman a taller, more sculpted version of her aunt. By now, he'd had several conversations with both. Relations with Katie were friendly, although he sensed she still had doubts about him.

When Robyn had returned from Miami, she'd issued an ultimatum. She wouldn't have called it that. 'Setting out my thinking' had been the phrase she'd used. Echoing one of Donald Trump's campaign slogans, she'd repeatedly asked, 'What have you got to lose?' It had worked for Trump and it had worked for Robyn. Sort of. What had helped to clinch the deal was Katie coming on board with more details about Eddie. Say what you like about the woman, she was a skilled detective. Her enquiries had begun with another nurse who'd worked in Carrigbrack. One contact had spawned another until she'd found the information she wanted. In what sounded like an unorthodox arrangement – was everything in Ireland slightly sketchy? – Eddie had been fostered, and subsequently adopted, by a woman named Joyce. They both lived in a town called Ballinlish in County Longford. The internet told Brandon that Longford was flat, rural and approximately seventy miles from Dublin.

He hadn't wanted to travel to Ireland straight away. 'I'm

busy at work,' he'd explained to Robyn. 'This isn't the right time for a vacation.'

'You're looking for excuses,' she'd replied. 'You figure that if you put the trip off for long enough, it'll all blow over. Am I right?'

His wife's week in Florida had taught Brandon that he couldn't be without her. That this sounded pathetic didn't make it untrue. He'd missed her enthusiasm and intelligence. He'd missed her touch, her kisses, her physical presence. He'd thought of the years he'd wasted by believing he was better on his own; the years when he'd grown so accustomed to loneliness that he'd no longer recognised its frosty grip. He'd been reading about twins. One line was repeated over and over again: *When you have a twin, you're never alone.* Every time, that line filled him with sadness.

The morning after Robyn's return, he'd called Katie and booked two tickets to Dublin.

Brandon worried that their marriage had been damaged by months of disagreement. He spoke to Robyn about his guilt, not all at once but in instalments. It was, he feared, impossible for her to understand. Her background was too conventional. She did her best but sounded perplexed. 'You were a *baby*,' she said. 'It wasn't your fault the dice rolled in your favour.' Beth probably had the best read of his emotions. 'Nothing about that system was fair,' she said. 'Everybody's trying to make amends for problems they didn't cause. But Eddie and Joyce are intrigued by you, and I think all three of you will feel better after you've met.'

Step by step, the journey back to Ireland had begun to feel less like an obligation and more like a choice. As Robyn liked to remind him, he was fortunate that his brother had been relatively easy to trace. 'Some people spend their entire lives looking down blind alleys,' she pointed out. Brandon couldn't say he felt an overpowering connection to Eddie, but he was curious, and for now that would have to be enough.

The news wasn't all good: it turned out that their birth mother, Linda Markham, was dead. In the early 1980s, she'd emigrated to Australia. Joyce and Eddie had tried to find her, only to discover they were too late. She'd died in a drowning accident in 1993. She'd been married but had no other children. Her husband knew she'd had twin boys in Ireland and that they'd been forcibly removed from her. She'd kept a photo of them, lying side by side in their crib. She'd said little about their biological father and had taken his identity to the grave. Brandon was stung by the cruelty of her early death. After everything she'd endured, Linda had deserved a long, comfortable life. But, as all of this had shown, not everyone got what they deserved.

Beth drove, with Katie beside her. From the back, Robyn and Brandon offered chit-chat about the flight and the scenery. Robyn did most of the work. Brandon's thoughts were flitting every which way. One minute, he was looking forward to the reunion. The next, he was rigid with nerves. We don't have to stay, he thought. If it's too awkward, we can leave.

'I'm glad you've spoken to Eddie,' said Katie. 'At least you know a bit about each other now.'

'Yeah, it was good to talk to him.'

'Would I be right in saying he wasn't what you'd expected?'

'I don't know that anything's been quite what I expected.'

'That seems to be the way with most of the people we've come across,' said Beth.

Their phone conversation had been brief. Eddie had told Brandon that not only had he been aware of his existence, he'd made every effort to find him. 'The files said nothing about where you'd gone,' he explained, 'so after a couple of years, I gave up.' During the call, he referred to his disability but didn't dwell on it. Like Brandon, he'd married late. His wife's name was Yvette, and they had a three-year-old daughter called Zoe. He was an administrator with the local council, while Yvette worked in a crèche.

Eddie's friendliness, and the fact that he lived a full life, had shattered Brandon's preconceptions. Was it wrong that he'd been relieved to discover his brother's disability was mild? Yes. Did this mean he was hopelessly shallow? Probably. Would others have reacted in the same way? Robyn wouldn't have. It was funny: Brandon remembered thinking that Ireland must be filled with people who needed professional help. Until now, he hadn't placed himself among them.

When he zoned back in, his wife was talking. 'Is this very strange for you, Katie?' she asked. 'Reconnecting with people after all this time?'

There was a delay, and when, finally, she replied, she

skirted around the question. 'Robyn,' she said, 'you've no idea how much it means to me that you've made this journey. When I sent both bracelets to Boston, I hoped that Brandon and Eddie would meet again. It's a delight when a story ends well.'

'Isn't it just,' said Beth. 'So, Brandon, what do you make of the place so far?'

'It's ... um ... green?' he replied, prompting laughter from Beth and smiles from Katie and Robyn.

'You're probably wondering where all the thatched cottages are gone, aren't you?'

'Now that you mention it, I am. And where are the donkeys? I expected donkeys. Oh, and leprechauns. We need leprechauns.'

'Stop messing, the pair of you,' said Katie, amusement in her voice. 'When I was growing up, there were quite a few thatched cottages left. My own grandmother – Beth's great-grandmother – lived in one. She'd no electricity and her water came from a well. And after we'd visited, our clothes smelt of smoke for a week.'

'Ah, the good old days,' said Beth.

Brandon was relieved when they fell back into silence. He needed to focus on the hours ahead.

To begin with, his other home was disappointing, just highways and fields, swathes of grey and green, grey and green. Slowly it changed – and kept changing. Lakes, rivers, marsh, bog, pasture, villages with quirky names and peculiar signs – what was the GAA Lotto? A 45 drive? A solemn novena? – blurred past. The picture was green, blue, navy, brown, red, yellow then green once more.

'It's lovely,' he said, conscious of the word's inadequacy.

'For a small country, there's a lot of landscape,' agreed Katie.

Brandon kept looking. He might never be back this way again, and he wanted to remember it.

Ballinlish wasn't an attractive town. In the early spring light, it appeared down at heel, vacant shops scarring the main street like missing teeth. On their journey, Brandon had noticed references to something called a 'Tidy Towns committee'. The Ballinlish branch needed to up its game.

Joyce's one-storey house was two miles further along, down a narrow strip of road. She'd lived there with her husband, Cathal, until his death five years earlier. Eddie lived in a new housing development on the other side of town.

Joyce had wings of white hair and small dark eyes. She was, thought Brandon, the sort of woman who could read every uncharitable thought that passed through your head. She wore a red sweater, a jade scarf and blue earrings. He wondered if the gaudy outfit was a backlash against the years when she'd been forced to wear black.

Katie embraced her, and for a time, they clung together. They were less like former colleagues, more like women who'd been side by side in the trenches.

'How long has it been?' asked Joyce.

'More than forty-six years,' replied Katie. 'And despite everything, I'd have known you.'

'Even without the veil?'

'Even without the veil. Though I haven't quite adjusted to using your real name.'

'If the occasional "Eunice" slips through, I won't mind. Please don't call me "Sister", though. That would be too weird.'

Katie blotted a tear while Joyce showed them into the sitting room. There to greet them was a man of medium height with mid-brown hair. His smile was cautious, his eyes blue, his nose a shade too long. Save for his thin legs and the fact that he rose with the help of a stick, he was Brandon's double.

Eddie spoke first. Like Joyce, his voice was soft. 'I saw your picture, but ... This is crazy. I never thought we'd be this much alike. It's great to meet you again.'

Words came slowly to Brandon. 'When you say again, does that mean you remember when we were together?'

'No, but because I've always known about you, I liked to think you were in my memory somewhere. I used to have this image of the pair of us crawling around the nursery floor in Carrigbrack, terrorising the other kids.' Another shake of the head. 'I guess that never happened.' He extended one arm. 'Come here. My limbs don't always obey orders, but I promise I won't fall on top of you.'

'I never—'

'You're grand. I'm used to people's concerns.'

They stepped forward and folded into a hug. Brandon couldn't remember the last time he'd shared a sober embrace with a man. He'd never been a tactile person, nor an emotional one. When they pulled apart and sat down, he saw that Robyn was crying.

Like her outfit, Joyce's sitting room was a riot of colour. Ordinarily, Brandon would have cringed at the patterned carpet, the lemon walls and pink drapes. He would have removed several of the paintings and questioned the need for so many photos. But, as he drank the worst cup of coffee he'd ever tasted, he decided the garishness worked.

'What I still can't grasp,' said Eddie, 'is that you never knew you had a twin. You wouldn't believe how much time I spent making up stories about you, wondering where you were and what you were like. It never occurred to me that you might have been sent to the States.'

Brandon explained how his parents had been kept in the dark. 'They applied for one baby,' he said. 'If they'd known about you, I'm convinced they'd have wanted you as well.'

Eddie shrugged, as if to say, *I'm not so sure about that.* Then he and Joyce explained how they'd come to be mother and son.

'I left the convent in 1980,' she said. 'By then, the regime in Carrigbrack was a little gentler. The mothers wore their own clothes. They were allowed to have visitors and make phone calls. They didn't have to earn their way out either.'

'Agnes allowed all that?' asked Katie.

'She was gone. As was Sabina. Did you know Sabina's still alive? She's in her nineties and living in a home in County Mayo. Imagine: when we thought she was as old as civilisation, she was only in her forties.'

'From the tales we've heard about her,' said Beth, 'she's enjoyed a far longer life than she deserved.'

Katie and Joyce swapped a look, but neither responded.

'When you left the convent,' said Robyn, 'was it to get married?'

'No. I met Cathal, the Lord have mercy on him, several years later.' Joyce sighed. 'I left because I didn't have a vocation. To be honest, I'd struggled for years. Somehow, I'd managed to convince myself that I could do good work in Carrigbrack.' She raised her palms to the ceiling. 'I know, I know. Given everything you've heard about the place, you probably consider that odd. Troubling, even. But I reckoned that if families were going to send their daughters there anyway, the least I could do was offer the girls some support. I'd like to think that, occasionally, I lived up to that aim.' She looked down at the technicoloured carpet. 'I fear there were other times when I failed – and failed badly.'

'You were always kind,' said Katie. 'Don't doubt that.'

'By 1980, the numbers in the home were dwindling, and other similar places had already closed their doors. I was increasingly disillusioned. I spent every day questioning whether I was living the right life. Oh, and there was another consideration. By then, both my parents were dead. They'd set such store by my life as a nun, I'd never been brave enough to tell them I wanted to leave. Finally, I felt I had to make a move.'

'What did you do afterwards?' asked Beth.

'I went to university and studied social work.' Joyce chuckled. 'They didn't get many thirty-something former nuns, but the other students – mostly young women – were very kind.'

'I was devastated,' said Eddie. 'I couldn't believe she'd abandoned me.'

'*Tuh*, I'd done no such thing, as well you know. It took a while to sort out the paperwork, that's all.'

'The best part of forty years later, and I can still get a rise out of her.' Eddie winked before sending an affectionate look in Joyce's direction.

'I'd no intention of leaving him behind. We were great buddies by then. He was a lovely fellow. Mind you, he could be a cranky devil when the mood took him. In those days, single people weren't allowed to adopt. At the same time, everybody agreed that Carrigbrack was no place for an eight-year-old and that I was best placed to look after him.'

Robyn tilted her head. 'Why hadn't somebody else adopted him?'

'A good question,' said Eddie. 'From what I've been able to gather, Agnes decided no one would want me.'

'That's appalling, and I'm sure it wasn't true, either.'

'I'd like to think you're right. For quite a while, I had a strange existence. The next eldest child was three years younger than me, and she was profoundly disabled. To be fair, the mothers were very good.'

'How did you learn to read and write?' asked Brandon.

'Joyce taught me. Once I'd picked up the basics, I read all the time. It wasn't as though there was much else to do. There wasn't even a television. To this day, friends and colleagues refer to childhood TV programmes, and I've only a sketchy idea what they're talking about.'

'I don't remember there being many books in Carrigbrack,' said Katie. 'What did you read?'

Eddie laughed. 'You've a good memory. The choice wasn't that extensive. Let's just say I know a lot about the lives of the saints, especially the female ones. Anyway, to go back to Robyn's original question, being left behind worked to my advantage. It meant I got to live with Joyce.'

'I became Eddie's guardian in 1981,' she said. 'And, before you ask, I'm aware there was something ridiculous about me being allowed to raise him when his birth mother hadn't been. Linda was treated shamefully.'

Brandon put down his coffee. 'This might be a lame question, and I don't want to offend anyone, but … were you trying to make amends? For everything that had happened in the home, I mean?'

While Katie shifted in her armchair, and Robyn examined her hands, Joyce appeared unperturbed. 'I couldn't tell you how many times I've been asked that, and I'll give you the answer I always give. To me the question makes no sense. It implies that Eddie was some sort of burden. A penance.

We'd spent eight years together in Carrigbrack and we were friends. I wanted him with me because I loved him.'

Brandon's cheeks burnt. 'I didn't mean—'

'Don't worry,' said Eddie. 'We know you didn't mean any harm. And listen, I probably did add a few white hairs to Joyce's head. When I was small, a doctor told the nuns I'd never be able to walk and I'd never talk properly. He said I'd probably have to spend the rest of my days in an institution. We were both determined to prove him wrong. Like she says, we were a team.'

'We were an unusual pair in Ireland in the 1980s,' said Joyce, 'but I had a job – I was working in inner-city Dublin at the time – and Eddie found a good school. And, of course, we realised that the doctor brought in by Agnes had been far too pessimistic. It turned out there were lots of therapies that could help. And then, in the middle of everything, I met Cathal.'

'Or Father Cathal, as some folks called him,' added Eddie.

Beth leant in, eyes bright. 'Don't stop there. This is quite a story.'

Joyce's face creased into a smile 'Yes, he had been a priest. But, like me, he'd left the religious life several years earlier. He was a national school teacher.' She looked at Robyn and Brandon. 'I think you call it grade school in the US. He applied for the principal's job here in Ballinlish ... and that's when we got married and adopted Eddie.'

'So there I was,' said Eddie, 'a disabled child living out in the wilds with an ex-nun and a former priest. I swear there isn't a joke I haven't heard. Some of the kids were as subtle as an ice cream van, and the word cripple was still in everyday use. But here I am.' He glanced at Joyce. 'Here we both are.'

The focus shifted to Brandon. By contrast, his story felt run-of-the-mill. His life sterile. He had achieved what someone of his upbringing was expected to achieve. No more, no less. Oh, he tried to make his job sound more exciting, his interests less banal, but for someone hurtling towards fifty, he had few anecdotes. He was relieved when the conversation flipped back to his brother.

Eddie revealed that Zoe's second name was Linda, in honour of the grandmother she would never meet. He also talked about his job. He was working on a plan to revitalise the town. It had been ravaged by the recession, he said, and recovery was slow.

'Make Ballinlish great again,' said Beth with a nod towards Brandon, and they all laughed.

No matter who was speaking, Brandon's eyes were drawn towards his twin. One part of him was relaxed. Why did I resist this? he thought. This is everything. Another part was overwhelmed. He wanted to run away and think. To measure their similarities and differences. That was why, when Joyce asked if he and Robyn would stay for a couple of days, Brandon changed the subject. He didn't know if he was ready. Returning to Dublin with Katie and Beth would be safer. There would be more room to breathe there. Robyn sent him a look of disapproval.

Katie was quiet. Perhaps she, too, was struggling to take it all in. She'd once worked side by side with Joyce, but that had been almost half a century ago.

Beth was more animated, outlining everything that she and Katie had been doing to reunite people with their birth families. Joyce was enthralled, oohing and aahing at several of the names. 'I remember him,' she'd say. 'He was an absolute dote.' Or, 'That's shocking. Completely shocking. She should never have been lied to like that.'

'We've encountered some amazing folks,' said Beth. 'A few difficult ones as well, but you get them everywhere.'

'What about my brother here?' asked Eddie, a teasing tone to his voice. 'Which category would you put him in?'

'Hmm. To begin with, he was a bit tricky, and we did have our differences. However, as the old saying goes, there was nothing wrong with Brandon that couldn't be cured by a good kick up the backside.'

'Beth!' said Katie, but Brandon found himself laughing, albeit nervously.

'And I think it's fair to say we've warmed to each other.'

'That's a relief,' said Joyce, mirth in her voice. 'Do you know, Beth, you remind me of someone I once knew, a young woman who spent time in Carrigbrack. In fact, I helped her to escape. Winnie was her name. She was younger than you, but she said the same type of thing. How she used to make me laugh. I often think of her.'

'Do you know what happened to her?'

'Unfortunately, we lost touch back in the late seventies. I

hope the years have been good to her.' She hesitated. 'There were a lot of casualties back then. Far too many casualties.'

The words obviously resonated with Katie, who closed her eyes and bowed her head. Before anyone could say anything else, however, they heard a car pulling into the drive. Within seconds, a little girl came skipping in. She had large golden-brown eyes and a cap of blonde curls. She was swaddled in a bright yellow raincoat and wore cerise wellingtons. Clearly, clashing colours were popular in Ballinlish. Her mother, a neat woman with angular cheekbones, was several steps behind.

'How's my best girl?' said Joyce.

'I'm good, thank you, Nana,' replied Zoe as she assessed the room. Her gaze halted briefly at Eddie. 'Daddy!' she said. Next, she plodded towards Brandon. 'Other Daddy?' she asked cautiously.

Eddie grinned and scooped her up. 'That's Daddy's American brother. Uncle Brandon. Remember how I told you he was coming to see us?'

'Oh, yes.' She risked another shy glance in Brandon's direction. 'Are you nice like my daddy?'

'I hope so,' replied Brandon.

Eddie kissed the top of his daughter's head. 'Sure how could he be anything else when he's related to us, huh? Now, what do you say to our guests?'

Zoe smiled, revealing tiny white teeth. 'Nice to meet you and welcome to Ballinlish.'

'Thank you, Zoe,' said Brandon. 'We're delighted to be here. I'm only sorry it took so long.'

Yvette took off her coat and sat down. 'It's no wonder the child's confused. You're the spitting image of each other. You could be the same man.' She had a pleasant, slightly husky, voice.

'We could,' said Eddie.

It was raw, this connection. It was complex, but in some ways, simple too. Once again, Brandon found himself thinking about the wasted years. About the years they'd had stolen from them – and the ones he'd chosen to fritter away.

He reached into his backpack, took out an envelope, removed a tiny paper bracelet and handed it to Eddie.

'This is yours,' he said. 'And I hope Robyn doesn't mind if I accept your kind invitation. We'd be honoured to spend the next few days in Ballinlish.'

Chapter 35

Katie

'Are you sure about this?' asked Beth.

'I am.'

'Because we don't have to do it today. I mean, we don't have to do it at all.'

Katie picked a piece of fluff from the duvet cover. 'I can't put it off forever, pet. The poor man's been dead for nine months. Someone will be glad of those clothes.'

'If you're certain,' said Beth, folding a suit jacket and placing it in a large paper bag.

'Well, maybe I'll keep one shirt. That would be okay, wouldn't it? Perhaps the pale blue one. That always smells so nice.'

'Oh, Katie. What are you like?'

'Hopeless, I know.'

Katie swung her legs onto the bed. She'd promised herself that this would be the week she cleared away Johnny's clothes. Beth had offered to help. In the end, she'd decided it would be easier if her niece did the physical work while she supervised. Otherwise, she'd spend the rest of the day sniffing and reminiscing. She'd get teary over some obscure event that meant nothing to anyone else.

That morning, they'd had their weekly meeting about the bracelets. Their task was petering out. Since their visit to Ballinlish three weeks before, they'd had only four queries. Two had fallen outside their time frame, while another had been from a man who'd just wanted to vent about the way his family had been treated in the 1960s. The final email was from a woman who'd been born in Carrigbrack but was reluctant to trace her birth mother. That some bracelets were likely to stay in the box was no surprise. Short of making a televised address, they'd never reach everyone on the list. Even then, there would be those who didn't want a reminder of their earliest days. And that was fine.

Katie worried that Beth would resurrect her proposal to help other adoptees. In many ways, it would make sense. There was something addictive about success. It wasn't, however, what Katie wanted. When she'd done everything she could to help the men and women whose bracelets she had kept, her task would be over.

Brandon and Robyn had spent four days in Longford. While Katie wouldn't claim that Brandon was a man transformed, he was definitely more at ease. Beth had taken to tormenting him about his Irishness. 'The next thing we know,' she'd said, 'you'll be saying goodbye ten times before hanging up the phone and buying a newspaper solely for the death notices.' Although he'd smiled, Katie suspected he hadn't understood a word she'd said.

With her, he remained slightly edgy. This was a shame, because she'd grown fond of him. She reckoned her affection was all the stronger because of how he'd struggled to accept his background. She also worried that he was too in awe of Robyn. She's your wife, she wanted to say, not some saintly reincarnation.

Earlier that week, she'd marked her seventieth birthday in low-key fashion. Friends had called and messaged while Margo and Con had sent an enormous bouquet of flowers. Beth had bought her a sky-blue cashmere jumper, the loveliest thing she'd ever owned.

Spring was in full bloom. There were shoots of life on the trees and daffodils were making way for bluebells. Soon, that brief period would arrive when Irish people switched from complaining about living on a damp rock in the North Atlantic to claiming there was nowhere else in the world they'd rather be. Pale skin would be scorched to a flamingo pink, and the smell of burnt meat would hang over the suburbs.

'Is that your phone?' asked Beth, lifting a white shirt from the wardrobe and placing it in the bag.

Katie gave what she hoped was an airy wave. 'Whoever it is can leave a message, and I'll get back to them later.'

She could guess the caller's identity. Since their reunion, Eunice – or Joyce, as she must learn to call her – had rung every few days. Katie had answered none of the calls. Nor had she responded to any of the messages. She would have to talk to her soon. Indeed, she feared the consequences of not doing so. But not today.

Later, she would bring Johnny's clothes to the nearest charity shop, and the job she hadn't been able to do would be behind her. The problem was, she'd replaced it with the conversation she didn't want to have.

Chapter 36

Gary

Gary continued to check the message board; not every day, but often enough to monitor developments; often enough that if something significant appeared, he'd see it. The conversation about Carrigbrack had slowed, the focus moving to other institutions. St Bridget's, Long Abbey, Rossallen House, Glenarra: the names might change, but the stories had a grim similarity.

Given what Katie had been able to tell him, his task should have been straightforward. Instead, after six months of searching, he felt like he was trying to isolate a single blade of grass in a football field. After he'd scratched Noreen from his list, he'd decided to approach the Adoption Authority. While he doubted they could shed any light on his case, he had to give them a try. If they failed, he'd seek the help of a private investigator.

In early April, he returned to Ireland for a few days.

On his first day back, he noticed a fresh message on the forum. The query didn't affect him, so he spooled on. Then he stopped, thought and returned. He read it, then read it again. The post was from a man named Luke. Was it a hoax? Or was Gary's mind playing tricks on him?

By rights, he should have brought it to Katie's attention. He decided to consult Ailish first. She messaged to say she was in London with Chrissie and would have a look later in the day. He called Beth, and when she didn't answer, he left a voicemail.

In LA, everything was moving quickly. The tour to promote the reissue of *Overboard* would be short, major venues only. A more substantial tour and a new album would follow. They'd spent time in the studio, and Gary and Anton were attempting to write together. He wouldn't claim it was easy. After almost four years of silence, their relationship had altered. Some days, they tried too hard to recapture what they'd once had. At other times, they were ill at ease, desperate not to offend, their conversation reduced to trite statements of the obvious. Then there were days when it all clicked. When they remembered why they couldn't have done anything else with their lives.

Once or twice, they spoke about Shanna. They did so with trepidation, as though rubbing the scar would reopen the wound.

In his downtime, Gary was working on a couple of his own songs. He was excited about one, a ballad called 'Big Sky'. He didn't usually write ballads. He'd always dismissed them as too syrupy. This was different. A bit more work, and he'd play it for Anton.

During the band's hiatus, a lot had changed. There were new Irish bands, guys who sang and spoke like they owed nothing to no one. Guys with a splash of talent and lashings of attitude. In short, guys exactly like Black Iris had been back in 1990. Meanwhile, the industry had become even more clinical, more cynical. More industrial. It was all about data and algorithms now. To bemoan this was to risk being labelled a dinosaur, so Gary told himself to focus on his music and his families, the one he knew and the one he'd yet to find.

Buoyed by their return, Frank was telling everyone that Black Iris were going to be bigger than ever. 'Authenticity is on the way back,' he'd say, 'and my guys are as authentic as they come.' Gary, Anton, Ray and Liamo rolled their eyes and pretended to be irritated.

In the main, Frank ignored the tragedy that had torn the band apart. One day, though, while they were getting a coffee, he turned to Gary and asked why he'd changed his mind.

'Three women changed it for me,' he replied.

The manager smiled. 'Aha,' he boomed. 'The old Gary Winters lives and breathes.'

Gary chose not to put him right.

The Winters family lived in a modest house on Dublin's southern fringes. Lilac Road was middle class, but not extravagantly so. As a teenager, Gary had chafed against its dull respectability. He'd been convinced that the real him belonged somewhere else. Now, in classic middle-aged style, he was mawkishly sentimental about the place. He had offered to buy his parents a bigger, plusher house, but they insisted on staying put.

In the mid 1990s, when Black Iris mania had been at its peak, obsessive fans had taken the 44 or 47 bus and scoured the neighbourhood for the band's childhood homes. Mostly, they'd focused on Anton's house, or Ray's, but occasionally someone had pressed the Winters's doorbell and asked for Gary. Bemused by such devotion, his parents, Shay and Lillian, had posed for photos. More than once, they'd provided tea and sandwiches. They'd answered questions, too: 'We bought him an acoustic guitar for his twelfth birthday,' they'd said, and, 'No, we could never have imagined they'd become so big,' and, 'Yes, we've known Anton since he was in third class. He hasn't changed a bit.'

As Gary parked his car, the message on the adoption forum played on his mind. He'd stay long enough to have a chat and drink the obligatory cup of tea: a quick 'God bless all here', as his old man would say. Then he'd give Beth another shout.

Walking up the path reminded him of something else: no matter what he achieved or how far he travelled, a visit home meant reverting to the age at which he'd last lived here. In 10 Lilac Road, he was permanently nineteen.

His parents were in the kitchen, his mother ironing sheets,

his father polishing shoes. Although they'd both retired, it was impossible to imagine them at rest. They were in perpetual motion, as if a minute's idleness would cause the house to collapse around them.

As much as he valued their relationship, he wasn't always open with them. It wasn't fear of shocking them that held him back so much as the desire to avoid hassle. 'Don't ask, don't tell' was his motto. Then again, they'd spent well over forty years pretending he was their biological son, so the balance sheet was even. They were dishonest in equal measure. While he'd told them about his falling-out with Anton, he'd never said how serious it was – or what it was about. Neither had he revealed much about the hunt for his birth mother. He thought he'd said enough. As he told them about his encounter with Noreen, he realised how wrong he'd been. It was clear they'd had no idea how extensive his search had been.

'So,' said his dad, voice cautious, 'for the past few months, when we were wondering what you were up to, you were actually pretty busy?'

'Not all the time, but I put in a lot of hours all right. The shame is I haven't got anywhere. Yet.'

'Why didn't you speak to us about your search?'

'I was nervous, I guess. It's obviously a difficult subject for you.'

His mother put down the iron. 'If we'd had any idea, we might have …' She tapered off.

'I was going to fill you in when I'd solid progress to report,' said Gary, starting to feel queasy about their reaction.

His father rubbed the heel of his palm against his forehead. 'You see, we mightn't have been …'

'… entirely straight with you,' finished his mother.

The smell of singed cloth hit Gary's nose. 'You'd better unplug that iron,' he said, 'and what do you mean by "entirely straight"?'

'I think we ought to sit down and talk about it,' said his dad.

And that was how the truth came spilling out. Over the next hour, Gary's parents told the full story of how he'd come to live with them. It was a very different tale to the one they'd spun eighteen months before.

'First things first,' said his father, 'you weren't born in Carrigbrack.'

'Then why did you tell me I was?'

'When Allegra was ill, we panicked,' said his mother. 'We never thought we'd have to answer questions about your background, and we didn't know what to say. If you remember, around that time there was lots of media coverage of mother-and-baby homes. All sorts of horror stories emerged. I read a newspaper article about a woman who'd been born in Carrigbrack and hadn't been able to find her birth parents. And …'

'… it felt like the easiest, most straightforward explanation,' continued his father. 'Easier than the truth, at any rate.'

'Hold on a minute,' said Gary. 'You said a cousin of yours was involved, and it was all arranged through her.'

'We may have embellished a little too much. But, like your mother says, we were in a flap and we didn't know what to do for the best. We were terrified that Allegra might die or be left with lasting damage. Suddenly, you were asking big questions, and we didn't have adequate answers.'

'Let me see if I've got this right: all this time, while I've been trying to trace women who gave birth in Carrigbrack, I've been on a wild goose chase?'

'Yes,' said his mother, tears in her soft brown eyes.

'What was so awful about the truth?'

'It wasn't so much that it was awful, although in a way it was. It was just unorthodox.'

'And illegal,' said his father, his voice barely audible.

'You'd better explain,' said Gary.

His mother took a deep breath. 'We'd wanted a decent-sized family. Not nine or ten like some people had in those days, but three or four certainly. Unfortunately, I'd been very sick when I was pregnant with both of your sisters. I'd also had several miscarriages, and the doctors warned me not to risk another pregnancy.'

His father took up the story. 'We wanted a boy and we were confident we could give another child a good home. Originally, we planned on going down the official route, but fate – or rather, a neighbour – intervened. The neighbour put us in touch with a local priest. He knew of a young girl who'd recently given birth. Her parents hadn't wanted to send her to one of the big mother-and-baby homes, so they'd packed her off to an aunt, and the baby had been born in a private nursing home. It's no exaggeration to say they were obsessed with secrecy. And, to be blunt about it, they just wanted to get rid of the baby so the girl could continue her studies.'

'We were the solution to their problems,' said his mother, 'and they were the solution to ours. Somehow, a birth certificate materialised containing our names and the name we'd chosen for you. It claimed you were born on the twelfth of August. Your actual birth was a couple of weeks earlier.'

Gary was having trouble grasping their revelations. Having accepted the initial story about Carrigbrack, he was no longer sure what to believe. Although he was angry at their deceit, he was hit by several other feelings too. Mostly, he was deflated. He'd squandered months searching for the wrong woman in the wrong place. Not only had he been wasting his own time, he'd led Katie and Beth astray. The energy they'd devoted to his case should have been spent elsewhere.

From his coat pocket, he heard the jingle-jangle of his phone. Whoever it was would have to wait.

'Okay,' he said. 'Let's go back. Who were this family?'

'We don't know,' said his father.

'Ah, come on. You must have some idea.'

'I promise you, Gary, all we know is what we've told you.'

'But why would they simply hand over a baby? You could have been a pack of gangsters, for all they knew. Or alcoholics or drug addicts. And why didn't they give me to the authorities or to an adoption society? I would've thought those folks were secretive enough for anybody. They wrote the book on secrecy.'

Gary's father straightened his back. 'Apparently, the family wanted it all handled quickly, with no comeback and no paper trail. We were told they were quite prosperous and were anxious to avoid a scandal. And, as far as our suitability was concerned, the priest and our old neighbour – Mrs Gallogly – vouched for us.'

'Right. So she knows my birth mother's identity?'

His mother sniffled. 'I'm afraid Rena Gallogly's a long time dead.'

'There's a surprise,' Gary said, the words like stones in his mouth. 'I take it the priest has also gone to his eternal reward?'

'Yes. Father Gleeson was his name. Finbar Gleeson. We saw his death notice in the paper about ten years ago.'

'And did my birth mother approve of her baby being adopted illegally?'

'We were assured that she did,' said his father. 'According to Father Gleeson, she'd no interest in being a mother at that point.'

'And her boyfriend? Did he have a say in the arrangement?'

'He didn't know about you.'

'She didn't tell him?'

'No.'

'What was wrong with him? Was he not respectable enough? Not rich enough? Not Catholic enough?'

'I think,' replied his mother, crying hard now, 'the opposite was true. Your birth mother's parents told his parents about the pregnancy, and they decided it would be better if he didn't know. It wasn't a serious relationship, and they worried his college work would be affected. Father Gleeson said he was very bright and had a wonderful career ahead of him.'

Gary stood and began pacing the kitchen. There wasn't much room for pacing. 'This shit is from the Dark Ages. You're telling me that, on the off chance I might have threatened this fellow's career prospects, he was never told I existed?'

'If you put it like that, it sounds very hard. I'm not saying what they did was right. We're just telling you what happened.'

'What a dreadful set-up.'

'It's not as though bad things don't happen to children now,' said his father, his voice becoming more prickly. 'Take a ramble into the city centre any day of the week, and you'll see youngsters who've been neglected. And what about all those lovely boys and girls being brought up in hotel rooms because their parents have nowhere to live? I'm not claiming the old ways were right. They weren't. But, let's face it, we don't have all the answers these days either.'

His mother cleared her throat and placed a hand on his father's arm. She'd always been the more conciliatory of the two, the one who'd prevented arguments from spiralling out of control or getting stuck in a swamp of whataboutery. 'We were lucky to get you,' she said. 'We've had so much joy from you. And I'm not talking about your success. Right from the start, we were delighted to have you as part of the family.'

Gary's thoughts swung back and forth. As much as he wanted to rail at his mam and dad, they'd been fantastic parents, far better than he'd ever been. If they chose to, they could point this out. But he knew they wouldn't. They were too kind. Too decent. It was then that he noticed a look pass between them. He wouldn't go so far as to call it furtive, but it suggested there was more to tell. He stopped his pacing and sat down. 'There's something else, isn't there?'

'I don't want you thinking we asked for it,' said his father, 'because we didn't.'

'That's right,' added his mother. 'We were thrilled just to get you.'

'You've lost me,' said Gary.

'When you arrived, a tiny scrap in a carrycot, we discovered a sum of money under the blanket.'

'How much money?'

'Two thousand pounds.'

'Nowadays, that would be a tidy sum,' said his father. 'In 1971, it was more cash than we could imagine.'

'Correct me if I'm wrong,' said Gary, 'but when babies were adopted illegally, was it not usually the adoptive family that handed over money?'

'Yes, but … we took it as further proof that they wanted the best for you. It also backed up Father Gleeson's statement that these were people of substantial means.'

'What were they? Bank robbers?'

His mother, whose crying had eased, gave a tepid smile. 'We also found a letter, saying the money was for your upkeep and for any little extras you needed along the way.'

'What did you do?'

'What the letter asked, of course. We spent it on you – and your sisters. Not all at once, obviously. It was wonderful to be able to give you the best of everything.'

'Such as?'

'Where do we begin?' replied his dad. 'Clothes and shoes; proper holidays, usually abroad; a great bicycle; music lessons and a quality guitar. And when you switched to playing bass, that was no problem either.'

A piercing pain had developed over Gary's eyes. 'I'd always assumed that we did okay because you both worked.'

'Take it from me,' said his mother, 'a part-time job as a school secretary doesn't pay for many luxuries. We were blessed to have that extra cash, and I'd like to think we made the most of it.'

'I'm ... I don't know what I am. Stunned, I guess.'

'We should have been honest with you when Allegra was sick. It was ... well, it all felt too ...'

'Shady?'

'Yes.'

'Have you ever wondered about my birth mother? From what you've told me today, everything happened quickly. Did she really have enough time to consider what she was doing? She gave away her baby with little chance of finding him again.'

'I think about her all the time. If she was at college then, she must be nearing seventy now.' His mother hesitated. 'I'm sorry that you've found out like this. We tried to do the right thing, but we didn't always succeed. I only wish we'd opened up about this a long time ago.'

Gary felt the remaining energy drain from his body. He attempted to drink his tea, but it had long since gone cold. His parents appeared far frailer than an hour before. His mother's cheeks had collapsed, and there was a grey sheen on his father's bald head. They asked if he'd stay for dinner, but he declined. He needed time on his own. That they'd had good intentions didn't matter. They'd lied to him – and lied again.

In the car, he tipped his head back against the headrest and closed his eyes. He'd wanted to be able to say, *Stop playing around. That type of thing didn't happen.* But it did. Over the past few months, he'd learnt that no story was too bizarre. No secret too dark. No cover-up too extreme. Children had been wiped from the record, and the practice hadn't been confined to institutions like Carrigbrack. Young women had given birth in nursing homes, and their babies had been spirited away.

Another thought hit him: the Adoption Authority was no longer an option. After all, what could he say to them? *Well, hello there. A wealthy family gave me away. They also placed a bribe in my carrycot and put my adoptive parents' names on the birth certificate. Obviously, all of this was completely illegal. Did they file any paperwork?*

It was unlikely he would ever find his birth mother. He would never know where the music had come from. Or whether Allegra's illness was hereditary.

His therapist wouldn't approve of the way he was framing what had happened. 'Is this the most appropriate response?' he would ask. 'Or is it overly negative?' Right now, however, it was the only response Gary had.

He decided to call Katie. She was entitled to know that their hunt had been futile.

It was only as he took out his phone that he remembered the message he'd spotted on the adoption forum. He squinted at the screen. There were eight missed calls: one from Frank, one from Allegra – and six from Beth.

Chapter 37

Ailish

In London that Saturday afternoon, Ailish was drinking tea with Chrissie and one of the women from the support group. Later, she was due to meet the rest of her family. She was dizzy with anticipation, examining photos of her half-sisters and brother, their partners and children until confident she could tell one from another.

She'd left Stevie at home in Kilmitten with instructions to spend the weekend studying. 'I'll be back on Sunday,' she'd said.

'Righto,' he'd replied. 'That gives me loads of time to clean up after the party.'

She wasn't fully sure he'd been joking and had to suppress images of the guards arriving while the house reeked of cannabis, drunken youngsters cavorted in the garden and the entire village was forced to listen to Stormzy.

Her deeper fear was that Keith would use her absence

to get at Stevie. Although she had changed the locks, she worried he would worm his way in. That this was unlikely, and that Stevie was far more skilled at handling Keith than she had ever been, didn't make the fear go away. She'd consulted a solicitor about getting a legal separation and was determined not to backtrack.

Since her husband's departure (at what point, she wondered, could she call him her ex-husband?), she'd been able to think more clearly. With the crystal clarity of hindsight, she saw how Keith hadn't needed to assault her to ruin her life, or the lives of their children. Punching her in the face had been just another step in his campaign of intimidation. He'd controlled and humiliated her until she'd stopped recognising the harm he was doing. His malice had contaminated the house. Ailish had long dismissed talk about self-esteem as the preserve of the young and the self-absorbed. An indulgence for privileged girls who'd nothing to do and all day to do it. 'I'm busy putting food on the table,' she used to say. 'That's all I've time for.' How wrong she'd been.

She also saw now that Keith enjoyed arguing. It was how he came alive, and it was unlikely he would ever change. He had revelled in belittling her and preventing her from being herself. She couldn't imagine that he'd disappear and allow her to get on with her life. She discussed this with Katie and Chrissie. They encouraged her, urging her not to fret about things that might never happen.

All the same, there were times when Ailish felt adrift, as

if all her moorings had been cut and her reference points erased.

The assault had left a dark bruise under one eye. While she'd tried to mask it with make-up, she'd only succeeded in making it more obvious. Her boss had called her in for a toe-curling meeting.

'I could make up a story,' Ailish had said, 'but I reckon you'd see through it. The truth is, my husband hit me. He's no longer in the house, so you needn't worry that it'll happen again.'

The boss, an officious young woman called Celia, had explained that while she had every sympathy for her employee's plight, a prestigious establishment like Rathtuskert Manor couldn't allow guests to encounter a housekeeper with a black eye.

'It's not the image we wish to convey,' she'd added.

'Make-up didn't work, and I can't clean the rooms in sunglasses,' said Ailish, fighting the urge to inform Celia that her empathy bypass had been a complete success.

'That's not what I'm suggesting. I'm asking you to take a few days away from work.' Celia paused. 'We will, of course, pay you during your absence.'

Ailish left the office feeling as if she'd done something wrong.

Since they'd last met, Chrissie's radiotherapy had finished, and she was getting stronger all the time. She was back doing work with the support group. 'The day I stop taking an interest is the day I'm in trouble,' she said.

She'd also invited one of the women, Gretta, to drop in while Ailish was there. 'I want to show you off,' she said. 'I hope you don't mind.'

Ailish didn't think anyone had ever said this to her before. 'Honestly,' she replied, 'you could invite every Irishwoman in London, and I'd be happy to meet them.

Just as Gretta arrived, Ailish received a text from Gary. There was a strange post on the adoption forum, he said, and he'd be interested to know what she made of it. Her first impulse was to look it up and reply. Then she decided to wait. It would be rude to get distracted while Gretta was there. She could talk to Gary later. She still found it remarkable, and not a little odd, that he was interested in her point of view.

The previous week, she'd received a letter from the authorities to say they were working on her case. She'd written back to let them know they were too late. Chrissie had been found, she said, and all was well.

Gretta had also been in Carrigbrack, but not at the same time as Chrissie. Her life after the mother-and-baby home hadn't been easy. By the time she was twenty-five, she'd been married and divorced twice. In her thirties, she'd married again, but her husband, an alcoholic, had died from a sudden brain haemorrhage. Then she'd gone through what she called her 'sterile phase', shutting herself off from the world. It was only now, in her mid sixties, that she could call herself happy. She had friends like Chrissie, and she was in love with a quiet Welshman called Alun.

'I do enough talking for both of us,' she said.

Ailish could well believe it.

In advance of Gretta's visit, Chrissie had outlined her background. 'Her baby died shortly after birth,' she'd explained, 'and from time to time, she still gets emotional. She wasn't allowed to grieve, and it took her a long while to get to grips with that. She has two sons, but the daughter she lost is never far from her thoughts.'

Ailish figured Gretta must be the woman about whom Chrissie had spoken in the newspaper interview. The woman who'd been upset by one of those witless 'celebrity gushes about baby' interviews. One of the other notable things about her was that, shortly after her daughter's death, she'd run away. Very few women had managed to escape from the home, and in Carrigbrack circles she was a legend.

'I couldn't have returned to my parents' house,' she told Ailish as they drank their tea. 'They'd have marched me straight back to the home. Luckily, there was this one nun who was kind to me. She wrote to my sister, who was already over here, and between them they arranged my escape.'

Ailish picked up her teacup. 'It can't have been easy.'

'One of the nurses used to make a regular trip into Ennis, so I hid in the boot of her car. God love the woman, she hadn't a breeze. We'd fixed it so I'd be able to climb out when the car came to a stop. For fear someone might recognise me, I'd changed out of my uniform into the clothes I'd been wearing on the day I arrived. Oh, and I wore a wig belonging to one of the other girls. I can still smell the damn thing. From there, I got the bus to Dublin and the ferry to

Holyhead. The whole time, I was petrified. I kept expecting to feel a hand on my shoulder, and to hear Agnes's cold voice saying, "Where do you think you're going?"'

'And your baby had died only a short while earlier?'

'Yes.' Gretta paused, rested her face in her palms then looked directly at Ailish. 'I can't say I've ever learnt to live with what happened. But I cope, and that's enough. I know what people think. They think it was only a short chapter in my life and I should've moved on. If only it was that straightforward.'

'People who speak like that haven't a clue,' said Chrissie.

Gretta took a mouthful of tea. 'In those days, moving to London was like moving to Mars. Once you arrived here, you didn't think you'd ever see home again. The way I looked at it, I could either hit the town or sit in the flat moping. So I went wild. Believe it or not, I was a pretty young thing back then.'

'Don't pay any heed to her,' said Chrissie with a grin. 'She's only looking for compliments.'

'As if,' said Gretta, with the rasping laugh of a long-time smoker.

If you asked Ailish, Gretta was beautiful, albeit in an offbeat way. The late afternoon sun cast a gentle glow over her face, highlighting her freckles rather than her wrinkles. She had shoulder-length silver hair and a wristful of bangles.

Despite the trauma she had suffered, she was spirited, entertaining, wise. She told other stories about her time in Carrigbrack, including an anecdote about the day the mothers had protested by refusing to stop singing. Her tales made Ailish stop and think. Although she should have known better, she'd tended to think of the women as one sad homogeneous group. That wasn't fair. Some had been gifted, some dull-witted, some hilarious, some kind. They'd been as gorgeous and glorious, as complex and difficult as any collection of young people.

Chrissie poured more tea. 'The nun who helped Gretta was the same woman who was good to me. Sister Eunice was her name.'

'No!' said Ailish. '*The* Sister Eunice? Did you know Katie and Beth met her only a few weeks ago?'

She explained that Eunice had left the religious life. She also told them about Brandon, the starchy American whose much younger wife had strong-armed him into meeting his twin.

'Isn't that a gas one?' said Gretta, whose speech was peppered with Irish words and phrases. 'Mighty', she'd said, 'grand, so' and 'get away out of that'. The fact that her accent no longer contained any trace of Ireland made the words strangely endearing.

Ailish took out her phone. 'I have a photo. Beth sent it to me. She's great at recording their successes. Do you want to see it?'

'I'd love to,' replied Gretta. 'We lost touch years ago. I've never forgotten her, though.'

'Bear with me a moment, and I'll get it for you.' Ailish scrolled through her photos before handing over the phone.

'Look, there she is with the twins, Brandon and Eddie. And there's Katie, too.'

Gretta studied the screen. She wrinkled her nose. 'Can I enlarge the picture?'

'Uh huh. Just tap it. Has Eunice – or Joyce, to use her real name – changed a lot?'

When she spoke again, Gretta's voice was thin. 'It's not Eunice I'm looking at.' She touched the screen. 'The other woman? You said her name was Katie?'

'That's right. It was through her that Chrissie and I were reunited. Well, through her and her niece. They're great women entirely. She was the one who kept the babies' bracelets. Why do you ask?'

'Was she originally from County Clare?'

'That's right. From Danganstown.' Ailish was confused. 'Have you come across her?'

'Yes, in Carrigbrack. She's someone else I've never forgotten.'

'I'm almost certain she only started work as a nurse after you'd left,' said Chrissie.

Gretta continued to stare at the photo. 'You're not following me. She wasn't a nurse. Not when I knew her. She was my friend.'

Chapter 38

Then, Patricia

Patricia had lost count of the number of times she'd been in Sister Agnes's office. She probably held some sort of record. By now, she could recite the title of every holy book on the shelves. She knew the scent of furniture polish and the slight creak of the heavy door. She also knew that, on the other side of Carrigbrack's high walls, the flowers were coming into bloom, the gentians and orchids popping up in gaps between the rocks. What she wouldn't give for a short walk through the Burren; for half an hour of birdsong, the perfumed breeze wrapping around her, the sun tickling her face. She promised herself that one day, when she was free, that was what she would do.

This meeting, she sensed, was different. The punishment wouldn't be short term. From the meagre amount she'd been able to gather, she was likely to be transferred to the mental hospital. That was often the fate of women considered to be untrustworthy or unpredictable. Once committed, it might be years before she saw the real world again.

With a wave of one pudgy hand, Agnes told her to sit down.

'Thank you, Sister.'

'You're very peaky. And thin as a scarecrow. Have you been eating? It's been two weeks since the unfortunate incident. There's no excuse for not eating.'

'I do my best, Sister.'

In truth, she felt a constant low-level nausea. Even fillet steak would have tasted like ash.

'The unfortunate incident' was Carrigbrack doublespeak for the night she'd almost died. Although she didn't know for sure that the others had been forbidden from mentioning it, she had her suspicions. If before that night she'd been unpopular, afterwards she was ostracised. She didn't mind; other people overwhelmed her. If she never used her voice again, it wouldn't bother her.

'Clearly, you need to try harder,' said Agnes. 'Have you been praying for guidance?'

'I have, Sister.'

'And has any wisdom been granted to you?'

'I think so.'

'Go on, then.'

Patricia raised her chin. The air around her appeared to quiver, like it would on the hottest day of summer. 'The boy to whom I gave birth has been accepted by a proper, loving family. It's right that he stays there and grows up with all the advantages of a legitimate child. I'm neither mentally nor morally capable of bringing him up. When I claimed otherwise, I was being selfish and immature.'

Agnes gave a single nod. 'I can see you've made progress.'

'Thank you, Sister.'

How much of her speech did Patricia believe? It didn't matter. She'd come to appreciate that people didn't want the truth. They wanted to be told they were right. Compliance worked. Deference was even more effective. All she had to do was tell them what they wanted to hear. Whether the words had any meaning for her was neither here nor there. Besides, even the smallest act of defiance would require more energy than she possessed.

She had loved Paul, but it hadn't been the right kind of love. It had been too intense. Too destructive. A line from her Leaving Cert English class came to mind: she had loved not wisely, but too well. She didn't, of course, share these thoughts with anyone. There was no point in confirming their suspicions that she was soft in the head.

No matter how often she told herself that yearning for her son was wrong, he pushed his way into her dreams. Every night, she woke to find herself whispering, 'Please go away.' She wished she could be scoured clean of her memories.

Agnes opened one of her desk drawers and took out a sheet of paper. 'One other matter: in the past, you expressed misguided notions about seeing the baby again. Do I take it you now accept that this would be wrong?'

'I do, Sister.'

'Very well. I have a form here. It may have been overlooked when he was adopted. I would appreciate it if you would sign it today.'

The form was headed *Certificate of Surrender*. Briefly, Patricia considered refusing to sign. But all that would do was create unnecessary rancour. Rancour she didn't have the strength for. She had been defeated.

'Thank you,' said Sister Agnes. 'Now, I have no wish to dwell on the unfortunate events except to say that they were extremely distressing for the community here in Carrigbrack.'

'I'm sorry.'

'As I understand it, this is what happened: you went to the nurses' office seeking pain relief. The nurse was called away. While this was unavoidable, she should have ensured that you had left the room. She should also have locked the door behind her. By that time, you were in agony. Not appreciating the consequences of your actions, you accidentally swallowed more tablets than your body could handle. At no point did you intend to do lasting harm to yourself. Had this been your intention, you would have committed one of the gravest sins possible, and I refuse to accept that any young woman who has received instruction here would be capable of such a sin.' She paused. 'Is that an accurate summary?'

Patricia looked down at the polished wooden floor. She wondered at the mental gymnastics that made it possible for Agnes to concoct – and believe – this version of events. 'It is, Sister,' she said.

Had she intended to die? Again, the answer wasn't straightforward. While her actions hadn't been premeditated, she would have been content to let go. She wouldn't have put up a fight. Also, if the circumstances arose again, she would probably do the same thing.

Her memories of the evening were jagged, half formed. She remembered lying on her bed, Paul's identity bracelet in her hand. Everything afterwards was a jumble of colours and sounds, of frantic voices and searing pain. Prominent among those voices was the woman who had found her: Sister Sabina.

Sabina, forever alert to breaches of the rules, had noticed that Patricia was missing. She'd tried several places before looking in the dormitory. Finding Patricia fully clothed and unconscious, she'd immediately raised the alarm. The nurse who'd left the office unattended had panicked, but her more senior colleague had known what to do. Somehow, she'd managed to force a tube up Patricia's nose and down her throat. Over the following hours, Patricia had retched and retched until there was nothing left inside her.

Even in her disorientated state, she'd been aware of arguments blazing around her. She'd heard a door slam. Then she'd heard sobbing. The nurse, she'd assumed.

When she was fully conscious, Agnes appeared. A deluge of questions followed. Patricia remained mute, and Agnes rounded on her. She was ungrateful, stupid, deranged, wicked. Did she know that Sister Sabina, a woman she had insulted and tormented, had saved her life? Did she understand how much distress she'd caused? Patricia, who still felt as if she was hovering between life and death, said, 'Sorry.' Her vocabulary was reduced to one word, and she said it repeatedly. She was genuinely sorry for creating a fuss and for getting the nurse into trouble. Otherwise, she couldn't claim to feel much of anything.

Later, she did as she was told and thanked Sister Sabina for coming to her aid.

'I did my duty, no more, no less,' Sabina replied. 'Hate the sin but not the sinner, that's what I say.'

Patricia regretted that it wasn't possible to choose the person who brought you back from the brink.

Only once in the following days did she cry. She was in the prayer room, where she'd been sent to beg for forgiveness, when Nancy found her.

'I saved this for you,' Nancy said.

It was Paul's wristband.

Patricia doubled over as if she'd been hit and wept until she had nothing left.

To her surprise, her parents were allowed to visit. True to form, there was no direct acknowledgement of what she'd done or how it might have ended. Her father told her that learning to endure was the mark of becoming an adult. If there was no softness in his speech, neither was there any scorn. Her mother, never robust, looked as if all the air had been let out of her. So determined was she not to mention the reason for their visit that she barely spoke at all. She spent more time lamenting the condition of her daughter's hair, which had grown back in a haphazard fashion, than she did talking about Paul. In her heart, Patricia knew her mother wasn't as shallow or unfeeling as she sounded. Rather, she was scared that a misplaced word would trigger a dramatic response. To avoid saying anything she would later regret, Patricia literally bit her tongue. She pushed her teeth in hard until her mouth filled with blood. Its coppery taste was oddly comforting.

Her parents did wish her a belated happy birthday. She'd been twenty-one the previous month. Like everything else in Carrigbrack, her birthday had not been celebrated.

Almost a year had passed since she'd entered the home. It felt more like ten years. A hundred years. She felt as though every part of her had atrophied. She could waste away. She could disappear.

Agnes drummed her fingers on the desk. 'So then, Patricia, your case presents a number of challenges. You have become a distraction to the other penitents, and it is, I fear, impossible for you to stay. However, neither can I permit you to return home as if nothing untoward has happened. You need further monitoring and guidance. Also, allowing you to leave with no consequences would send the wrong message to other girls.'

Patricia could guess the next part. She was being sent to the psychiatric hospital. Where once this prospect would have terrified her, now all she felt was a weary resignation. Shouldn't she feel more?

When she tuned back in, Sister Agnes's monologue had veered from its expected course.

'While life in Carrigbrack isn't easy,' she said, 'and nor should it be, there is scope for compassion. Having discussed your failings with my fellow sisters, we concluded that hard work would aid your spiritual rehabilitation. Like so many modern girls, you spend far too much time dwelling on your supposed rights and not enough on your responsibilities. To this end, Sister Eunice, a most enlightened young woman, has put forward a suggestion. Before your downfall, you were training to be a nurse, is that correct?'

'Yes, Sister, only I'm not certain ...' Patricia came to a halt. She couldn't see where this was leading.

'Thankfully, the hospital authorities are unaware of the true reason for your sudden departure. Your parents, saints both, have made a number of enquiries, and it appears you can return to complete your training.'

For half a moment, Patricia wondered if she was being set free after all.

'Following that, you will come back to Carrigbrack and you will work here as a nurse for as long as I see fit. In that way, you can discharge your debt to the home.'

Patricia's mind was lumbering and slow, and she'd have liked time to consider the implications of Agnes's announcement. She wanted to feel something, yet, still, there was nothing there. 'When am I to leave?'

'This afternoon.'

'Thank you, Sister. Just one thought, though: won't it be strange for the other mothers if I come back as a nurse?'

'I don't envisage you returning before next summer, and 1970 seems to be rushing by at such speed that I'm sure the summer of 1971 will be here before we know it. I'm hopeful that by then all our current penitents will have moved on. Unless someone breaks a confidence, there's no reason why any of the new mothers should know your history.'

'I understand.'

'I should have stated that, as you'll be here in a professional capacity, you'll be known by your original name. It's Kathleen, isn't it?'

For the first time, she looked Agnes in the eye. 'People call me Katie,' she said.

Chapter 39

Now, Katie

Why?

The same word over and over again.

Why bother with other people when you should have been looking for your own son? Why wasn't he your top priority? Why live a life of secrecy? And most of all: why didn't you tell us?

Katie had known that something was up when Beth disappeared without saying where she was going. Two hours later, she'd returned with Gary. They'd been gentle at first, reticent even. Their queries centred on a message board post. Gradually, the questions acquired more edge. Beth, in particular, used words like 'deception' and 'devastated'. One moment, she crackled with anger. The next, she was downcast, barely able to articulate her thoughts. Her reaction was understandable. Katie had let her down.

'Strangely enough,' Katie heard herself say, 'it's fifty years this week since I first arrived in Carrigbrack: April 1969. If you'd told me then that all these years later it would still be part of my life, I'd have …'

Her voice trailed away. When she was twenty, she wouldn't have cared about what might happen when she was seventy. Seventy had been beyond her imagination. That was the blessing, and curse, of being young: you could only see short term.

They were in the sitting room, Beth and Gary on the sofa, Katie in the armchair beside the fireplace. They'd been here for more than an hour. She'd done most of the talking. She could have claimed ignorance. She could have said, 'Nope, means nothing to me.' But that would have been a lie too far. Besides, one look at the post, and her entire body had trembled. She'd known exactly what it meant. And Beth and Gary weren't stupid. She was cornered.

Slowly, methodically, she'd brought them through her time in Carrigbrack. Her first time, that was. They'd already known about her second spell in the home. She'd told them all about Paul, the day he arrived and the day he disappeared. She hadn't stopped there. Perhaps they hadn't needed to hear about her job in the laundry, or the day she'd had her hair cut off, or Diane's burial. Perhaps they hadn't needed to hear about Sabina or Winnie. Or Mike, for that matter. Once she had started, however, she'd been compelled to continue. Memories she'd thought were buried kept rising up in front of her.

Now, she wanted the two of them to leave. She wanted

to be alone so she could mull over the forum in peace. She wanted space to consider her response. But neither showed any sign of going, and she could hardly blame them. In the same circumstances, she would have had a million questions.

Beth hugged a cushion to her chest. 'What I can't get my head around is why your parents agreed to send you back to Carrigbrack. You'd obviously had a breakdown. You'd attempted to kill yourself, for God's sake. Why didn't they say, "No, she's been through enough. Let her go."'

'They were dutiful people,' replied Katie, knowing how inadequate this must sound. 'I presume they didn't see an alternative. I remember my father telling me that when it got difficult, I'd have to offer up my suffering for the souls in purgatory.'

She didn't add that her parents' house had quickly become her personal purgatory. She hadn't been allowed to leave a room without one of them asking where she was going and what she intended to do there. By contrast, the nurses' home was pure heaven. Always hanging over her, though, was the knowledge that when her training finished, she would have to return to Carrigbrack.

'Why didn't you refuse Agnes's rotten deal?' asked Beth. 'Or, if you weren't brave enough to stand up to your mam and dad, why didn't you simply run away?'

That word again. Why? Why? Why?

'Beth, love, it was far from simple. For starters, I'd hurt them enough. Plus, I was completely flattened by the experience. Even a year later, I'd no more energy than the day I left Carrigbrack. Eventually, that changed. By the time Johnny arrived, I was ready to make my move.'

Gary scratched his stubble. He looked as worn out as Katie felt. 'I haven't met Eunice, or Joyce as I suppose I should call her, but according to everything you've said, she's a good woman. Why would she come up with a plan that forced you back to that godawful home? That was inhuman.'

'Not if you consider the alternative. She thought I was about to be sent to the psychiatric hospital. She was trying to make sure that didn't happen. She was taken aback when I returned. She'd been convinced that, given the chance, I'd run off and renege on the deal.'

'What about my mother?' asked Beth. 'How much did she know about what was going on?'

'It's not my place to—'

Beth shot up as though spring-loaded. 'For God's sake, Katie, did she know or didn't she?'

'I doubt she was fully in the picture at that stage. She was only a child. But later? Yes, she knew where I'd been and why I'd been sent there.'

'No wonder she flew into a tizzy when we told her about the bracelets.'

Katie didn't reply. The situation was difficult enough without whipping up further friction between Beth and Margo.

Back in 1969, when Katie had broken the news of her pregnancy, Margo had been eleven years old. Their parents had dispatched her to a relative so they could deal with the situation in secret. She must, though, have asked questions. Five years later, she'd told Katie that while she knew the truth, she would never say anything. 'The scandal would kill Mam and Dad,' she'd explained. To the best of Katie's knowledge, the only person she'd ever confided in was Con. Until last Christmas, the name 'Carrigbrack' had rarely been spoken.

Outside, the sky was an ugly pewter grey. A steady drizzle was falling. You could always rely on the rain. Some people thought of it as beautiful. Katie wasn't among them. She'd seen too much of it.

The silence stretched and grew uneasy until it was broken by Gary. 'Where does Johnny fit into this?' he asked. 'Did he know?'

'Everything I've said about him is true. We first met in Lahinch in the summer of 1972. When we met again, I'd been through a bad few days. Agnes was being extra pernickety with me, and I was taking out my frustration on the mothers. I felt wretched about it. I couldn't stop myself from telling Johnny. He gave the obvious response: "Why don't you leave?" I flimmed and flammed until, finally, I told him the full story. I remember thinking, he's going to walk away. Even so, it was a relief to have unburdened myself to someone. To my great surprise, he was sympathetic. More than that, he was angry on my behalf. "We've got to get you out of there, Kateser," he said. I'll never forget those words. The third time we met, he proposed.'

'And did you go to Sister Agnes and hand in your notice?'

'It wasn't that straightforward. When I asked, she told me I couldn't leave. The nurse who'd been there the night I took the overdose was gone. The midwife was due to retire. And, as you can imagine, young women weren't exactly queuing up to work in Carrigbrack. Johnny went to see her. He explained that we were engaged to be married, and still she said no. She claimed I hadn't yet paid my debt to the home. Johnny, bless him, guessed that Agnes wouldn't fancy being on the wrong side of the law. So a couple of weeks later, he put on a plummy accent and called her pretending to be a solicitor. He invented all manner of legal mumbo-jumbo about my continued presence in Carrigbrack breaking some law or other. I didn't think she'd fall for it, but she did. I left just before Christmas, and we got married shortly afterwards.'

'How did your parents react?' asked Gary.

'Mam was the more sympathetic of the two. Left to her own devices, she'd probably have come to the wedding. There was no reasoning with Dad, though. As time went by, Mam thawed further towards Johnny. It was hard not to. But Dad? I don't think he ever accepted the way I left Carrigbrack. And that meant he never accepted Johnny.'

'Far be it from me to side with your father,' said Beth, 'but was marrying someone you hardly knew not a bit risky?'

'I knew enough. I knew he was kind.'

'Is kindness sufficient reason to marry someone?'

'There are far flimsier ones.'

'I don't remember Grandad very clearly,' said Beth. 'I was only six when he died, and Mam doesn't say much about him.'

'He was … of his time.'

To say that Katie's parents had lived limited lives sounded unkind. That didn't make it untrue. Their existence had been stunted by poverty and blind deference to authority. Oh, she knew that others had challenged those constraints. Not everyone had tugged the forelock. But the O'Deas had possessed neither the gumption nor the imagination to defy Sister Agnes. They'd been waiting for the meek to inherit the earth.

Beth punched the top of her head, as though the bizarre nature of the conversation – and the scale of Katie's duplicity – had only just struck her. 'This is insane,' she said. 'Beyond insane. And we're still none the wiser as to why you decided to forget about Paul.'

Katie did her best to sound calm. 'I never forgot about him. You can say anything else about me, but that's not fair.'

'But can you not see, Katie, that none of this makes sense? We've spent six months trying to unite mothers with their children. And despite having scores of opportunities, you never mentioned Paul. You never said, "This is why it matters to me." Surely you can understand why I'm upset?'

Before she could answer, Gary intervened. 'Listen,' he said, 'I've had a rough day. I can appreciate your feelings, Beth, but for my sake can we step back from the family argument? We still don't have the full story. Katie, why don't you tell us what happened after you and Johnny got married?'

Although Beth pulled a face, she stayed quiet.

'No matter that Paul was always in my thoughts,' Katie said, 'I'd come to accept that he was no longer mine.' She hesitated before continuing. She doubted that either Beth or Gary would understand her reasoning. 'Johnny's family were in many ways more outgoing ... more generous ... than mine, but they were traditional too. Hearing that I'd already had a child would have coloured their view of me – and not in a good way. The rules were explicit in Carrigbrack. Outside, they may have been less clearly stated, but they were there all the same. Johnny and I agreed that we'd move on and have a family of our own. And I thought, yes, let's put the past behind us.'

'Did you really think that would be possible?' asked Beth.

'I don't know. In my defence, I was only twenty-three. And I wanted it to be possible.'

In the beginning, Katie had hated claiming not to have children. Denying Paul had felt wrong. After a while, it had become easier. There were times when she forgot she was lying. She consoled herself with the knowledge that nobody showed their true self to the world. Who chose to parade their wounds? Even today, when honesty was supposed to be prized, how many women devoted a large part of their lives to constructing an idealised version of themselves?

'I remember telling you about Gráinne Holland,' said Gary, 'and the way she'd cut her son out of her life. At the time, I thought you were too charitable towards her. Now, I understand why you said what you did.'

His tone was flat, and Katie realised that his view of her would never be the same. Fleetingly, she recalled the last time he'd been in this room, when he'd spoken about Shanna Ellis's death. She wished she could rewind to that night. Back then, she'd still had the chance to tell her own story in her own way.

'I didn't cut my son out of my life,' she said. 'He was taken from me, and I had to deal with that. As I said to Beth, I never stopped thinking about him.'

And that's what I want to do now, she thought. Please go, so I can have the space I need. Please.

She bent down and picked up the red box. She'd been looking through it when they arrived. There were only nine identity bands left. Well, nine plus one. She removed the plus-one and handed it to Gary.

'Boy,' he read, 'Paul. Eighteenth of August 1969. Ten pounds four ounces. Mother: Patricia.' He sighed and passed the bracelet to Beth. 'Another Paul.'

'My cousin,' she said, as she examined the tiny letters.

'I hadn't thought of him like that,' said Katie.

'There's a lot you haven't thought of, though I can understand why you guarded the box so carefully. If I'd seen its contents, I'd have asked why one of the bracelets was different. God, I feel like such a mug.'

Katie took back Paul's identity band and returned it to the red box. She knew what it was like when everyone pretended your baby didn't exist. She knew what it was like to collude in a lie. That was why she'd kept the bracelets. They told the truth.

Beth had another question. 'Are you sure you weren't coerced by Johnny? Like, if it was up to you – and you alone – would you have looked for Paul?'

'The decisions we took, we took together. If anything, I was the one who was more anxious to push on. You've got to understand, I … I'd had to try and rebuild myself. To start again as though I'd never had a baby. I also felt that, whatever I'd chosen to do, someone would have found fault. To this day, there are plenty of people who judge women mainly by the number of children they have. That number is always either too many or too few. And some of the sharpest, smuggest critics are other women. You know that better than anyone.' She looked at her niece, hoping to find common ground while fearing it was too late.

Beth bit her lip. 'When you and Johnny didn't have children, did you not reconsider?'

It had taken Katie several years to accept that what had happened by accident with Mike wasn't going to happen with the man she loved. In those days, medical attitudes to infertility had been less sympathetic. In some cases, a lot less sympathetic. One doctor had sat in front of Katie, picked a crumb from his moustache and announced that the fault must be hers. She hadn't been able to stop herself from revealing that, out there somewhere, she had a seven-year-old son. You'd swear the devil had popped up in front of him.

'Well,' he'd said, in his south Dublin drawl, 'you'll know all about adoption, then.'

Bruised by that experience, Katie and Johnny had left it a while before seeking help again. They saw a specialist who decided there was no obvious problem with either of them. They were just unlucky. 'It happens,' he said. Nowadays, in the same circumstances, they would have been able to try IVF. But in the early 1980s, IVF wasn't available in Ireland. Over the years, they tried everything: every tip, remedy and old wife's tale. They tried being clinical, they tried being lackadaisical. Finally, when Katie was forty, she discovered she was pregnant. Thrilled – and scared – they kept the news to themselves. After almost five months, she suffered a miscarriage.

Her baby would have been twenty-nine now, the same age as Beth. She remembered going to Beth's christening and forcing herself to pretend that everything was great.

Katie had learnt then that there were myriad ways in which life could be cruel. Twice, a much-wanted child had been wrenched from her. Later, she decided that if life had punished her, it had also been kind. It had given her Johnny. And, when she'd needed a friend, it had given her Beth. She considered explaining all of this, then decided that some of it was too personal.

'Did I have a change of heart about looking for Paul?' she said. 'By then, he felt more distant. I'd already missed too much. I'd missed his first tooth and his first steps. I hadn't been there when he started school and made friends and learnt to read. I hadn't been there when he needed me. Also, and I don't have to explain this to either of you, I doubted I'd be able to find him. The nuns still had all the files, and there was no chance of them giving me any details. When I was working in Carrigbrack, I considered attempting to find my file. But I was terrified what would happen if Agnes caught me.'

Beth gave a look Katie had seen many times before. In the past, it had been reserved for those who'd written to the Carrigbrack Nurse account with half-baked theories about the women who'd given birth there or the nuns who'd been in charge. It was a look of impatience mixed with bewilderment.

'I still can't understand why you didn't come clean to any of us,' she said. 'Seriously, aside from Mam, who was going to be upset with you for telling your own story? You've spent six months listening to other people talking about their lives. How could you not want to talk about what happened to you?'

Four days before he died, Johnny had asked if she regretted not searching for Paul. At the time, he'd been propped up on a bank of pillows, his eyes sticky, his face the colour of a wizened Golden Delicious. She'd looked at him, noble and good-natured despite his suffering, and squeezed his papery hand. 'No,' she'd lied. She'd hoped he would urge her to find her son, but the conversation had meandered on to another subject.

'I couldn't say anything after Johnny died. It would have felt disloyal. We'd made a decision together. If I'd wanted to change my mind, I should have done it while he was alive. And, like I've told you, he wouldn't have had any difficulty with that. At the same time, I kept looking at the bracelets and I knew I had to do something. Then you came on board, and the whole exercise took off in a way I hadn't expected. Everyone we met was so interesting, and I felt so useful.' She folded her hands neatly, one over the other. 'I'm sorry that you haven't had any success yet, Gary. You will, though.'

'I probably won't,' he said, 'only that's another story.'

Katie wanted to ask how he could be so sure, but this wasn't the time. She'd concluded that his bracelet must be one of those she hadn't been able to collect.

'Nothing you've said explains why you didn't prioritise Paul,' said Beth. 'I can sort of understand why you were reluctant before. I get that you'd been damaged. But now? When you'd seen the joy of other reunions? When you'd witnessed how Ailish's life had been transformed? Why couldn't you cast aside the secrecy and go for it?'

And there it was, the thorniest *why* of all. There was no logical answer, nothing she could say that would satisfy her niece. If she had to pick an explanation, it was this: she hadn't been brave enough. She'd been scared that Paul wouldn't be interested in her. Scared that she'd be a disappointment to him. Scared that he'd be a disappointment to her. What if the real Paul bore no resemblance to the man in her imagination? What if he was unkind? Arrogant? Mean? What if they met once and didn't like each other? What if she couldn't find him? What if he was dead?

In there too was something she didn't like acknowledging: a deep ingrained shame. The logical part of her knew this was wrong. How many times had she told others they had nothing to be ashamed of? And yet she couldn't lose the feeling that, all those years ago, she'd messed up and let people down. She hadn't been a fit mother.

'It felt safer like this,' was all she said.

'What about when you began contacting others, like Rita Farragher – and Joyce? They knew you as both Patricia and Katie. Surely you must have worried the truth would come out?'

'I asked Joyce not to mention Paul. Robyn and Brandon didn't know anything about him, I said, and it would be awkward if they were ambushed by the news. I told her that I'd been trying to trace him. When it became apparent that you didn't know about him either, she was … I won't say angry, but concerned. That's why she's been calling me.'

Katie hadn't returned Joyce's calls. That was something else she needed to rectify.

'I used to wonder,' said Beth, 'why there were times when you struggled to cope with what was happening around us. Like, I remember how quiet you were on the day Brandon and Eddie met. I assumed it was because you felt guilty about working in Carrigbrack. Or because you'd never had children of your own. Or even because you were missing Johnny. If only I'd known the truth.'

Gary peered at his phone, which had been buzzing insistently for most of the evening. Was it still evening?

There was no clock in the room, and Katie hadn't dared look at her watch. It was black outside now, and rain was throwing itself at the sitting room window. Cars made a skeetering sound as they sped along Griffin Road. It could be any time between eight o'clock and two in the morning.

'Ailish is looking for me,' he said. 'I'm going out to the hall to talk to her. I asked her to run an eye over the message board. She deserves to know what's going on.'

Katie hadn't realised that he'd remained in touch with Ailish. 'Did you speak to anyone else?' she asked.

'No,' he replied, his voice suggesting that the question offended him.

Announcing that she wanted a drink, Beth disappeared into the kitchen.

Katie drew the curtains before taking the opportunity to pull out her phone and re-examine the message. Not that she needed to see it again. It was him. It had to be.

Hi. My name is Luke. I was born in Carrigbrack in August 1969 and adopted through the St Saviour's agency. I grew up in Dublin and still live here. My adoptive mother and father have been brilliant, and until recently I didn't feel the need to track down my birth parents. But you know the way it is, you get older, your own kids start asking questions, and you decide the time has come to find out more. As many of you will know, the Carrigbrack files are a disaster.

Mine are even more puzzling than usual. The records show that my original name was Paul. The problem is, my birth mother's name was scratched out. There is, though, a later note to say that she returned to Carrigbrack – to work – in the summer of 1971. Luckily, I was able to find my birth cert in the register office. It told me that she was from a village in east Clare. It also gave her full name. Obviously, I won't include it here, but her initials are KOD. My dilemma is this: somebody went to the trouble of trying to conceal her identity. So should I leave her alone? Or should I try to contact her?

Katie considered his name: Luke, one of the four Evangelists. Did it mean his adoptive parents were religious? Or had they simply liked the name? She was comforted by the fact that he described them as brilliant. She would hate to think that, like Ailish, he'd grown up in a cold house. Almost fifty years later, he was still wrapped around her heart.

Re-reading the post cemented a feeling she'd had earlier. Luke had guessed she was 'Carrigbrack Nurse'. He was attempting to smoke her out. Otherwise, why make her identity clear? This prompted another question: was he upset by what she'd done? Did he, too, wonder why he hadn't been top of her list?

From the kitchen, she heard Beth stamping and sloshing. If it was possible to pour wine aggressively, that was what her niece was doing. Katie thought of all the work they'd done together. All the emails. All the conversations and journeys. She couldn't blame Beth for lashing out.

She tried to eavesdrop on Gary, but picked up only the occasional word. It sounded as though Ailish was doing most of the talking.

Beth returned and handed her a glass of wine. Katie hoped this was a positive sign, an indication that they could talk this through.

'I was at school with Mike Langan's granddaughter,' said Beth. 'Her name's Bronagh. Mam never had a good word to say about the family. She claimed they were trashy. Of course, I thought she was being a snob. Little did I know what was actually going on.'

Katie took a sip of her drink. It tasted like turpentine. 'I spotted him at the back of the church on Christmas Day. It's odd to think he's almost eighty. Vera's a long time dead. A stroke, I think.'

'Do you ever speak to him?'

'No. What would we say?'

'You could talk about what happened between you. You could talk about your son.'

'It's far too late for that. I met him shortly after I left the home. He asked how I was, like I'd had the flu or something. I … I couldn't bring myself to talk. I can see now that I was too depressed to handle the situation. We never spoke again. I gather there were other women along the way.'

At the time, Katie had been trying to focus on her nursing

training, hoping that something might prevent her return to Carrigbrack. Every day had been a struggle.

Beth ran a finger around the rim of her wine glass. 'Did anyone else in the village know?'

'A few may have had their suspicions, but only one person knew for sure. Mam confided in one of her sisters, your great-aunt Esther. You wouldn't remember her. She provided the wig.'

'I see.'

'And I suppose it's possible that Mike told Vera.'

'Possible but unlikely. Now that I think about it, Mam may have muttered something about him being a womaniser.'

'I haven't always been fair to Margo. Growing up, she can't have had an easy time of it. At least she was a daughter Mam and Dad could be proud of.'

'Was she really?' said Beth.

'They don't come much more respectable than your mother. She was everything they wanted.'

'I don't think of her like that at all. The more I hear about your parents, the more I reckon they would have disapproved of her life. They sound like simple, frugal people whereas Mam has a mania for material perfection. In a way, spending has been her rebellion.'

Katie had never looked at it that way. With hindsight, however, she could see how Carrigbrack had also helped to shape Margo's life. If nothing else, it had given her a heightened fear of the judgement of others. She was about to say as much when Gary returned. He sat down, placed his elbows on his knees and rested his face in his hands. For a minute, maybe more, he said nothing.

'Is something wrong?' asked Beth, before quickly revising her question. 'Well, obviously, everything's wrong, but is Ailish okay?'

'Uh huh. She spent most of the day with another woman who'd been in Carrigbrack. A woman called Gretta.' He looked at Katie with questioning eyebrows.

'Winnie?' she whispered, scarcely believing what he'd said.

'Uh huh.'

'How is she?'

'Good. Shocked to find you like this, but good.'

Gary passed on what Ailish had told him. Beth offered no opinion on Gretta. While Gary and Katie spoke, she drank her wine and stared at her hands. In opening the box, Katie had always known that the truth might emerge. And, in the deepest crevices of her brain, hadn't that been what she'd wanted? Hadn't she hoped that, one way or another, the bracelets would lead her back to her son? Along the way, she'd been surprised that no one had guessed her history. Some days her injuries had felt so visible she might as well have been covered in scars. What she hadn't foreseen was that she'd grow to love Beth like a daughter.

'Can I ask you about something else?' said Beth. 'Your reluctance to extend the search – was that because you were scared someone might recognise you from your first stint in Carrigbrack?'

Katie had dreaded this question. 'Yes.'

'Right, so some of those on the message board – and I'm thinking in particular of the people born in 1969 and 1970 – you might have been able to provide them with information?'

'Yes.'

'Did any of the stories sound familiar?'

'The man who believed his birth mother was from Limerick? I have a feeling his original name was Lorcan. In the home, his mother was called Jacinta. Her real name was Marian Purcell and she was from the Ennis Road.'

Apart from the tap of rain against the window, the room was silent. When, finally, Beth spoke again, her tone was firm. 'He's the guy who was sick. He was frantic, and you didn't help him.'

'I should have done.' Katie wanted to cry but knew she had no right. 'I'll contact him tomorrow.'

'What if it's too late?'

Gary, who appeared increasingly uncomfortable, went to say something.

Beth stopped him. 'Were there any others?' she asked.

'There's a message from a woman who lives in South Africa. From the details she provided, I'm nearly certain that, in Carrigbrack, her mother was called Imelda. She looked after the babies at night. She was very kind.'

Katie shut her eyes. She was determined the tears wouldn't

escape. When she opened them, her niece was rocking back and forth, her face rigid with distress.

'A great wrong was done to you, Katie,' she said. 'You should have been allowed to keep Paul. You would have been a wonderful mother. But—'

'Maybe we should leave this for tonight,' said Gary. 'Maybe we should talk about it tomorrow after we've had time to consider everything.'

'No,' said Beth, her voice vibrating. 'Katie, I feel sorry for you, you've got to believe that. But what happened back then doesn't excuse the way you've behaved over the past few months. I mean, I thought you were a heroine. There you were, a woman doing a good thing when you didn't have to. I watched how you connected with people and how you seemed to care about them. But you lied to me. And to them. And then there were the folks you could have helped, people who were desperate, and you did nothing. It's all such a mess. Do you not see that?'

Katie felt as if a canyon was opening between them. 'Please, pet, don't judge me too harshly. You can't—'

Beth raised a hand as though directing traffic. 'I'm trying not to judge, but I can't help how I feel. I understand what it's like not to get on with your family. I understand what it's like to feel different and to be on the outside. I was honest with you. I told you all about myself. You could have been honest with me. You had chance after chance, and yet I had to find out the truth from an internet forum.'

Katie recoiled at the strength of her words. 'Please ...' she started.

Beth got to her feet. 'Listen, I need some time to think about this. Everything we did together feels so different now.'

'I'm very sorry, Beth. I was entirely in the wrong. I admit that. Please don't leave.'

Gary also urged her not to go. 'This is a shock,' he said, 'but don't walk out like this. If you don't want to spend the night here, you can stay with me.'

She was at the door. 'I'll collect my belongings and give you back your key in the morning.'

Katie realised that the more she pleaded, the more she was likely to irritate her niece. Instead, she tried to focus on practicalities. 'It's lashing rain, and you've been drinking. You can't drive and you can't walk anywhere in this. You—'

Beth was already gone.

Chapter 40

Katie

His full name was Luke Patrick Flannery. He was six-foot-ish with toffee-brown eyes and dark hair stippled with grey. He was married to Jen and they had two daughters, Róisín and Sadie. They owned a dog called Ben. Luke worked as a probation officer, and when he spoke, he tended to lean in as if explaining the merits of a crime-free life to a freshly released prisoner. He'd played Gaelic football (but not very well) and would like to write crime novels ('Believe me, I have lots of stories').

He'd been seven when his parents told him about his original mother and father. The other mam and dad had loved him, they said, but hadn't been able to keep him.

'Like Tatters?' he'd asked, and they'd agreed.

Tatters was the Flannerys' black-and-white cat. The previous spring she'd had five gorgeous squirmy kittens. Luke and his sisters had wanted to keep them, but, one by one, their eyes still blue and their miaow barely audible, they'd found new homes. For a day or two, Tatters had looked everywhere for her brood. She'd unleashed a tirade of mewls at Luke's mother, as if to say, *Where have you put them?* His mam had gone to Quinnsworth for a tin of rabbit-flavoured Whiskas (the cat's favourite). Two hours later, the kittens had been forgotten.

While Luke's amnesia hadn't been quite as severe as Tatters', neither had he obsessed about the people who'd given him away. His parents had been great and, apart from one secondary school knuckle-dragger, no one had given him a hard time about being adopted. He'd tried to live most of his life in the moment, allowing the past and the future to take care of themselves. 'I was practising mindfulness before it became popular or profitable,' he liked to say.

Then he got older.

People started talking about mother-and-baby homes. His wife and daughters asked questions. He read and he listened. He saw that the past wasn't a foreign country; its repercussions were all around. Well, he'd already known that. How many prisoners had fathers and grandfathers who'd also served time? What began as mild curiosity grew into a burning need to find out where he'd come from.

He decided to trace his birth mother.

There was one other fact about Luke, a fact that turned Katie upside down and inside out: he'd spent most of his life within a couple of miles of Griffin Road. For the past decade, he'd been closer still. The Flannery family lived only a handful of streets away. They shopped in the same supermarket as Katie, used the same post office, caught the same bus. There was every chance that Luke and Katie had stood side by side in a queue or passed in the street. They might well have greeted each other with a generic comment about the weather. She might have admired his dog.

Should I have recognised him? she thought. But she hadn't been looking. She'd expected him to be in the west of Ireland or America or Australia, not within touching distance. She wished there'd been a tracking device, a GPS of the heart, something that could have alerted her to his presence. But even science fiction hadn't allowed for such an invention.

The day after the confrontation with Beth and Gary, Katie had replied to Luke's message, asking him to contact her via the Carrigbrack Nurse email. Her hunch had been correct: he was on her trail. One of the others on the message board had revealed that the woman sending out identity bracelets was called Katie. The dates she'd worked in Carrigbrack tallied with the information he'd received about his birth mother.

'I was putting two and two together and getting who-knew-what,' he said, 'but I thought it was worth a shot.'

'You could have emailed me directly and asked if I was the right Katie O'Dea.'

'I considered it. What if I'd been wrong, though? Putting the request out there was easier. I was giving you some leeway. If you were the right woman, and you wanted to contact me, so be it. If I hadn't heard from you, I would have tried something else.'

Of course, he'd been flummoxed by the fact that she'd helped others yet hadn't attempted to trace her own son. She'd done her best to explain. What she'd said hardly deviated from what she'd told Beth and Gary, yet it had felt different. Context was all, she supposed. It probably helped that Luke spent his working life dealing with people whose behaviour made little sense. Whatever the reason, he accepted her explanation.

Everything she knew about Luke she had garnered from two emails and two long phone calls. Despite their proximity, they had held back from meeting in person. Katie didn't know how he felt, but she was nervous. Part of her longed to see him. Another part felt as if she was trespassing. At the end of the second call, they arranged to go for tea in the Gresham Hotel, the place where she'd first met Gary. It was where her mission had begun and where it was likely to end. Several weeks had passed since the Carrigbrack Nurse account had received a genuine query. Should one arrive, Katie would have to help, but she wasn't sure she possessed either the heart or the drive. It had been a job for two people, and the other half of the team was gone.

She'd contacted Rory, the man she believed to be Jacinta's son, and Lynette, the woman she believed to be Imelda's daughter. Thankfully, Rory's health had improved a little. While both had been grateful for the information, neither had yet found their birth mother.

She spotted Luke as soon as he entered the lobby. True, she was helped by the photos he'd sent, but there was more to it than that. There was a familiar bounce to his walk, a familiar cowlick at his left temple. He was Mike Langan's son all right. As he got closer, she saw that she was there too, in his round eyes and thin nose. For a moment, she felt as if every sound was amplified, as if she was breathing different air. Her heart took off: *rat-tat-tat-tat-tat*. She wanted to examine every hair on his head, every line she hadn't been able to watch develop. How absurd was it that she'd never seen his childhood face, his teenage face, his face on the day he'd got married? She didn't know how he'd done at school, whether he'd ever been ill, how he liked his coffee, how he voted.

Two arms enveloped her, the embrace tighter than she'd expected. Tighter, perhaps, than she deserved.

'My boy,' she said, 'my boy.'

In an instant, every promise she'd made to herself flew away. She'd pledged not to get emotional, not to make him uncomfortable. But as soon as she touched him, those pledges evaporated. He was there and he was real. No longer just a memory, no longer just a sliver of paper in a box.

As they drank their tea, they exchanged pieces of personal information. Katie told herself to savour every moment. He might not want to maintain contact. There might not be room for her in his life. All the same, her mind kept flashing back to the last time she'd seen him. He'd been completely dependent on her then. Or so she'd thought.

'The girls are dying to meet you,' he said.

'Really?' It was the first time he'd mentioned meeting the rest of the family. She felt a burst of pure, uncut joy. Then, a tiny voice at the back of her head warned against getting carried away. She'd urged other people to move slowly, and that was what she ought to do too.

'Yes,' he said. 'Sadie in particular. She's fourteen and feels very strongly about everything.'

'Didn't we all at that age?'

'True, only because of what happened to you, well … she views you as a heroine.'

'Oh, dear. I hope I don't disappoint her. I don't think anyone could call me a heroine.' Beth had used the same word, and Beth had been wrong.

Oh, Beth.

'That's not how Sadie sees it. She has a list of questions for you. But don't let that put you off. Jen was wondering if you'd like to visit next weekend. Or if that would be too soon, that's fine. I mean, you don't—'

'Next weekend would be wonderful.'

Luke smiled. Katie was pleased that his smile belonged neither to her nor to Mike Langan. It was entirely his own.

'I thought you might like to see these,' he said, reaching into his jacket and removing a wallet of photographs. 'I know I emailed you some photos, but they're much better like this, aren't they?'

Katie shuffled through the pictures, shaking her head and exclaiming as she went. There he was: with an uncertain smile on his communion day; with a terrible haircut as a teenager; goofing about on a caravan holiday in Wexford; laughing during a snowstorm. And there was the rest of the family: his parents with their generation's trademark diffidence; his sisters, their hair as blonde as his was dark. And there were his daughters, her granddaughters: pretty little things with the waterfall hair and caterpillar eyebrows that all the girls favoured nowadays.

'I'm overwhelmed,' she said. 'Thank you for showing me these.'

Luke ran his hands along his thighs. 'I meant to say that Beth is welcome to come with you next weekend, if she wants to. I know she helped you with the bracelets and I'd love to meet her. We all would.'

'Ah. That mightn't be possible. She lived with me for a while. She's moved on, though. I don't know if she's around. I could check …'

She couldn't check because she didn't know where to find Beth. Her niece had left without saying where she was going. She didn't return Katie's calls or reply to her emails. Katie had written to express her regret and to let Beth know she loved her and was desperate to rekindle their friendship. *Of all the mistakes I've made, not being honest with you was the greatest*, she wrote. She'd sent the letter to Beth's work address. The following week, it had returned unopened.

Margo's reaction had been unexpectedly restrained. Even her 'I told you so's had lacked their usual bite. 'I did warn you,' she said, her speech punctuated by tuts and sighs, 'but you didn't listen. As soon as you started delving into other people's stories, it was likely that yours would be revealed. Still, I've thought about this, and it doesn't really matter now, does it? The world has changed. To be blunt, nobody cares about these things any more.'

It did matter. It mattered to Beth – and to Katie. She couldn't bear the silence. She couldn't bear knowing that Beth was out there, hurt and angry. She hadn't expected the high of finding her son to be offset by the low of losing her friend. She also found herself becoming irritated by Margo's laissez-faire attitude. *Nobody cares about these things any more.* What was Katie supposed to do? What were all the women supposed to do? Shrug their shoulders and say, 'Everything's fine now because society has decided we weren't filthy harlots after all?'

'It matters,' she'd found herself shouting at the kitchen sink.

Who would dare to tell Gretta it didn't matter? Gretta, who'd been forced back to work three days after her baby's death. Gretta, who'd fled to London at the age of sixteen because her own family would have returned her to Carrigbrack.

'I owe you a wig,' had been the first thing she'd said when Katie had called, immediately dispelling fears that they'd struggle to find common ground. Fifty years ago, they'd known each other for three months, but their friendship had been forged in such intense circumstances that the bond was still there.

'I can't believe we found each other again,' Katie had said, tears rolling down her face, 'and that you've survived so much.'

'That's me,' Gretta had replied. 'Cracked but not broken.'

And who would tell Gary that it didn't matter? Gary, who'd been handed over like an unwanted puppy, his birth mother hidden away, his birth father oblivious to his existence. It was unlikely he would ever find out where he'd come from. He could try, he said, but he feared he'd be entering another maze with no guarantee of finding his way out. Despite this, or perhaps because of it, he'd been conciliatory towards Katie.

So had Ailish. 'It's a lot to take on board,' she'd said. 'An awful lot. You've got to give Beth time.'

Katie didn't agree. She worried that all time would do was allow Beth's hostility to harden and that their estrangement would become permanent.

She chided herself for thinking about this now. She couldn't allow the day to be soured by her separation from Beth.

Johnny was also in her thoughts. It was a shame he'd never met her son. They would have got on; she was sure of it. If only she'd been courageous enough to do this sooner. If only, if only …

'Will you tell your parents I said thanks for taking such good care of you?' she said to Luke. 'I often fretted for fear you'd been given to people who didn't love you enough.'

'They said to say hello to you.' He paused. 'Would you like to meet them?'

'Yes, I think I would.'

He pulled at his ear lobe. Her father's ears, she thought. 'I was very nervous coming here today. I couldn't sleep last night.'

'That makes two of us,' she said. 'But why?'

'You sounded great on the phone, but I worried that in real life you might be strange or damaged, and I wasn't sure how good I'd be at handling the situation. I can see now what an idiot I was. I mean, you're so … so normal.' He immediately thought better of what he'd said. 'Jesus, that sounded terrible, but you know what I mean, don't you?'

Katie remembered a line from Chrissie's newspaper interview: *It's not every town that has a story. It's every village. Every street.*

We're your neighbour, she thought, your friend, your aunt, your mother. We're the women who left and the ones who stayed. Some of us have been able to talk. Others may yet get the chance.

She didn't say any of this. Instead, she smiled and squeezed Luke's knee. 'I know exactly what you mean. Can you stay for another cup of tea?'

Chapter 41

Katie

Ailish had been nervous about the idea.

'You might think it's a terrible suggestion,' she'd said. 'If you do, that's fine. But it came into my head, and I thought I'd ask.'

None of them had considered it a bad idea, including Gretta. And it was her opinion that mattered most.

That was how they found themselves on a shimmering September morning walking towards Carrigbrack, the grass still in its summer green, the hedgerows ablaze with hawthorn berries. In the near distance, a fox went slinking by. A kestrel hovered overhead. It was that time of year when every fine day felt precious because you knew that winter was lurking. It was a time of endings and beginnings.

This was Gretta's first trip to Carrigbrack since the morning she'd climbed into the boot of Rita Farragher's car. It was also the first time Chrissie had returned. Chrissie's husband, Iggy, was with them, as was Gretta's husband, Alun. Ailish was accompanied by Stevie. Despite his volatile home life, he'd secured a great Leaving Cert and was due to start university later in the month. At eighteen, towering over his mother, he radiated a confidence that had always eluded her.

'If I didn't remember the day I squeezed him out,' she said, 'I wouldn't believe he was mine either.'

'Ah, Mam,' said Stevie, 'you're forever embarrassing me.' His tone, not to mention his presence, made it clear he was joking.

Ailish didn't mention Keith, and Katie followed her example. There were days to talk about him, but this wasn't one of them.

Gretta was carrying a bunch of red roses to place at the spot where Diane was buried. Not the precise spot, obviously. That had been obscured by time. Chrissie would say a few words because, as they all agreed, she was best with words.

Gretta was quiet. She was wearing a russet jacket, a cream skirt and bronze sandals. When Katie complimented her outfit, she said she'd wanted to make an effort for Diane. To tell whoever or whatever was out there that her daughter had been worthy of respect. Katie's mind flashed back to the morning the baby girl had been wrapped in white cloth and placed in the ground. She recalled what Gretta had said then: *Just because I couldn't keep her, it doesn't mean I didn't want the best for her. I wanted her to be brilliant. She deserved to be brilliant.*

They'd been reunited during the summer, when Katie had gone to London for a long weekend. She'd stayed with Chrissie, and the three of them had laughed and cried over a roast chicken and two bottles of Sauvignon Blanc.

'If only Agnes could see us,' Chrissie had said.

'She'd definitely cut off all our hair,' Gretta had replied.

Luke was with Katie today, as was her younger granddaughter, Sadie. Katie had wondered if this was a wise idea. Sadie was at that age where everything mattered and every injustice tore at your heart. Wasn't there a danger she would find Carrigbrack too upsetting? She had a word with Luke, who told her that if he didn't bring his daughter, she'd probably stow away like Gretta and pitch up anyway. Although they both laughed, it was unsettling to think that, at the same age, Chrissie had been imprisoned here, her name taken, her life changed forever.

They were midway along the lane, almost at the place where Carrigbrack's boundary wall began, when Katie heard an engine. She turned to see two ... no, three cars, their windscreens glinting in the sun. As the occupants emerged, she recognised Gary's loose-limbed walk. The woman beside him – seventy-ish, with the complexion of someone who rarely saw sunlight – was unfamiliar.

Next came Joyce, Eddie, Yvette and little Zoe. At the rear were Brandon and Robyn.

'I hadn't expected everyone to come,' said Ailish, her fox-like face aglow with pleasure. 'But when I told them what we were doing, they all said they would.'

Gary introduced them to Noreen, one of the women who hadn't been his birth mother.

'After he came to see me, we kept in touch,' she explained. 'He told me what was happening today and asked if I'd like to come. I hope I'm not intruding.'

'Of course you're not,' said Chrissie. 'I remember you. The nuns called you Gloria.'

'That's right,' said Noreen, her eyes misty. 'And I remember you. You were the little girl, the one they called Hanora.' She smiled. It was a wonderful smile.

If Katie was taken aback by Brandon and Robyn's presence, she was even more surprised to see Gary. The tour was due to begin the following week.

'Yeah, this time next week we'll be back on stage,' he said. 'As chance would have it, the opening night's in Boston.'

'I hadn't realised that,' said Katie, glancing towards Brandon and Robyn. She was an awful liar. She knew most of the dates, including when Black Iris would be in Dublin (17 and 18 December). She knew their next album would be called *Catching Fire* and that it would include a song written by Gary about the women whose children had been taken. She'd signed up to the Black Iris website, which as far as she could gather was the twenty-first-century equivalent of joining a fan club.

'And we're going to the Garden to see them,' said Robyn. 'Isn't that great? We met earlier for coffee – Ailish put us all in touch – and Gary invited us. I'm so excited.' She linked arms with Brandon, who looked scared.

'Mam's going too,' said Stevie.

Katie felt her mouth forming an O. Ailish studied her feet. The rest of the group resumed walking.

Gary laughed. 'It's compensation for the night she spent nine hours getting home from Slane.' He turned to Katie. 'By the way, I have news,' he nodded his head towards the others, 'but we'd better get moving. I'll tell you later.'

They snaked towards the home, seventeen of them in all. A collection of mothers, sons, daughters, partners and grandchildren.

One person was missing. Katie had written again, this time sending the letter to the Linnane family home in Danganstown. It had returned, unopened, in a large brown envelope. An accompanying note from Margo advised her to leave Beth alone. *She's still upset. If anything changes, I'll let you know.* For all Katie's delight at finding Luke, she felt her niece's absence more keenly than she could have imagined. Where once she'd spent her days wondering what Johnny would have said about something, now she did the same for Beth. At least Johnny's death hadn't been her fault. With Beth, the wound was self-inflicted.

She kept telling herself that she had to walk on, that she couldn't become overwhelmed by her mistakes. But the house was too quiet. She missed their banter, their in-jokes and rituals. She'd taken to sitting in Beth's old room, thinking of new ways to try and make amends.

One of the many surprising developments was that she'd become closer to Margo. They'd never be best friends, but they were more at peace with each other. Shortly after Katie's first meeting with Luke, the sisters had had a long conversation about Carrigbrack. For the first time, Katie had spoken about how her treatment there, and the loss of her son, had scarred her for life.

'I did everything I could to recover,' she'd said, 'but I was never the same afterwards. How could I be?' She'd spoken too quickly, the words tumbling out, but she'd been waiting most of a lifetime to voice them.

In response, Margo had become emotional. 'I wish we'd talked about this before. I wish you'd been honest with me.'

Increasingly, Katie found herself thinking about the way her ordeal had affected her sister. In some ways, Margo too had been forced to live in Carrigbrack's long shadow. Katie had been wrong when she'd said it was too late to try and understand her. It was never too late.

As they approached the gate, Joyce squeezed her hand. 'Any word?'

'I'm afraid not.'

When, finally, Katie had confessed, Joyce had been sympathetic. She'd even offered to intercede with Beth. Katie had declined. After she'd told Luke, he'd made the same offer, and she'd given the same response. If she knew Beth, and she liked to think she did, an outside intervention would only push her further away.

Carrigbrack was even more dilapidated than the last time Katie had visited. Time and the elements were chipping away at it. Nature was taking over, wrapping its tendrils around the stone and slate, jutting through what remained of the roof.

Compared to a year earlier, when she'd found every step difficult, she was calm. She wouldn't describe the visit as cathartic. That would be going too far. But she was fascinated by the reactions of others. When they reached the plot and its single headstone – *In Memory of the Little Angels* – she looked around. There was Joyce, deep in thought. There were Brandon and Eddie, exchanging stories. There was Zoe, clutching a drooping toy rabbit, taking ballerina steps around them. There was Sadie, crouching to take photographs. And there was Gretta, as dignified as the day fifty years ago when her daughter had been buried.

The previous weekend, Ailish, Stevie and two of his friends had removed the worst of the brambles and weeds. While the site remained bedraggled, at least there was a clearing where they could stand and remember.

Chrissie spoke briefly about Gretta and about other women she knew. Gretta placed the flowers beside the wall, then turned around.

'I wasn't going to speak,' she said, 'and I haven't prepared anything. I just want to say thank you. I haven't met most of you before, but I know Carrigbrack is part of your story too. I hope today brings as much comfort to you as it has done to me.'

Afterwards, they split into small groups, shuffling from one foot to the other, swapping reminiscences. They were due to go for lunch at a nearby pub. It was like a proper funeral, thought Katie. She noticed Noreen talking to Joyce and Yvette. Robyn and Brandon were playing with Zoe. Ailish, permanently on duty, was clearing away more weeds. Stevie was helping. As was Sadie.

Katie was with Luke, his presence still such a novelty that she had to stop herself from staring. Every time they spoke, she discovered something new. She'd learnt that he'd once been in a bad car accident, that he'd spent a year travelling in South America and that before marrying Jen, he'd lived with a woman called Heidi. Sometimes, she overanalysed their conversations. She read too much into throwaway comments. She worried that she said too much. She worried that she said too little. She was, she supposed, scared of losing him again.

Gary tapped her lightly on the arm. Katie felt for him today, the only one among them with no connection to Carrigbrack.

'So,' he said, removing his sunglasses, 'do you remember late last year when I signed up to a couple of those DNA databases?'

'I do.' Katie had been sceptical. She'd read about long-lost family finding each other through the wonders of science, but the success stories were always far away. In America, usually.

'I didn't think anything would come of it. And to begin with, it didn't. To be honest, I'd so much else going on, I forgot about the DNA sites. And then, last month, I received a notification to say there'd been a match.'

'Go on.'

'I assumed I was going to find a sixth cousin three times removed or something. But, and I still can't quite believe this, the match was with my biological father.'

'No!'

'The guy who didn't know you existed?' said Luke.

'The very man ... only eventually he had found out. Someone in the family had let something slip, and he'd badgered his folks until they told the truth. By that stage, he'd lost touch with my biological mother. When he tracked her down, she confirmed it all. I get the feeling the scenes weren't good.'

'And did he try to find you then?'

'We're talking about twenty years ago. Like me, he didn't think it'd be possible. He'd been given hardly any information, and everyone he asked was vague as hell. Oh, and he was thousands of miles away. He was a doctor in the Mayo Clinic in Minnesota, an expert in the endocrine system or some such. His name's Peadar, by the way. Peadar Gilligan.'

'At least his career wasn't affected by your untimely birth,' said Katie.

Gary smiled. 'Yeah, that was one of the first things to occur to me too. Anyhow, recently, he decided to try again. He sent away his saliva, and up I popped.'

'That's amazing,' she said. 'Come here, I've got to hug you. I'm actually ... I'm at a loss for words.' The others had found their families through hard work, perseverance and a sprinkling of luck. This was different. This felt like a miracle.

'Thanks, Katie,' he said, as they pulled apart. 'It's not all straightforward. I gather my birth mother's life hasn't been easy, and I'm not sure if she wants to meet me. I'll have to play it by ear. But at least part of the puzzle has been solved.'

'And are you going to Minnesota to meet Peadar?' said Luke.

'Ah, there's the thing. He retired a couple of years back and returned to Ireland. His wife was originally from Galway, and that's where they're living. As chance would have it, that's also where Noreen's from. So I'm going to drop her home, and then I'll go and see the Gilligans. And tomorrow I'll go back to the States.'

'You're a quick mover,' said Katie.

'Yeah, I know you'd probably advise me to take it more slowly. But if I don't go to see them today, it's probably going to be a few months before I get another chance.'

'Don't mind me. I'm the woman who told you all to be honest but didn't take her own advice. Was Peadar surprised at who you turned out to be?'

'Totally. Apparently, I have two half-brothers and a half-sister, and one of the guys is a fan of the band.'

Around them, the huddles were starting to disperse. People were drifting back towards the lane. 'I'm so pleased,' said Katie, still tingling from the news. 'So pleased. Does ... does Beth know?'

'I emailed her a couple of days ago, but I haven't heard

back. I'm surprised, because she was so enthusiastic about my search.'

'Maybe she's away.'

'Maybe,' said Gary, his tone revealing that he didn't believe this either. 'Listen, you can't let Beth's absence ruin the day.'

'That's what I told her,' said Luke.

Katie took her phone from her bag. She didn't plan on returning to Carrigbrack. It had swallowed enough of her life. She decided, however, that she'd like a photograph. Not as a reminder, for how could she ever forget? Rather, she wanted it as an acknowledgement of what had happened. She wanted to look at it and know that this place no longer had power over her.

She handed the bag to Luke. 'I'm going to take one photo, then we can head on our way.'

'Grand. Do you want me to take a picture of you standing in front of the building?'

'Yes. Why not?'

She gave him the phone and turned to face the lane. As she did so, she saw a fair-haired woman with large sunglasses striding through the gate. The woman stopped to embrace Gary, then walked over to Katie.

She spoke the way she always did, as if there was a tremendous amount to say and not enough time to say it. 'I'm sorry I'm late,' she said. 'It took me forever to get out of Dublin. The traffic was terrible. Isn't Gary's news fantastic?'

Katie ran a finger along the back of her son's hand. 'Luke,' she said, 'this is your cousin Beth.'

Acknowledgements

Many, many thanks to all the people who helped bring *The Paper Bracelet* to the page.

In particular, I'm grateful to my editors, Ciara Considine at Hachette Books Ireland and Sherise Hobbs at Headline. Thanks also to Jane Selley for the copy-edit.

As always, thanks to Joanna Smyth, Ruth Shern, Breda Purdue and Jim Binchy at Hachette Ireland. Thanks also to Elaine Egan and Susie Cronin.

Much gratitude to my agent, Robert Kirby, and to Kate Walsh and Amy Mitchell at United Agents.

In writing the book, I was helped by a number of newspaper articles, especially those written by Conall O'Fatharta and Alison O'Reilly. The websites of the Adoption Rights Alliance and the Clann Project were invaluable.

I'm grateful to my RTÉ newsroom colleagues, especially all the gang on *Morning Ireland*.

A big thank you to the readers, bloggers and booksellers who have been so supportive.

Massive thanks to my parents, Tony and Ruth English.

And, finally, more thanks than I can say to my husband, Eamon Quinn.

Author's Note

For the first time, Beth was seeing how the sins of the past reverberated around them. She'd realised that the story wasn't confined to black-and-white film and bleached-out Polaroids. The women weren't exhibits in a museum.

More than twenty years ago, as a young reporter, I interviewed several women who'd been born in a mother and baby home in Cork city. All were trying to trace their birth parents, and none were making progress. Even basic details about their backgrounds had been denied to them. No matter that they had been adopted by loving families, they felt as though a vital part of their identity was missing. I've never forgotten those women, and not just because of the power of their words. For the first time, I was forced to think about the sheer number of people whose lives were spent wondering about their earliest days and whose attempts to find out more were stymied.

Meanwhile, thousands of women were continuing to live with a bitter legacy, and many were doing so in secret. These were the women who had been treated like criminals when some were the victims of crime. Their children had been taken from them and they'd been warned that any attempt to find their son or daughter was illegal.

Of course, Ireland wasn't the only country where single, pregnant women were ostracised. Unwarranted shame and stigma can be found everywhere. Neither was the country alone in sending women to institutions. Nor was it a uniquely

Catholic practice. Where Ireland did differ was in the scale of this practice. A report carried out by a group called the Clann Project details the experiences of women and children who spent time in the homes. Apart from the personal testimonies, one statistic stands out: In 1967, 97 percent of children born to unmarried mothers in Ireland were the subject of adoption orders. It's such an astonishing figure that I decided to include it in Chrissie's newspaper interview.

Something else made clear by the Clann Project report is that most of the women were effectively incarcerated. They had little or no control over what happened to them and their children. Those who ran away were apprehended and returned by the Gardaí. Many mothers say their babies were taken without consent. They were also discouraged from having contact with their families.

So, while Carrigbrack is fictional, the details are based on real homes. Women were stripped of their names (officially this was to protect their identity); pain relief during labour was frowned upon; children disappeared without warning; graves weren't properly marked. It's also true that women, some heavily pregnant, were forced to carry out hard manual work. There are relatively few accounts of day-to-day life in these institutions. One of the exceptions, a book called *The Light in the Window* by June Goulding, details her time as a nurse in Cork's Bessborough home (the place where the women I interviewed in the 1990s had been born). She witnessed mothers plucking the grass from a lawn by hand. Others were forced to tar a driveway.

To this day, it can be hard for women to talk about the secretive system that treated them so harshly. I spoke recently to the head of the Adoption Authority in Ireland who lamented the fact that their contact register contains the names of relatively few birth mothers. Also, while many women went on to rebuild their lives, others found it more difficult. A considerable number, like Chrissie, left the country.

Tracing a birth parent isn't easy. Most of the references to this in *The Paper Bracelet* – from the missing files spoken about by Beth to Gary's bogus birth certificate to the way Ailish was given the runaround – are based on real life examples. There's still considerable controversy about the way adopted people are treated by the state. Compared to their counterparts elsewhere, they have few rights, and legislation to change this has been a long time coming.

In recent years, the story of Ireland's mother and baby homes has become better known. There has been considerable international news coverage of the Tuam home where, following the work of local historian Catherine Corless, the remains of hundreds of children's bodies were discovered. There has also been worldwide interest in the stories of babies, like Brandon, who were sent to the United States. In these less deferential times, it can be particularly difficult for younger people to understand why families behaved the way they did and why these practices continued for so long.

I grew up in the 1980s when, too often, the women who appeared in the news were there for tragic reasons. I remember fifteen-year-old Ann Lovett who died while giving birth on open ground; Joanne Hayes, a single mother wrongly accused of killing her baby; and Eileen Flynn who lost her job as a teacher because she was living with a separated man. A few mother and baby homes, including Bessborough, were still open. I'm conscious that to younger readers such events might seem like ancient history. But, like the stories of the women whose children were taken from them, the consequences continue to reverberate. It's only in the past few years that some of those who knew Ann Lovett have felt free to talk about her. It's just two years since the State apologised to Joanne Hayes.

My background as a journalist tends to seep into my writing, and it's easy to become ensnared by too much research. While writing *The Paper Bracelet*, I read histories, listened to old radio programmes and scoured message boards. Eventually, it occurred to me that I was like an interviewer who's overly keen to display their knowledge. I had to remind myself that I wasn't writing about an issue, but about characters. I had to keep asking myself: What must that experience have been like? And what is it like to live with the consequences?

I also wanted to try and bring the mothers and the women who ran the homes to life. It's too easy to portray the nuns as caricatures of evil and the mothers as devoid of wit and personality. As Ailish says when she meets Gretta:

Although she should have known better, she'd tended to think of the women as one sad homogeneous group. That wasn't fair. Some had been gifted, some dull-witted, some hilarious, some kind. They'd been as gorgeous and glorious, as complex and difficult as any collection of young people.

I hope I've done them justice.